NATURE TRIUMPHANT

Peer emerged into the park, but the feeling of reassurance she often had when she walked among the bushes and trees was absent today. On the contrary, her sense of displacement, of not belonging, increased dramatically. The trees seemed to grow closer to the canal than before, and mean twigs scratched perforated lines of blood in the skin of her arms. Soon she was running, certain that other footsteps followed; but too afraid to look back and see. Her bare feet hurt as they pounded down into the dirt. She tried to dodge sharp stones or broken glass, but she could feel and hear the wet slap of her bleeding feet as she sprinted for the next bridge.

The canal was unused and unkempt, a clogged artery through the sickly town, and rushes grew in abundance. Just before Peer reached the bridge they parted, and a knot of ducks flew straight at her. She stumbled in their midst, lost her footing and started to fall, positive that she felt several cruel prods from angry beaks in the flurry of waving limbs and dancing feathers. The birds careered low across the park and disappeared over a clump of shrubs towards the lake, calling loudly back at her. Peer rolled to break the fall, but still she cried out as her knees and elbows took the brunt of the impact. Spots of blood were already bleeding through muddy skid marks on her arms.

The park seemed to laugh. Birds sang in triumph. Trees whispered their pleasure with a breeze from nowhere. Squirrels sat at the bases of trees, watching her dispassionately, turning nuts in their claws as they gnawed.

Even the grass looked sharp.

THE
NATURE
OF
BALANCE

Tim Lebbon

LEISURE BOOKS NEW YORK CITY

A LEISURE BOOK®

October 2001

Published by

Dorchester Publishing Co., Inc.
276 Fifth Avenue
New York, NY 10001

ISBN 0-8439-4926-0

The name "Leisure Books" and the stylized "L" with design are trademarks of Dorchester Publishing Co., Inc.

Printed in the United States of America.

Visit us on the web at www.dorchesterpub.com.

For Tracey and Ellie, with love

*I'd like to thank the following wonderful editors
and friends, without whom . . .*

Anthony Barker, Darren Floyd, Andy Fairclough, Peter
Crowther, Jason Williams, Stephen Jones, Ellen Datlow,
Don D'Auria, John Pelan, Jeremy Lassen, Steve Lockley,
Mark Chadbourn, Steve Savile, Richard Chizmar, and
Stephen Calcutt at Anubis.

Chapter One

The Little Dead Girl

The dead girl holds her mother's hand.

She does not seem dead. In fact, she is the very image of a pretty, lively child, all suntanned limbs, glinting eyes and knees grazed by adventure. Even her hair appears drunk on her life force, swaying where there is no breeze and bouncing with each step.

But the girl *is* dead, existing only in this strange place, unmissed and forgotten elsewhere. And although her mother clasps her hand tightly, and their palms are fused by sweat, there is no real connection.

The road is cut into a mountainside. To their right, trees cling tenaciously to the edge of an almost vertical drop, roots shriveling where earth has fallen away into the valley below. They are evergreens, but mostly brown. The road is dusty from lack of use, any line markings long since scoured into veinous patterns by the abrasive wind. Their footsteps thump into silence.

The dead girl feels safe. There is nothing here to harm her. The road behind them is empty, while ahead there is only a virgin surface ready for them to disturb.

But there is something wrong with the trees. Those at the roadside are slanted slightly toward the valley, evidence of the land's insidious downward movement, but they are also twisted into other, less logical shapes. They seem to turn away from the sun, seeking darkness rather than light to provide their sustenance.

The dead girl knows that this is very wrong.

Her mother increases their pace and the girl looks up, but the sun is glaring down into her eyes and she can see only a haze where her mother's face should be. She glances down and sees that they are no longer leaving tracks in the dust. With startling clarity, the little dead girl realizes that all the trees are now leaning in toward her. Following her along the road, like the eyes of a sickly portrait.

Something drifts above the path. It is a huge bird, wingspan that of a heron, but its beak and feathers scream carrion. It settles into a nest made of stained white bones, jerking its head as it regurgitates its own insides to feed its slovenly brood. As they pass by the great bird turns its head and stares at her. Then one of the fledglings pecks out its mother's glazed eye, and it stares no more.

"Mummy," the dead girl wants to say, but she cannot speak. The heat has melted her voice. She tries to scream, but there is no pressure in her throat, no movement in her chest. She is afraid and recognizes that she always has been. There has been something constantly there, lurking just beyond her perception, like a vulture awaiting her demise.

The little dead girl finds that she is no longer holding her mother's hand.

The air changes. It becomes heavier, cooler. The girl shivers; then she knows that there is someone standing behind her. To her left and right, bushes and trees fold in on themselves like polystyrene splashed with flame. The road begins to undulate, but the girl feels no movement. Whatever unnatural shape the world is assuming, she is transforming with it.

There is a sudden pressure on her arms. Strong hands grasp and lift her from the dry earth. She tries another scream, but it goes inward, shaking her bones, rattling her insides.

For the first time the girl is aware of the huge drop to her right. The valley is wide and flat, stitched into uneven squares by hopeless farms scattered across its floor. Walls and hedges divide the fields, trees huddle here and there in small groups, as if plotting escape from the confines of the man-made landscape. The farmhouses are white, reflecting the sun up toward the mountain road. From this height they all seem very small.

The girl is lifted higher, and then thrown.

Air rushes past her ears, through her hair, rippling beneath her clothing. She spins and sees the mountain behind her, the road empty in both directions. From here, the brown trees look almost as nature intended.

As she rises high and then plummets toward the

fields, she realizes that the crops are unknown to her, the trees twisted and cancerous, hedgerows bulging like blocked veins. With seconds to go before she strikes the ground, she knows that the land is deformed beyond hope of redemption.

Here, nature no longer holds sway.

Not real, a voice says. She starts; the words must have originated somewhere. Perhaps from the wind rushing past her ears?

It's not real, the voice says again. *Wake up, Peer. Please wake up.*

Why should I wake up when I'm already dead? the girl wonders. What good would it do to open my eyes again?

Look below you. Look around you. You have to wake up. This isn't real. But it could be, unless you . . . wake . . . up.

The dead girl tries to open her eyes. It is not easy, because they're open already, and what she sees makes her want to do the opposite. But suddenly the rush of air stops, the view vanishes into stagnant darkness. For an instant, she thinks that she is staring down into her own grave.

Then she realizes who she is and where she is, and the darkness is welcome. She draws in a grateful gulp of air, glad that she can taste her own breath once more.

Chapter Two

The Distance

The dreams were always the same. The little dead girl walking hand in hand with her mother, loving her mother, but never being loved back. The girl did not realize what was happening, but when Peer woke up she always knew. It often made her cry, although she could never come to terms with who the little girl was. The obvious answer was that it was her, but the dream girl was dead, and associating herself with that was far too disturbing to dwell upon.

She sat up in bed, holding her head and wondering whether she'd cried out. There had been no thumping on the cardboard-thin wall, no cursing from the girl next door, so she assumed that her sore throat was caused by sleeping with her mouth open rather than by screaming. She massaged her temples to squeeze out the sticky remnants of the nightmare. She'd been falling, flung from a cliff, plummeting toward farmland that was all wrong. Then someone had woken her, just before she struck the ground. Dragged her from sleep with ambiguous whispers. She felt groggy and disorientated, as if she'd been shaken awake.

Peer turned on the bedside lamp and squinted into the searing light. The room was in its usual state of disarray; she had come home drunk and dropped her clothes wherever she took them off. She'd tried cooking some supper, and the small alcove kitchen looked like it had been hit by a hungover poltergeist. She hoped she hadn't left the stove on.

She eased herself out of bed. Underwear and a T-shirt did little to fight the cold as her feet touched the floor. Her head began to thump in protest, insisting that she go back to bed, sleep, let it get over last night.

She should be at work, should never have gone out last night, however much Jenny had begged. Now she was going to be late, and if she didn't take care she would end up losing this job as well. Thrown back into the pit of unemployment, after spending so much time and effort trying to crawl out. And it would be nobody's fault but her own.

Peer glanced at the clock and sighed with relief when she saw that it was still only three in the morning. Still, the memory of the dream unsettled her, as if somewhere the little girl was still falling and waiting to strike the earth.

She had realized why Jenny had been so keen to go into town when she'd arrived at the Quill & Quail, only to see her friend standing between two geeky guys at the bar. By then Jenny had spotted her and waved, and both men had thrown appreciative glances her way. The evening did not begin well, and it took a sharp turn for the worse when one of the men said he was sure he'd seen Peer before, perhaps she remembered? Had she ever been to Greece? Did she go to the Planos bar when she was there? Her answer to each question had been an emphatic "no," but insistence seemed to be his forte; he was trying to wear her down into a casually forged friendship. In the end Peer had left the pub without looking back. Jenny had come after her, telling her not to be so rude, asking her why the hell she didn't appreciate anything done for her. Get out of that dreary flat, she had said. Stop being so bloody introspective and have a good time for a change, she had shouted.

It had descended into a bawling match in the street, with Jenny stalking back to the pub and Peer desperate to avoid an early return to her lonely home.

She groaned when she saw the full results of her late-night cook-in. The stove had been attacked by a fry-up, caked baked beans hanging from its sides and globular splashes of tomato peppering the surface like recent wounds. Saucepans and plates overflowed onto the worktop, testimony to eyes bigger than stomach. A plate had smashed to the floor in front of the stove, and the dried food stuck to its surface, giving it the appearance of a crushed crab. The greasy smell made Peer queasy. She turned her back on the mess and vowed to clear it up later, when she felt more able. She went to the bathroom and drank from the tap, splashing her face and neck in an effort to drive away the heady feeling that she had been shaken awake. Her mother had always told her never to wake someone up when they were dreaming, otherwise they would go mad. Or, depending on exactly what it was they were dreaming, they might carry it over into the waking world. Her mother had been full of such stories, and however ridiculous Peer knew them to be, they still carried a certain resonance. Sometimes, she wished her mother had simply told her the truth.

She sat on the loo, rubbing her head in an effort to ease the hangover, staring down at the smudges of nail polish on her toes. It's pathetic, she thought, how a scrape of paint could be all that was left of the last good time she remembered.

It had been with Jenny. In the country for a day, the two of them had both graduated from the point of casual remark, to daring, to a firm determination to learn to ride a horse.

"It's a girly thing to do," Jenny had said, "and we're girls."

"It'll be wonderful, viewing nature from nature's viewpoint," Peer had said, laughing when Jenny aimed a quizzical stare. And so, for divergent reasons but with the same faith in the outcome, the two friends had gone straight to the nearest riding school. As if to make the day perfect, the riding instructor had been a plum-in-the-mouth, dictatorial, tight jodhpured nightmare.

The day had been wonderful. Neither of them had fallen off, and they'd progressed farther than they thought possible. Waving good-bye to the instructor, promising to return, the friends had confirmed to each other that it was one of their best times ever. That night, for no other reason than childish vanity, they had painted each other's toenails. Peer did Jenny's pink. Jenny, insisting that she had the right of choice, splashed shiny black polish onto her friend's toes.

Only three weeks ago, but it seemed like forever. The dream had come several times in the intervening period, and something else had begun to happen. Peer was confused at first, could not explain it, and that made it all the more unsettling. The best way she could put it was that a distance was growing around her. She was withdrawing into herself, and the rest of the world—her friends and colleagues included—were not expanding to fill the vacuum left behind.

Peer heard a groan from the next flat. Privacy must have been intentionally excluded by the building's designers. Another groan, then a bedspring adding its own voice.

"Oh, no, that's all I bloody need," Peer whispered. She shook her head, rubbed her temples. Sat up straight when the scream came.

There followed a silence so profound that she wondered whether she'd dropped off for an instant and dreamed the scream. The stillness seemed too complete to have been disturbed so recently; there would be surely be echoes of the sound, ripples of the disturbance. Then there was another groan from next door and a further scream, this one long and loud and lacking any pretense at control.

"Kerry!" Peer shouted, more out of shock than concern. She heard a thud and recognized it as her neighbor's bedroom door being thrown open. She pulled up her knickers and ran for the front door, stubbing her toe on the settee and cursing loudly as the next scream came from farther away. Kerry had left her bedroom and must be making her way through the flat.

"Kerry!" Peer shouted again, uselessly. She and her neighbor had never exchanged more than a few mumbled formalities, and Peer's entire knowledge of Kerry came from what she overheard through the thin walls.

Peer teetered on the verge of panic. She felt suddenly dizzy and explosions of light danced before her eyes, trying to hypnotize her into falling into a faint. She leaned against the wall adjacent to her front door, lowered her head and took in several deep breaths. Her hair dropped around her face, darkening her vision, tickling her cheeks. Maybe she had imagined it all.

Should she phone the police? And tell them what?

Open the front door? Take a knife?

Her thoughts were scattered by a frantic hammering at the door.

Peer leaped back and almost fell. Her room was suddenly alien, meaningless, the accumulated junk of a lifetime only serving to show how that life had been frittered away. She no longer felt at home; she was disassociated from her own belongings. Distance intruded once more.

"Peer!" The scream was loud, high-pitched, reverberating through the timber door as though Kerry had her face pressed tight to the other side. "Peer! It's Keith, Peer. It's Keith!"

Peer unlocked the catch and grabbed the handle. For a moment, brief but wholly serious, she considered re-locking the door. What if Keith was out there now? Should she expose herself to such a danger? Or should she look after herself? But Peer was a woman of impulse, and she acted before good sense could veto the decision. She hauled open the door.

A demon entered.

"Oh, shit!" Peer fell back under the attack, arms and legs pinwheeling as she tried to remain standing. She hit the ground hard and the breath was shocked from her lungs.

Kerry was covered with blood. And more than blood. Gunge. Gore. Peer's neighbor looked as if she had been in a road accident with a meat wagon, sustaining injuries and hauling herself through the detritus of the wreckage. Her pretty face was contorted with a strangled scream that refused to come, smeared with dark blood and lumps of something else. She was naked, but clothed in things that belonged inside a body, not outside.

Peer shoved at Kerry in a reflex action, not wanting to touch her where she was injured but disgusted by this bloody thing. The girl tumbled onto her side, and the impact forced out the trapped scream.

"It's Keith!" she shouted, scrabbling on the floor, trying to beat Peer to her feet. "Keith's dead! He's all bloody and . . . exploded!"

"Exploded? Bomb?" Peer could make no sense of the girl's ramblings; nor could she look away from the gore-spattered woman.

"Peer, please help me. Keith's dead." Her voice was quieter this time, still edged with the promise of panic but tempered, perhaps, by the presence of someone else.

"Are you hurt?" Peer asked, and instantly felt like laughing. Adrenaline was flooding her system, heightening her senses and dulling her memories at the same time, protecting her against the worst of what could happen, or had happened. Coupled with her strange sense of remoteness, it gave everything a dreamlike quality. Although as yet, there was no little dead girl.

Kerry looked around wide-eyed, as if realizing for the first time that she was no longer in her own flat. "It's Keith," she said again. "I think perhaps he's dead. Maybe I should call my mother?"

Peer reached out and held Kerry's face in her hands, holding her steady, trying to catch her eye, trying also to ignore the wet mess beneath her palms. "Kerry? Did Keith hurt you?"

Kerry paused, seemed to become lucid for one brief, calm moment. "No. Of course not. He's dead." Then her eyes began to flutter shut. Peer caught her as she slumped and eased her to the floor, trying to steer her toward the patch of carpet already smudged dark with blood.

She did not want to go next door. She wanted to call the police, tell them what had happened, mention all the blood. The blood, Peer thought, would confirm the seriousness of the matter. It hinted at cutting things, not just a nasty accident or a fight. Cutting, slicing things.

Exploded?

The distance decided for her. Peer retreated back into herself, viewing things from a way off, almost dispassionately. It was the rush of panic, she knew, but it was also the aloofness she had been feeling for weeks. As if she had known that this was going to happen, and the knowledge had given her system advance warning.

Glancing down at Kerry, she saw a little girl covered with blood. The image shocked her *(little dead girl?)* but kneeling she could see that Kerry was not so little. Her breasts lay flat on her chest, one of them displaying a bunny rabbit tattoo through the rusty coating of blood. Peer touched the girl's forehead, eliciting a troubled groan. She turned the unconscious girl onto her side in case she puked, then stood and slipped from her front door.

There was no one else in the lobby. She was still wearing only knickers and a T-shirt, but if nobody had come out to investigate the noise by now, then they were probably too scared to be bothered.

The door to Kerry's flat stood wide open. There was a smell wafting out; rich, indefinable. Peer paused at the threshold, thinking of all the bad films she'd seen over the years where the girl chases the horror instead of running as fast as she can away from it. But something, perhaps a remnant of the bad dream, told her that this was a sight she would inevitably have to face. Now, or in the near future. Here, or elsewhere.

She grimaced and entered the hallway.

The flat was mostly silent. The only noise was an uneven dripping from the bedroom. She noticed, vaguely, that no two flats ever look alike, no matter how similar their layout. Kerry's was furnished with cane furniture, the walls boxed with tatty posters of five-year-old films and movie stars long in decline. A real eighties throwback, Kerry.

A louder sound from the bedroom; a heavy drip, then a wet thud.

Peer paused and brushed her hair back over her shoulders. She looked at her hand, saw the flaked smear of drying blood there and wondered whether she'd given herself a punkish streak. Her legs had begun to shake and she wanted to pee, even though she'd only just been. In fact, she wanted to do anything other than step into Kerry's bedroom, from where the sounds were coming, and the smells, and the sense of something terrible having happened.

She closed her eyes, walked through the doorway, opened them again. In that one step normality, or that portion of it she liked to think she inhabited, fled her life forever. Nothing could be normal again. Nothing ever would.

She found Keith in the bedroom. At least, she assumed it was Keith. She had never realized that there was so much blood in one body. He was lying on the bed. Bits of him were slowly sliding down the bedspread and dropping to the floor. It was George Romero's worst nightmare.

Peer spun around and shrieked as she caught sight of her reflection in a mirror. She turned again and tried not to look at what had once been Keith, but curiosity overrode common sense. She could see his ribs. That's what concerned her the most.

Banging and screaming came from far away. Peer frowned and darted to the window, trying not to step on the spreading dark patch on the carpet.

She could see his ribs.

"Help me!" a voice whimpered, the scream defeated by distance. Peer shielded her face against the glass, held her breath and looked down into the street. An old woman was kneeling on the pavement outside the row of shops across the road, shouting and crying, while behind her the bedroom window of her house seemed to exude a red-tinged light.

Blood red.

There was a loud thump from her own flat next door.

Peer ran from the room, wanting to puke, desperate to react in some way to the terrible sight she had seen. She stole a final glance at Keith's shattered rib cage. Her brain felt deadened, composed, almost accepting the horror as readily as if she was observing it all on television, not firsthand.

Something was terribly wrong. There were noises. The world was waking, but not in the way it should.

Kerry was on Peer's living room floor, lying in a spreading pool of blood. Her head was deformed, flattened on one side, and once more Peer picked up on a small detail. Perhaps this was her mind's method of diverting her attention from the full, awful picture.

One of the dead girl's eyes lay six inches from her head. It was still attached by a stringy, frayed cord. It sat on a slowly spreading pile of scarlet fluid, which resembled the guts of a cracked lava lamp.

Kerry's dead, Peer thought. *On my living room floor. With an eye out of its socket and her brain leaking onto my carpet. And her boyfriend is dead in the next flat, smashed up on the bed as if a ghostly juggernaut had decided to use the bedroom as a thoroughfare. And I could see his ribs. And there's a woman crying in the street. And I can still see the smudges of the last good times I had on my toenails, black and faint now, but still there. Maybe I'll never wash again.*

From outside, as if in sympathy with the old woman on the pavement, more screams erupted. A terrible dawn chorus.

Chapter Three

Deadweight

Tonight, as usual, darkness was home. It hid confusion and shielded inadequacy from public scrutiny. It made where he was seem like the whole world. Blane loved the dark.

Clouds dampened the starlight. In the woods the darkness was almost total, and solitude was guaranteed. Blane spent most nights here, sitting naked on a fallen tree trunk, whiling away the hours as the world slept around him. He would close his eyes, let his mind wander and wonder, encouraging it to explore the past and probe the deep recesses of unknown memory. But this, too, was hidden by clouds.

At night, more happened than most people knew. He loved to listen to the sounds of nature: the exuberant cries of mating; growls of the hunt; screams of the kill. A family of foxes lived nearby, and when the sun sank behind the hills to the west they emerged from their hiding places. Beyond the gaze of humanity, away from its influence and the scars it had wrought on the planet—both physical and spiritual—the animals frolicked and killed and mated, screaming like lost children and frightening those unable to sleep in the nearby village. Blane would sit among them, eyes closed, experiencing with them and enjoying the intimate comfort of the occasional warm body brushing against his shins.

Birds slept in the trees, but sometimes there would be a frantic rustling as a predator found its way to a nest, or discovered a fallen fledgling calling for its mother on the soft leaf carpet. Owls haunted the dark, flapping by like giant moths and questioning the night air. Badgers lumbered through the bush, hissing and spitting. Sometimes a deer would venture down from the hills, and on those occasions Blane sat with his eyes open; such a creature held beauty that had to be seen in starlight, as well as heard and sensed.

He never truly slept. His eyes would close and his breathing slow down, but sleep was always elusive. Blane had not slept for many years, not since the day that defined his life, the event he knew had made him the person he was today. The day he could not recall. Where memory should be there was only blankness, a hole in his mind through which the truth of his existence had slipped. Sometimes he could slip a finger into the hole and widen it almost enough to touch what he was seeking, feel its warmth, encourage its rebirth; but most of the time the hole was locked tight. The darkness helped, he knew, and the proximity of nature around him, as if this could in itself take him to wherever the memory had gone. But for years, he had never been close enough.

Occasionally, when he thought his past was there for him to touch, something happened. The night felt different, the animals overactive or silent altogether. The trees reached creakingly down for him, or strove for the stars. The ground beneath his feet would be colored with the smell of fresh flowers, or acidic with the stench of decay. These moments were not dictated by the seasons. They followed him.

Tonight was one of those nights. He sat on the same old trunk, clothes thrown carelessly to the ground, skin prickled by goose bumps and invigorated by the cool breath of the forest. He was frowning at the sudden inactivity, straining to hear the bark of a fox or the snuffling of a wandering badger. There was nothing. The night was so silent that he could hear the hum of life from the village across the fields, occasional cars and midnight strollers. And, less often, the whimper of tamed pets, cosseted and unused to true nature.

He waited for a long time. He kept his eyes closed, letting his other senses reach out. The forest smells were normal, the tang of pine and the sickly stench of a dead thing, overlaid with the pleasing knowledge of spring blossom. He stuck out his tongue and tasted the night, but even here it was corrupted by the poison waste from motors and machines. Disappointed, Blane opened his eyes.

The deer was standing before him. It started, as if only seeing him for the first time as he saw it. A flash of memory suddenly snapped at Blane—an awareness of importance, a sense of belonging everywhere at once, homeless, baseless—but the creature whined and coughed, and as it hit the ground the memory was stolen away once more.

Blane stood and darted to the deer where it lay squirming. It still whined, but the sound seemed involuntary, as if produced by instinct rather than intention. It sensed his footsteps and tried to stand, but its legs were no longer able to hold its weight.

"Deadweight," Blane whispered. The deer howled in reply.

He knelt by its side. His knees popped in protest, and for the first time that night he realized how cold he was. He was suddenly aware of his nakedness and looked around guiltily. He felt certain that strange eyes were upon him. The deer whimpered again as if to recall his attention, and Blane touched it.

It died. Quickly, noisily, messily. It arched its back and coughed, spitting a black clot from its frothing mouth. Blane leaned back, then placed his hands on the fluttering body, ashamed of his temporary squeamishness. The animal's eyes glazed, excluding what little starlight found its way through the clouds and the budding tree canopy. Blane felt a sinking sensation in his stomach; perhaps he could have saved the animal, had he acted quicker.

On examination, he knew that this was not the case. The creature's neck was crushed, bones ground and splintered by whatever force had done the deed.

"Roadkill." It always made Blane seethe. The word itself was repulsive to him, but he felt he had to speak it to properly air his anger. "Roadkill."

The road was half a mile away. It was a wonder that the deer had managed to walk at all, let alone this far. The resilience of nature never failed to amaze him.

He stood suddenly, almost tripping over the dead thing, as a noise cut through the darkness. He was never afraid here—never—but this sound raised his hackles and sucked his balls up into his body. He exhaled and stood motionless, barely breathing in case the noise came again. It had been low and deep, quiet but menacing; a malign chuckle.

Silence.

Not far from Blane, standing sentinel over the forest clearing, an old oak tree grasped at the dark. It was magnificent, its trunk enfolding the past within its rings, holding traces of lost times ready to be discovered. Blane revered this tree, imagining the layers of history contained inside: dust from the Krakatoa explosion; dead remnants of the Black Death; the stored screams of the millions killed in the last war. A living testament to life, and to its end.

He wondered what the tree would know of today in a hundred years' time.

Gathering his clothes, he felt spied upon, set upon, victimized. He dressed quickly, garnering a comfort from being clothed that was unusually keen. Normally for Blane natural was best, but tonight his clothes were a barrier against whatever had happened here. As ineffectual as a blanket over a nightmaring child's head, perhaps, but still heartening.

There were no more sounds from between the trees. The world was still unnaturally silent. A smear of light bled across the hills to the east.

From the village, a single scream murdered the peace.

Chapter Four

Chewing Grass

Blane craved solitude. In his unseen past he had never been alone, he was sure of that at least. But his new self, his modern, confused self, sought no company.

Things were happening now that would change that.

More screams floated across the fields. He stood in the clearing, unsure of what to do, uncertain whether to intervene. These were the screams of nightmares, waking ones, not the ambiguous grizzles of sleep.

He could stay here, wait for the disturbance to pass.

Another scream. This one a child, androgynous in high-pitched panic.

It took several minutes to move to the edge of the woods. Once in the fields he hurried through the tall grass and glistening bracken, even now realizing the beauty in nature. Spider's webs, perfect creations unmatched by any clumsy construct of man, had caught the dew, and they reflected the dawn like memories of better yesterdays. There had been better times passed, Blane was sure. He simply could not remember them.

The path worn into the field curved around a clump of trees, then headed straight across to the stile by the village church. As Blane started toward the ancient edifice, increasing his speed as the sounds from the village became more frenetic, he thought he saw someone in the churchyard. The early morning mist, rising in natural sun worship, might have distorted his view, but for a second there was someone standing among the leaning gravestones. Someone staring through the mist, across the field at Blane.

The shape was shockingly familiar, as though sight inspired memory in the same manner as smell. Blane recalled a musical laugh that sent birds shimmying and dancing through the air, and time spent at work and play in unspoiled woodlands.

The figure vanished suddenly, folding up in the sea of gravestones, or perhaps becoming one. The church took on a menacing aspect. Blane carried on, discomfort rising in tandem with his speed.

As he reached the stile there were more screams from the village. The square itself was hidden by the row of trees bordering the churchyard, but he did not need to see to know what happened next. The growl of abused gears; an engine protesting at such an early awakening; a crash, a shout, silence, followed by the cough of fire being birthed.

Blane looked up at the church and knew that it was tainted. He could taste it in the air and sense it in the way the light seemed loathe to touch the ancient stone. As more shouts came from around the village, and the whimper of fire turned into a roar, he saw what was in the graveyard.

Where the silhouette had stood there was no living thing, but there lay several dead ones. A cat, a badger, a magpie, a small boy, his pajamas shredded in sympathy with his soft flesh. Blane gasped, breathed in the stench of death and swayed on the stile. He could have gone either way, and later he wished he had fallen backwards, away from the church, away from the scenes that awaited him in the square. But fate pulled him into the graveyard, and fascination and disgust took him over to where the dead things lay. They had been arranged in a starlike pattern, heads pointing inward, feet out. The boy was at its center. They were all terribly mutilated. One bore obvious teeth marks.

Chunks of flesh had been gnawed away from the boy's neck. Blood merged with the dew on the grass, catching the rising sun and turning black.

Blane knelt by the dead boy, tears in his eyes for the other creatures as well as the lad. They had all been bitten or slashed, and none had died easily. He touched the child's forehead, wiped away a splash of blood that was drying there. The boy's eyes were still open, staring in sightless agony at a dawn he should never have expected not to see.

The gate to the churchyard burst open. Blane stood, ready to ward off a panic-stricken parent, stepping over the dead boy in an effort to hide the mutilation from whomever had come searching for him. But the person running between the graves seemed to have no interest in Blane, nor the grotesque arrangement behind him. It was a woman, middle-aged, her nightgown flowing around her ample form like ghostly gossamer.

"What's happening?" Blane called to her. She did not see him, nor seem to hear. "What's going on?" His voice sounded alien to him, desperate, filled with a terror that had, as yet, failed to completely reach his brain. He felt aloof, apart from what was happening, though he was certain it was not simply the usual remoteness he felt from humanity. He was normally caring and concerned, if distant. Today he had taken one whole step back.

He looked down at the dead boy once more. Who had been in the graveyard? They must have seen this horrendous display. And suddenly he knew that the person he had seen had arranged it.

More memories. The laughter again, a song thrush joining in and adding its own wonderful voice. Surely that laugh could not belong to someone capable of such destruction?

"Wait!" Blane shouted, and raced after the woman. He was short, but she was large, and he intercepted her at the church doors. She glared at him, eyes wide and white and empty in the red landscape of her face.

"Slow down," he said, holding out his hands, palms up.

She stopped. "It's horrible," she said, and fell heavily to her knees.

Blane knelt by her side, reached out and placed his hand gently on her head. He was not used to such close contact, not with people. He did not know whether the sticky mess in her hair was caused by wounds to her own body, or other's. He wondered whether she was the instigator of the terrible murder back among the graves, but he instantly saw how ridiculous this assumption was. She was mad, not insane.

"What's going on?" he said. "I heard screams. There are . . . dead things in the graveyard."

"You're that weirdo from out on Pond Road, aren't you? From the prefab?" Blane nodded, hardly concerned with the "weirdo" label. She was right, in a way. He knew how he was usually perceived, and weird was not so bad.

"Davey always tells me you're odd," she said. Her eyes glazed, and Blane recognized the signs of shock settling over her system like a possessive ghost. "Weirdo, animal lover, layabout. Davey is quite opinionated, you know. He's dead."

"I'm sorry." Blane was unused to grief, so he was unsure of how to handle it. To him, death was a natural part of living. "How? Is that why there's lots of screaming? Is there . . . an animal in the village?"

The woman frowned, hands clasping and unclasping at her sides. A dribble of blood found its way from her great mop of hair and trickled down her temple, onto her cheek. She seemed not to notice. "He's in bed. Dead. Bloody. In bed. Dead and bloody." She looked up at the front of the church, squinting at the broken sunlight reflected from old stained-glass windows. "I think maybe I should pray."

Blane wanted to help her, hand her over to someone who could look after her properly. But she stood, nudged him aside, hurried over to the church door, tried the handle and found it locked.

"Father!" She banged on the door. "Father!" Another bruising knock. "Father!"

"Come with me, please, we'll find—"

"Father! Father! FATHER!" The woman continued striking the door, her whole body vibrating with each impact.

There were more sounds of disruption from the village, and a cloud of greasy smoke was forming in the still morning air. Blane stood undecided, wanting to help the woman but also drawn by the sounds of chaos from beyond the line of trees. He had to find someone, tell them about the dead boy. And the animals. And the person he had seen in the graveyard, the murderer—

—*the laugher.*

He walked to the gate, unable to purge his mind of the sight of the dead boy and animals accompanying each other into stiffness. Nature had no morals, he knew, not of the human kind. The morals it did hold true were way beyond the comprehension of many, inspiring phrases such as "nature is cruel," "nature is indifferent." Blane had seen as much death as life, and knew it to be a balancing force. But he had never known it dealt in such a meaningless and vicious way as this. In nature, death was food for the body, or protection of family. What lay in this sick graveyard was sustenance for a perverted, turned mind.

He paused at the gate. What he had seen and heard in the graveyard should really have prepared him for the sight confronting him, but shock immobilized him for the few seconds it took to take everything in.

The village square was no longer quaint. The pond at the far side, beyond which lay the road leading up to his home, seemed to be the focal point for wandering, screaming, crying people. Some of them were hugging, most were sitting alone, one of them was floating dead in the pond. The others appeared unconcerned. None of them noticed Blane, or if they did they failed to acknowledge him. The burning car lay to his left, its front end huddled around a telegraph pole, its insides a mass of voracious flame. Its tires were melting across the cobbles. He could not tell whether there was anyone still inside. No one was even trying to douse the flames. In the small pergola on the green, where the village tramp Saint often spent warmer nights sleeping and plotting his next day's odd-jobbing, there was something huddled in the corner. It looked like a pile of rags that had been dipped in red paint, then flung carelessly across the timber floor of the small building. Two dogs, animals Blane recognized from the village, were fighting over whatever the rags contained.

He could see no other dead bodies. But death itself hung heavy over the village.

"Mr. Blane." The voice was quiet, fragile, full of a restrained emotion that constantly threatened to flood through. It belonged to one of the kids from the village; he was standing half-hidden beneath the church conifers. "What's happened, Mr. Blane?"

"I don't know. You're Slates, aren't you?"

The boy nodded. "That's what my friends call me. Mum and Dad . . . Mum and Dad don't . . ." He trailed off and stared through Blane, lost somewhere in a horrible memory.

"What happened here, Slates?"

The boy started, focusing once again on Blane's face. "Mum and Dad are dead. I was reading under my duvet, you know, secretly . . ." He trailed off again, looked across at the pond and the body marring its surface. "That's Mrs. Greenwood from the village store. I nicked a Mars Bar once and she didn't tell Mum and Dad. She said one little misdemeanor shouldn't scar a life for life, but more than one would destroy it. I didn't nick again. Stupid. Stupid old woman." Slates's face, strained like a taut drumskin while he had been talking, changed shape. His cheeks rose, mouth tensed, eyes wrinkled almost shut. His long hair, hooked behind protruding ears, shimmered as he tried to hold back the tears. He shouted out once, loud and incoherent, as if a pressure valve of emotion had snapped open. Then he began to cry.

"Slates, come on, come with me." Blane held out his hand and gently touched the lad on the shoulder. He was hot through his T-shirt, too hot. Burning up with terror.

"Mum and Dad are dead," Slates said, and it was as if stating the fact again had opened the floodgates. The boy began to talk, drowning his tears with words. "I was reading under the covers, couldn't sleep, then I heard a noise from across the street in Mr. Simpkins's house, like a sort of crash, or a bang, or something. I looked out the window but couldn't see anything. It was dark."

Blane walked alongside the boy, hand on his shoulder, listening and looking around at the same time. He steered toward the people by the pond who, although in a group, did not seem to be together. He wondered whom he could tell about the dead boy, wondered also whether any of them would even listen. This morning, it seemed, grief was endemic.

"So I got back under the covers, but the book began to scare me after I'd heard the sounds. I thought there was something in the room with me, waiting to make the same noises. I'm not usually afraid, you know, but last night seemed . . . pregnant with danger."

Pregnant with danger, thought Blane; *the lad should have been a poet.*

"That's from the book I was reading," the boy said, with an oddly flat pride. "Mum and Dad were both snoring in the next room. They always did. Mum said it's how they stayed together so long, not being able to hear everything they both said in their sleep. She was only joking."

Slates was panting now, almost spitting the words out, forcing his fears into the open, perhaps thinking that if he kept talking he could keep the reality of what had happened at bay.

As they approached the pond some of the milling people noticed them. They looked up with red-rimmed eyes, stared straight through the man and boy, looked down again at their hands or the mess of blood on their clothes. One of them, a middle-aged man, was lying with his face pressed into the grass, mouth opening and closing, chewing the turf like a dog trying to make itself sick.

"So when I heard the bang from next door, I really jumped, threw back the covers. I went into

Mum and Dad's room, because I thought one of them had fallen out of bed or something. But when I saw them . . . when I saw them . . ."

Blane and the boy stopped beside the pond. Reeds reached for their knees. Ducks paddled in quiet disregard of the human tragedy unfolding around them.

"There was blood. And bits. Other bits. And Dad's face was . . ." Slates could not finish. He fell to his knees, shuffled across the damp grass to the nearest person and flung himself into her lap. She did not seem to notice. She began absently stroking the back of his head, murmuring, rocking back and forth, her eyes seeing something far different from this early morning scene.

The sun had risen behind the church and now sprayed golden dawn across the village, shimmering separately in a billion drops of dew and a thousand shed tears. The sky turned red. Shepherd's warning.

"There's a dead boy in the churchyard," Blane said quietly.

"Everyone's dead, why should he be different?" The man who had been chewing the grass turned and sat up, chin and teeth stained green and brown by the sod. "My Janice . . . she's gone. Dead. I don't know . . . her back's broken." He frowned in amazement.

"Has anyone phoned for ambulances? Police?"

"I have," a woman said from across the pond. She was standing near the water's edge, letting soft black mud ooze up between her bare toes. "I heard a noise from next door, where Mr. and Mrs. James live. I knocked, but there was nothing. So I rang for the police and an ambulance. They're quite old, you know." She looked at the people gathered around the pond, frowning as if she did not recognize any of them. "Then I saw everyone out here . . . the car, burning . . . blood. And I came out. What the hell is going on?"

"There are dead people everywhere," Blane said. He was going to mention the shape he had seen in the churchyard, but the memory felt suddenly personal, like an undisclosed sin. The laughter and singing birds made it so, perhaps. His own unknown memory.

"Dead how?" the woman asked, taking a long drag on a cigarette. She had cropped ginger hair, dangling earrings, adult echoes of a teenaged punk. The short hair revealed ears large enough to attract a second glance, and it seemed that the haircut and earrings dared anyone to mention them. Her eyes held a sparkling intelligence, where once there might only have been rebellion. Her pale expression seemed soft and vulnerable, even though her voice held a certain note of control. Nobody answered her question, so she asked again: "How? What happened? It'll help when the ambulances get here, you know, if the paramedics have some kind of idea what they're having to deal with." She stared at Blane, meeting his gaze. He did not recognize her as a villager. Perhaps that was why she treated him as an equal rather than an oddball.

"How did the boy in the graveyard die?" Her voice demanded an answer.

Blane thought it unwise to supply it. "The same way as everyone else, I guess." He did not mention the bite marks in the flesh. Nor did he hint at the dead animals, arranged around the body of the boy like ancient spiritual guides into the next world.

"Which still tells us nothing." The girl squatted on her haunches and flicked a fly from her sweatshirt. She glanced around at the others sitting or standing around the pool, examining each of them closely, eyes finally coming to rest back on Blane. Another pull on the cigarette. "Who are you?" she asked.

"My name's Blane. I live out on Pond Road." He casually indicated the direction, waiting for the snide remarks, giving her ample opportunity to realize who he was, if she hadn't already.

"In the prefab?"

Blane nodded.

"You're like me, then. Alone. I've only lost friends, today." With that the woman stood, slipped on a pair of cheap sneakers that had been dangling from her hand by their laces and walked around the pond. She threw her cigarette butt into the water as she went.

Blane had a chance to observe without being observed. The woman was tall, at least three inches taller than him, probably nudging six feet. Her baggy clothes held a bulky body, but she was heavy boned rather than overweight. She walked with a steady grace, a confident step, arms swinging as if they were constantly seeking something to do.

Blane glanced over at Slates, who was still being absently cuddled by the woman. Neither seemed to be aware of the other's presence, but there was definitely a joint sharing of comfort that he was loathe to disturb. Instead, he moved off quietly to meet the woman.

"Talk with you?" the woman said as they drew together. She indicated the pergola with a nod of her head, and the two of them moved away from the pond.

Blane looked down at his feet as he walked, imagining that he was still in the woods. There were clearings in there where the grass grew up through last year's blown leaves, and snowdrops and daffodils had already shown their tentative faces. Sprays of dew erupted from around his shoes, turning the light leather dark. If he concentrated—ignored the shadow of the woman where it clung to his feet; tried to forget the terrible sight of the dead boy surrounded by the mutilated creatures; thrust the fleeting, haunting shape in the churchyard from his mind—he could imagine himself safe within the secret arms of nature. Comforted. Protected. Shielded from petty human delusions of grandeur and the childish squabbles of politics and nations.

A growl came from ahead, low and throaty. He looked up quickly, reminded of the sound he'd heard in the woods after the deer with the crushed neck had died before him. Another growl, then a flurry of barks and yaps from the pergola as the two stray dogs fought. Between the slats in the side of the wooden structure Blane could see that they had something in their mouths, and were performing a canine tug of war.

"Maybe this is far enough," the woman said. "Shoo! Psshhhh! Out of it, go on!" She clapped her hands and stomped several paces toward the pergola, until she was staring in through the slats. She paused, her big shoulders slumping slightly. "Oh,

Christ." The dogs threw her a desultory stare and trotted slowly down the steps and away. They had stopped fighting; whatever had been the cause of their argument had apparently ripped in two.

"Blane, there's a dead person in there."

Blane nodded. "I think maybe it's Saint."

"Saint?"

"He lives around the village."

"I know Saint." The woman walked back to Blane and stopped, staring down at the ground between them. "The dogs were eating him."

Blane said nothing. There was nothing to say. The dogs were strays. They were opportunists, but he knew this was not the best wisdom to come out with right now.

"Just what the fuck happened when the lights went out last night?" For the first time since he had seen her, the woman seemed touched by the circumstances. She did not appear as big as she had, grief and fear molding her body into their own withering shapes. Her face had paled, and her fists were opening and closing at her side, trying to grab onto something solid to explain the tragedy they had all woken to.

"I have no idea," Blane began. "I was in the woods for most of the night."

She gave him a strange look but said nothing.

"I spend a lot of time in there. Living with nature. Keeping away from . . . human trivialities."

"This isn't trivial. Have you noticed? No sirens yet. I rang over an hour ago." She hugged herself, clasping her upper arms as if holding on to whatever sanity remained. "Maybe I should try again?"

"Maybe they're busy. What's your name?"

"Holly."

Together, Blane and Holly turned to look back at the people gathered around the pond. Blane glanced sadly at Slates.

The boy's body jerked once, hard, as if struck by a massive invisible weight. An arc of blood powered from his nose and mouth, soaking the woman who had been stroking his hair. He twitched briefly, limbs thumping a tattoo on the damp earth, forcing his head from the woman's lap.

Then he was still. Dead.

Chapter Five

Blood Red

Mary hated the people she chose to be with. But then, she lived a life she didn't want, so the hatred went both ways. She had once been an attractive young girl with ambitions and prospects, but a combination of drugs, cynicism and feuding between heart and mind had reduced her to a shadow of her former self, a void, a nothing. Her personality bounced around inside, lost. She tried to fill this emptiness with the notion that Roger really needed her and loved her. Even when he loved her with curses and fists, this premise persisted.

Inside, Mary knew that she had died years ago. But she had long chosen to ignore her inner voice; it told the painful truth, and truth was as wanting as hope.

The bedroom walls hung with tattered posters from a decade ago, so familiar that they went unnoticed. Painted faces stared from them, pouting arrogance into the staid atmosphere of the room, vacuous expressions promising equally inane music. There were other things on the walls, but Mary did not like to look at them. Not unless she had to, not unless Roger or Jams made her. Then she tried to shut the photographs from her mind, but eyes were thoughtless things, and they transmitted all the terrible truths straight to the essence of her quailing soul. The floor was scattered with gruesome mementoes of the gang's work. Some of them stank. The latest one, from earlier that night, hung from a nail on the back of the bedroom door. It was drying, but it shed a dark dribble that had almost reached the floor before hardening into a crust.

The room was filthy. It bore testament to a monstrous fascination, a perversion enjoyed by Roger and Jams and the others, but only indulged by Mary because she so wanted to belong. The room had no morals. It was a bad room.

Mary was like this room, where she was supposed to be sleeping but could not. Memories of the previous night held her far from the land of dreams, stirring her with stabs of guilt and a sour, bloodred taste of self-loathing. Yes, she was like this place, where she cried so often, in the dark: hollow; superficial; abandoned.

Roger lay beside her, snoring quietly from within his own dark dreams, a potential of hard love and violence and wickedness rolled up in one abused and abusive body. Mary raised herself on one elbow and stared at the man who purported to be her lover. There was a sheen of sweat on his skin, catching a ghostly green light from the stereo display, which picked out his angles and curves. She imagined a knife put to his skin, parting flesh from bone, wondered how he would like it. She could see his penis in the half light, nestled within tufts of dark hair, and meditated on whether he thought of his own while mutilating others. If she were strong, she could ask him. Hold one of his filthy knives there, wake him up, ask him.

But she was not strong, she was weak. She was a wagon and Roger the engine, guiding her easily and mindlessly to whatever future awaited her. Occasionally, very occasionally, she thought of her family. Her mother tired and limp, offering a vague grimace through cigarette smoke and apathy. Her father huge and drunk, not really bad, just indifferent. She realized not for the first time that whatever warning her childhood had sent her had not been heeded. And the feeling upon that realization was always the same; anger at herself. A dilute anger, because Mary rarely felt anything to the extreme.

She closed her eyes and remembered the horses from last night.

Roger had driven. Jams sat in the back between Helen and Mary, and in the front passenger seat Rupert rolled joints and took swigs from a bottle of cheap whiskey. Jams had his hand down the front of Helen's knickers, and Mary stared from the window in discomfort. But it was dark outside and all she could see was the reflection of her own sad face, and Jams gnawing Helen's neck.

Helen seemed unperturbed by the rough attention. She had told Mary her story once, years ago, and for a while it had seemed that she regretted the terrible things she had done. Now, sitting in the back of a stolen Escort, happily being fingered by the sort of person her parents were regularly being paid by the state to give legal advice to, the girl seemed beyond help. Her soul had become ugly.

Mary wished she was like Helen. She would have taken a different path, because with the girl's intelligence and erstwhile vivacity, dropping out should have been such a great adventure, not a descent into the blankness they now inhabited. "I love this life," Helen would say. But she rarely smiled any more. Her eyes were hard, her voice roughened by cigarettes and bitterness. She knew the truth, and the truth hurt.

They were traveling too fast. The clanking of metal came from the trunk as they skidded around a corner in the lane, reminding them all of what they were about to do.

"And now, I blood myself once more," Rupert said solemnly.

"You're a complete fucking arsehole!" Roger shouted, struggling with the steering wheel as the offside tires clipped the grass verge.

"Drink?" Rupert held out the bottle to Roger. "Nearly there, everyone."

"Whose are we doing?" Jams asked, glancing up from his exploration of Helen's secrets.

"Some prig's," Rupert replied, snatching the bottle back from Roger. "Rich bastards, hunting at the weekend, a bit of interfamily fucking at Christmas, lunch with the local MP, ohh, marm, you do look delightful tonight, may I bribe one into letting one's son off one of those awwwful little charges?"

"It's not the animal's fault," Mary said quietly,

but if anyone heard they did not even bother to reply. She was as good as a ghost.

"Wait 'til you see those things scream and holler! God, they'll cry and screech and go crazy-ape shit!" Roger was slowing the car now, looking in the dark for the gateway. The one working headlight passed across hedgerows like a searchlight, seeking out new victims for the gang's crazed habits. The inside of the car stank of apathy and sweat and sex, and Mary lowered the window, breathing in grateful gulps of fresh air to clear her sinuses. She almost felt like crying, but tears would not come, and what was the point of crying if there was no one to see or care? *If I cry,* Mary thought, *and nobody sees, does that mean I don't really cry?*

"Rabbit!" Rupert yelled.

"Woah, hold still you, little shit!" The creature was briefly illuminated by the car's headlight, frozen in the middle of the lane like a misplaced garden ornament.

"Funny how they seem to welcome death," Helen said mildly.

Roger adjusted the wheel slightly and the car jumped. There was a sound like a plastic bag of jelly and biscuits being popped, and Mary banged her head on the window frame, yelping in pain.

"The gate's back there." Rupert was straining in his seat, even though there was only darkness and a dead rabbit behind them. "I'm sure."

Roger slammed on the brakes, and the three back-seat passengers sprang forward. Helen cried out and pushed herself back, driving an elbow into Jams's chest.

"Not my fault," he whined insolently, reclaiming

his hand and holding it to him as if afraid she would cut it off.

"That hurt, you stupid shit."

"Not my fault."

"Well, it hurt."

Roger turned and stared through the back window, slipping the gearstick into reverse and flooring the accelerator. Mary tried to catch his eye—to smile, blow him a kiss, raise an eyebrow, confirm her own existence by eliciting some sort of response from him—but he did not see her.

Mary had started to shake. She knew what was about to come, how gruesome the next hour was going to be, and she hated herself even more for feeling a rush of adrenaline that she could not kid herself into believing was purely down to fear. It was excitement, the sort of anticipation felt before watching a graphic horror film, only this was real. Stinkingly, retchingly, bloodily real.

Rupert was first from the car. He derided Helen when she talked of dropping out, insisting that he was different, he had *moved on*. His, he said, was the greater challenge: to forget a previous life and concentrate on a new, living death, like Helen, took little more than a realization that humanity provided all the artificial rules; to do what he had done, shun all the trappings of money and wealth, to form his own art, took genius.

Mary thought he was a pretentious wanker, and the drugs he took merely reduced him to a pathetic, philosophizing fool. But she could never tell him that to his face. Not that he would really listen to her thoughts or opinions, or put any value in them if he did. He might simply choose to hit her for thinking.

She liked to pretend that she was the only one here through necessity and fate. While the others were all manufactured failures, she was one of life's genuine runts.

She opened her door and fell out into the cool, fresh dark, standing still for a moment so that her night vision could adjust. The glare from the head-light made the night even more impenetrable, and the moon and stars were hidden from view by low, dense clouds. *Just as well,* she thought. *They wouldn't want to see what we're about to do.*

"I want the chain this time," Jams said. "You've had it the last two times."

"Pussy!" Rupert mocked. "You're just scared of getting too near. Frightened of smelling the fear as the knife goes in." He hefted something from the boot, an old broom handle on the end of which was strapped a thick, long kitchen knife. He reached back in and grabbed something else, standing and throwing it to Jams in one fluid movement.

"Watch it!" Jams leaped back as the chain rattled to the ground in front of him. He bent down and picked it up almost reverently, careful only to touch the long handle, not the metal links themselves. There were a dozen sharpened blades welded onto the chain along its length, curved and barbed for added ripping effect. The whole thing was rusted blood red apart from the blades' cutting edges, which were silver and razor sharp.

"Roger, hit the lights." Rupert stepped to the gate in the overgrown hedge, stared out into the field, across to where a dark building huddled in the shadows at the far side. "You're sure they're still in there?"

" 'Course I am. I was out here yesterday, watching that sweet little tart stroke them and comb them. Looked like she was enjoying it, too. Looked like she couldn't wait to get them back into the stable." For Roger, this was sex, this was filth. Mary knew that later he would want her, soothing her and whispering sweet nothings beforehand. Sex was a duty for Mary. One that made her feel important, if only for the few seconds when Roger screwed up his eyes and muttered some name, even if it was not hers. Those few seconds were important enough.

"Sick bastard," Jams said, but he was giggling.

Roger leaned into the car and flicked off the light, plunging them into utter darkness. He hurried from the car and strained at the gate, waiting for Rupert to give the signal to head off across the field. "Here, horsey," he said, then mused: "Wonder if she *has* ever fucked them."

"For Christ's sake, Roger," Helen said, but she did not really mean it. She liked to listen, stand back in the field and hear the noises from inside. Mary suspected that she would just as gladly listen if there were two girls in the stable instead of two horses. It would appeal to her rebellious side. Law was for the masses, Helen would say. Morals are human conceits. Fuck morals. Fuck humans.

"Let's go," Rupert said. "Got the flashlight?" It took several seconds of silence for Mary to realize that he was talking to her, and she sensed a sudden wave of hostility directed her way. Sometimes she railed under this, other times she lapped it up. They thought she was nothing because she had no reason for being here. They thought that by creating their own petty, pathetic myths, they made themselves special. There was nothing special about being nothing. At least Mary could admit it to herself.

"It's in the trunk," she said.

"Hurry up," a voice growled, and in the darkness it was androgynous. It could have been any one of them hating her.

Across the field, kicking up diamonds of dew, and to the stables. Rupert snipped the padlock with a pair of bolt croppers. Helen stood back a few paces, and Mary could see her eyes wide and glinting in the night. Jams swung the chain at his side, giggling and breathing heavily. Rupert looked around, nudged Mary none too lightly and indicated that she should enter first. Jams turned and gave Helen a good-bye kiss, as if he was going to work for the day. She ignored him.

Inside, it stank of horses. Mary turned on the heavy flashlight, splashing the walls with a dirty yellow light. The two animals stomped in their stalls, snorted, staring at her with only a vague interest. She stepped forward to try to pat one of the long snouts, but the horse turned and casually plucked a mouthful of hay from a hanging feeder.

"Ignore me, will you?" she said quietly.

"They there?" Rupert stuck his head around the door and grimaced when Mary shone the light into his eyes.

"Yes. Both of them." Rupert, Jams and Roger filed into the stable. Roger motioned Mary back against the wall, arranging her like a mannequin so that the light pointed at the right place. Not once did he speak to her.

But later, after the blooding and the taking of trophies, he would. He would whisper and cajole as she did what he asked of her. He would talk of the night, excite himself again with visions of grandeur. Mary knew this, and from it she took the only comfort she could find in her meaningless life.

Roger coughed in his sleep, mumbled something incoherent and full of malice. Mary stared at the back of his head, thinking how amusing it would be to stick the stiffening horse's tail there while he was sleeping. Would he be disgusted when he woke up? Disturbed? Probably neither. Probably just angry that she had touched his trophy and ruined it by clotting the hairs with sticky tape.

His back was broad, muscled, shadowed with old tattoos. Aching to be split with a knife.

Mary closed her eyes. She was still propped up on one elbow, so she knew she would not fall asleep. But within minutes, the despised room had receded and been replaced with a wide-open space, a field in summer, a harvest of rape spraying a bright, dazzling yellow far out toward the horizon, like a field of butter.

There is a horse in this field, a huge stallion, blazing white and regal. It is undoubtedly the king of the horses, the fittest, the fastest, the model for all horses, the mold from which their imperfect shapes are cast. It is waiting for Mary to mount it. She jumps up easily, though there is no saddle.

At the edges of the field dead trees stand in misery, holding out jealous arms to where the more fertile ground supports the harvest. The horse walks slowly at first, gauging the weight on its back, allowing Mary to become accustomed to its natural rhythms. She moves with the horse as if they have been together forever. The animal turns its head, looks at her with one of its huge, bottomless eyes. Then it breaks into a canter.

The field flows by like a golden sea in a gentle breeze. The horse's hooves swish through the crop, throwing hazy clouds of dried stalks and stems into the air behind it, leaving a smoking trail across the field.

It looks back again, sees that Mary has fallen easily into the rhythm, and suddenly begins to gallop at the horizon. The end of the field remains a lifetime away, the dead trees rushing by on both sides. Mary looks up at the sky and shouts with joy, sure that the sparse cirrus clouds can hear her, certain that within its boiling heart the sun has a place for her for all eternity.

The horse looks back one last time. Its eye has changed from watery to dry, wide to narrow. It turns and points its head at the trees. From this distance they look thin and fragile, but as they rapidly approach Mary can see that their dead branches are dried into ripping, grabbing, slicing fingers.

She cries out. What? What's happening? She should be foolish to expect an answer, but nevertheless one is forthcoming, silent but sure: She is urged by some inner sense to look back over her own shoulder. She does so, and immediately becomes unbalanced. The horse picks up speed, dodging great swathes of rotten rape until there is more dead than living, upon which it begins to dodge the living.

The horse has no tail. There is a gaping wound where the proud white tail should be, *had* been, as if it has been gouged out with a blunt knife.

Mary looks back toward the trees. They are much closer than they should be, but woman and horse now seem to be taking an age to reach them. The animal is frothing at the muzzle, puffing splatters of blood-flecked saliva from its nose and mouth and letting them splash back into Mary's face and body. There is a rending, tearing sound, and a gash opens in the animal's back. Blood gushes through the tear in the beautiful coat, turning the glorious white to an instant, grotesque red. Another rip opens in the skin, curving jaggedly down toward the creature's belly. Mary feels herself slipping in blood; she tries to grab onto the horse's mane but finds it pulls through her hands and slices them open. The hair at the mane is hot and sharp, like cheese wire.

She slips some more. She is falling, the sensation is inescapable, and inexplicable because she is still holding on to the animal's flanks. Its hooves pound the dry earth into showers of dead and rotting rape, pummeling both itself and Mary relentlessly toward the scabrous line of trees.

More slashes appear in its body, coils of innards peering through as if seeking their own freedom. Mary lets go. It is the only thing to do.

She falls. Air rushes past her ears and twists her hair into swishing shapes, but still she is attached to the horse. She sees that her thighs and knees are sinking into the animal, being eaten up and frozen in place in the gashes now appearing all across its body.

Wake up!

The trees are closer now. The animal has stopped running, as if the pretense is no longer required, yet still it speeds toward the woods. Perspective and distance are fluid, and Mary is sure that across to the trees is actually down.

Wake up, you stupid bitch. Wake up, whore.

The voice comes from nowhere, but still seems more real than what she is seeing and sensing here.

Wake up, I need you, Mary. You can help me, Mary. You have skills. You have . . . passion. A snicker, half hidden in the sudden sound of clashing branches and clattering twigs. The horse opens its mouth and bellows, pain and triumph combined.

Mary's head jerked forward and hit the pillow. Her eyes snapped open. For an instant the cruel giggle was still there, hanging in the air like an echo of an echo. Then silence.

Roger jerked in his sleep. It was a movement more violent than mere muscles would cause. Then there was a loud, reverberating thud, like a bag of potatoes striking concrete. Roger was flung onto his back, his left arm and leg twisting around his body and snapping with the machine-gun rapidity of Chinese crackers. The side of his head bent inwards, squashed by an invisible force, and then burst.

"Oh." Mary could not talk, move, breathe or believe. A flash of memory hit her, the horse's splitting skin from her dream. Roger's chest now looked the same. Blood was welling in the wound, glistening in the tentative starlight peering in between the ill-fitting curtains. It overflowed and darkened the sheets, spreading slowly across the bed toward her like some living, malevolent thing.

There was a sound from next door, two thuds, almost instantaneous. Then a slow, wet slithering as something dropped onto the floor. Jams's and Helen's room.

Mary pushed herself from the mess that had been Roger, scrabbling in the sheets with feet and hands until she became truly entangled and pulled the sheets onto the floor with her. She cracked her head on the bedside table and her teeth clanged painfully, forcing a bright agony through her gums and into her temples.

Her hands smarted. When she looked she saw thin red lines seeping blood.

Is it going to happen to me?

"Oh, God, no, God, no, God, I'm sorry," she ranted, but even Mary knew how pathetic it all sounded now. The horses had come to get them, all of them, and now they were kicking in their heads while they slept, cracking skulls open like coconuts and letting the juices inside seep away to waste. Roger was steaming.

Mary huddled back against the wall. She would have pulled the sheet up over her head, if she had not noticed the spray of blood fanned across its surface. She shoved it from her, pushing it as far away as she could with her feet, tears blurring her vision and making Roger's shattered corpse move fluidly, as if he was coming for her as well.

There was a noise from the hallway. Footsteps, running. Or hooves.

"No!" Mary shouted, hurting her throat and doing it again. The pain seemed right, somehow, told her she really was awake. She checked the bed to see whether she'd had some dreadful nightmare brought on by last night. Roger's head had slowly drooped to one side, and now his remaining eye glared balefully at her. It was filling with blood.

The hooves were right outside the door. They began pounding.

"I'm so sorry!" she shouted, nails raking at her throat to drag out more apologies. "I'll never do it again, I only held the light, I'm so so so so sorry!"

The door swung open. A shape stood there. It clucked, imitating again the sound of horse's hooves.

"Don't be sorry," the shadow said. "Be glad."

Chapter Six

Death by Design

They laid Slates on the grass, next to the drowned woman whom they had already pulled from the pond. Blane took off his pullover and draped it gently over the boy's ruined head. The stench of blood was everywhere; he did not need to see it as well.

He and Holly had gone back to the pergola, but there was too little left of Saint to make it worthwhile attempting to move him. It would have taken them several trips. As for the car, it was still smoldering, and the blackened shape in the driver's seat looked ready to disintegrate at the slightest touch. They left him, or her, to cool down on their own.

Holly had barely spoken since Slates had died. She cupped her elbows in her hands, hugging herself, keeping noticeably close to Blane, smoking an occasional cigarette. Two hours had passed since she had rang for the police and ambulance service, and further attempts by others encountered constant engaged tones, whether they tried local or emergency numbers.

"How many emergency lines are there?" the grass-chewer had asked. "How many calls do they have to have to make them engaged?" Nobody bothered to answer, but each of them was quietly considering the implications of what he had said.

The villagers remained by the pond, which already felt haunted. They were waiting for something to happen, the atmosphere tense to the point of tearing, but nobody moved. Closeness seemed to bring some comfort, and shock acted as a drug.

The sun rose high and cast its spirited gaze across the landscape, disregarding the dead people scattered across it. The ducks on the pond became more animated once the sun struck the water, fussing and calling for food from the people assembled in the square. A soft haze of steam rose from damp grass and thatched roofs, slowly dissipating like the specters of those who used to live there.

Blane wondered how many dead people there were in the village that morning. There were nine survivors around the pond, he and Holly included, and the fact that they had all decided to gather here could mean one of two things: They were in the minority, or they were the only ones left.

"There's a little dead boy in the churchyard," Blane muttered. "I'm going to fetch him." He stood and left quickly, feeling suddenly uncomfortable close to so many people, living and dead. He so wanted to be back in the forest listening to nature shouting and screaming, whispering and rustling, waiting patiently for the dark when the land would really come alive. But even there, in his favorite place in the world, there was the dead deer, tingeing his memory of last night with unexpected death and the strange, half-heard sound from the dusky dawn.

He had almost reached the gate to the churchyard when he realized that Holly was following him. She still had her arms crossed, her face a maze of tears. She seemed used to affording her own comfort.

Blane did not want her to see the dead boy. Slates dying had been bad enough, but he had not had his throat chewed and torn. He was not arranged like the boy in the graveyard. Not on display.

"Maybe you should go back to the pond," he said.

Holly blinked rapidly, but she did not move. "I don't just want to sit there," she said. "It's too hot. Too quiet. Spooky. I don't want to sit there . . . with them."

Blane was unsure whether she meant the bodies, or the survivors. "Stay here, then, while I fetch the boy."

"No." Holly shouldered past him, nudging him aside, hands still cupping her elbows. "Don't tell me what to do. Last I heard, you hardly ever spoke to anyone, so don't start now by giving orders."

Blane watched Holly enter the graveyard, indecision holding him back. There was no explanation for what had happened to the boy, or why he was surrounded by dead animals. And there was no point telling her of the shadow he had seen from across the field. The shape that, along with the voice in the woods, inspired a niggling memory struggling to be recalled, as though déjà vu was stuck in the routes and byways of his mind. Whatever past Blane spent his nights trying to recall had taken one step nearer that morning.

He suddenly felt an overriding terror, not simply of what was happening, but also a fear for his soul, an icy finger working its way in between ribs and lodging there, burrowing ever closer to his heart with each breath.

"Where's the help?" the grass-eater shouted from across the square. He stood, waved his arms, stumbled around, punch-drunk by so much death. Blane knew, more than anyone, that death was the most natural consequence of living. Most people hardly ever realized that.

He glanced through the gate. Holly was standing over the dead boy, hands flexing in and out of fists, body tense with shock.

The deer in the forest had a broken, crushed neck. The nearest road had been almost a mile away. He'd seen roadkill before, a hundred times, and the victims were always stained with the car's exhalations: radiator marks; oil splashes on bloodied hide; tire marks splayed carelessly across crushed ribs. No, something else had killed the deer, something other than a car. And then that something had sent it to Blane.

Perhaps the same something had killed the boy.

Blane entered the graveyard and walked quickly past the church, away from where Holly was standing. He hardly noticed the woman huddled up against the door, tapping insistently with a red-raw fist, calling, ". . . Father . . . Father . . ." He climbed the stile without looking back, and he was pleased that there were no pleading calls from behind him. Soon he was in the field again, and the forest, his home, beckoned.

Holly could not move.

The sun stroked the back of her neck, but she was stone-cold. Nervous sweat ran cooly down her sides and pooled at her waistband. Goose bumps prickled at her skin. Her knees began to shake. She wanted to bring her left foot forward, stand properly, but terror had broken the link between brain and limbs and she simply stood there, staring down at the carnage before her.

The boy by the pond had been bad. She'd seen dead bodies before, but never an actual death. Not like that. Not so strangely. Like someone had hit him with a bus.

This was worse. Worse than if she had actually seen it happen, because the mystery of the child's death remained, and not knowing somehow made it even more awful. This had design to it, intention. This was a display aimed at people like her. The perpetrator had wanted it to be seen. His wounds were clotted into chopped-beetroot patches on his skin, his arms thrown out in a casual display of affection for the dead animals surrounding him. A tableau.

The presence of the animals was even more disturbing. Why surround a dead boy with dead creatures? And why was the boy the only one of them to bear obvious teeth marks?

She wanted to pick the child up, hug him to her, imbue him with some of her warmth in the hope that it would inspire a vanished life to return. But she was cold, and she was certain that there was not enough warmth in her own weak flesh to go around. That's how Tommy had put it when the doctor told her she was sterile. *There's nothing wrong with you,* he'd said. *You just haven't got enough life to go around. You need it all yourself.*

Poor, dead Tommy. Holly hated him for dying. But she resented herself more for not being able to keep a part of him back. He'd always wanted a child.

She tried to turn away, but the scenario held a horrible fascination. She had seen such human nature at work before, been subject to it, watching from a crashed car in disbelief while the whole motorway slewed and slowed to see blood. Seeing eyes flit over her living form to the covered mess at the roadside.

She fell to her knees, vomiting, turning and cricking her neck in a desperate attempt to direct the puke away from somebody's dead son. She went down onto her hands and knees, spitting out the last square meal she had eaten before something had gone sour with the world. She hung her head, wishing she had long hair so that it would hide what she could see from the corner of her eye. Dangling earrings tickled her cheeks, precursors of the fresh tears which inevitably came. She waited that way for a while, expecting Blane's comforting hand to fall on her shoulder any minute. But when he did not come she sat on a nearby grave and turned away from the dead boy.

There was no sign of Blane. At the church door, a woman was crying and shaking and tapping against the wood, mumbling and suffering her own private grief with the rest of them. Holly wanted to go and help her, hold her, but she would have felt like an intruder. The woman was in a world of her own, and Holly did not know that place.

She looked at the marker for the grave she was using as a stool: MARY-JANE ELIZABETH, LOVING MOTHER, ADORED WIFE, *1897–1974*. At least she had a gravestone. Tommy, her dead boyfriend, had little more than her own memories to mark his passing. And perhaps a rose on a bush in the garden of remembrance. But she would never know, because she refused to go there. No use aggravating wounds barely healed.

She stood and walked away from the boy. It crossed her mind that she had come here with Blane to fetch him and take him down to the pond, lay him out with the others, but the thought of picking him up was suddenly abhorrent. And if Blane had decided to leave, then why shouldn't she?

The sound of an engine crept in from the distance. At first Holly thought it might be the first of a fleet of ambulances, and they'd come in and clean up and tell them all that there had been some terrible accident, but it was all right now.

But the boy was lying there with dead animals around him; there was no accident here; there was only murder.

Holly trotted to the gate and out into the square just in time to see a tractor come trundling down from Pond Lane. It was towing a trailer, and even from this distance she could see the bloodstained bundles jumping on the boards. She remained by the church. She knew what was to come, and she could not bear it.

The man driving the tractor had wild hair, a beard that hung down to his chest, thick National Health glasses held together with layers of sticky-tape of varying ages. When he came into the square, saw the people around the pond, saw the two bodies on the grass, Slates's blood darkening Blane's pullover, the tractor jerked to a clumsy halt. The farmer stared in disbelief. He glanced over his shoulder at the bed of the trailer, and when he looked back there were tears spilling out from behind his glasses.

"You too?" the man said. He spoke quietly, but his voice carried, because there was no sound other than the indifferent singing of birds to drown it.

Blane went into the woods. The solace he sought was not there.

Instead, silence welcomed him. As he approached the trees the cacophony of birdsong slowly died down, until the only noise to mark his arrival was the sound of his shoes on last year's rotting leaves.

Blane loved nature. He could not recall a time when it had failed to love him back. But now he felt as if he was being shunned, as though nature had turned its back on him and left him standing alone in a cold, empty place.

He found a familiar path and quickly passed into the shadow of the trees, eager to lose sight of the church and the village altogether. An occasional breath of wind passed overhead, shaking the highest branches and brushing newly budding leaves together in secretive whispers. Blane looked up, but he could discern nothing in the canopy overhead.

He could see no squirrels or birds, no butterflies flitting from tree to tree. The familiar springtime scent of the woods seemed jaded and somehow old; the tint of new life had faded into a memory of the smell of something aged, vaguely musty, dried and desiccated. Blane bent to pick a bluebell from a cluster between two old sycamores, but when he put it to his nose and inhaled the smell was distant, a ghost of what it should be.

A tension had lifted when he left the village, the pressure of nearness to other people, which often set him on edge and sent him into a clumsy flush. Guilt accompanied the easing of this tension, but shock did much to override the guilt, and Blane found it easy convincing himself that he was doing the right thing.

But a different kind of stress bore down on him as he passed within the influence of the trees. He felt shoved from all sides so that as he walked, he was buffeted by opposing forces. The trees exuded an authority over him, nudging him here, urging him there, steering him in every direction at once. And they seemed to be growing closer together than they had before, forcing out emptiness and filling it with more of their own gnarled certainty. They were shouting to be heard, or perhaps eager to hear. Either way, Blane felt further from nature than he ever had. Today, he was a stranger in these woods.

He could not help thinking that what he'd seen in the graveyard had made him so.

He stopped, sat on the damp ground, lowered his head and shut his eyes. There was an incredible urge to leave, to run to his dilapidated home, flee from this place where he had spent much of his life.

The deer had been killed and shown to him, and then the shape in the churchyard had watched him coming across the fields. He had been lured to the display of the child and the animals with a teasing glimpse of buried memories.

What was happening?

He tried to imagine the singing birds and musical laughter he had recalled earlier that day. But all he heard now was the low, throaty chuckle that had followed the bloody death of the deer. And still he could hear no birds.

The atmosphere changed suddenly, from loaded to threatening. What before had been an absence of the normal forest noises fell instantly into utter silence. Blane kept his eyes closed, his head bowed, though the temptation to look was becoming unbearable. He wanted to see how such a wonderful, alive place could be so quiet and still.

A sourness entered his mouth, either the taste of fear or something from outside. He opened his eyes a fraction, and the leaves beneath him shifted. They slid sideways, as one, as though he were on a great carpet being tugged at one end, though he could feel no movement. They did not move again, but now they looked wrong; they were the same shape, the same pattern, but suddenly they no longer seemed to belong here.

Things had shifted.

There was a noise from his left, a shape rattling through the branches up above. Then something fell to the ground to his right, shrieking slightly as it hit, then silent. He looked up, stared about wildly, for some reason expecting a shape with teeth and claws to come racing at him. But it was only a woodpecker, its glorious colors faded and dirty in death. One wing still twitched, trying to haul its broken body back into the trees.

There were several more thumps as birds struck the leafy ground around him. Some of them fluttered briefly, calling to each other in confusion, then seemed to turn and stare at him. One, a robin, opened its beak and let out a loud hiss, a sound it should not be able to make.

Blane stood, turned and ran. Behind and around him more birds fell from the trees, calling and hissing and squawking, not one of them singing. Blane was being chased from the place where he felt most content, but the change that had been wrought here terrified him. He had to leave before he saw any more.

He took a circuitous route that brought him out halfway down Pond Lane. As he emerged from the woods, the sense of panic that had consumed him evaporated like sweat. He turned and stared back through the trees, where shadows hid secrets he had once thought he knew, and history was wrapped tightly within old trunks. As if his leaving was a signal, the twitter of birds ended the silence. Soon the sounds were almost as familiar and comforting as the feel of the old oak in his favorite clearing.

It felt like the birds were mocking him.

He reached his home after five minutes of rapid walking, a time in which he tried without success to hear the birdsong as it had once sounded; beautiful, soulful, magical. Magical, like the laughter he had remembered. But the singing now sounded as grim and dark as the chuckle he had heard in the woods that morning, as if the passage of that sound through the air had polluted whatever it touched.

He opened the front door, the familiar creak of rusting hinges welcoming him in. But even here, he no longer felt at home.

The echo of the closing door was askew, coming back from all the wrong directions. He stepped across the main room, unfamiliar creaks rising from previously sound floorboards, mysterious chirps and snicks sounding from within the walls. A monotonous dripping reached him from the back boiler, and the one radiator in his living room gurgled as if constantly being replenished. It was cold to the touch.

A window had cracked. From sill to head, the thin white line zigged jaggedly through the dirty glass. Moisture had bled in from outside and run down onto the frame, staining it dark with mold, as if it had been this way for years. The ceiling bowed downward, cracking plasterboard and opening an upside-down network of valleys and ridges in which earwigs and spiders went about their business. His bookcase, previously piled high with texts on natural history, mankind's progress through the technological era, theological studies of the harmony between nature and God . . . had rejected its contents. They lay scattered across the threadbare carpet, already yellowing and shrivelling as though subjected to an intense, sustained heat. The bookcase stood empty and defiant. Even the footprints of the books in the dust had vanished.

His world had rejected him. Blane left his home for the last time.

Chapter Seven

The Absent They

Peer had nowhere to go. But she had to go somewhere.

She shut the door to her flat after picking up her keys and hauling on a pair of dirty jeans from the washing basket. Shutting Kerry in, so no one else would have to see her. Then closing Kerry's front door as well, so she would not have to see Keith's ribs again.

Calmness had emerged from somewhere, a strange calm like the temporary peace at the eye of a hurricane. Control took over and started telling her what to do, guiding her actions with a dispassionate eye, steering her across the echo chamber landing to the flat opposite. She rapped on the door, although she could hardly imagine anyone still being asleep after Kerry's murderous screaming. There was no answer, so she knocked again, louder.

"Mr. Stapleton? Could I use your phone? I need to call an ambulance. And the police." Still no answer, no voices, no sounds of movement from behind the heavy door. In fact, Mr. Stapleton's flat exuded an unnatural stillness. Or perhaps it was just because everywhere else seemed to be a source of grotesque noise. Perhaps the Stapletons were in there now, huddled under a blanket, cuddled together in the sure knowledge that thirty years of companionship would guard them against whatever had ruined the night. Peer hoped that was the case. She could not imagine them dead. "Could you ring them for me, Mr. Stapleton? Please?"

Peer jumped as a shout erupted from the open lobby two floors below. It was incoherent, a roar of terror and woe, someone screaming in tongues at a God who could have let something so appalling happen. Peer composed herself quickly; that buffer zone again, pulling her back from the infected area of thought and calming her by distancing her from things.

But some things cannot be tempered. On the way down the final flight of stairs fear bit in abruptly, richer and sweeter than any she had yet experienced. It stretched her skin, tingled in her nipples and at the base of her neck, and still she had to see. If anything, she moved faster.

In the lobby a naked fat man was veering from wall to wall, screaming, slapping blood from his huge stomach and face and chest. Peer sat down heavily and began to shake. The distance was still there, but while she was one step removed from what was happening, she realized that the shock of what she had seen had finally forced through.

73

There was blood all over her flat, probably leaking through the floorboards into the room below, and something had crushed Kerry without actually being there.

She shivered; Kerry's blood on her T-shirt had cooled enough to kiss coldly onto her skin. She peeled the shirt from her chest, wincing as it stuck there momentarily.

"Is something wrong?" she asked suddenly, surprising herself. The fat man continued to shout, gradually bruising himself against door handles and the fire extinguisher, paying her no attention. She was sure she could see the whites of his eyes. The blood did not appear to be his own.

What was going on? This couldn't be happening everywhere; it was too crazy, too unbelievable. But here she was, sitting on the staircase just before dawn with a dead person in each flat upstairs, a madman slowly trying to batter down the lobby, blood drying on her clothes and skin, and she hadn't even rung the police.

There was screaming in the street. The woman, kneeling in front of her house. Shouts from farther away, the surprised clamor of a world waking to a nightmare.

Jenny. Peer had to go to her place. They could help each other understand what all this was about, hold each other, sit and wait for the police and ambulances to arrive at the flats to take away Kerry, and Keith, and this fat man's wife.

And the Stapletons?

She glanced at the four doors on the ground floor, handles greased with blood from the screaming man. She wondered what scenes they hid this morning.

The man seemed to be tiring. He slumped as he hit each wall, winding down, before forcing himself away and onto the next one, slowing every time, panting, the screams quieter and higher pitched.

Peer stood and stepped unsteadily down the last few stairs. "Please stop," she said. "Calm down, keep still, stop." The man looked at her and his eyes rolled in their sockets, like those of a fighting dog appraising its next target. Peer stepped back, ready to turn and thump up the stairs if the fat guy did so much as raise a hand. But his unsteady gaze went right through her, eyes dilated in the semi-dark, still seeing whatever it was that had driven him to this state. His mouth slowly opened and he began to wail, and Peer took her chance and ducked past him.

"I'll call an ambulance," she shouted, just in case he could hear her. But when she opened the heavy door from the lobby to the street outside, she guessed that the ambulances were busy this morning.

The street was lined on both sides with three- and four-story Victorian buildings, most of them converted into flats of varying quality, from squalid upward. The council had tried planting trees last year, with a view to adding an "Avenue" to the street name to make it sound more exclusive. Local kids had enjoyed a brief period of tree-swinging and now the pavements were pocked with weed-infested squares, out of which stuck sad dry stalks like paupers' gravestones.

About one out of every twenty lights was on.

The remaining windows were dark, exuding an aura of death. Pigeons sat only on unlit window-sills. The screaming woman had vanished, presumably back into her own flat, but the light remained on. It still retained its red tinge.

There were several people in the street. One man was calmly walking his dog along the opposite pavement, whistling softly, the only indication that something was amiss was the fact that he was still wearing his pajamas. The dog was marking corners and wagging its tail in delight at this unexpected early morning stroll. Opposite the local shop, two people stood hugging and crying, both of them talking incoherently in an apparent attempt to comfort each other. Peer headed toward them, only realizing now that she had forgotten to find a pair of shoes. Her bare feet made slap, slap sounds on the pavement. Dead fish hitting a worktop.

"Hello," she said when she reached them. Two women, both middle-aged, both tightly wrapped in nightgowns. One of them had curlers in her hair, and Peer felt an irrational compulsion to laugh. She tried to hold it back, but it came out as a groan and turned quite naturally into a stuttering sob.

"Oh, no," one of the women, the one with the curlers, said. "Not you too."

"My neighbors are dead," Peer said through fresh tears. Maybe the distance is closing, she thought. Although now was when she needed it—whatever it was—most of all.

"I know, dear, I know," Curlers said.

I know?

"I've got to phone for an ambulance, though, because, you know, it's remarkable what the human body can withstand." She remembered Keith's ribs pointing at the ceiling. Kerry's eyeball sitting like a billiard ball on her living room floor.

Curlers broke her hug, but kept one hand on the shoulder of the woman next to her; she was staring at the ground and shedding a steady rain of tears at the pavement. "I've already tried that, dear. No use. I've been getting engaged for an hour."

"I tried," the other woman said suddenly, looking up and presenting Peer with a face devoid of any color save the bright red smudge of hastily applied lipstick. Even her eyes were like a sepia-tinted photograph. "I got through, too. But when I asked for an ambulance, the lady at the other end said they were too busy. She asked me for my number, then hung up."

"Too busy? How can the emergency services be too busy? My friend's lying in a pool of guts, her boyfriend's dead and there's a naked fat man in my lobby, covered in somebody else's blood. Shouldn't the police be out trying to find out who's doing all this? What if—"

"I think it's happened everywhere, dear," Curlers said. She leaned over and whispered just as loudly as she'd been talking. "I heard Mrs. James here crying, knocked on her door. Her husband was dead in the living room, with the telly still on, watching one of those nasty films, you know? There was lots of blood. Awful!"

"What about you?" Peer asked.

"Not married, dear. I just like to help. I think my work's cut out this morning, don't you?" She nodded over Peer's shoulder at a group of people walking up the street, many of them bloodied, some carrying dripping bundles of clothes that could only contain children. The blood contrasted with the other colors, fading them into weak background tints.

"I have to see if my friend's all right," Peer said. "When they get here, could you tell the ambulance men that there are people in the top flats at number thirty-eight?" Curlers nodded, then guided her friend past Peer and toward the shuffling group of stunned humanity.

Peer should be joining them, but the remoteness was still there, as if she was watching a well-made film and becoming so engrossed in the story that she imagined herself within it. She felt no real connection with these people. No real link. But still, she had to find Jenny.

The streets were mostly quiet, but Peer could hear crying behind locked doors. A pack of dogs fought over something in an alleyway and she hurried on, not wanting to see what it was they were scrapping over.

Whatever had happened had seemed to turn the streets into a place of extremes. The silence was deep and profound, but when it was broken by a scream or a shout the noise would reverberate between buildings like an explosion. Once or twice Peer heard sirens, but they were from a long way off, and she saw no blue flashing lights. Cars passed by occasionally, some of them obviously being driven in a blinding panic: one had both back doors open, displaying a bloody bundle on the rear seat; another was using other parked cars and lampposts as guides, coughing out showers of sparks each time it careered across the road to bounce from the opposite side. Its windows were smashed in, and Peer could only see the shadow of a driver. It looked like a kid.

She stepped back into a doorway in case the car found a gap and mounted the pavement, but it scraped by, giving an old Beetle a screeching kiss as it passed. Gears crunched inexpertly as the incline dragged at the engine. The hospital was on the other side of the hill. People were taking matters into their own hands.

She tried to imagine the scene at Accident and Emergency this morning. She closed her eyes to shut out the image, but sightlessness sent her imagination into overdrive.

Overhead a helicopter thumped its way across town, coming from the direction of the rising sun. It was low and quite slow, and Peer recognized it as one of the local police choppers brought into use recently to track joyriders. Waving her arms she stepped out between parked cars, checking both ways beforehand. The helicopter slashed the silence into angry fragments, cruising above the street at a hundred feet, dark against the dawn. Its dead searchlamps hung like bombs on either side of the cockpit. It was nearing her and she continued to wave, swinging her arms back and forth over her head as she had seen desert island castaways do on television a hundred times before.

The machine passed her by. She saw the passenger staring down through the glass panel in his door. The police markings were plain, as was the fact that they had no intention of helping.

Peer felt abandoned, spurned, just like those desperate desert island dwellers. She watched in dismay as the helicopter followed the road up the incline toward the cathedral, then veered away suddenly and disappeared across the rooftops.

They were heading away from the hospital now, toward an emergency more important than her own. Where were the ambulances, and the police? Where was order? They were supposed to be ready for things like this, have contingency plans to put into effect any time there was a major accident or disaster. They were supposed to help. Peer had worked in a hospital for a while, answering the phone on a casualty ward, making appointments, taking complaints, and she had seen two major accident practices.

Day patients were cleared. The unit was flooded with nurses, some of them wearing triage vests. Doctors hurried in wearing golf clothes, shorts, jeans. Beds were cleared, gurneys were lined up like horses set for the off. There was control there, organization, an adeptness at handling the unthinkable and the terrible that had both impressed and comforted her.

The police had passed her by, even though she'd been waving her arms for help. Surely that was an offense?

Peer realized with a sense of emptiness how much the everyday person relies on the faceless They in times of upheaval. And if They chose not to deliver the goods—or *could* not do so—then the masses were left on their own.

She decided to walk along the canal path to Jenny's house. It would take slightly longer, but it was away from the obvious danger of the roads, and it passed through one of Peer's favorite places, the park. Maybe that would calm her, ease her worries, because surely things couldn't be as bad as they seemed. There must be a disease or something, one of those exotic hot viruses from Africa that caused a rapid bleed-out, no time to help, nothing to cure. She recalled a film she had seen on that subject; the final solution they had to the problem then was a big bomb.

She walked quickly toward the canal, her own bare footfalls echoing behind her as she passed through the narrow alley leading to the towpath. A dog scampered ahead, sandy snout darkened and wet, eyes frenzied. Away from the shouting, and the wandering people, and the dangerous driving, she tried to imagine normality. But she could not. Even this alley had changed, or rather the things in it: the moss on the old brickwork was rank and foul; pigeons sat quietly along the tops of walls, observing her progress with pinprick eyes; the dog, well groomed and sporting a thick collar, looking like a wild animal after the kill.

Peer hurried through the alley and came out onto the towpath. There was a body in the canal. A man, floating facedown, a long coat billowing around him. On the opposite side lay a bloodied parcel of sheets, hair splayed from one end like spilled straw.

She stared down at her bare feet, set off toward Jenny's place, dodging dogshit and trying so hard not to look around and see what was happening. She was breathing fast and her heart thumped in her chest, and she knew that it was not entirely from the exertion.

She emerged into the park, but the feeling of reassurance she often had when she walked among the bushes and trees was absent today. On the contrary, her sense of displacement, of not belonging, increased dramatically. The trees seemed to grow closer to the canal than before, and mean twigs scratched perforated lines of blood in the skin of her bare arms. Soon she was running, certain that other footsteps followed in exact synchronicity with her own, but too afraid to look back and see. Her feet hurt as they pounded down into the dirt, but it was a numbing pain, flaring briefly, then settling into a background throb. She tried to dodge sharp stones or puddles of broken glass, but she could feel and hear the wet slap of her bleeding feet as she sprinted for the next bridge.

The canal was unused and unkempt, a clogged artery through the sickly town, and rushes grew in abundance. Just before Peer reached the bridge they parted, and a knot of ducks flew straight at her. She stumbled in their midst, lost her footing and started to fall, positive that she felt several cruel prods from angry beaks in the flurry of waving limbs and dancing feathers. The birds careered low across the park and disappeared over a clump of shrubs toward the lake, calling loudly back at her. Peer rolled to break the fall, but still she cried out as her knees and elbows took the brunt of the impact. Her teeth clanged shut, her limbs hurt. Spots of blood were already bleeding through muddy skid marks on her arms.

The park seemed to laugh. Birds sang in triumph. Trees whispered their pleasure with a breeze from nowhere. Squirrels sat at the bases of trees, watching her dispassionately, turning nuts in their claws as they gnawed.

Even the grass looked sharp.

Peer stood and ran the last few paces to the bridge, clambering up the well-worn path and hauling herself over the stone balustrade. Only when she was out of the park, safely surrounded by faceless concrete and glass facades and aware once more of the shouts of desperate people, did she stop to assess her wounds.

She was Girl Friday on this terrible Tuesday morning, leaving a trail of bloody footprints behind her on the pavement. She lifted one foot to look at the damage and could not bear to look at the other. Her elbows and knees were cut and bruised, she could feel the cool dribble of blood running down her left leg and out onto her bare foot, the world was going mad around her. . . .

She should get to Jenny's. Then she'd sort herself out.

Jenny was dead.

She was lying naked on her Laura Ashley duvet, a cigarette burnt down to the filter between her fingers. It had raised tiny heat blisters on her skin. There was a faded rose tattoo on her left breast, the prickly hint of dark hairs on her shins and biscuit crumbs nestled in the nape of her neck. The television was still on, emitting an uncomfortable hiss. There were no other marks on her body at all. But she was dead, pale and cool. Her eyes were squeezed shut, her mouth stretched into an everlasting grimace of terror. Whatever had killed her, she had known it was coming.

Peer did not want to touch her, but she had come this far and she felt she owed her friend that, at least. She sat on the bed and stroked the dead woman's cheek.

Later, she stood suddenly and fled the room, thundered down the stairs and somehow did not fall. She opened the front door and ran into the street. Now, she was just another running person.

Peer had nowhere to go.

Chapter Eight

What's in a Name?

"Be glad that I need you," the voice said, and Mary was glad.

The woman walked into the room accompanied by the rattle of chains. At least, Mary thought it was a woman. The voice was androgynous, deep and dry; it must have hurt to speak. There were two fine chains, hanging from pinched skin at her temples, curving past eyes and over cheeks and passing into the corners of her mouth. They had been there for a long time, because they had rusted. The chain Mary heard rattling was the one they had used to flay the horse's flesh that night. The woman swung it by her side. It dripped fresh blood, even though they had been back for hours.

Her hair was long and thick, might once have been blond but now hung mousy and gray with dirt and grease. Her face seemed scarred by time, wrinkles clustered around her eyes and mouth like dried noodles. When she walked, her shapeless clothing whispered around her, offering no clues. But she carried herself as a woman, stood like a woman. Pouted like a woman when Mary began to cry.

"I'm sorry," Mary said quietly, "were the horses yours?"

The woman laughed, a dry cackle that completely failed to manifest itself in her expression. "In many ways, I suppose so. Yes, you could say so."

"Oh."

"But I'm glad," the woman continued. She nodded, pursing her lips as if contemplating a timeless work of art. She stroked the chain against her leg, the sharp blades pricking threads from her loose trousers. "You did a good job."

Mary glanced over at Roger, still swimming behind her tears. The woman followed her gaze.

"He did a good job, too, I suppose. But it's you I wanted, Mary. You're the one I need. You're the one I decided to . . . wake to your potential." She sat on the foot of the bed, unconcerned at the blood-spattered sheets. "I admire you."

"Me?" Mary felt her shaking subside, the fear diluting in the presence of this strange woman. She did not want it to happen; she wanted to be afraid, if only because she could not bear change. But already, the bloody mess on the bed was losing meaning. Just as the steaming bodies they left in the stables and fields and pens lost meaning so soon after they had seemed so important. Roger was fading to a dead memory; he just happened to still be here.

"You." The woman leaned forward, and Mary realized that the chains were not pierced into her temples. There were small, rusty bolts holding them there, apparently screwed into her skull. Unreality swept across the moment, changing how things were now, altering things, for Mary, forever.

"What happened to you?" Mary asked, with a reverence that felt entirely natural. "What are those chains?"

"These?" The woman tugged at one of the chains, jerking her head and encouraging a teardrop of blood from the old wound. It trickled down the chain and hung suspended by her cheek. She seemed unconcerned. "These are a secret."

"Why do you want me?" Mary had started to feel good. Not just well, or less fearful, but good inside. A feeling she could not remember experiencing for years, a sensation showing its tentative face from within the folds of her darkened soul.

"Mary, how can you say that? Surely you can see how useful you are. How special." She frowned. "Do you mock me by asking why I would want you?"

"No, no, I don't mock you, I . . ." She was not sure what she was going to say, but it felt vaguely daring.

"You what, Mary?" The woman leaned forward some more, and Mary realized now that she was foolish to have ever doubted her gender. Not only was she confident and sure, she was also quite beautiful. Her eyes were green, the color of life, and though her sallow skin contrasted sharply with this appearance, her breasts hung heavy and full beneath her shirt. Mary had an obscene, tingling image of suckling at them, and the woman's smile hinted that she knew what Mary was thinking.

"Well, you'll be able to say it in time." She sat upright again, reaching down for the chain at her feet. "Now then—"

There was a shout. A shape lurched into the doorway and leaned against the frame, its moaning accompanied by the uneven patter of escaping blood on the floor. It was Rupert. He looked as if he was trying to talk, but his jaw chewed gore. The side of his head was strangely flat and wet, and his left eye did not move with his right.

"Sleeping," he spat, ". . . hit me."

He saw the woman on the bed, Roger dead behind her. "What . . . ?"

The woman did not even honor him with an answer. She stood and swung the chain. It wrapped itself around Rupert's throat and he muttered in surprise as the blades bit into his skin. The woman held the handle with both hands and pulled.

Mary was fascinated. The woman tapped her on the shoulder seconds later, jerking her back to attention. *His throat*, Mary thought gleefully, *just gone.*

"As I was saying," the woman said, "I need you to do something for me."

"What? What?" Right then, Mary would have gladly used the chain on herself. For this woman who made her feel so wanted, she would have flagellated the skin and flesh from her own back and offered her spine for appraisal.

Mary was handed the chain. "First, I'm sure you're pretty good with this. Yes?"

"I've never—"

"Good, I'm sure." The woman's voice bore a trace of impatience now, but Mary had to know more.

"What's your name?"

The stranger stared at Mary for a long time, eyes piercing, chain twitching as her scalp flexed in thought. "I suppose it won't hurt you knowing."

What's in a name? flashed across Mary's mind.

"My name's Fay. I'm here to save you. And this is what I need you to do."

Chapter Nine

Arguing with Instinct

He is cold to the bone. Someone has left the aircraft door open and frosty air spins through the cabin, rattling parachute lines, laden with snow. The sound of the engines, pumping choking fumes into the slipstream and straining against the thin air, drowns everything else.

He is sitting with his back against the fuselage, hands clasped on his knees. There are others there with him. All wait in the same worshipful attitude. He wants to talk to them, but they are bags of bones, flashes of skull showing under spiderwebbed hair. They have been waiting forever.

He goes to cry out in frustration, but then his mother appears from the cockpit. She is dressed as she had been for his wedding. The colors of her exquisite clothing shout out against the dead blandness of the aircraft, melt their way through the assembled army of skeletons and seem to imbue them with a jerking, tentative life. Bony hands lift like a marionette's, helmeted heads raise and aim empty eye sockets at him. Impossibly, the skeletons grin.

The airplane banks violently and a storm of snow blasts through the open door, instantly camouflaging the movement of living bones. He tumbles from his seat, cries out as he realizes what is happening, claws his hands in the vain hope that he will grasp onto something before the void claims him.

He is falling.

He has no parachute, because he does not belong here with the others. Wind freezes his hearing. Above him, through the angry snow, he can see the tail of the aircraft drifting into the distance before it fades away behind a blanket of white, disappearing into nothing.

He spins, limbs flailing like independent living things. He cannot breathe; air rushing past his face sucks out what breath he has. He wants so much to scream, but his chest is an agony allowing only an unspoken dread. He remembers his mother, not as she had been on the plane but as he had last seen her, waving at the airport, a splash of exuberant color among the burned pink hides of the tourists.

His fall levels and now he can see below. A great whiteness is sucking him in, drawing him toward itself as implacably as death follows life. He finds a breath but does not scream; the impulse has left him, replaced with a certainty that there really is nothing too much to be afraid of here. Here he is alone, allowed to reflect upon things at his own pace, using his own thoughts. He can consider his life, and what went wrong. He can see Jenna's face below the water, eyes nibbled by fish. Here, he is himself. So often he exists purely as others see him.

A landscape carves itself from the plain whiteness, like a drawing slowly appearing on a blank sheet of paper. Texture first, hills rising slowly to meet him, valleys shying away. Then trees and walls, speckled with the snow yet still distinguishable from this height.

The last few seconds speed by. The ground rushes up, eager to meet him.

He strikes. There is no breath to be knocked from him, but still the jarring is massive, the impact on arms, legs and torso driving great spears of pain into his spine. He is instantly enclosed in blackness, wiping out the glaring white as effectively as a funeral shroud hides the dead from the living.

He thrashes wildly, waving his arms and legs in an effort to shift the snow which has covered him.

Wake up, son.

He was still buried beneath the snow. There was a hint of light, but it barely found its way between his sticky eyelids. He shoved at the blanket holding him down and the air hit him, cooling his sweat and bringing him gasping awake.

Paul sat up, panting at the cold and the shock of the strangely vivid dream. A sudden rush of emotion swept through him, a relief so palpable that he could not believe he had been asleep for the last six hours. The snow had enveloped him, eaten him, cushioning his fall and trying to crush him in the process. But it had also been a shield behind which he could hide and belong to himself. The coolness still lingered on his body, spreading through the fine sheen of sweat and prickling his skin into goosebumps. He thought briefly of Jenna; wondered whether she had been in the dream; said a silent hello to her.

Paul jumped from the bed and rubbed his arms briskly to restore some warmth. He'd always been a fast waker, either through a love of life or a weariness toward it; often, he could not decide which. His arms and legs ached; his back was sore in several places. He cursed the cheap mattresses they used in these holiday cottages.

He dressed quickly, vowing to wash later but eager now to simply retain some warmth around his body. As he hurried downstairs, he wished he had saved enough loose change to replace the Calor gas canister in the mobile heater. Switching the kettle on for the first of his several early morning mugs of tea, Paul's thoughts suddenly snapped back to the strange dream.

So vivid. His mother, smiling at him in the plane. The strange skeletons, sitting there in eternal readiness for an arrival that would never come. The ground rushing to meet him, snow cushioning his fall and spreading the impact throughout his body, into his legs, arms and back, all aching now, all displaying signs of having recently been struck a heavy blow.

Jenna, giving him a fluid stare through mutilated eyes. He blinked, shook his head, trying to forget. But dislodging the memory of Jenna was like trying to escape his own shadow. All he could do was keep her in the dark, where she didn't show so much.

He pulled up the sleeves on his left arm and twisted in the dawn light. Beneath his smooth brown skin there were several areas where bruising was already forming, swelling and pushing outward from the bone. "Shit." He must have been thrashing so hard in the bed that he'd struck himself on the frame.

The kettle boiled and he poured himself a huge mug of tea, two teabags, four sugars. The milk smelled suspicious, but there were no lumps in it as yet, and it was only a day out of date. It was either this or walk down to the village to buy another pint. Besides, he had a cast-iron constitution.

He strolled through to the cluttered living room—his study for the duration of his stay—and opened the curtains. A smile came unbidden at the sight that greeted him, a sense of peace tempering the ache in his muscles. He was still cold, but the tea was melting the dream from his body and warming him to the day.

The woods began at the far edge of the field in front of the cottage. They rose to the right and rolled gently down to the left, following the line of the valley into Rayburn. In the distance, over the heads of the trees, Paul could see the faint outline of the Cotswolds peering through the early morning mist. The sun shone from behind the house, throwing the untended garden into shadow and lighting only the true wilderness of nature. The field was fallow, left to the whims of nature by a farmer too traditional or too wealthy to bother with an awkward-shaped field on sloping ground. Along its side ran the path Paul took every day, lugging his rucksack containing food and drink, a camera slung around his neck, notebooks and pencils folded carefully away in a leather folder strapped to his belt. Already he had worn the grass down to a flattened trail, temporarily rescuing a path back from nature.

He had been here for just over a month, since the early flowers pushed their way through the frost-hardened soil, to catalogue and observe the profusion of plants and animals inhabiting the woods. They were among the most densely populated in the country, with an even greater span of species than many manufactured wildlife reserves. His colleagues at the Wildlife Heritage Trust seemed to view his excitement as more than a naive enthusiasm for the job, and cracked smart remarks about him having someone on the go in the area. One or two of them had made other veiled comments, painted as humor but instilled with an age-old prejudice. These he had tried to ignore. It was never simple to do so, but when the Trust had approved his four-month stay just outside Rayburn Woods it was easier.

The truth was, Paul was fascinated by nature. The area was intriguing, and it offered him the perfect isolation. There were so many species of bird and small mammal here, that it almost seemed unnatural.

This morning, however, something was different. Paul frowned through the steam from his tea as he took another mouthful. Things were slightly askew, though he could not discern precisely what. It was as if a familiar landmark had been removed overnight, leaving a glaring gap in the landscape.

"Now what's wrong here?" Paul shivered, the last remnant of the dream fleeing his body. *Goose on your grave,* his mother would have said. He felt disturbed on a level far too remote to name. Everything was normal, he was sure, and yet there was something niggling at the back of his mind, like a name long forgotten but aching to be recalled. If he went to make more tea—diverted his attention—he might suddenly realize what it was. And yet he was fascinated with this sensation, this feeling that something in the scene was out of kilter. He shook his head, closed his eyes, opened them again. The view was the same, familiar yet lacking. Or, perhaps, there was more than was normal out there.

"Bruised arms," he muttered. "What about them? Bruised back, too, by the feel of it." He placed his fingertips on the window and gently tapped the glass, willing the fault to make itself clear, trying not to analyze the details of the scene too hard in case he was missing the big picture.

It seemed so natural to link the strange dream with what he was sensing now, that he did not question it.

"Nope." He turned away, frowning, and stalked slowly back into the kitchen.

It hit him just as he was filling the kettle for the second time. "Too much," he said. "Too much going on." He ran back into the living room and looked through the window again. As was often the case, he chatted to himself, as if verbalizing everything for posterity. Some would have told him that this was a sign of loneliness.

The view was wonderful. Beautiful. But flawed.

"Birds everywhere. All sorts." They darted across the field, twisting in the air in peculiar flight patterns, diving into the long bracken and emerging with some squirming breakfast morsel. Blue tits and green finches twittered and argued along the fence between the garden and the field. A woodpecker leaped around near the garden gate, inspecting the cracks in the concrete path. A pair of buzzards drifted high up, watching the proceedings.

"They're hardly singing. And when they do, it's barely normal. More like shouting. And those rabbits."

The family of rabbits sat at the fence, staring in. Staring in, at him.

There were several magpies in the old apple tree at the corner of the garden. They sat apart, calling to each other intermittently to ensure they had not been abandoned. They were all watching the house. Their heads jerked slightly, as if plucking insects from the air.

"Seven. Must have a secret."

Sometimes a bird would leave its place on the fence and disappear over the top of the house. Another would instantly flutter down to take its place, as if filling the blank spaces in a defensive wall.

"Weird." Paul was not especially afraid. He'd been studying nature for a long time, ever since his mother had bought him a subscription to a natural history magazine for his seventh birthday, and he knew that there was a reason behind everything. Apparent randomness was the lifeblood of nature; each event went to make up the balanced whole. Many of these designs had yet to be perceived by man, but nature had a way of dealing out what was right. Paul was certain of this, and it had become his faith, in the same way that his mother believed in her benign God who still seemed to take everything personally.

Order was how nature controlled itself. There was an order to everything, not in some fated way—fate was a human conceit, a fall guy for good or bad—but in a certainty derived from millions of years of evolution and survival. The things living on Earth now inhabited branches on the tree of nature, and when the boughs became too heavy and began to break there would be a disease, or an asteroid, to balance the trunk once more. It was an analogy he liked, because it seemed to fit circumstance so well. Humanity had a branch at the top: thin, new, still bending in the wind, still molding itself to its final shape. Paul only hoped that it did not become too large and bring stress to the tree. A stress that would demand action.

Though in many ways, this was already happening.

"Weird," Paul said once more. "Damn weird. Hello, birdies. What are you up to today, huh? And you, Mrs. Rabbit. Shouldn't you be back inside now, dodging us ghastly humans?" Now that he had realized what was amiss, or rather different, he could perceive it more and more. The birds on the fence, the magpies, the rabbits; even a few badgers sitting at the base of the old oak out near the woods, staring up the field. All of them, staring at the house.

"Fucking weird." A coolness had settled over Paul's skin again, as if he was still buried in the snowdrift of his dreams. He'd heard about that once, someone falling from a plane but landing in snow and surviving with cuts and bruises.

Bruises. His arms were swelling, tender to the touch. He flexed his shoulders, and felt a nest of pain settled in between his shoulderblades.

"Breakfast can wait." He put his mug down by the sink, adding to the steadily expanding chaos of unwashed crockery, and hurried upstairs for his jacket. He pulled on another pair of socks while he was there and stuffed some gloves into his pocket.

But when he arrived outside, he found that most of the coolness had been within. The sun had just tipped its head over the cottage and down into the garden, and as he stepped from the shadows he felt the still heat wash over him. He undid the jacket, keeping his eyes on the retreating flurry of animals, noticing that several of the birds remained on the fence not ten steps away. They were often more trusting in the country, he found, but not this tame. The only time he had ever had a bird feeding from his hand was in the bad winter several years ago. And that memory recalled the white dream once again, and aggravated the pain.

There was a definite change in the atmosphere. The air felt altered, wilder, and even though he often shirked the company of others, he decided that a trip to the village would be beneficial. Besides, he tried to convince himself, he needed some bread and milk, and he could have a fried breakfast in the pub.

And those birds were still acting strangely.

Paul looked back, expecting to see a line of rooks sitting patiently along the cottage ridge line, seagulls swarming overhead, circling as if he was one of many ants in a huge nest. There were none, however, and silently and gratefully he cursed Hitchcock.

For the first time in his life he felt unsettled by

nature. He was often in awe, a sensation he believed was not experienced enough by people in these modern days. Now, awe was reserved for the cinema or computer, not out in the open where it should be felt, allowed to grow and expand organically with the wonders of the world that inspired it. He had been frightened too, several times, a healthy fright that he attributed to his more natural, instinctive side than his educated humanity. Once, he had faced a wild cat in Scotland, a big old tom with scars decorating his snout like some mysterious hieroglyphic. Paul had wanted to run, but instinct told him to stay. The cat had hissed, darted at him, veered off and disappeared into the woods. He had been both terrified and ecstatic.

Now he was experiencing an uneasiness which, if he did put it down to instinct, scared him more than anything. There was no reason to be frightened. Nature faced him, as it did every morning, but this time he was being stared at rather than skirted around.

Fear kept the warmth from his bones.

Leaving his rucksack inside the front door, he dropped his coat back on the hook and set off for the village. As he closed the garden gate he felt suddenly exposed, naked under the glare of a million eyes. It was as if the whole world were watching him. He glanced around, truly fearful, expecting at any second to be attacked from the sky or the hedgerow. But nothing came, and silence had once again descended across the landscape. Looking back into the garden, he saw only the sights he was used to. Birds fluttering around the hanging baskets of peanuts, the secret dashing of rabbits in the field. Normality.

He hurried down the road, watchful and alert. The lane was so rarely used that weeds and grasses grew along its center hump, and Paul kept to this in an effort to hide the sound of his footsteps. He smiled uncertainly at his actions, but the fear was still there, nestling in his stomach and warning him, with indelicate twinges, that everything was not right with the world today.

The lane fell slowly down into the shallow valley, curving around hedgerows and hillocks, old stone walls on either side held up more by the plants piercing them than by design. The day seemed to be in tension, sprung with some massive event waiting to be unraveled, heavy with the promise of future strangeness. Paul wondered what the hell had happened during the night. He no longer felt at home walking down this lane. Rather, it seemed that he was an outcast, excluded by nature and turned into an intruder. He felt an unreasonable sense of betrayal; unreasonable, because nature did not deal with such pettiness as vanity and that, in truth, was what Paul was exercising. He mourned the loss of his place. He grieved the shunning of his love; a love given freely, because Paul knew he could love nature without having to worry about the feeling being reciprocated. And perhaps that was why he felt so hurt: He had thought it could never happen this way.

He passed Milligan's Pond. It was silent this morning, the usual chirrup of crickets and the covert splashing of fish or frogs absent. The surface of the water was still and undisturbed, mirroring the clear, bright sky. Paul felt the sun on the back of his head, drawing sweat from his body beneath the two pullovers, coaxing the final reticent buds to open on the trees and plants around him. He passed the pond quickly. He wanted to reach the village, chat with Mrs. Greenwood in the shop, spend a couple of hours in the company of his own kind.

Maybe he'd been shutting himself away for too long, avoiding the company of other people in the vain belief that he was closer to nature than they. Could he really think that, and still be the reasonably minded person he took himself for? Was he being conceited, hiding away in the woods with his clipboard and an air of natural superiority? Was he full of shit?

"Full of shit." Paul shook his head. As he rounded a bend in the road he saw an ambulance. It sat at the T-junction of the lane and the main road through the village, idling, puffs of exhaust rising into the still air. And, as if to amplify the feeling he had been trying to shake this morning, there was something very wrong.

The front cab doors were open. There was no one inside. The engine was still running, waiting for a getaway, but nobody seemed ready to jump in and go screeching off on some lifesaving errand. Indeed, apart from the steady grumble of the engine, the vehicle was as quiet and eerie as the fields surrounding it.

Paul trotted the last few steps and leaned in the driver's side. There was a smear of blood across the white paintwork next to the door. The vehicle stank of sweat. There were sandwich wrappers and squashed drink cartons scattered in the footwells, drifted against the gearstick housing like wind-blown refuse. As if the missing paramedics had had a busy night.

"Hello!" Paul cupped his hands around his mouth and hollered, thinking that perhaps they were off treating someone; a fallen biker, a clumsy farmer who'd become entangled in his own barbed wire. He circled the van once, looking out into the fields and along the road toward the village. Nothing. He walked to the overgrown hedge between the road and the pond, expecting to lean over and see some sort of rescue operation already in progress.

Nothing. A dead cat lay in the hedge, slowly drying and melting down into the landscape. But there was no sign of any ambulance men. No sign of life.

Paul went back to the vehicle and climbed in the driver's door. He didn't want to have to touch that smear of blood, or even pass it. It was proof that something had gone badly wrong. "Pretty normal in an ambulance," he said, eager to disturb the spooky silence. "Got to be expected. Probably in a field somewhere, behind a wall, can't hear me calling. Treating a runaway kid with exposure or some loony-toon, wandered away from their nursing home, hairbrush in one hand, melting Mars bar . . .

"I wonder what's in the back." He did not really want to know, of that he was sure. But he was equally certain that the same inquisitiveness that directed him to sit in the woods for weeks on end, cataloguing and recording and counting, would now urge him to open the back doors and see. Human nature, to be nosy. That was what made us powerful and superior, many said. Paul would argue that humanity was inferior, rather than superior, but in this case he could not argue with instinct.

The doors were not locked. They opened easily. There were no bodies inside, but Paul wished there had been.

Rather that, than all the blood.

It looked like someone with a grudge against white had taken to the interior of the ambulance with a spray gun full of blood. Walls, ceiling, floor, all glistened with new, or shone with the faded sheen of old blood. There was one trolley, covered with a mish-mash of bloodied blankets and used, caked bandages. It stank like a butcher's shop first thing in the morning. Open, fresh meat. Insides.

Paul turned away, gagging. "What the hell?" he said, staggering back around to the cab, supporting himself against the vehicle. The engine died. It coughed, gave out a couple of shuddering gasps, then cut out. Jumping into the cab, more to sit down and calm himself than anything else, he glanced at the dashboard. The fuel gauge was flashing red. "These guys don't forget to fill up," he murmured. Then he saw the radio.

He'd never used one before; all he could get was blank static. He twiddled knobs, depressed buttons, shouted into the mouthpiece, but nothing happened.

Abandoned. It didn't sound good—it sounded decidedly bad, to be truthful—but it was the only word that seemed to fit. An ambulance, idling away until the fuel ran out. Full of blood. Abandoned.

The village was not far away. Paul decided to run.

Chapter Ten

Wake Up Falling

Blane felt lost.

The lane headed in opposite directions: to his left, it led back down to Rayburn and all the heartache resident there this morning; to his right, it wound its way past the forest and the pond, up the hill and out into the open country. He was torn both ways, between the comfort he yearned from nature and peace, and the solace he might yet find with the other victims of this tragedy.

He stood on the verge in front of his house, undecided. Wondering how he could *possibly* decide.

The skin on the back of his neck prickled. He looked once more at the front facade of his home. The plastic gutter had tipped at a jaunty angle, giving the house an expression of pure mockery. He could recall living nowhere but here, yet this place felt truly alien now.

Blane stared up into the cool blue sky, watching a bird circling high on updrafts of warm air. It seemed to hang suspended, drifting slowly to and fro, never once having to use its wings to gain lift. He used to be like that, he thought. Rambling along on the rush of nature, being swept in whatever direction it chose to take him. Kept warm and dry, cosseted by the implied love that nature could impart to those who loved it. Now, he had been sucked into a downdraft. He was plummeting toward rock, and he had no wings. He had the sudden, painful awareness that the direction he took now—to or from the village—would decide whether or not he was broken when he eventually struck the ground.

He closed his eyes. The torment did not recede.

The sound of pounding footsteps snapped his eyes open.

There was a man running down the lane, flicking up puffs of dirt behind him as though he were racing ricochets. He was tall and strong-looking, like an athlete, and he took long, graceful strides. But his face showed that he was ill at ease. He slowed as he neared Blane, then stopped altogether, panting but never dropping his eyes.

"You look scared," Blane said.

Paul nodded. "It's been a weird morning."

"It has, at that."

The two men stood there for a while, sizing each other up, both wondering how much to say about what had happened. Nature was silent about them, holding its breath.

"Aren't you the scientist? Staying up in the holiday cottage?" Blane had heard about this man, his counterpart in many ways, who spent much of his time in the forest. The villagers seemed to accept him with the same good-humor as they did Blane, raising their eyebrows and staring skyward if he was mentioned in passing in the village store. Perhaps it was their constant nearness to nature, living within it, that made them take it so much for granted.

Paul nodded. "Hardly a scientist, more a counting boy. But yes, that's me. Paul Toré." Normally he would have held out his hand, but today was not normal. After a while, having not heard a name in reciprocation, he asked: "You are?"

"Blane."

Paul nodded. "Heard of you. You're a forest fan too?" He tried to sound ironic, but it came out all wrong.

Blane nodded. The banter was light but necessary. He was not used to meeting people in such a casual, unexpected manner, and he sensed a similar distrust emanating from this tall man, perhaps borne of the strange day they had all awoken to. They were assessing each other as well as making their introductions.

"I love the woods," Blane said. "I virtually live there. I watch things, rather than documenting and counting. I don't need a reason to be there."

The two men looked at each other. Both could see a glimmer of distress in the other, an uncertainty slowly growing and propagating in the strange atmosphere hanging over the fields and woods.

"It's quiet," Blane said. "Strange."

"The birds were watching me outside the cottage," Paul burst out. "Squirrels too, and rabbits. The pair of buzzards? Sitting there, watching me. Spooky." He was fisting his hands at his side, still panting from his sprint, sweat beaded on his forehead like clear boils.

Blane frowned. "In the woods . . . birds fell from the trees. Most were dead. Those that lived didn't sound like birds at all. Everything's wrong today."

"I know," Paul said. "All wrong." As though a barrier had been broken, Blane sensed that Paul wanted to tell him more. They had never met, but already there was a curious sense of kinship between them. In time, perhaps, they could talk some more.

"Coming down to the village?" Blane asked. Paul nodded. "Well, we'd better go. They're waiting for help."

Paul stopped cold. "The village?"

"Things are bad in the village."

"What things?"

Blane diverted his eyes. "People are dead."

"I just saw an ambulance," Paul said, breathless. "Back at the junction with the cottage lane. Abandoned." That word again. It sounded so final.

"No drivers?"

Paul shook his head. "As I said, abandoned. Empty. Just . . . covered with blood."

Blane stared at the man for so long that Paul thought he was being accused of some nefarious crime, perhaps suspected as the root cause of all of this. He was about to defend himself, protest innocence, when Blane spoke again.

"We'd best get to the village."

"How did the people there die? Oh God, who?"

Paul seemed to slump, shrink where he was standing.

"Last night," Blane said. "I was in the woods. It was . . . strange. You know. Then I heard a scream, ran to the village. A few of them were around the pond." As he described what had happened, remembering details that had passed him by the first time, he realized how surreal and out of kilter all this was. How ridiculous it sounded. He wished Paul would laugh at him, mock him, but he seemed to be taking it all in with a stunned, wide-eyed acceptance.

Blane did not mention the shape in the churchyard. The sound of its laughter.

The men began walking toward the village, Blane continuing to prepare Paul for what he would see when they got there. "There was a car burning in the square. Dead woman in the pond, looked like she'd drowned. Another dead kid in the graveyard."

"How had he died?"

"I don't know," Blane snapped, a little too sharply. "He was just dead. I think some dogs had got at him. They'd got at Saint, too . . . you know Saint? . . . in the pergola in the square. Other people had died in their houses, and their wives and husbands . . . and kids . . . were wandering around in a daze. A young boy was there, Slates."

"I've met him," Paul cut in. "Saw him in the woods sometimes. Nice kid. He seemed genuinely interested in what I was doing. In a slanted sort of way. Laughed, but kept coming back."

Blane did not talk for a while, and both men took

comfort in the sound of gravel crunching beneath feet other than their own.

"Slates died," Blane said, eventually. "Badly. Fell asleep and just died. Like something had hit him while he was sleeping. Crushed his head."

"On the green?"

"Yes, by the pond there."

"In front of everyone?"

Blane nodded.

Paul shivered and flexed his shoulders.

"Everyone's waiting for ambulances and the police," Blane continued, "but from what you were saying, they may have a long wait. They all tried the emergency services, usually got an engaged tone. One got through but was told they were too busy and they'd be called back."

"What?" Paul said in disbelief, his voice high. There were so many questions that they all tumbled over each other and ended up in a hazed mess in Paul's mind. He felt stunned, shell-shocked, and walked on in silence. Neither man mentioned the strange stillness about them.

"Where are you from?" Blane asked after a pause.

"The Dominican Republic. Lived here since I was six, though."

"A lovely place," Blane said.

"Which part did you go to?"

Lush mountainsides covered in rich tropical growth; banana plantations spread across hillsides; the smell of distilling rum, drifting from long, low factories. Blane frowned, and shrugged. "Never been there," he said. "It just sounds nice."

"It is." Paul said no more, but felt that something

had just happened that belonged to the day. Something strange.

Blane would have agreed with him.

Holly felt lost the moment Blane disappeared.

He had brought if not a sense of calm, then at least a semblance of control to the terrified people in Rayburn's village square. He'd seemed removed from what was going on, concerned with something else. As he left and the farmer drove despairingly into the square, panic rose once more, like a malignant mist from the ground.

The grass chewer had run away from the pond, screaming and shouting that he was coming home, it was all right, Daddy was coming home. They could still hear an occasional scream.

The woman who had held Slates as he died stood, walked calmly toward the still-smoldering car and seemed ready to throw herself upon the twisted wreck. Holly ran to her, grabbed her around the shoulders and hauled her back onto the grass. The woman protested at first, with a vehemence that almost scared Holly into letting her go. *If someone wants to die so much,* Holly thought, *who am I to stop them?* Then the woman's screaming faded and she began to cry, and Holly had been cuddling and cajoling her ever since.

The farmer lifted the three bloody bundles from his wagon and laid them lovingly on the ground by the pond. He kept them slightly apart from Slates and the drowned woman, as if the dead could spread infection. Then he sat next to them, touching one after the other, in turns whispering and crying, rocking on his heels and going down

111

on all fours. His glasses had fallen off, but he seemed not to notice. He was blind with grief.

A terrible stillness sank down across the village, and hopelessness reflected in the eyes of those still alive. Holly wanted to do something to help, suggest some wise course of action, but shock had bitten into her harder than she would admit, even to herself. She felt as useless as she had trapped in the car years ago, watching her boyfriend's blood dry in the afternoon sun as firemen cut her out and motorists stared with wide-eyed fascination at the blanketed figure at the roadside. Then, as now, she needed someone to help her. Perhaps she was not as strong as she made out. Even in her sweatshirt, she was cold.

And then Blane came back. He walked into the square from behind the stalled tractor, a tall black man next to him, both of them wide-eyed, as though they had been chased by something impossible. The tall man glanced back up Pond Lane as they entered the square, saw the bodies and the burning car and the shattered people sitting or standing around, and he could do nothing but stand and stare.

Blane walked straight across the grass to Holly. She felt a tingle of satisfaction at this, pleased that he had singled her out. The woman in her arms looked up, then down again at the grass, sobbing dryly.

"Blane," Holly said.

He smiled but seemed unused to it. "Sorry I left. I . . . it was the boy in the churchyard." He glanced at the bodies by the pond.

"I left him there," Holly said. "I didn't want to move him. The animals, you know?"

Blane nodded. "I don't blame you. I think that's why we *should* move him."

Holly frowned, but no explanation was forthcoming. Blane smiled again—that same forced smile—and headed off toward the church. Holly glanced back at the man he'd walked in with, and motioned with her head that he should come over. She was feeling more able now that Blane was back, and she sensed her usual outward dominance rising to the fore once more. The man stared at her as though she were a moving statue, and she smiled to put him at ease. He walked toward her; small steps, hesitant, looking about him as he came.

"I'm Holly," she said quietly as he came closer.

He looked down at her but could not hold his gaze there for long. There was too much to look at, to take in. Too many dead people.

"What the fuck happened here?" he whispered. "Is there someone doing all this? Shouldn't we be—"

"I saw someone die right in front of me," Holly cut in. The woman squirmed in her lap, but it had to be said. The last thing they needed now was a panic to spread, the thought that there was some madman cruising the village and killing people at random. If that happened, the likelihood was that the first rescue personnel into Rayburn would get lynched. "No one killed him. He just died."

"Slates?"

"Blane told you?"

He nodded. "I've seen the lad in the woods a few times. Nice kid."

"What's your name?" Holly tried to keep his attention, gauge his condition. Shocked, certainly, but it seemed a controlled shock, not crazed. "I've introduced myself; surely a gent would do the same back?"

He frowned at her for a second, then his face relaxed. Not a smile, exactly, but better. "Paul. Paul Toré. Nice to . . . well, meet you. Not nice, but you know."

Holly shrugged, and then he did smile. The expression suited him. She thought he did it a lot. "I wish circumstances were different. Did you, um, lose anyone?"

"What? Lose? No . . . no. I'm staying alone in the holiday cottage on Pond Lane. Surveying the wildlife in the woods." A shadow passed briefly across his face, and he glanced over her head, past the church and across the fields to where the woods posed starkly against the sky.

"It's lovely in there," Holly said. "I've been meaning to take a walk in there for weeks, but I've never got around to it. I suppose I'm an armchair nature lover. *Wildlife On One.* David Attenborough, that sort of thing. You know?"

"Hmm." Paul squatted down next to her, and the severity of his gaze froze her mid-speech. "I passed an ambulance on the way in." He paused, waiting to see whether the woman in Holly's lap had heard. She did not stir; she was somewhere else. "It was abandoned. Nobody about. Engine ran out of petrol while I was there. The back was, well, pretty messy."

"Messy with blood?"

Paul nodded. "Hey, wake up!" He nudged the

woman—more than a nudge, more like a slap—and she stirred, mumbling something incoherent.

"Let her sleep," Holly said.

Paul frowned, pursed his lips. "I think it's best not to," he said meticulously, as if testing an idea as he spoke. He stood and followed Blane.

Holly watched him go. She looked over at Slates where he lay bleeding his heat into the ground. And although she did not really believe, she prayed that she would see no more dead people today.

The woman was still sitting at the church door. She had stopped banging on the old oak and now nursed a bloodied hand. She took no notice of the two men. Her eyes barely flickered as they walked past her into the graveyard. She was a sleeping mannequin.

"Good place to die," Paul said. Blane did not answer.

When they reached the dead boy, neither spoke. Blane had seen it before. Paul could find nothing to say. A mixture of emotions—anger, dread, dislocation—vied for supremacy in his mind, leaving him confused and shaking.

The lad could not have been more than ten years old.

Blane picked him up, wincing as the dried blood on his throat crinkled as his head tipped back. He averted his eyes from the wounds, but he could see their ghastliness reflected in Paul's eyes.

"Get the gate for me, will you?"

Paul nodded, pleased to walk on ahead. "What were those animals doing with him? Someone arranged that. It's like . . . an offering, or something."

He did not look back at Blane, but talked just loud enough so he could hear.

"Don't know," Blane said sharply.

"Anything else like that around?"

"Not that I know of. Not that anyone's mentioned." A raucous twitter of scrapping birds erupted from one of the trees stretching above the gate, and the memory of a joyful song flashed across Blane's mind once again. How he so wanted to recall what that was about. Whose the laugh was. Why it was there. And why he should connect it with the silhouette he had seen in the graveyard.

"Did you hear anything weird in the woods?" he asked suddenly. He watched the back of Paul's head shake.

"Haven't been in today. Got up, opened the front door, came down here as fast as my legs would take me. Why?" He stopped and turned, looking for the root of the question in Blane's face.

But Blane gave him nothing. "No reason."

They walked slowly onto the green, Blane first with the boy, Paul following and smiling grimly down at Holly as he passed. Blane lowered the body gently to the ground next to Slates and quickly stretched a flap of his bloody jacket across the boy's throat and face. As much to hide his glaring eyes as his wounded flesh.

"There's some stuff you all need to know," Blane said loudly.

Paul glanced back at Holly, who raised her eyebrows and shrugged. She tried to prise the woman from her lap, but succeeded only in rolling her onto the grass. Paul went to help.

"Listen to me," Blane said again. He was standing next to Slates and the other dead kid, trying not to look down but finding his eyes drawn that way anyway. Two young lives. Shattered. Ripped away. And by what? For what? There were no reasons in nature, he knew. They were merely forms from the same mold, and when death came they went back into the stuff of future bodies. And in the end, the very end, they would all go back to the stars. So, death was meaningless.

But still he raged inside.

The people around the pond had started to pay attention. The farmer who had driven his dead family into the village sat close to Blane and looked up at him, apparently glad to have something else to focus on, for a time at least.

Blane was silent for a while, suddenly unable to begin, hardly knowing where to. He looked around at the villagers; bloodied, stunned, ashen-faced. Holly caught his eye and nodded, smiled. Paul stood next to her, arms crossed, frowning, eyes flickering around the square, then back again, as if watching for something.

"Something terrible, and strange, has happened," Blane began.

"Telling me," a woman said. She sat cross-legged close to the pond, wringing her hands between her knees. Her head shook as if possessed of some sonic vibration. "Telling all of us something we know."

"It's something terrible, but it's something we're going to have to help each other out of," Blane continued. "Paul here came into the village from the holiday cottage. I met him outside my house. On his way in, he passed an ambulance with its engine still running, doors open. It appeared to have been abandoned."

"The engine cut while I was checking it out," Paul said. "Petrol ran out."

"Maybe they were away treating someone," a small, frail-looking old woman said. She was swaying gently from foot to foot, as if nursing an invisible baby, her nightgown stained green where she had been sitting on the damp grass. Her eyes were glassy marbles in her leathery face.

"No," Paul affirmed, shaking his head. "I called out. I looked. There wasn't anyone within shouting distance. And the back was covered with blood. It was awash with the stuff."

"Were there bodies?" the bearded farmer asked, glancing back at his family lying beneath bloody sheets.

"No, no bodies."

"None of us have been able to get through to the emergency services," Blane continued. He did not have to raise his voice. He had their complete attention. He was an outsider, and perhaps it was this that gave him a semblance of authority in the eyes of the villagers. That, and the fact that he had no family member laying dead nearby. "That in itself is worrying enough. Either there's a fault in the line between here and the exchange, or all the lines are busy."

"There must be a fault," the old woman said, "maybe a line fell down. Was there a storm in the night? Did anyone hear thunder?"

"There's no line down," Holly said. "I got through, remember? They said they were busy. That was hours ago. Anyone heard anything?"

Heads shook. A few faces turned to the road leading out from the village, down to the main bypass that twisted along the base of the valley. No ambulances appeared, drawn by will. No cavalry came to rescue these sad people, besieged by strangeness and death. All was silent.

"I don't think anyone is coming," Blane said. "I think we may have to go to them. But the main thing is... is anyone injured?" Again, shaking heads. "So, we're a village of living people and dead people."

"Nice way of putting it," said the farmer bitterly, but he only shook his head and stared down at his feet.

"I've got some ideas," Blane said. "Some things we could do. We *must* stay together, find a house that's empty, make some phone calls. Try to find out what's going on, and whether it's just happening with us. Pray to God it is."

"God?" the farmer hissed.

"He helps people, whether He's there or not," Blane said quietly. He stared at the man. "Believe in whatever will help you. If that's anger and rage, then hold on to it. I think there's something very wrong with the world today." He spoke up, so that they could all hear. "The animals are acting strangely, as well."

"What do you mean?" the woman from near the pond said. "Who gives a shit about the animals?"

"I do," Blane said, "and so does Paul there. We've both noticed some weird behavior from them today. Unusual. Certainly nothing I've ever seen before." He thought of the dead animals surrounding the boy in the graveyard, the fleeting shape he had seen there. He considered mentioning it. But it was something personal, particular to him, and telling them of what he had seen and heard would have felt like baring his soul to them.

"What have they been doing?" the farmer asked, half rising. He had something to tell them, Blane was sure. He was also sure that what the farmer said would make things a whole lot worse.

"Birds hissing, squirrels and rabbits staring at me. They seem, I suppose, less afraid than they used to." Paul shivered slightly at his own description. "The animals seemed unfrightened, as if instinct now told them that there was no longer anything to fear from Man."

"It's the Terror," the farmer mumbled.

"What's that?" Blane wanted to hear what he had to say, afraid that it might affect them all more than they could imagine.

"A story I read, once," the farmer continued. "Horror story. Horrible. The Terror, when the animals rebelled against man because he was destroying the planet with war. He'd removed himself from nature. But what the hell happened to my family? Why are they all dead, just because the animals . . . ?" He trailed off so that his new tears did not distort his words. His beard trembled, shedding old tears like stale rain.

"I was coming to that," Blane said. He squatted on his haunches; standing in front of these people, talking to them so openly, seemed bizarre. "What happened to all your people?"

"I was awake," the old woman said, "couldn't sleep. Making tea. Sitting down, watching telly. Thump from upstairs. George . . ."

Someone else, a man who had been quiet up until then, raised his hand to speak. He stood and began without preamble. "I was in the toilet. My wife screamed, once, then I heard a terrible sound. I don't know how that sound could come from our bedroom. There's nothing that hard there. Nothing that solid, to do what it did to my wife. To do . . ." He stared away past the church, still talking, voice reduced to a mumble.

"Slates told me, before he died, that he had been awake, reading under his blanket," Blane mused, almost to himself. "Everyone who died was asleep."

And in the woods. I had my eyes closed when the deer appeared before me.

"I had a bad dream," Paul said. He stepped forward, unsure of himself among these strangers, wondering whether he had any right to intrude into their grief. He felt foolish, certain that what he had to say would be laughed down, but there was proof. He had proof.

"A bad, bad dream." He told them. He left out the fact that his wife had appeared, swollen by the river water and crisscrossed with darting fish. But he relayed the rest of it: the fear he had felt in the aircraft; the terrible cold; the tumble through the air, and the impact on softening snow. Finally, when he had finished telling them, he showed them. He peeled off the two pullovers he had on and turned around, so that they could see the damage to his body.

His ebony skin had puffed out and swelled between the shoulder blades, as though pushed by a hand from inside. The swelling was a violent purple color, like thunderheads just before the unleashing of a storm. They had all seen worse that day, but gasps of surprise rang around the group.

"That happened in your sleep?" Holly asked, dumbfounded. Paul nodded.

"When Slates fell asleep . . ." Blane said, looking at the woman Holly was still comforting. But he did not have to complete his sentence. They all remembered.

"So what? We can't sleep?" said the farmer.

Blane shook his head. "Whatever else we know, I think that's clear. I think Paul survived, because . . . he hit snow."

"You think everyone is dying because of their fucking dreams? Are you crazy? Sorry, of course you are, you're the nutter who spends his nights in the woods, fucking the animals. For all we know, you're the one—"

"Shut up, June," the farmer said. "He's hit it on the head. I was awake when they all died."

"What about Slates?" June scoffed. "He didn't fall."

"I think he did," Holly said. She looked over at Blane, who nodded to confirm the impression they all had.

"The ground," Paul said. "The ground hit him."

"Don't you remember the stuff when you were kids," Holly exclaimed, a glint in her eyes that was a mixture of excitement and terror, a terror at something that forbade comprehension. "That thing we used to tell each other, the urban myth? That if you died in your dreams, you died in real life?"

A couple of people nodded. Blane stood expressionless. He did not remember his childhood. For all the good his memories did him, he might as well not have had one.

"I recall it differently," said Paul, "and not just because of what happened to me." He shrugged back into his pullovers, wincing as he lifted his arms. "I seem to remember it being something about, if you have a falling dream, and you hit the ground, you die. Perhaps I woke up falling."

Blane had been taking all this in, evaluating, trying to perceive where the connection was between the animals and the dead people, the dreams and the wildlife. He could find none. In a way, he hoped there was none. That was just too terrible to comprehend. Did animals dream? Was the same thing happening to them, in slightly different ways?

"I think," he said, "for the present time, that we should ensure that no one nods off. Agreed?"

They all agreed. Even June.

"Meantime, let's make some phone calls."

Following Blane, letting the stranger lead them toward the village post office, the villagers left the green, and the red-dappled bodies lying there beneath a bright blue sky.

Chapter Eleven

Agitated Ghosts

A car was lying on its roof at the Castle roundabout. There were dead people inside. One man hung half in, half out of the windscreen, his blood darkening the tarmac like spilled oil.

How many dead people?

As Peer crossed Newport bridge toward the roundabout, an ambulance and two police motorbikes came screaming past from behind her. Their sirens were silent, and one of the policemen flashed her what seemed a casual glance. No problems here, it said. All under control.

The small convoy slewed onto the roundabout, bypassed the crashed car and disappeared between the King's Hotel and the train station with a smear of exhaust fumes.

Peer should not have been surprised, but still she stood agog. What was going on here? There were dead people in the middle of the road and the ambulance had not even slowed down. She hoped that when she drew near, the car would have a POLICE AWARE sticker splashed across the shattered, bloody windscreen. She hoped, but she did not believe.

Maybe they'd decided to pick up the bodies later, after they'd done all the other things they had to do today. Like pick up all the other bodies.

How many dead people?

Peer was becoming more and more disturbed. Not only were people dying everywhere, and her friend lay dead in bed with a broken neck, but things were changing. Crumbling. The calmness with which she had used to approach life, believing that there were always people there to keep control, whether they did it well or not, was slowly being chipped away. Perhaps this calm acceptance was a facade, behind which chaos hunted unhindered. Now the facade was weakening. And although the curious distance still kept her on something of an even keel, she could feel the panic building up inside her, storing itself for an eventual, cataclysmic release.

Jenny was dead, but when Peer had made a frantic phone call to the emergency services from the nearest call box, she had heard a pre-recorded message. Nobody seemed to care. She was alone, abandoned. One step removed.

All lines are busy at present. You're in a q-queuing system, and your call will be taken as soon as possible. P-please wait. The female voice had sounded high and edgy, as though it had only recently been recorded. Peer had queued, and waited, and queued, and listened to the apology five more times before slamming the phone down. Then slamming it down again, and again, trying to draw attention, desperate to talk to someone.

There were people in the streets, but they seemed more confused and terrified than she. One man had walked straight by her as she tried to stop him, shoving her arm gently but firmly out of his way. He was carrying a rucksack, which leaked redly down his back. "I'm taking our baby home to my wife," he said. "She has to see our baby."

Now, panic was building like a stifling cold, tightening her chest and pounding an ache into her skull. Something kept it at bay somewhat, but that just made it worse. It all felt like a bad dream, but she still had Keith's blood on her T-shirt, and that was no dream. And Jenny's head had tilted sideways with a dry-biscuit crunch that no nightmare could conjure.

Peer had led a simple, relatively normal life, drifting from job to job, with boyfriends here and there, in what her parents had told her was a dreadful waste of her intelligence. But it was a life she had thought she enjoyed; meeting new people meant a lot to her. The jobs were tiresome and often boring (the boyfriends likewise) but the people were mostly fresh and enlivening, and if she ever became bored with her work colleagues as well as the job, then she'd simply move on. She had lived and worked in Newport for four years. Jenny had been one of her best friends, and theirs was a friendship that had looked to last forever. Never, before this morning, had she seen a dead body. Even her parents had merely been innocuous boxes after their deaths.

The world was coming to life around her, but it was the most abnormal beginning to a day she had ever seen. For a start, there were hardly any people.

There was a bang. It could have been a lorry opening its doors, or a train shunting into a siding at the nearby station, or a car backfiring. But the way Peer's mind was attuned, it sounded much like a gunshot. She paused on the bridge, unable to determine the direction it had come from, unsure of which way to go. Her intention had been to head to the town center, find help, tell someone about Jenny and Kerry and Keith, direct aid to her street. But events were rapidly turning this into a bad idea. If there was no help for a car full of dead people, surely she was on her own.

How many more people were on their own today? Husbands kneeling by dead wives, children shaking bloodied parents, unable to wake them? To her left, looking south, smoke smudged the horizon. A bad day for everyone.

She listened, trying to filter out the strange sounds echoing around this mausoleum of a town: shouts; screams; the squeal of brakes; smashing glass; barking dogs; the thump of running feet; car horns and burglar alarms; a full concerto of chaos. Her body was tense, tearing itself both ways. Her conditioning told her to go toward the center of town, find a policeman and call for help. Her common sense tried to convince her to get out of Newport as quickly as she could, flee the madness and head out into the country.

Take away three square meals, and you're left with anarchy. The thought came unbidden but seemed to meld in comfortably with what she had already seen this morning. Something terrible had obviously happened, and people were handling it in different ways. And just what had happened? Its bizarreness and suddenness had distracted her so much that she had really not stepped back and considered what was occurring. In some ways she still felt partly removed from it all, as though it was happening in a country far away and she was merely visiting. But from other angles she felt inextricably enmeshed in events, deeply touched. Almost responsible.

And that was just crazy.

Gas? she thought. *Chemicals? A disease?*

Her gaze fell once more on the crashed car. It was a Volvo. The man in the windscreen was topless because his pajama top had been ripped off by the jagged glass. An atlas had spilled out onto the road, destinations he could never visit pinned with rosettes of drying blood.

There was a bang. A hole the size of a fist appeared in the Volvo's side door and the driver twitched in death.

"Was it you?" a voice shouted. "Huh? Was it you?" Another bang, a tire shredded. Peer ducked down onto her haunches, looking around desperately for cover but finding none. There was a man walking around the elevated roundabout, fresh cuts gaping on his naked legs and genitals, baring bloody flesh to the air. He carried a shotgun, smoke curling from both barrels, and a carrier bag full of cartridges slung over one wrist. Other than that he was naked, pale and shriveled in the cold. As she watched he broke the gun, plucked out the spent cartridges and reloaded. He stalked closer to the ruined car, bending down as he approached so that he could see the driver shielded from above by the hood.

"Was it you? Killed my Helen? Huh? Was it you? Maybe it was." He pointed the gun at the man's head and fired.

Peer turned away just as the shadow beneath the Volvo's hood erupted. Among the echoes of the blast, she heard a noise like the heavy patter of penny-sized raindrops.

"Oh, maybe it wasn't you!"

She looked back, trying not to see the mess splashed out into the road. The man was loading his gun again, glaring around through a veil of tears and secondhand blood, walking around the car.

"Who was it? Who the fuck was it?"

Peer began to scurry back the way she had come.

"Maybe it was you!"

She glanced over her shoulder. He had seen her. He was aiming the gun.

Whatever fate saved her left her with the gory memory, like a part-payment for providence. She would remember it forever, because death was like that. The shotgun exploded in the man's hands and sent him stumbling back against the upturned car, his face all raw meat and ruptured eyes. He opened his mouth to scream, but his throat had gone, and instead he slumped to the ground and twitched his life away.

"Oh, God!" Peer gasped, running, tripping, tangling herself in her own terror. Her bloodied elbows and feet received another shock, leaving exclamation marks of blood on the paving slabs.

She finally found her feet and her voice, and ran screaming from the bridge.

There were several people ahead of her, clustered on the pavement outside the old film college. As she ran blindly toward them, they held out their arms, as if trying to redirect a herd of cattle. "It's all right," they were saying, "calm down, you can come with us, we're going to the hospital now." Peer heard but did not comprehend; what she did understand was that nothing would get her back across that bridge. Over the river was real horror. Splashed across the road. Awaiting her return. Peeled shotgun smoking in readiness.

She dodged the arms, ran out into the road and sprinted away. She passed familiar names: the Riverside Tavern where she had drunk on occasion; Kentucky Fried Chicken; KwikFit. Memories fading into history already, although their shells remained like ghosts.

Long minutes later she came to a halt and slumped down in a pub doorway. It smelled of stale beer and piss, echoes of a time before this madness had begun. Last night people would have left this place, laughing and feeling well with the world, the germ of a hangover already planted in their heads. Peer wondered how many of those people were still alive now; how many hangovers stung them this morning? Or were they dead, spread across their own or someone else's bedroom? She had a brief, chilling vision of the future: mold speckling the insides of used glasses; dust settling over full ashtrays; food rotting, then drying into hard husks in display cases. She shook her head to disperse the images, but still they came, scaring her, draining her. Everything was changing. Nothing would be the same again. The world had shifted, and the direction of shift—forward or backward—had nothing to do with those few who survived. Control had been ripped from the hands of humankind. The survivors would have a new fight on their hands.

She so wanted to be one of those survivors. She remembered the little dead girl of her dreams, moving and animated but so desperate for recognition and love. She did not want to be that girl, although she knew she was. And there was something else that strove to protect her as well, a deep-seated feeling in her gut that seemed peculiar to her. It urged her to stand, move, get out of Newport and find refuge in the country. The town was a dangerous place, it told her. After this—for a while—people would be dangerous as well.

It was logic talking, and the instinct for survival, but also an impulse of another kind, something she could not identify. Something from outside her own mind, alien yet comforting.

As she stood she caught the first whiff of smoke. It was acidic and rich, subtle but definitely there. Automatically she glanced over the rooftops, searching for the telltale smudge in the air that she'd seen minutes before from the bridge. She was used to the undercurrent of smoke and smog in the town—there was a steelworks not far away, exhausting relentlessly into the atmosphere—but this was more overt. This was a fire.

A car roared down the street, heading for the bridge she had just fled. Wide-eyed passengers stared at her through the windows, faces full of dread, pleading an understanding that might never come. Lots of faith would be challenged today, she thought, in many ways. Faith in the relative comfort most people inhabited, a firm belief that water would flow and electricity would be there when required, and order was constant and undeniable.

And spiritual faith, too. How could God let this happen? Peer shook her head, let out a laugh that was half sob. God had never been a close traveling companion, but He was always there in her background, a sneaking misgiving that she was wrong to doubt more than an actual, active presence. Now, she felt He had slipped even farther into the shadows. Ironic that she felt even less in control of herself, as though God had chosen to distance himself from her to encourage fresh belief.

But she was moving as if there was another, stronger hand controlling her fate. That, she had faith in.

A second car came careering along the street, clipping the side mirror of a parked vehicle and sending it scattering across the tarmac. The driver braked for an outrageous few seconds, as though considering leaving a note on the damaged car's window. So sorry, broke your mirror, you can find me at the hospital. Then they knocked down a gear and accelerated past Peer. A woman was hunched over the wheel, seat slid all the way forward, face almost pressed against the windscreen. Peer caught a fleeting glimpse of shapes in the back seat, bundles of clothes, blotched red and for all the world resembling the picnic blankets of fairy tales.

Peer needed a car. She had to get out of Newport; she was more sure of that than ever, because everything was going bad. Where there was one man with a shotgun there would be ten more, and twenty with knives, and a hundred with grudges against society. She had never passed her driving test but had taken a series of lessons in her early twenties, and she was sure she could pick it up again. Like riding a bike, she hoped. Or walking.

She started down the street, heading toward Maindee, deciding almost without thinking that she would leave via the eastern side of Newport and head for Chepstow. Perhaps subconsciously there was the hope that by heading toward London, she would find more order.

She passed a side street and decided to venture down it in search of a car. The thought of stealing was abhorrent to her, but she could really see no other option. It was unlikely that public transport was operating a normal service today.

The street curved around to the right. Houses stood in bland serried ranks, many curtains drawn, only one home displaying any signs of life: a woman, walking in through her front door, out again, in again, never disappearing for more than three seconds before emerging back into the light. Peer called, but she seemed not to hear. Her mouth was hanging open, her eyes wide and unblinking. Peer thought at first that she was dressed in a red sari but then realized it used to be white. The woman stepped back into the house, reappeared again, looking straight through Peer as she passed on the other side of the street.

There were five cats sitting on the pavement. They were normally solitary creatures, and Peer could not remember ever seeing this many together before. Staring. Watching. Waiting for her. They were silent. One of them, a fat old tom, had fresh scratch marks on his face. Blood hung on his whiskers like desperate dew. It was this, more than anything, that made Peer turn around and step back to the nearest door. She had seen enough blood for one day.

She banged on the door, keeping her eye on the cats. Pigeons fluttered overhead and settled on the sills of houses opposite, but the cats seemed unconcerned. There were at least thirty town birds, all fattened up on chips. A bee buzzed at her ear suddenly, startling her into an air-waving pirouette. The cats stared. A sparrow hawk landed among the pigeons but looked only at her.

She banged again, using the heels of both hands. There was no answer. The echo from inside sounded muffled and dead. She glanced at the window, saw that it was not double glazed.

The cats and birds watched with disdain. The woman—into her house, back out again—provided the only real movement in the street.

Peer prised up the corner of a cracked paving slab. Even half smashed it was heavy, and she had to heave with all her might just to raise it up to chest level. She flung it, ducked to escape the noise, and remained on her haunches as glass clattered to the stone sill. The pigeons took flight at the sudden crash but soon came down again in the same spot. The cats merely stood, looking even more threatening than before. The sparrow hawk surveyed the street with its jerky glare.

The woman across the road paid no attention. She wandered in, out, as if working up the courage to actually go all the way in, see what confronted her there. Her clothes were drying black.

The window had been painted shut, so Peer had to remove jagged shards of glass before carefully easing herself through the gap. She was as cautious as she could be in her agitated state, but she still managed to add to the cuts on her feet as she stepped gingerly onto the carpet. She pulled the curtains wide, listening for noises from within the house, ready to defend herself should the need arise. She hoped the house was truly empty, or the inhabitants dead upstairs. Rather that than have to face a petrified father, protecting his family against an intruder from the obviously mad world outside.

The carpet was old and threadbare, the furniture torn and tatty. A television stood in the corner, an old fake wooden monstrosity with heavy protruding buttons and cup marks on the top. Peer had a sudden urge to turn it on and see what was being transmitted, if anything. But she was terrified that there would be a blank screen, a low hum, a white dot. Nothing.

Jesus Christ stared down at her from above the fireplace, a huge, gaudy painting portraying him with hands outstretched, as if to encapsulate the terror at large in the world this morning.

Peer hoped these people had a car. She swept her hand through her long hair, lifting it back over her shoulder, before calling: "Hello? Anybody in? I'm not here to steal, I just wondered . . . anybody in?" She was here to steal. Already she was lying. What would she be doing next?

There was no answer.

Her words fell heavy in the silence, sucked up by

the damp walls. In the hallway, folds of wallpaper hung like the wrinkled skin on an old body. Shelves held knickknacks and ornaments, all of them religious in nature, most of them tasteless and exploitive. The house stank of dampness and age. The staircase was carpeted with remnants, no one step matching the next in pattern or shade. Peer edged slowly toward the back room, unintentionally rubbing her arm against the wall. She cringed; it was greasy with slimy damp. It smelled of rot.

In the next room, adjacent to the kitchen, a man sat in an armchair. His eyes were closed and he seemed at peace. There was even a shadow of a smile on his old, spittle-encrusted lips. His head rested on his left shoulder. He was dead, Peer was sure. He must be. But she did not go to him to check.

She let out a sigh, her body relaxing, and realized how tense she had been. Her arms and legs began to shake, her stomach rumbling. She ran her hand through her hair again. It seemed easier this time. She sat on one of the dining chairs, taking the weight from her painful feet, and looked around the room.

She didn't even know whether he had a car. And if he did, which one was it? And where were the keys? Fate answered her questions for her. Next to the back door there was a key hook. Hanging on this was a large bundle of keys. She snatched it up and recognized the old, sweat-stained leather key ring immediately. A Morris.

She took a final look at the man. He must be dead because he was smiling, and the expression looked alive on his time-ravaged face. She left the house through the front door. It seemed the right thing to do, as did locking the deadbolt after her. It could be that nobody would ever enter this house again.

The stench of smoke was stronger now, unmistakable, and she was sure that the air was hazier than when she had broken and entered minutes before. Looking back down at the main street, she saw a bus trundle by. It was empty, apart from the driver. She wondered if he was stopping at every stop and smiled bitterly at the thought. If he was, he was mad.

The cats had gone. The pigeons were still there, but much of their attention seemed to be taken with the woman across the street, still walking back and forth. The sparrow hawk hovered above the street, beak pointing down at the top of the woman's head. Peer did not want to wait and see what happened. There was violence in the air, as well as smoke, though she could not make out whether it was the sense of trouble past, or the promise of pain to come.

She searched along the row of parked cars for a Morris, and spotted a Marina several spaces away. It was white, tatty, the paint crazed and peeling from the bonnet and roof. The first key she tried opened the door, and she jumped in with a gasp of relief. It smelled similar to the house; the old man's scent, stale and rich. She wondered whether he would sit in his armchair for all eternity, head on his shoulder, the smile on his lips slowly stretching into a rictus grin as decomposition did its wet work.

The car started first time. Peer closed her eyes and muttered a thanks to nothing in particular, then felt for the clutch. There was none, and a moment of panic bit into her. Then she saw the gearstick, realized she had picked an automatic and thanked whatever was looking over her shoulder today. She performed a clumsy six-point turn in the street, crunching into a parked van on the final reversal. Nobody complained. Her feet hurt terribly and she berated herself for not looking for shoes in the old man's house. But there was no way she could go back in there now.

As she rolled cautiously to the junction, she glanced in her rearview mirror. The woman appeared from her house, hands twisting together in front of her as if trying to rid themselves of a stain. Then she turned, ignoring the pigeons lining the sills above her, and went back in.

At the junction Peer turned right, aiming out of Newport. She did not look back.

There was little traffic. An occasional car passed her going in the opposite direction, but other than that the streets were comparatively deserted. Of humans, at least. Animals, it seemed, were reveling in the unusual silence. Dogs trotted in menacing groups, drifting across the street in an arrogant display of dominance. Cats crept along gutters and slunk in and out of doorways. Birds hurried through the air, often in flocks, or sat watching to see if there was movement in the street. Peer was tempted to stop every time she saw someone on the pavement, but after the man with the shotgun she was afraid she'd wait for the wrong person. When a woman darted into the road, waving and pleading, Peer had to swerve the car and narrowly avoided mating it with a lamp post. She drove on without looking in the mirror. She did not want to see the woman's face.

As she passed through Maindee, the smell of burning became heavy and more obvious. Smoke drifted lazily across the road, swirling in her slipstream like the agitated ghosts of the town's dead. And as the fire came, so a descent into hell seemed to begin.

On the pavement, three men were raping a woman. Peer slowed, then drove by. She had to. She could do nothing else. Tears masked the full view of what they were doing, but not the knowledge. She sped past a scarlet mess in the road, and only realized at the last minute that clothes were mixed into the gory smudge. A minibus sat face-first in a shop window, mannequins and bodies scattered across the pavement in surreal abandon. Some of the bodies still moved, clawing glass from their eyes, holding insides in.

Ahead, over the heads of the shops and houses lining the road, she could see a monstrous blur of smoke against the blue sky, dark and expanding. The road made a slow bend to the left and she eased the speed. As the buildings on the right opened out into a small green, Peer stopped the car. She sat, openmouthed, looking down a slight slope toward the hill half a mile distant.

The fire was widespread. It began at the far end of the side street she was looking down, where a frantic fire crew was working on a row of blazing houses. Windows blew out, slates popped and showered the area with lethal shrapnel, the ribs of roofs showed through dancing flames. From where she sat she could see a network of streets, roads and factories, leading across the shallow valley and lifting gently as they reached the slightly raised area of Ringland. Many of these streets seemed to be ablaze, sending columns of thick smoke up into the still air. It seemed as if the whole area had been carpet bombed with incendiary devices, blasting houses and shops into maelstroms of fire and crumbled ruin. Some of the streets must have been burning for hours, because there was little of the actual buildings left to be seen. The fire had taken a firm, tenacious hold, spitting skyward in walls of flame fifty feet high. There were no signs of life anywhere, save for the struggling firemen. And their battle was already lost.

Peer moved slowly on, alternating her attention between the road and glimpses of the conflagration between rows of shops and houses. She could already feel the radiated heat in the car, and she resisted the natural inclination to open the windows. Rubbish danced across the road as air was sucked into the base of the ever-hungry fire. Soon the car itself was being buffeted by the increasing winds, and one word made her press her bleeding foot firmly down on the accelerator.

Firestorm.

Shops gave way to large, bay-fronted semidetached houses, and between each couple Peer could see the fire. The farther she went, the nearer it seemed to be. Down the next side street, the destruction began a dozen houses along, another set of windows and doors bursting outward on limbs of flame even as she watched. She drove faster. Something darted into the road—something smoking—and the car lifted and bumped down again as she ran it down. It had looked like a big dog. She hoped that was what it was. *Just a big dog,* she told herself. *Just a dog.*

She could see the end of the next row of shops. Light danced at the junction, flashing from windows and sending a glare out across the street that promised fiery death. Peer did not hesitate. Her knuckles turned pearly white as she gripped the steering wheel, pressing her foot down as hard as she could, willing the car to suck out another burst of speed from its old engine. She winced at the glassy pain of her cut feet.

She passed the entrance to the street at about fifty miles an hour. She had to look.

The whole world was ablaze. A car parked at the corner exploded like a bomb, twirling gracefully in the air, spreading liquid death across the tarmac. Fire flowed in the gutters, and drain covers blew into the white-hot sky. Even the road itself seemed to be aflame, melting around the shells of destroyed cars, bubbling against the crumbling bricks of those buildings left standing.

"Good-bye Newport," Peer muttered. She willed the car faster, holding the wheel firmly against the winds howling across the roads, turning on the wipers in a vain attempt to clear her view of old chip wrappers and flattened cigarette packets. She roared past a pub on her left, where she and Jenny had once both tried alligator steaks. A petrol station flashed by, three cars clustered around a manhole where a woman struggled with a hose pipe.

Peer thought about stopping, warning them of the danger. But as she glanced in her rearview mirror, she knew it was more than obvious.

The sky was on fire.

Half a mile later, Peer was faced with the choice of risking the motorway or staying on the A roads to Chepstow. She chose the motorway, and it was only four miles later that the car gave up the ghost. It coughed, jerked and died with a crunching rattle of broken parts.

She hauled herself from the vehicle, realizing only then how close she had come to being incinerated. She began to shake, goose bumps rising on her arms in sympathy with the near miss. Her teeth clattered and she hugged herself, as though holding in the relative safety her body had found. Looking back toward Newport, half the sky seemed full of smoke. Ash fluttered and drifted down, turning the verdant landscape into monochromatic blandness.

The entire driver's side of the car had been virtually stripped of paint. The metal had warped out of shape in the heat, the glass cracked, the tires bulged out.

She opened the trunk. She found a long iron bar, which she slid into her belt, and an old trenchcoat that had seen better decades. She slipped it on, welcoming the smell of stale sweat and mustiness wafting from it. It was a human smell.

Looking down at her sad, bloody feet, trying to shut out the pain, Peer began walking along the hard shoulder. She soon realized that this was where all the broken glass and sharp stones lay, and resorted instead to the inside lane.

There was little danger of being run over, she thought.

Traffic was light today.

Chapter Twelve

Laying the Demons to Rest

Mary would remember her journey through the house for the rest of her life. There was blood clotting in the carpet and dead bodies screamed silently at the walls. A rich stench hung in the air, and she recognized it as insides turned out. She felt frighteningly alone, but also smugly triumphant at being still alive.

Mary loved it.

Stepping over Rupert first of all, kneeling to have a closer look at the mess the chain had made of his throat. Then into Jams's and Helen's room. Helen was in a dark puddle on the floor. Jams was lying on his back on the bed, arms and legs spread, head thrown back as if baring his throat to be chewed. His skin seemed whole, but he was distorted all out of shape. She remembered the night before, when he had moaned that he never had the chains. She giggled, twitching the handle at her side, letting the blades snag on Helen's hair.

Before she left, she fulfilled his wish and let him have the chains. A dozen times. Practice makes perfect.

Fay had rescued her. Dragged her from the stifling pit of hatred she inhabited alongside these meaningless people and set her in a place of her own, at Fay's side, wanted and needed and taking up space in the world. Before she had been a vacuum, a nothing wandering the landscape and waiting for death. For a long time she had not sensed any warmth, any feeling of belonging; everyone and everything seemed to hate her. The gang had shunned her in the cruelest way, ignoring rather than offending her, disregarding her entirely.

But now Fay had come and reordered her life. She had opened up whole new vistas of experience, showed Mary the ease and the beauty of death, and the art involved in dealing it. Rupert had been right, in a way: Art was what it was all about. But he had been an amateur, with no knowledge of technique or method, no potential. Mary had the tools and the inspiration, her muse in the memory of beautiful Fay, and the pledge that they would meet again soon.

Before she departed, Fay had smiled and promised her a future, a future where Mary would have meaning: *There will be plenty of opportunity for you to practice your strokes.*

Mary left the house, liberated. The air was clearer, the sun shone brighter than it had for a long, long time. She slammed the front door and recognized an immediate change in her life, as if she had just hacked off a monstrous growth that had been dragging her down for years. She laughed out loud, surprising herself with the sound. It was genuine and held real humor. It was something she had not heard for many years.

She did not feel a sliver of pity for the dead people inside, even Roger. She was happy that they were dead. She hoped it had hurt.

She wanted to burn the house down. The idea had been simmering ever since Fay had left an hour before. She was sure she would be able to find petrol and matches, and refuse was piled against the rear of the house as usual, waiting for one of them to be bothered to move it out for the dustman. But as she stepped into the light and felt the clearness rushing through her body, chasing all the dark demons away—or at least into dusty corners from which they peered, and schemed—she realized that she could never go back inside. There was too much bad stuff in there. Much of it was imprinted on her mind forever, and every nook of the house would inspire these dark memories to rise up and haunt her. She did not want to be reminded of her years of not belonging so soon after her deliverance.

"Rot, you bastards," she shouted, and suddenly that seemed a much more befitting fate for those who had hated her. "Rot, get eaten, be home for maggots and worms." She swung the chain around her head, careful not to lose control and wrap it around her own neck. It whispered in the air, grumbling like the wheezing breath of a hungry animal. She let the momentum slow and turned as the chain dropped. She wanted to strip, run across the garden

naked, revel in the freedom granted her by Fay.
And if anyone saw her, gaped, pointed, she would
ignore them.

Suddenly, she noticed the silence.

The house sat next to a railway line, spiderweb
cracks in the outside wall testament to the busyness
of the route. It was the main line from Newport to
Bristol, but there had been no trains.

Mary felt no fear, only excitement. She remembered Fay's words.

*There are going to be a lot of confused people out there
this morning. Things have changed. The emphasis has
shifted, and it's time for people like you to grab the opportunities this affords. Understand me, Mary? Never
has the chance been so clear for your art to be practiced.
I'm here to create my own particular masterpiece, but
you . . . you, I want to be my understudy.*

Mary walked to the rotten timber gate between
the house and the railway embankment. She
smiled, and remembered the young summers she
had spent with her cousin in the country. He had
taught her how to listen for oncoming trains; said
it was how the Indians did it. She climbed the gate
and almost fell as the timber crumbled and collapsed. There was a slight rise to the railway track,
strewn with litter and bits of decomposing animals
discarded from the house. Jams had always said, if
anyone finds anything they'll think it was killed by
the trains. Jams always was an idiot.

Mary bent to the line, brushed her hair out of the
way and placed her ear against the metal. She
winced at the coolness, but then let out a deep
breath and remained motionless.

Nothing.

She turned and sat on the gravel-strewn embankment, kicking at a desiccated piece of dog fur as she did so. The chain rattled against the stones, providing the loudest noise against the silence of the morning. She jerked the handle and listened to the sound, relishing its random musical cadences, wondering whether this was what death sounded like. It was for Rupert; the jangle of chains as his throat was torn open by Fay's strong tug. Mary smiled at the memory, closing her eyes because that way it was easier to picture.

When she opened her eyes again, there was a dog sitting at the bottom of the embankment. It was watching her, tongue lolling and dribbling, ears pricked up, listening to the silence. It was an old mongrel, brown and barrel-shaped. One ear had been torn in a fight and now consisted of little more than a sharpened point aiming skywards.

"Spike," Mary named him softly. "You'll be Spike. Here, boy. Come on." She rubbed her fingers together, as if offering the mutt money, and it trotted gaily up to her. Before, she would have watched the others flay the creature alive. Before her freedom, she would have held the torch while they attacked with clubs and the chain, often breaking the animal's legs first so that it could not fight back or flee. She glanced down at the bit of fur she had kicked away and wondered whether it had been a cousin or brother of the dog before her now.

The dog reached her and licked the hand she proffered. It was panting and dribbling, but she laughed and tickled its undamaged ear with her other hand. It growled, and Mary tensed and reached back down for the chain. But the growl had

147

been a groan, one of comfort and satisfaction, and she continued with her petting.

She sat with the dog for half an hour, patting it, stroking it, playing with it, at one point letting it gnaw gently on her fist. She had found a friend, and she would do her best to keep it. Two new friends in one day. She was so lucky.

"Hungry, Spike?" she said. "Does Spike want some breakfast? Huh? Well, we've no doggy food, but something better. It tastes sweeter, for me as well as you. See this, Spike?" She picked up the dried fur between thumb and forefinger and waved it in front of the dog's nose. He sniffed it disinterestedly, and gazed back up at her as if asking what he was supposed to do. "You know who did that, Spike? I do. Come on." She stood and tapped her leg, leading the dog back down to the house and around to the flaking back door.

"Ever tasted revenge, Spike?" She opened the door. The dog entered. She shut the door and leaned against the wall, listening. In the extreme silence, she could hear the mutt sniffing around the kitchen. Then the sounds stopped for a while, and she heard the padding of paws on the stairs.

Oh, sweet revenge.

A few minutes later, after Mary had made sure the Escort had a full tank of petrol, she opened the back door and called for the dog. For a terrible few seconds she thought he would not come. She feared she had lost him. There was no way she could go back in. She would have to leave him there, perhaps lock him in for his disobedience, let him eat the rotting bodies until they poisoned him and he died.

Then he came thundering down the stairs, ear

flapping, tongue lolling a different color.

"Good boy," Mary said. "Who's a good boy, then? Breakfast good?" The fur around his snout was dark and tacky, and his breath smelled of fresh meat. Mary smiled. She laughed. Art.

She opened the back door of the car and the dog jumped straight in, as if aware of her need to leave. She wondered whether Fay had met and spoken to the dog as well. She did not smile as much as she could have at this strange thought.

"Let's go, Spike," she said. She turned into the road without checking for other traffic and drove straddling the white lines, whooping, touching the chain handle with her left hand and trying to picture its next victim.

I need you, Fay had said. And for that, more than anything, Mary loved her.

Chapter Thirteen

The Taste of Memory

The post office had two telephone lines. Holly and the old woman volunteered to try them, and Blane was not about to argue. He found it hard enough talking to people face to face.

Holly tried the emergency services, while the woman—who had introduced herself as Elizabeth—opened a local directory and tried numbers in the surrounding towns. Holly heard only engaged tones, or the occasional recorded message telling her that she was in a call-waiting queue. She waited for an hour.

Elizabeth held out her receiver as she dialed each number. Usually an unanswered ringing was the result, but sometimes an answering machine cut in and told them all to leave a message. They never did. Blane shivered when he heard the fake-cheerful voices talking awkwardly to people they did not know or could not see. He wondered how many of these people were still alive this morning.

When they had arrived at the post office, a couple of people had drifted away. Now there were only six of them, huddled together in the small shop, each anxious for the calm voice of authority to reach for them down the phone lines. But none came. They tried for an hour; local numbers, emergency numbers. Anything else—anything farther afield—was too awful to contemplate. In the end, Holly dialed a London number at random, held up the receiver so they could all hear. The call was answered immediately.

"Hello? That the ambulance? Oh, God, thank God you called back, please hurry, I think he may be dead, I think, but—"

"It's not the ambulance," Holly called clearly into the mouthpiece. "Hello? I'm not the ambulance service. Who is this?"

"What?" the voice called, anxious, stunned. "Wrong number. Get off the line. I'm waiting for—" She hung up even before she finished her sentence.

"Where was that last number?" Blane asked.

"London, I think."

There was silence for a while, as the enormity of what they had heard sank in.

Henry stood and walked slowly to the door. "Have to find my brother. Got a young family. Two girls." He stood in the doorway for a moment, staring out at his family where they lay dead by the side of the pond. "Twins." He closed the door and passed the windows on his way back to the tractor.

Nobody went to stop him. None felt they had the

right. Besides, they could barely move with the weight of dread crushing their guts and wringing their brains with cool, tenacious fingers.

"Maybe we should try farther afield," Paul said, staring at the phones. "Here. Let me have a go." He was thinking of his mother. He had been all the time they'd been in this little room, but now he had to try. He had to. He thought of the dream—his mother the only hint of color in a nightmare of gray dread—and a lump came to his throat.

Oh, to hear her cheerful voice crackling from thousands of miles away, berating him for wasting money on a phone call.

He grabbed the handset and punched in the number from memory. It rang. And rang. Then rang off.

The line went dead. He hung up and tried again, but this time there was not even a dial tone. He felt like he was listening in on the eerily still bedrooms of a million victims this morning.

"Line's gone."

He closed his eyes, and conjured up the dream image of his mother. He had to keep it there. It might be all he had left. A tear squeezed from the corner of his eye, but the others were kind enough not to notice.

"What does that mean?" Holly said, frowning. "Why the fuck has the line just gone?"

No answer was forthcoming, because nobody had one.

"We should move," Paul said, "leave the area. Drive until we find help. Maybe Gloucester? South to Chepstow? We can't just hang around—"

"I'm not leaving my George," the old woman

said, shaking her head and stamping her foot like a petulant child. "He's never left me alone, and I can't leave him alone, even if he is . . ."

"Well, I'm all for going," said June. "I want to leave this place. There's only dead people here now. We don't belong here anymore."

"Blane?" Paul asked the short man who was leaning against the window, forehead pressed against the glass, searching the village for the fleeting shadow he had seen earlier that day.

Blane felt suddenly cold, spied upon. He watched the farmer kneel by the side of his dead family, tenderly touch their heads through the stained sheets and then climb onto his tractor. He headed across the square and disappeared down the main street without a backward glance. Blane hoped he would find his brother and family alive, not dead like everyone else.

"Blane?"

What was happening? The animals, his animals, were turning, and all around him bodies were stiffening into the shapes that would carry them into decomposition. The world had flipped sideways. While he was sitting in the woods last night, something basic had changed, a natural law that maintained order had dropped a function, allowing in a dose of true, unbridled chaos.

And who the hell had been in the churchyard?

"Blane!" Paul almost shouted, and Blane turned around suddenly. His eyes were wide, as if he had been startled from a dream.

"Daydreaming," Blane said lamely.

Tim Lebbon

"Do you think we should leave?" Paul was asking him as a leader, an adviser.

"Who put me in charge?" Blane asked, instantly regretting it when he saw Holly avert her gaze and frown. "I'm not even a villager. Neither are you, Paul. Elizabeth, perhaps you should decide—"

"I'm asking you because you know better than us what's been happening these last few hours," Paul said.

Blane could not answer. Paul was wrong. He was so wrong.

"I can see it in your eyes. The way you're always looking around. Like you're searching for someone."

Blane shook his head. "You're so wrong. I know less than anyone." He glanced back through the window at the churchyard, recalling the sickly chuckle in the woods and the gay laughter tormenting his memory. "I think by knowing more, I know less."

"What do you mean by that?" Elizabeth asked. Her gray hair hung lank over her forehead. Her husband was dead. Blane wondered how she could possibly handle something like that. He suddenly felt in awe of these people who had lost family and friends. He could never recall losing anyone in his life. There was a void, true, before memory began, and this he mourned desperately. But could he ever really equate that with losing someone near and dear?

It was as if another voice provided his answer. *You have lost someone near and dear. You just don't know it yet.*

"More answers breed more questions," Blane

said, and left it at that. He nodded at Paul. "I suppose Paul's right. We should go for help. South, I think, toward Chepstow. If it's bad there too, we've got a choice of direction from there. Into Wales, Newport and Cardiff. Or over the old bridge, Bristol, then London."

"Why even bother?" June said. "After what we've heard, why bother?"

Blane shook his head. "I don't think we should assume anything from what we heard." But he knew his voice betrayed his own sense of hopelessness.

They were silent for a while, five shattered people who had been rudely awoken by a nightmare. Around them, brash advertisements exhorted the merits of National Savings Bonds or stamps in books of ten, and on the counter a rack of National Lottery Instants shouted in loud colors that the next one would be the winner. The place stank of the normality of yesterday: cold coffee in a mug behind the counter; a pack of paperclips, spilled across the floor like robot confetti; the cardboard smell of secret parcels, piled at the collection point and destined never to be delivered.

"Chepstow it is, then," Paul said quietly. Heads nodded. Elizabeth, small and cold and shaking, was the first to the door.

The population of Rayburn had once been over five hundred. It seemed that there were few survivors.

"I've got to stay," Elizabeth said. "You all go on. I'll only be a hindrance, anyway, old woman like me."

They were standing in the square, not far from

155

the pond. Blane and Paul had gone on a walk around the village, shouting and banging on doors. The sun was high and strong, gazing down on the world as if nothing had happened. If there had been no survivors at all, it would have done the same.

"No, you must come." Holly could not bear to leave Elizabeth behind. The place was full of dead people, she would be almost alone, and besides . . . besides, everything felt wrong. Holly was sure that they were not doing the right thing, and that if they took Elizabeth with them, it would make everything seem better.

"I'm staying, young lady!"

Holly held her hands out, palms outward. "Elizabeth, please, okay! But promise me you'll stay indoors."

"Why should I have to do that?"

Holly went to tell her but realized she had no valid reason. "Just a hunch."

"Well—"

"Elizabeth, something terrible has happened. We don't know how far it's spread. There may be people around, desperate people, survivors, who would do anything."

"You don't have much faith in human nature, do you, Holly?" The woman's eyes were severe but kind. Shadowed by a grief whose full impact she was trying to delay by staying here talking.

Holly shook her head, shrugged. "I've always believed we were on a knife edge. That's just the way things exist. I never dreamed we'd fall off."

Elizabeth looked at her intensely for a few seconds, then grabbed her arm. For a small woman she was strong, and Holly had to tense her lips to hold in a gasp of pain. "My George always said that there's one thing that set humans aside from the animals, Holly—being human. We're so different in all sorts of way. I know all the arguments about thumbs, or language, or whatnot. But inside, here"—she tapped her head—"there's a basic kindness that doesn't exist in nature. An awareness of others. Why do you think we're all here, in this square, instead of home with our dead or running around like idiots?"

Holly shrugged.

"We care about each other."

"But animals—"

"They care too, yes. But not for long." Elizabeth let go and turned to watch Blane and Paul walking back alone, shaking their heads. "You come back for me," Elizabeth said. "When you've got help, bring them back. I think I will have said my good-byes to George by then."

She reached up and patted Holly on the shoulder, then turned and walked away. She merely nodded at Paul and Blane, and Holly could tell by their expressions that she was crying.

"I wish she was coming with us," Holly said.

"Never persuade her," June said. "Stubborn old bitch."

Holly glanced at the woman. June stared back, as if ready for a confrontation. Holly said nothing.

Four of them left the village. They took time to collect belongings, but there was a general feeling that none of them wanted to spend time with their dead. Most merely left in the clothes they wore.

Paul, Blane and June went in June's car, a Mondeo. Holly followed in her Mini.

From the window of an old cottage, unseen, Elizabeth waved them off.

Paul drove; Blane sat in the passenger seat. June exuded disaffection from the back. She had refused to drive.

"There's going to be hell to pay," she said. "When the press finds out about this, the lack of response from the emergency services. Hell. Heads will roll. I'll make damned sure of it." She glared at Paul in the rearview mirror as if it was all his fault.

"I've already seen an ambulance, I told you," Paul said. "It was—"

"Abandoned, yes. Well, there's more than one, isn't there? What about Derek? What about my husband?" Her voice hitched on the last word and descended into a series of harsh, bitter sobs.

"I'm sorry," Paul said. June did not answer.

Can't adapt just like that, Blane thought. Whatever had happened had affected a wide area, changed the very nature of things. Even now the hedges bordering the roads seemed to be crowding in on them, appearing heavy with autumn growth rather than young and keen as spring. Birds flurried to and fro ahead of the cars, as if preparing an ambush at any moment. Even though the sun burned bright ahead of them, darkness gathered beneath the trees, and there was a genuine coolness in the car.

As they left the village behind, Blane felt an unaccountable loss. He had only ever felt at home with nature, and to him nature was homeless. A valley in Scotland was as welcoming as a shaded cove in Cornwall; a common in London held as much allure as a hilltop in the Lakes. True, he had been in Rayburn for years, but the woods were his real home, not the rundown shack he had been so suddenly and completely excluded from. He tried to analyze his feelings and could truly feel no real emotion of loss when he considered the village itself.

Perhaps it was dread. Maybe whatever he had seen in the churchyard waited for him out here, and the village was the only safe place for him now. Lightning never struck the same place twice . . .

. . . Except it did, he knew that. Today more so than ever.

As if conjured by his thoughts, a shadow emerged from beneath the trees a hundred yards ahead and darted across the road.

"Deer!" called Paul.

"No. Stop the car." Blane had seen it. It had not been a deer. It had looked like one, yes. Had the guise of a deer. But it had been something else entirely.

Singing again, in his head, high and musical . . .

"It's only—"

Laughter, tinkling like ice drops into water. "Stop now."

Paul saw and heard how serious he was and braked the car to a halt.

"What is it?" June asked.

"Something." Blane jumped from the car and glanced back at Holly in the Mini. Before anyone had time to stop him, he ducked between two trees, emerging into a ditch. He heard crunching footsteps from farther along, but tree branches conspired to hide his view. Paul's concerned voice called from the road, but Blane headed on anyway, determined to catch up with whomever, or whatever, was following him.

Following? It's always ahead of me.

The ditch was shielded on both sides by shrubs and trees, forming a natural tunnel that curved to follow the line of the road. There was no standing water, but the compressed leaves of past years had rotted down into a pulpy, damp layer on the ground. The smell of rot permeated the air, even though spring was here. Some of the plants were shriveled and distorted; the bark of small trees hung dry and brittle from the dead wood beneath. It was as though some great heat had come this way, killing everything where it stood.

Blane's old leather shoes were soon darkened with moisture, and dirt stained his trousers halfway to his knees. He could hear birds ahead of him and behind, but as he moved along the ditch a zone of silence accompanied him. They were still there, though. He could feel them watching.

The ditch opened out suddenly to the right, the hedge giving way to a gap facing into a field. Blane squinted at the sudden glare of the sun. There was a fallen tree not far from the hedge, and someone was straddling its dead back. For now, they were merely a silhouette. This was enough.

Memories, both good and bad, exploded into Blane's mind. The sudden input was so intense and loud that he gasped, clasping his hands to his head to hold it together against the pressure. There was laughter, bitter and low, though he could not tell whether it came from the shape on the tree or his own curtailed visions. Images and smells and sounds vied for his attention, forming a glut of sensory data to clog his perceptions. Scents inspired recollections of motion; the sound of splashing brought the taste of salt to the air; a laugh prickled the skin of his neck with a gentle touch. Reality and memory became one, so that even though Blane was on his knees with his eyes shut, still he could feel damp sand between his toes as he ran through frothing surf. The thumping of hooves and the smell of a million migrating caribou made him raise his eyes to the stillness. Everything was here, now, and it was all too much. Try as he might, he could not grab onto one definite memory, draw it to him, treasure it and store it for future reference.

First there was everything.

Then there was nothing.

The visions were purged from his mind, like gasps into a vacuum. The shock was stronger than before, because emptiness is so much larger than anything else.

"Who are you?" Blane managed to mutter. He could still make out nothing of the person sitting on the dead tree; the sun hung behind their head like a halo, dazzling Blane and throwing their features into deep shadow.

"My, you've let yourself go. Put on weight, I'd wager. All those bad meals. Sitting around in the woods." The voice was low, throaty. The sort of voice that could so easily have chuckled that morning, when the deer had died before him.

"Who are you?" he said again.

"Got your gang together, I see? Right little orgy

you could have now, though I don't think June would be up for it. Holly, though ... I'll bet she likes it hard and fast, with one at either end."

"Were you in the graveyard? Did you do that to the boy?"

"Graveyard?" The voice was mocking, full of false bewilderment. "Boy?" The speaker stood and walked to where Blane was still kneeling on the damp ground. The shape slowly resolved itself against the sun, and for the first time Blane could see who he was talking to.

She was tall, haggard, hair long and knotted. Her eyes were glazed and dead. Her body was shapeless beneath loose-fitting clothes. And she had rusted chains piercing her temples, running down into her mouth. Recognition shouted for him to grasp it, but doubt crowded in as well.

"I've seen you before," he said, trying to phrase it as a question.

She laughed. A low, growling chuckle. He shivered, remembering the deer twitching in its bloody death. He looked at her hands where they hung by her sides, trying to imagine them twisting the animal's neck. They looked thin but strong.

"You may have seen me, once or twice, from a distance. But ... I can't tell you any more. I'm enjoying this as it is." She smiled, but it did not fit well onto her face.

"What? Have you lost someone? In all this?"

The smile faded, relaxing her face into its natural sad posture. "Oh, yes, someone very dear to me. Long, long gone."

"We don't know what's happened, but—"

"You, of all people, should know," the woman

cut in. "It's easy. It's the ruin. The end."

The chains moved as she spoke, stretching, raking her skin. Blane could see now that the skin at her temples was not only pinched, it was pierced by two small screws.

"What are they?" he asked.

She bent down close, her face only a few inches from his. Her eyes looked dark and flat, devoid of emotion. Her smell was more basic than animal. "It's a secret, don't you know."

"Do I?"

She stood again, shook her head, snorted. "You've gone way downhill, Blane." She picked at her mouth. "I'm so sad." She plucked something from between her teeth, held it up to the sun and examined it.

"You know my name?"

"Damn hair." She shook her hand, then abruptly turned and ran across the field, arms pummeling the air, feet pounding and throwing up clots of dried sod behind her.

"Wait!" Blane called, standing and starting after her. But she had already crossed the field and disappeared into the trees at the other side. Branches swayed slightly, then became still once more. As though she had never even been there.

"Wait," he said, quieter, fighting tears of shock.

"Blane." Paul emerged from the hedgerow behind him. "Who are you talking to?"

"You didn't see her?"

"See who?"

"Strange woman," Blane said, then walked unsteadily past Paul and headed back toward the road.

Paul looked across the field, past the fallen tree, scanning the wooded perimeter. All was still. No birds, no rabbits, no squirrels. No woman.

Too still.

They found the tractor around the next bend.

Henry was spread-eagled in the cart, arms and legs pointing at each corner. Paul and Blane jumped from the car. The Mini stopped behind them. Holly opened her door and leaned out, frowning over at Paul.

Blane stepped to the cart.

The tractor was parked on a slight incline and Henry's blood dripped steadily onto the road, running in rivulets across the tarmac.

He had been killed, violently. His shirt had been ripped off in the struggle, and deep scratches scored his chest and stomach, welling blood. His head was thrown back, the darkness of his tattered throat peering out from beneath his thick beard, an insane second smile. The flesh was ragged and torn.

Scattered across the base of the cart were red gobbets of chewed flesh. Whatever had killed Henry hadn't liked the taste.

"Oh, for fuck's sake," Holly moaned. She sat back down in the Mini and gripped the wheel.

"Henry?" June was standing next to the Mondeo, leaning on the open back door, eyebrows raised. She looked angry at him for being dead.

Paul went to her and tried to block her view, but she shifted to one side. He held on to her arms. "June, he's dead. You don't need to see."

"I do! Let me go!" She tried to shrug him off, but he grabbed tighter until she squealed with pain.

"Believe me, it's not nice. I wish I hadn't—"

"Let me go, you black bastard!" She shouted it out, drawing glances from Holly and Blane.

Paul paused, then let her go. "I hope you like what you see."

June stepped around him without catching his eye, approached the cart, groaned. She started to shake her head, denying what was set out before her, shuffling backward until her legs touched the hood of the Ford. She sat down heavily, rocking the suspension. She could not drag her gaze from the scene.

Around them, the world was silent. It was holding its breath.

"What did this, Blane?" Paul said, passing June and touching the short man on the shoulder.

Blane shook his head.

"Don't know?"

Blane did not answer. He did not move.

"Or won't say? Who was the woman, Blane?"

Blane turned and walked back to the car, ignoring June where she sat on the hood. He slumped into the passenger seat and stared past Paul. At Henry.

"Anyone ever driven a tractor?" Paul asked. Nobody replied, but he saw Holly shaking her head, her pale face and wide eyes begging him to help her, hold her, remove her from the path of all this death.

He turned. He tried not to look, but his eyes were drawn to the grotesque display before him. He felt sick to his stomach, terrified, but his scientific mind still analyzed, even as his body rebelled. He had no idea what could have done this, in this country,

165

other than a wild dog. He walked around to the cab, convincing himself that a mad hound was loose, ignoring the insistent voice that kept niggling at the back of his mind: *It's sacrificial. He's spread out like an offering to some insane god. He's in the cart, not the cab. He'd have been safe in the cab, from a dog, at least. And what's wrong with Blane? Who was the woman?*

"He's a weird one," Paul muttered, glancing over his shoulder through the open back of the tractor. June was staring up at him, an unreadable expression on her face, tears distorting whatever she was trying to impart. Blane remained motionless in the car, staring off to the side as though he could read the truth of things in the hedge bordering the road.

As Paul started the engine the trees alongside the road burst into life, startling him. Birdsong struck up, drowning the engine, piercing and shrieking the day apart. A cloud of blackbirds darkened the sky for long seconds, circling the vehicles before heading off across the fields.

They had been there all along. Watching, listening as the humans did what humans do; arguing, shouting, becoming emotional. Hundreds of them, all silent, hardly moving.

Henry's throat had been torn out.

"Get back in the car!" Paul shouted over the sound of the engine. "Whatever did this might still be around." June averted her eyes and complied. He knocked the tractor into gear and moved forward, the tow bar clanking as the cart rattled on its poor suspension. The motion soon smoothed, and he nursed the vehicle along the lane until he came to a wider part. He drove as close to the hedge as he could, trying to tuck the tractor and cart in far enough to be able to slip by in the big Mondeo.

The two cars had followed him. June was driving her Mondeo now, Holly the Mini. Paul parked the tractor and turned off the engine, pocketing the keys with a misplaced sense of security. He walked past the passenger side of the Mondeo, noticing that Blane barely blinked as he did so, and climbed into the back.

June did not turn around, but he could hear the tension in her voice.

"I am sorry," she said quietly. "I didn't mean that. I've never spoken like that. I'm not like that." She trailed off, staring rigidly ahead, easing the car between the tractor and the hedge.

"Don't worry," Paul said. *I've heard it all before,* he was going to add, but it hardly seemed appropriate. "No offense taken."

"Thanks." She caught his eye in the rearview mirror, and they offered each other a strained smile. "Do we just leave Henry like that?"

"We can't take him with us," Paul said. "There's nothing to cover him with. And when we find help, we'll send them back this way. To pick up his body."

"Okay."

He's going to be here forever, Paul's thoughts spat, *because there is no help, and the animals will eat him and the birds will peck out his eyes—*

"Henry loved the countryside," June said, "he won't mind staying here."

Paul could think of nothing to say.

Blane rocked with the motion of the car. He seemed to have slipped away from reality, staring blankly through the windshield, subsumed by some inner turmoil that excluded everyone else.

Paul had a lot of questions for him. He would ask him soon, but not just yet. Now he seemed one step removed.

And, perhaps, Paul would not want to hear the answers.

Chapter Fourteen

A Chorus of Cries

Five minutes after leaving the broken-down Morris, Peer heard the sound of car engines.

She stepped gingerly onto the hard shoulder in plenty of time for them to pass. The grumble of engines seemed alien now, shattering a silence that itself was far from natural. No birds; no dogs; no mutter of wind. The sun had risen as usual that morning, but the land it shone down upon was changed.

Two cars approached side by side, keeping well below the speed limit. Both had roofs stacked with suitcases and black sacks, looking like grotesque boils. One of them, a big old Mercedes, had two bikes tied across the hood. The other seemed more suited to this day, carrying countless dents and scratches like the scars suffered by so many this morning. It was a Cavalier, a recent model but looking as if it had been through the crusher already. The front bumper was missing, and even from a distance Peer could see that the windshield had vanished, leaving a ragged maw where it should have been.

Peer was certain they would not stop. She held out her hand, thumb up, feeling foolish but unsure of what else to do. She wondered what image she would present to the occupants of the cars: disheveled; bleeding from multiple lacerations; heavy metal pipe protruding from her belt like the wounded guts of a deficient android. The trenchcoat would not help, either, the archetypal garb of the Hollywood villain. She went to smile but feared it would manifest itself as an insane grimace. She looked sad and pathetic instead. The expression took little effort.

The cars passed, both full to capacity. Peer counted seven people in the Cavalier, and the Mercedes seemed similarly loaded. She sighed.

They flashed at her with their brakes and drew to a halt. The Cavalier winked its surviving reversing light and labored back up the inside lane at her.

Peer tensed, ready to fling herself into the deep ditch. *Did you kill her? Was it you?* she remembered, the words of the mad naked man ringing in her head. The skin and flesh on her back should have been flayed and stripped by lead shot; only fate had helped her then. She doubted it would do so again.

The car stopped thirty feet away. The driver held it with the foot brake. A head stuck from the passenger window, eyes wide and cautious. It was a young man, probably still in his teens, head shaved and rings and studs twinkling from ears, nose and eyebrow. He looked terrified.

"You own that Morris a while back?" he asked.

Peer nodded, deciding it was easier than trying to explain. The boy gave her the once-over, pausing in his examination as he saw the pipe in her belt. He glanced down at her feet.

"Hurt your feet."

Peer felt a sudden lump in her throat at the concern in his voice. She had not heard a tone like that for days, let alone since all this started. "Yes," she said, "like shit."

"Hang on." The head disappeared back inside the car. There was a pause of a few moments, then the door opened and the boy stepped out. He reached back in, never taking his eyes from Peer, and his hand came out holding a sawn-off shotgun.

"Oh, Jesus!" Peer screamed. She could not move. Fear had disconnected her brain. "Oh, no, please don't!"

The boy looked startled, then sheepish. "Hey, don't worry, missus. Hey, sorry." He handed the gun back in the car and held his hands out, his eyes wide, his expression gaunt with guilt. "Hey, no harm intended, missus. Christ, I'm sorry, it's just that . . ." He shrugged, nodded back at the black cloud above Newport. "Had a run-in with a gang back there."

Peer could hardly talk. Her limbs suddenly felt like lead, holding an insubstantial body hundreds of feet above the soft ground. She went to her knees, holding her head in her hands, shaking uncontrollably. Yet again, she was faced with a shotgun. And once more, it seemed, she would survive.

The boy approached her cautiously, but she could tell that there was no threat here. He seemed as afraid of her as she was of him.

"You come out of Newport?" he asked.

She nodded. "Only an hour ago. Is the fire still going?"

The boy nodded vigorously. "We came over the hill from Caermaen. The whole town is on fire. Christ, all of it. It's like doom in there, hell, burning people everywhere. A gang was charging people to get by on Chepstow Road. There were dead people in the gutter, and . . ." Whatever else he had seen was too awful to utter. "We only just got out."

"I wonder what caused it?"

"What caused any of this?" The boy's voice suddenly seemed different, and when Peer looked up she could see he was on the verge of crying.

She wanted to comfort him, but she did not know who was in the car. She didn't want anyone thinking she was crowding them out. "I've lost friends today," she said. "All dead. All . . . dead in their sleep."

"Sleep!" the boy said, suddenly. "That's what's done it. There're thirteen of us here and none of us slept last night. It was only the ones who were asleep that it happened to. Like my mum. Happened to her." His eyes glistened, then spilled over. He walked into Peer's natural embrace, and she locked her hands behind his back. He smelled of sweat and fear. She held him, and gained as much comfort from the contact as he seemed to. "It's all gone shit," he said. "It's like dreaming. Except if we were, we'd be dead anyway." His earrings scraped against her cheek.

She recalled her recent dream, just before she had woken with a start and heard the noises from next door. Something about falling. Being thrown. Then a voice. *Wake up, Peer.* Pleading with her, protecting her from the ground rushing up to meet her, bringing her back toward the darkness of her room. *This isn't real. But it could be . . .*

"I was asleep, then I woke up," she said.

"Were you falling?"

The shock stole her voice. She could only stare at the boy as he pulled away and nodded at her stunned expression.

"Yep," he said. "There's a young girl in the Merc. She's got broken legs. We're taking her to Chepstow, to the hospital. Newport hospital's full, and there're police stopping anyone else getting in. She was asleep, she says. Says she fell out of a haystack in her dreams. Hit her legs on a tractor."

"How . . . ?" Peer had so many questions that they blended into one, unspoken, unspeakable.

"Heard her screaming," said the boy. "I broke down the front door in the end. Her parents were dead. I carried her out. Met up with the Merc just outside her house, cruising slowly down the street. Dave—he's the driver—reckons we should go to Chepstow."

"Why?"

The boy shrugged. "He says there's help there. None of the phones are working, did you know? And on telly, there's only some old music. Opera. Always did give me the creeps."

"No, I didn't know that." Peer could barely take it all in. "Chepstow?"

The boy looked suddenly sheepish again. "Thing

is," he said, "there just isn't any more room, at all, in the cars." He stepped back slightly as he said this, perhaps afraid that Peer would whip out the metal bar and bash his brains in for having the impertinence to refuse her a lift.

"Right," she said. She knew he was right, she could see from where she stood, but still she felt let down.

"What we thought, though, was that we could meet up at Magor services. Only a couple of miles down the road. We'll find another car there, ease up the pressure on us lot." He nodded back over his shoulder. The Cavalier revved twice, obviously a pre-arranged signal, for his face changed and his eyes widened again.

"You go," Peer said. "I know you have to now. But please, do as you said, wait for me at Magor. I'll be there as soon as I can." She glanced down at her feet.

"Oh, God, I'm sorry," the boy said. "Here." He bent down to undo his shoelaces, and the car revved again. "Hang on!" he roared over his shoulder, and Peer could not help laughing.

The boy looked up at her as he struggled with his knotted laces. He was attractive, wide brown eyes and a skull shape that cried out to be shorn of all hair. His image suited him. He smiled.

He gave her his sneakers and ran back to the car. "I've got another pair in my bag," he called. "See you at Magor!"

"Thanks!" Peer said, waving. The Cavalier moved off until it was adjacent to the idling Mercedes; then they both accelerated smoothly away, leaving the hint of exhaust in the air.

Peer sat awkwardly on the rough tarmac and examined her feet. The left was worse, having seemed to steer itself toward the sharpest pieces of glass in both the forcible entries she had made that morning. There was a deep cut at the junction of big toe and foot, and the thick, rough skin of her heel had been slashed right across. The cut welled like a pouting mouth. She could see her flesh, pulpy and pink, squeezing to escape the confines of her skin.

She did not look anymore. There was nothing she could do, so she had to make the best out of what she had. She had to walk, to reach Magor services, to join up with the group that had just passed her by. There was no alternative. She was sure she would not be able to walk much farther that day, nor at any time in the near future, so she had to push herself this final distance.

She tried to think of what she had to strap her feet up with. In the end it came down to her knickers, so she eased herself down the bank on her rump and peeled off her jeans and underwear. She relieved herself while she was undressed, unaware until now of how much she had wanted to pee. The jeans felt rough as she dragged them back on, and she wished she had not been so inclined to buy tight jeans. Who was going to see her looking good in them now? Would she even want anyone to think that?

She tore her knickers into three uneven strips, used two on her left foot and one on her right. The makeshift bandages seemed to stem the bleeding somewhat. She hoped there were medical supplies in the Merc and Cavalier, and berated herself for feeling so self-pitying; there was a little girl with two broken legs in the Mercedes. How must she be hurting? Would they find anyone to treat her?

None of the phones are working, the boy had said.

The sound of a speeding car suddenly broke the silence. Peer hauled on the sneakers, wincing at the pain and their moist warmth. Then she pulled herself up the bank on her bum, pushing with her hands and feet, but only as much as she had to. She reached the top just as the car flashed by. As she stood the brake lights flashed on, and the car left four screaming skids on the tarmac as it slewed sideways to a halt. It turned and drove back to where she stood, facing the wrong way now, the driver handbraking when he reached her and spinning the car through ninety degrees.

A sudden flush of dread turned her mouth dry. Her hand moved fractionally toward the deep side pocket of the coat, where she had stowed the bar after dressing again.

Had a run-in with a gang back there, the shaven-headed lad had said.

A boy opened the driver's door and stepped out. He must have been all of seventeen, six feet tall, muscular. His eyes were wide and a sparkling blue, his left hand clasping a bottle of Vodka. "Hey, babe," he said. "Want a ride?" His eyes passed over her T-shirt and down to her crotch, lingering there. "Woah!"

Peer hauled the bar from her pocket and brought it down heavily onto the car hood. "Not with you, bastard! Fuck off!" She was shaking with adrenaline rush, wondering exactly what she would do if the boy came for her. Would the bar hurt him enough,

with one smack, to stop him? It would have to. She was certain she would never get in more than one blow.

"Christ, only trying to help!" he screamed, his voice high-pitched and childlike. He sounded genuinely hurt. He jumped back inside and revved the motor, and it was only then that Peer realized the car was pointing directly at her.

She went to jump back, squealed as her feet twisted and pain flared up her legs. The car reversed and handbraked again before heading away, the boy honking the horn well into the distance.

It took her several minutes to compose herself and let the white-hot pain in her feet fade to red. For the first time she had a good look around, taking in her surroundings far as well as near. The fields lay in a neat pattern across the landscape, sprouting circles of trees here and there like hairy moles on an otherwise unblemished face. She noticed a wildness about the hedgerows that she had not seen before, an almost primal insistence to branch out, spread themselves, devour the countryside around them. In several places the hedges had broken completely from their uniformity, bleeding into the fields like blood from a broken vein rushing into neighboring flesh. She had never seen this before.

Across the fields nearest the motorway sat a huddle of farm buildings, built in a circle to shelter each other from winds rippling across the flat landscape. They were well kept, in a decent state of repair. Smoke was curling lazily from the red brick chimney, spiraling skyward without a care.

A herd of cows bayed noisily at the gate to their

field. They were waiting to be milked. One of them was stepping in a circle, crying out, tail raising and lowering. From this distance, Peer could hear only the combined chorus of their cries; not individual voices, but the sound was forlorn and lost. Pained.

She felt that she should be doing something to help them. But there was nothing she *could* do.

She turned away and stared back in the direction of Newport, hidden behind hills but still spouting smoke. The cloud was charcoal black against the clear blue sky, smudged at the edges by distance. Even from here, several miles away, Peer could smell it. Rich, cloying, the smell of annihilation.

She wanted to cry again, but she was all cried out, and the tears would do no good. Instead, she started shakily along the hard shoulder, always listening for the sound of cars behind her. Two more passed without stopping, staring faces haunting her with desperate expressions.

An hour later she reached the exit ramp and breathed a sigh of relief.

She paused to take stock. Her feet were an agony, and blood had seeped between the stitching of her borrowed sneakers. Her elbows and knees had not been given a chance to scab, and her scrapes and cuts still dribbled the occasional tear of blood. The bar was a comforting weight nudging her thigh.

From here she could see the service station. The hotel was silent, curtains still drawn in a stillness Peer recognized already. What mess awaited the chambermaids today? There were no lights on in the restaurant, but she could detect signs of movement behind the tinted glass. A Marks & Spencer lorry sat in the petrol station, cab door open, rear doors yawning, a mess of paper and cartons and clothes fanned out on the ground behind it. There was no sign of the driver; neither did there appear to be any activity in the petrol station kiosk.

Peer hobbled down the access road, cutting across the grass and skirting rose gardens gone wild. Thorns promised plenty of pain. As she walked she scanned the parking lot for the Cavalier and Mercedes. There was no sign of them.

The automatic doors still worked. For some reason she had been expecting them to be shut off, but their senseless operation instilled her with a warm, welcome flood of relief. Not all humanity was dead. There were still the things they had made, things still striving to make their lives that much easier.

There were about twenty people in the restaurant area. Nobody seemed to be serving behind the darkened counters, and the mess of sandwich wrappers on the tables indicated that the lorry outside had been the source of food for those here. Some sat in groups, conversation muted. Others were alone, staring into space, apparently surprised by what they saw. A couple had dead eyes, as if they had been resurrected and were not too happy about it.

Footsteps approached from behind and Peer turned, hand closing around the pipe in her pocket, to see a middle-aged man pass her by. He offered her a sad smile and then sat down alone. He picked up a photograph from the table and began turning it over and over, as if reviewing the image every few seconds would renew the life it had recorded.

Peer walked to the food serving area and searched for something to drink. She remembered she had no money and felt a vague twinge of guilt, but no one even seemed to notice. The soft drinks dispenser was still working, though when she tasted the fizzy orange it was tepid and flat. The gas had run out and not been replaced. She found a spare table and sat down gratefully, conscious of several sets of eyes following her every movement. An involuntary groan escaped her as the weight was taken from her abused feet. She looked around for the boy with the shaven head, but she could not see him. He had given her his sneakers. He had promised to wait for her here.

"Excuse me," she said, loud enough for the whole restaurant to hear, not too loud to sound aggressive. Most heads turned, though nobody said anything. "I wonder if any of you have seen some people traveling in a Cavalier and a big Mercedes. A girl with broken legs, a boy with a shaven head. I was supposed to meet them here."

There was a tense silence as the whole place seemed to hold its breath. Several people were on the verge of speaking; a big man with a ponytail broke the tension. "Been and gone," he said flatly. "Left ten minutes ago."

Peer frowned, feeling extraordinarily let down by the boy who had issued such a casual promise. "But he said they'd wait for me. We were going to find another car . . ."

"Plenty of spare ones about," a young girl said. "Hotel's full of dead people."

"Sorry, love," Ponytail continued, "but they just shot off quickly. Actually, it was my fault. I told them I'd just come up from Chepstow. Then I told them what was there. And off they went. Pointless, really. I'm sure they didn't believe me." He looked down at a half-finished carton of orange juice, pinching the end of his straw, picking up liquid, releasing it with a gurgle that could be heard across the restaurant. "No point going anywhere, from what I hear. I'll just stay here."

"What is there?" Peer asked, knowing the answer before she spoke.

"Well, it's not on fire like Newport," the young girl said. "Other than that, it's much the same. It's full of dead people."

Peer closed her eyes. Something nuzzled at her left hand. She jerked the bar from her pocket, tangling it in the material of the coat.

"Hey!" a voice said. "Only my dog. He's friendly, you know. Loyal. He needs me. Everyone needs someone. Even dogs. Here, Spike!" The dog sauntered away, sniffing at table legs and pissing against a plant pot.

Peer looked over and saw a pale, thin face peering above a low partition. The woman was holding an open packet of sandwiches in one hand, a cigarette in the other. Peer had given up smoking years ago. Now she craved one.

"Want to share?" the woman asked. She waved the sandwiches like a lure.

There was a lorry full outside, begging to be plundered, but Peer welcomed the invitation of company. She nodded and walked around the partition, sitting at the messy table and staring in disbelief at the range of food scattered across its surface. There was hardly any table to be seen. "Thanks."

The woman smiled across at her. "I'm Mary," she

said. "I'm not contrary, and I've never had a garden." She held out her hand.

Peer snorted a laugh, noticed the spiked chain on the seat next to Mary, realized she was still holding her iron bar. "Peer," she said.

"Dig in!" Mary grabbed another unopened packet of sandwiches and ripped it apart, throwing one of them to the obedient Spike. "They're free."

Peer thought of the lorry outside, doors open and its insides torn out. "I suppose so."

She ate. The woman watched. The dog dribbled from messy jowls, tattered ears pricked up in readiness for any more scraps.

"I'm glad I found you," Mary said.

Peer was suddenly too hungry to listen to anything else. Or to register just how peculiar this statement was.

Chapter Fifteen

Dead Rainbows

He will have a woman with him, Fay had said. *If he hasn't when you find him, then he soon will. It's the way things must be forced to proceed, it's an inevitable event. It's the route he'll have to take. He may not know his own mind—he will not understand his own drives—but this will fall into place around him: He will have a woman. And this woman will be dangerous, to you as well as me. Watch her. Mark her. Wait for the right time.*

Mary had not asked how she was supposed to recognize this Blane. Fay implied that she would know him when they met, and so she left it at that. She had felt unable—unwilling—to question Fay, because the woman with chains was so right, so correct, so totally aware of Mary. How do you question the person you love? Why should you?

Mary drove away from the house without once glancing back. She was leaving her old self there, her whole history, decaying into dirt and filth along with the bodies of those who had used and abused her. She mourned nothing. The dog sat behind her, panting foully into her ear, eager for a sniff of air from her partly open window. In the side mirror she could see him dribbling onto her shoulder, his saliva thick and tinged pink. She did not care. Nothing mattered, except the job she had been given by Fay, the woman who needed her.

Go north: you'll find him. Fay had said, stroking Mary's hair like a mother nursing a child. *He'll be heading south, and he'll probably have others with him. They'll be confused, wary. The fools don't know what's happened, not even him. But I can let him know. If there are others, your job may be more difficult. But not impossible. Nothing is impossible, Mary, with love.*

"With love," she muttered, enjoying the words, relishing something so important, so honest in her mouth after so long. Spike ignored her, eyes squinted shut in the breeze as he sensed a thousand breakfasts waiting to be eaten.

She headed north, away from the coast, driving carelessly. She had not been in control of a car for years, and she reveled in her newfound freedom. Roger had never let her drive, insisting that she would not be able to, making her believe she was useless with his insistent mockery. How she wished he could see her now.

She eased the car blindly around corners, unconcerned as to whether there was anyone coming the other way, sure that there would not be because she had a job to do for Fay. Fay would not let her die in any petty, meaningless way. If she had to go it would be glorious, a death that everyone would recognize as that of someone significant. Not a runt of the litter of mankind. Not a worthless piece of shit, as Roger had so often said.

Mary was someone!

She drove up from the marshy flatlands until she hit the motorway, and then suddenly realized how hungry she was. Now she could eat what she wanted, not only what the others happened to be eating. She had a choice.

She glanced down at the motorway as she circled the elevated roundabout; it seemed deserted in both directions. No signs of any cars, buses, lorries, motorbikes; nothing that a normal weekday morning would bring. Nothing. Silence, desertion, abandonment.

Mary did not find it difficult to accept what had happened. Fay had touched her. Understanding came in a flash. There was nobody in the world she would miss, and the ripple of shock she felt initially was soon overwhelmed by the realization that she had survived. She was superior, now, to the millions of dead lying rotting in their beds. More important. More beneficial to those who had survived; especially Fay.

"Well, and how the world has changed," Mary said, scratching behind the dog's tattered ear as it stuck its head between the seats.

She turned the engine off for a moment and breathed in the silence, taking deep breaths as if purging her lungs of foul smoke. Imbuing her body with the changed state of things. Noticing, for the first time, how wonderfully fresh the air tasted today.

She started the motor again and rolled slowly

Tim Lebbon

down into the service station. There was a food
lorry in the fuel area, back doors standing wide
open. She accepted the invitation and dragged arm-
fuls of food into the restaurant, making two trips
before settling down for a feast. She ignored the
other people there. They were meaningless, echoes
of the passing of humanity. They had no idea who
she was. Besides, she had nothing to say. She had
not truly communicated with anyone in years, apart
from Fay.

The dog sat with her, accepting food, trotting off
to mark out new territory. Nobody approached her,
or complained about the pissing dog. She hid herself away behind a partition, defiant but still
slightly intimidated. The dead she could gloat over,
certainly, but the living might still hold her in low
regard. She saw that in their eyes, sensed it in their
whispers or the way they looked away quickly, disregarding her totally.

The only sound came from the humming lights
and the occasional shuffle of feet or crinkle of food
packaging. Less often, a quick, whispered sentence.
Shock had all but stolen the gift of speech. Mary
smoked, throwing the butts on the floor. Nobody
objected.

Soon after, a woman entered the restaurant, hob-
bling, clothes bloodied and tattered.

I don't know what this woman will look like, Fay had
said, *but she'll be powerful. Rich in nature. Clothed in
the colors of dead rainbows, waiting to be enlivened
again. The power will not be visible, but now, I think,
after this talk . . . well, you may see it. You may not. If
you do, remember to exercise caution. But also, propagate
hate for this woman. She would threaten me. You may,*

eventually, find a moment when you can rid me of her.
You'll know when.

"Rich in nature," Mary mumbled, staring at the
woman. She seemed lost and forlorn, but there was
a power in her eyes, a glimmering awareness yet to
be realized, even by its owner. Mary could see it.
She could sense it because Fay had told her so. And
the woman, who spoke to the others without seeing
her, was clothed in gray, lax light. The light of dead
rainbows. The negative radiance of wonders waiting to happen.

For an instant Mary wondered just how this
woman could threaten Fay. But then she saw: This
woman was good, in the true definition of the
word. Fay was good also, but in a different way.
Good for herself. Good for Mary. Not necessarily
good for others; like Rupert.

Mary giggled, then stood. "Hey!" she called. The
woman was about to brain Spike, send a pound of
iron into his head. "Only my dog. He's friendly,
you know. Loyal. He needs me. Everyone needs
someone. Even dogs. Here, Spike!" The dog pissed
on some plants and ran back to her, sitting patiently
by the table for more scraps. She waved the packet
in her hand; the woman looked hungry. She looked
suddenly dangerous, too, with the metal bar
clamped in her fist. "Want to share?"

The woman nodded and walked around to her
table. Mary's heart was racing. It was a long time
since she had enjoyed any real, one-to-one company. Always forgetting Fay, of course, but she was
so different, so much more. This would be dis-
course on the same level, mutual appreciation

rather than a one-way monologue finished off with some abuse, then rape.

Fay had done so much for her.

"I'm Mary," she said. "I'm not contrary, and I've never had a garden." The woman laughed. Mary remembered the garden back at the house, scattered with the bones and moldering parts of dead animals. Sometimes, Roger had made her clear it up and bury the incriminating evidence in the mud. That was the only type of planting she had ever done. No pretty maids would grow from there, that was for sure.

"Peer," the woman said.

"Dig in! They're free." Mary lobbed Spike a chicken tikka sandwich. He snapped it from midair, like an unwary bird, and swallowed it whole.

"I suppose so," the woman, Peer, said.

Spike sat watching them. One day, Mary thought, her dog might breakfast again. Chew into the throbbing throat of this bitch who would deign threaten her saviour, her mistress Fay. Tear out her pulsing, fucking throat, swallow the blood, bite into her tits, rip out great chunks of dripping flesh, slashing her skin with his carrion-sharpened teeth.

She watched as the woman ate, sensing the power inherent in every movement but finding, to her surprise and delight, that she did not fear it. Rather, she loathed it. Her body shivered with the desire to end it here and now, but Fay's words echoed in her mind, and she would never disobey Fay.

Watch her. Mark her. Wait for the right time.

"I'm glad I found you. The light loves you," Mary said. The woman looked up, surprise registering in her bright eyes. "It caresses your skin."

"Thank you," Peer mumbled through a mouthful of sandwich.

For now, it only touches your outsides, Mary thought. *When my Spike has his time, and I command him to do my Fay's bidding, he'll lay you open.*

Then it will touch every bit of you.

Chapter Sixteen

Open Wounds

Fay had lost many of her old powers, yet she was still far greater than most. She mourned the loss, laid blame where she thought it was due, but revelled in what she had left.

For what she needed to do, it was enough.

She could only observe the larger power at work around her, with perhaps a finger dipped in here and there if it suited her purpose. She enjoyed seeing it exercised, smiled at its twisted cadences. She could sense it coursing through her body, circling molecules in their place and subtly altering them, changing her into something new, changing everything. Many would not notice until it was too late. Few would have any comprehension of what was happening, or the ability to halt things if they did.

Fay knew. She wanted it to happen. She found it amusing.

There had been a time when her joyful laughter had set the world singing, a jubilant echo of the wonder she felt. The birds had perched in the trees and serenaded her across forest floors. In the valleys, deer had bounded from cover and leapt around her, and rabbits had frolicked in the long grasses at her side. The world had flowed into and through her, filtering itself and emanating only the true rightness of nature. The very idea of her had set nature on a straight, ordered route, and kept it there.

No longer. Now a smile from her would tumble a squirrel dead from a tree, its innards pulped and leaking from every orifice. A laugh could strafe through woodlands like high-velocity bullets, smacking birds from their roosts and throwing them at the ground, already dead from shock. Deer froze helpless in her path and shrieked as they died of fright. If they were lucky.

At first, she had not wanted it like this. But she had no control, and if this was how things had to be, then she would make the most of it. With loss of reason went a distortion of love.

It was not the true power she possessed, but an echo, caught from the person wielding the genuine vigor. A throwback to the womb, perhaps, though the womb that had birthed Fay was long lost and deformed through the passage of time. Nature had begun when Fay had begun; a long time ago. It continued now, but its course was being irrevocably altered. And she was glad. Glad because she was bored, tired of the same old thing, and now she savored the taste of change in the air.

She could almost see it. The air itself shimmered

with anticipation, transmitting the change via its agitated particles, the message of revolution moving on and ever onward. It swept across farmland and hillsides, bathing the land in its invisible, tasteless and odorless perfume, encouraging the first signs of change. The trees obeyed; the animals obeyed; the people, slipping from the heady heights of their ascendancy, obeyed.

Fay loved it. She enjoyed watching. Especially, like now, when what she was observing had direct consequence on her own bit part within the mighty play of nature. She was high in a tree, sitting at a junction between branch and trunk, one hand clawed into the dying bark. A nest of woodpeckers had died with fright as she climbed, but a rook sat on her biceps, gazing at her through sapphire eyes, its head jerking from side to side. Its feathers were unhitching and splaying, shedding the microscopic barbs that allowed flight. Soon it would only walk. All part of the change.

Fay had seen the cars stop just as they pulled from the motorway. People had darted from the doors and gone behind a hedge to urinate.

She felt a wave building. Behind her, in the field, there was a rustling and an air of disorder; around her, those creatures still alive in the trees hissed and spat in their confusion, eyes turning toward the cars. The air was charged. Fay's hair stood on end with the static of promised violence.

In the field, she heard the waterfall patter of an entire herd of cows voiding their bowels at the same time, the stink wafting up through the trees.

It had not happened yet, she knew. Not completely. But now seemed to be the time for it all to begin. Perhaps it was because she was there, the echo she had of the true power urging those affected just over the precipice. Whatever the reason, Fay was ecstatic. An almost sexual thrill passed through her as she heard the sound of cows pushing through the hedge below. Barren thing that she was, her stomach tingled with expectation.

Fay touched herself, gasped, laughed as one of the cows glanced up at the noise. Its eyes began to roll. Foam flecked the whiskers around its mouth. There was blood in the foam.

The trees suddenly came to life, as if the leaves themselves had a mind of their own. The rook on her arm fluttered awkwardly to a branch nearer the road. Other birds—sparrows, finches, tits of all kinds, a group of magpies, several sparrow hawks and a pair of huge, powerful buzzards—flowed through and above the trees, as if fleeing a bushfire. But there was no fire; not externally, at least. The only flame burned inside the mind of every animal here. The flame of hatred, the white heat of madness. The agony of change.

Fay knew that the cars would be found. She knew who would find them. *He* would find them, along with his band of cronies, so sure that they could drive their way out of this madness. If only they knew.

Oh, it would be a true work of art. Part of her Renaissance.

"Go, then," Fay whispered.

The cows forced their way through the hedge and stood glaring wetly at the cars, both loaded down with people and their meager belongings. The people stared back, across the expanse of road separating them like a fire stop. But nothing could contain this conflagration.

The cows moved hurriedly across the road. Birds burst from the trees around Fay, splattering her with shit and tangling in her hair. She cried out with joy, and the noise seemed to spur them on even more. Squirrels, rabbits, badgers, stoats, a family of foxes, all flowed against and through the hedge, a living, jumping carpet of animals.

Their complete silence made the scene all the more frightening.

Curious voices called out from the cars, then fell silent. A toddler asked for his mummy. A woman screamed. A boy came from behind the hedge, shaven head gleaming with the sudden sweat of fear as he saw the tide of creatures bearing down on the parked cars. He had forgotten to do up his zipper.

The cows struck first, battering into the cars like a tank assault. They dented metal, rocked the vehicles on their suspensions, starred glass. Just as they hit, a door opened and a figure emerged from the Cavalier, holding a short black object. He was crushed between the door and the car body, arms going skyward as his ribs were shattered and punched inward. He opened his mouth, but screamed only blood. The gun discharged, pumping pellets uselessly at the sky.

Other cows piled into the first, crushing them into the cars, leaping up and pounding into their cousins in a parody of rough rutting. The cars slid sideways, leaving squealing black skids on the road. The animals remained silent, apart from the occasional bay of pain and the snap of bones.

The birds and other creatures hit then, darting between the stamping legs of the cows, climbing into smashed windows, fluttering through an open roof light in floods of feathers.

The real screaming began.

The shaven-headed youth turned and ran, bare feet slapping the tarmac. He managed quite a distance before he was caught.

Fay sat on her branch and grinned. She cried out as the people in the cars cried, trying to match their screams of agony with her own moans of false pleasure. They deserved it, she knew. They all deserved it. No exceptions, no questions. If it weren't for them, she wouldn't be who she was today. She would still be perfect.

The back doors of the Mercedes opened and two women darted out. One of them tried to force her way through the far hedge. In seconds she was engulfed in a mass of biting, scraping, tearing birds and small mammals, and her screams lasted only as long as she remained upright. Then there were only sounds of feeding. The other woman ran. She was chased. She was caught by a fox, which snapped into her ankle like a bloodhound and held on as she fell. Birds dive-bombed her, pecking, clawing, drawing red hieroglyphics of agony into her exposed skin. Then the other ground creatures reached her and set to, ripping clothes from her body with hooked claws, tearing flesh. She stood and screamed, looking back at the cars as if expecting help from there. Then a buzzard swooped down and plucked her left eye from its socket. She crushed a rabbit as she fell, breaking its back with her knees. Its feet drummed a death tattoo on the roadside as the woman was killed next to it.

The cows were climbing over the cars now, dropping themselves heavily onto the roofs, breaking their legs and rolling off to allow others to continue the assault. Screams, androgynous with terror, fought their way through the rolling wave of animals engulfing the vehicles. There was hardly any metal or glass to be seen. And all the time more creatures arrived, attracted by the noise and called by whatever strange signals had enraged the first.

The engine of the Mercedes suddenly burst into life. The horn sounded, but the animals took no notice. The vehicle began to move, a macabre mobile sculpture of biting, clawing animals, their fur speckled with blood. It crawled along the road, crunching over the twitching bodies of creatures injured in the attack, picking up speed until it hit the flailing mass of the woman on the verge. The wheel struck what was left of her head and stilled her misery.

Two cows fell from the roof of the car. Glass had burst from all the windows, and these openings were now crawling with life. There were screams from inside, and the driver's door opened. A figure fell out as the car was still rolling. It squirmed in the road as if trying to smother burning clothing, but this fire was the blaze of open wounds. Soon the shape had stopped moving. Seconds later the Mercedes drifted to the right and tilted gracelessly into the ditch alongside the road.

There were no more screams. From the Cavalier, moans drifted over to Fay for several minutes. The sounds only seemed to enrage the frantic animals even more. Back legs kicked at the air as they fought their way inside the car, and then inside what was inside.

Fay watched them for an hour. By that time most of the animals had drifted away, gorged and bloodied, swaying across the road with eyes full of a manic confusion. Blood dripped from their whiskers. Pink flesh clung to their teeth. The cars were ruined; their interiors were a gruesome mess, split and torn and emptied of their stuffing. Blood dripped from bent metalwork. Bones gleamed in the afternoon light. A hand, half stripped of flesh, clung to the doorpost of the Cavalier.

Fay let herself slowly down from the tree and walked away. She did not need to see close up. She had seen enough.

Enough to know that Blane would see it. Enough to know that the message—the tiding of the end of things, and the beginning of something else—had been well and truly sent.

Chapter Seventeen

Rebellious Ghosts

Peer was not completely at ease with her new traveling companion. The girl seemed too casual about what had happened, almost dismissive. But she needed company—she craved it—and Mary had been the only person in the service station to offer it.

The car began to shake as it reached sixty miles per hour. Mary insisted on driving at seventy. The dog, Spike, sat with his head protruding between the two front seats, panting bad breath, dribbling thick drool. Peer thought that the mutt had still not forgiven her for almost taking a swing at its head. Any time she turned, it seemed to be staring at her. It would glance away but look back at her if she did not divert her attention. It was unnerving.

Aside from that, there was also the matter of the spiked chain that Mary carried around with her. She had thrown it into the footwell of the passenger seat before Peer climbed in; Peer now sat with her feet resting on the cool metal. Over the last half hour she had been trying to take a good look at it without being too obvious. She was certain there was dried blood on the blades. In many ways, she did not want to know for sure.

She remembered the man in Newport, the one with the shotgun. How many people would be driven mad by something like this, shoved over the subtle dividing line between eccentricity and insanity?

Or were the few survivors mad not to be mad? Perhaps the welcome embrace of derangement was the only real escape from this dreadful reality.

"Don't let me nod off," Mary had said as they started out from the services. She laughed, and Peer almost joined her, but then she remembered what the people from the two cars on the motorway had said. About how only those who had not slept last night had survived.

And remember the dream, Peer. The falling. The ground, waiting to crush you.

And she had said, "Yeah, me too."

At least Mary talked. Incessantly. A defense mechanism, Peer thought, telling a complete stranger about the way she had found her parents dead in bed, almost relishing the elaborate descriptions of their shattered corpses. Peer had once gone out on some dates with a man who, by his own admission, was peculiarly sensitive to other people's emotions and states of mind. He had taught her how to spot a lie, by varying methods, from the way a person's head is tilted as they talk to the words used to relay certain falsities. Unfortunately, he had been too good at his own particular gift. When Peer's interest waned, her attempts to embellish it turned into a huge, pounding guilt. Eventually, the man had imagined a lie greater and more important than the sad truth, and he had left.

Mary was rattling off at the mouth. Her descriptions of her dead mother and father were intricate and detailed. She emphasized the loss she felt but seemed to enjoy doing so. She made a point of catching Peer's eye as often as she could, sometimes to the detriment of safe driving. The only thing she did not do was touch Peer's leg as she spoke.

Mary was lying. Everything she said, Peer was certain, was a complete fabrication, created on the spot and expanded with a childish enthusiasm as her imagination got the better of her. She seemed so pleased with her own peculiar little tale that Peer did not mind. It seemed to make her happy, and Peer was pleased to hear a human voice doing something other than screaming or crying.

"And Mr. Hopkins next door was dead in his bathroom," Mary said. "And that's where I picked up Spike. He was in there, sniffing around old Hopkins's head when I went in. Oh, I always have a spare key for next door, because Mr. Hopkins is old and frail. And I check on him every day. So I went in and saw he was dead, and Spike followed me out as I left. I couldn't just leave him. Could I, Spike? Eh?"

The dog glanced at Mary as if to acknowledge what she had said. It drooled, just to be different.

Mary continued her monologue. Peer half listened, but most of her attention was absorbed by thoughts of her distant family. Her mother in New-castle—what would she be doing now? Was she still alive? Peer had not seen her for several years, and now petty family rivalry seemed the most fool-ish concept ever. It was always too much trouble to telephone, she never seemed to have time to write a letter, even though she knew just how much her mother would have loved to hear from her. She wanted to say she loved her, send a note and go to stay with her. For a weekend, at first, because longer might be too much. Then, maybe, reconcili-ation and friendship. She so wished she could have the chance, but at the same time she was certain the time had passed long ago.

"Peer? I said I think we should go through Chep-stow anyway. What do you think? Are you listen-ing to me? I was thinking of heading north."

"Why north?" Peer had no real plans, just a vague idea to find help. But the farther they drove from Newport, the more unlikely it seemed that there was any help to be found. There was hardly any traffic. No signs of the emergency services any-where. They saw an occasional vapor trail high in the sky, or the telltale flicker of sunlight from a he-licopter's rotor blades, but these things seemed far removed from what was happening on the ground.

"North, well, I just thought it would be for the best. And I've got family. In . . . Cheltenham. A brother. Maybe it's all right there, who's to say?"

"All the phone lines are down," Peer said.

Mary did not reply at once, and when she did it was with another question. "So, Chepstow it is, then?"

Peer nodded. "Fine. Only dead bodies there,

though. That's what the girl in the services said."

They drove on in silence. It seemed that Mary was all lied out.

Peer thought that she and Mary had some things in common. They were both rootless, for a start; she had never felt this more so than now, when calamity had struck and she had nowhere to go. Her best friend was dead and she was estranged from her mother, unable to communicate with her even if that was not the case. And there was no one special, no lover, nobody left to turn to. She had no home, no place of comfort where she could at least wait out this catastrophe until everything was put back as it should be, and normal service had been resumed.

Mary, at first glance, appeared the same. Peer was sure that if she did have parents she had not just come from their home, and she probably knew as much about them now as Peer did about her own mother. Maybe there had been a boyfriend, but now she was alone. The spiked chain testified that she could look after herself, but there was also a frantic vulnerability about her, shimmering below the surface like a child trapped under ice.

Two lone survivors together. Peer hoped they could help each other.

Mary had not spoken this much to one person in years. Peer was the one, she was sure, the woman whom Fay had told her about. Whatever quirk of fate had brought them together Mary blessed it, and hoped that Fay would be equally as happy. Mary was silently intimidated by Peer's presence and the ease with which she carried her power, almost as if she did not acknowledge its existence. But she also found she hated her, wishing so much that now was the time to let her Spikes—both the dog and the chain—loose on the bitch's putrid flesh.

Fay had preached caution, however. Mary must wait until the time was right. And she would never, *could* never disobey Fay.

She needed to tell Peer a story, paint a make-believe background so that she would not betray Fay with any casual questions. So she thought up a dead family, a dead neighbor, the dead neighbor's dog, escape from the home and flight toward Cheltenham in the hope of finding her brother alive and well there. In truth, she knew that they would get nowhere near Cheltenham before seeing Fay once more. The transparency of the lie mattered little.

As she took the exit ramp from the motorway, Mary experienced a sudden, intense flush of dread. Her skin prickled, her stomach rumbled. She felt as she had for the last few years, closed in with Roger and his sick gang, turned into one of them by the endless mockery and the foolish, useless urge to make herself wanted. She slowed the car and started to ease it onto the hard shoulder. From the corner of her eye she saw Peer look up.

"Anything wrong?" Peer asked.

Mary shook her head. She did not want to talk to her, could not. Something terrible nestled in the pit of her stomach, twisting her guts and promising much, much more pain to come. She felt an instant of dissatisfaction, and she was honest with herself for the first time in a long while. Like a drowning woman she relived a dozen instances from her life, all of them bad. The here, the now, suddenly felt the same.

The car swung around the roundabout under its own momentum, and Mary helped it on its way around the corner and down between the fields.

Seconds later, as if placed there to reinforce Mary's confidence in her new self and her absent mistress, she saw what awaited them.

She's been here, Mary thought, and a rush of baseless love shoved her doubts aside. "Something nasty here," she said, trying hard to keep the note of eagerness from her voice. She stopped behind the first car.

Peer looked up. "Oh, Christ."

A flurry of activity animated the scene for a few seconds, birds and animals darting guiltily away. Then all was still. The bloody mounds in the roadway that might once have been people. The smaller dead things, animals half eaten or still twitching in death throes. The steam rising above the wrecked Cavalier, like reticent ghosts unused to haunting.

Spike growled, sniffing at the window. Mary so wanted to let him out; he must be hungry. But she did not think that Peer would approve.

"I was supposed to meet those people," Peer said, "at the service station. They were the ones I was looking for. The boy . . . Oh, no." She leaned forward in her seat and pointed out a white-and-red mess just behind the Cavalier.

Mary looked. She could make out the vague shape of a person amid the ruin of tattered clothing and gashed flesh. She wanted to giggle; Roger and Rupert would have been amused, no doubt. She had seen these wounds before, and the purple-scarlet of exposed guts held little repulsion for her anymore. The fact that these were humans, not animals, seemed immaterial. What fascinated her more was the stench. Cow crap, spilled petrol from a ruptured tank, human shit, the tang of blood, the meaty smell of opened bodies. Underlying it all, the strange new spring freshness of fields and hedgerows. She breathed it in, tasting it, letting it touch the back of her throat. She wondered why Spike was not in a frenzy.

There were two cows huddled down on the road, broken legs protruding from beneath their massive bodies. Their flanks and bellies were torn and bleeding where hundreds of tiny teeth had bored them. Their eyes rolled wildly, throwing continuous ironic stares skyward. As well as the wounds so evident on their bodies, their udders were swollen and close to bursting. They were raving, riddled with pain. Mary thought of the chain and spikes, even glanced down at it where it sat between Peer's feet. But that would give the wrong impression.

She needed Peer to trust her.

They walked to the wrecked cars together, Spike wandering on ahead, sniffing at the ruins scattered right across the road.

"Here, Spike! Bad boy!" Mary called, but Peer could hear the humor in her voice. Spooky.

The cows reminded Peer of the herd she had seen and heard baying at the farm gates, viewed from the silent motorway. Whatever farmer owned these was, no doubt, dead in his bed. Never to be milked they would die here, like this.

"Do you have a gun?" she asked, suddenly sure

that she would never be able to pull the trigger.

"Of course not," Mary said.

"Sorry. Only, I was thinking . . ." She did not need to say any more. Mary nodded in sympathy, but as she looked away the corner of her lip twitched. She ran over and pushed Spike away from a dead rabbit. He dragged it with him; it was impaled on his teeth. Peer only hoped he did not transfer his attentions to the dead people, and the thought shocked her rigid.

"I'm sure they're all dead," she said, suddenly wanting to leave this place far behind. This was the worst she had seen all day. Dead people, dying people, Kerry with her eyeball sitting on the floor, Keith's exposed ribs. Far, far worse. Because these people had been killed, actually slaughtered as they tried to escape whatever it was doing the killing. And from what she could see—the slashed flesh, the teeth marks in bare bone, the various dead animals both inside and outside the cars—it looked as though the animals had done all this.

"Mary," she said, "I think we should go. I think the animals are dangerous." Mary looked over at Spike with an almost wistful look on her face, and for a moment Peer just wanted to turn and run. She knew nothing about this person. She had hardly spoken to her, and now she was traveling in a car with a faded, pale woman who obviously lied about her past and had a murderous chain and a creepy dog for company.

Jenny would have smiled at this. *Just like you to hook up with a loser, Peers.*

Choice was removed from her then, however, when the sound of engines rattled the still air.

Around the slow bend ahead of them, past the ruins, two cars appeared.

Mary trotted back to the Escort, called Spike to her and reached in for the chain. Peer backed away, more from the terrible mess around the static cars than with apprehension over the approaching ones. When she turned around, she gasped. Mary was standing legs astride, left hand on hip, right hand swinging the chain to and fro. The blades *swooshed* in the air. Spike sat at her side like a living extension of her weapon. She was gazing past Peer at the two cars, her eyes those of a shark, emotionless yet full of menace. She looked terrifying.

"I'm sure they're not dangerous," Peer said.

"So the animals are, and a roving band of survivors isn't?"

"Well, look." Peer pointed around her, at the bloody scene. At the same time, she remembered the shotgun-man in Newport, and the threatening boy in the car. "They can't all be bad," she said, to herself more than Mary. "Things like this don't just drive everyone over the edge. We're still civilized."

Try as she might, she could not shift the seed of doubt planted in her mind by Mary. It grew quickly as the cars neared, and by the time they halted fifty feet away, just beyond the wrecked Mercedes in the ditch, Peer was ready to turn and run. It was a feeling she was having a lot lately.

They did not switch off their engines. This sent Peer's alarm bells ringing. Spike growled behind her. Mary's breathing was heavy, fast, fear or anticipation flooding her blood with oxygen in readiness for action. The lead car, a Mondeo, shifted on its suspension as the back door opened and a tall black man stepped out. He was smiling, but with trepidation rather than good humor. His face was strained, the smile false like a clown's.

"You all right?" he asked, glancing about at the destruction.

"Fine," Peer said. "We just got here. Found this. We weren't a part of the group or anything."

The tall man did not speak for a time. He took in his surroundings, frowning as the wounded cows bayed at the new arrivals. He leaned back into the car, moving stiffly, and Peer heard the murmur of discussion. She could make out no words, but there were three voices involved: his own; that of another man, quiet but firm; and a woman, who seemed to be arguing with whatever the tall man was saying. Finally, he stood back away from the car.

Peer was waiting for him to raise a gun. The image seemed so likely, so certain, that she half ducked. Mary took in a breath behind her, startled by Peer's movement rather than anything the others were doing. The dog growled, and Peer heard the sharp scrape of nails as it crouched forward, ready to attack.

"Hey, hey, no problems here, ladies," the man said, hands outstretched, palms up. "We're not here to cause trouble, believe me. No problems. My name's Paul. We've come from Rayburn, little village in the forest. Where are you from?"

"Newport," Peer said. "Is there anyone left in Chepstow?"

"Nothing there," Paul said, averting his eyes. "People wandering around, waiting for the emergency services. We saw a few police, but they seemed to be doing the same thing. They told us some things. How about Newport?"

"When I left, it was on fire."

"All of it?"

Peer shrugged. "Probably, by now. My friend died. And my neighbors."

Paul nodded. "Lots of people have. Have you heard anything on the radio? Been able to phone anyone? Have you tried Nine-nine-nine?"

"Who's in the car?" Mary cut in, her voice harsh and mistrustful. The chains rattled as she spoke, and Paul glanced down at the weapon in her hand.

"Blane," Paul said. "Hop out, let's show the ladies we're not meaning anything nasty here."

Blane! The name hit Peer, though she did not know why. Strong name. Powerful. At the same time, the strangeness of the situation struck her: having a conversation across a spread of corpses.

Blane stepped from the car. Short, wiry, balding, his eyes haunted and dark from lack of sleep. He smiled. The expression did not work. His eyes did not stop their exploration of the scene around him, lingering here, squinting there, taking everything in like a video camera.

"Blane," Mary whispered. Peer glance over her shoulder, but the woman's eyes were set on Blane.

"Know him?"

Mary shrugged. "No. Just the . . . No, of course not."

"There are four of us here," Paul said. "Myself, Blane. June here, driving the Mondeo. Back there in the Mini, Holly. We're to send help back to the village. When we find any."

"I don't know where I'm going," Peer said, and

the expression was stark, laying herself open for this man she did not know. "I had to leave Newport, and since then—"

"This is bad," Blane said. "Bad. The animals. Remember in the woods, Paul? How it all felt wrong? Well, it's getting worse. The animals did this."

"Like Henry?"

Blane shook his head. "No. Henry was . . . something else. Though . . ." he trailed off, looking around, crouching on his haunches when he began swaying. "Maybe she was here."

"How about we go across the bridge?" Paul said. "Go to the services. Find some food, and maybe an incident room will be there. Or something. There must be someone doing something about all this."

Peer nodded. "But if it's anything like Magor services, it'll just be full of people hanging around. Waiting for something to happen."

"We can try." Blane walked back to the car and climbed in, his eyes wide and panicked. Mary threw her chain into her car and waited for Peer to go with her. For a moment, Peer wanted so much to go to the Mondeo and travel with them, ask questions, find out more. They seemed in control, if control was at all possible now. Mary was the opposite: unstable; volatile; violent, waiting only for a direction in which to aim it.

Peer's decision was made for her. The Mondeo moved slowly past them, closely followed by the Mini. Peer returned the cautious smile of the driver, then hurried back to Mary's car, which was already coughing into life.

"What do you think?" she asked.

Mary looked at her, eyebrows raised. "About?"

"Them."

"I think we have to be with them," Mary said, and spoke no more.

Peer gazed down at the Severn as they crossed the old Severn bridge. The river was high and swirling its deadly currents in random, hypnotic patterns. Thousands of tons of silt were swept along in the waters, stripped from upriver, deposited here into new shapes and new ideas. She remembered going fossil hunting on Severn Beach with an old boyfriend, picking up rocks shaped like teeth and pretending they were from a real Tyrannosaur's mouth. Every stone they found could be a story, and they both ensured that they were.

She had discovered an ammonite hiding inside a stone the size of her fist. When she broke it open the delicate whirls and spirals of its shell were revealed, cast forever in stone, and a feeling of incredible loneliness had washed over her. The boyfriend had been farther along the beach, and she had stood for a few moments staring out over the water, trying to imagine the world as it had been all those millions of years ago. Time touched her then, not just passed her by. The realization that she was the blink of an eye, the beat of a heart in the lifetime of the planet filled her with mixed feelings of dread and, curiously, satisfaction. The sense that there was an overall scheme to things was immense, and this similarly led to the comfortable thought that whatever she did in her small, short life, could only help this scheme.

The waves washed into the beach, and out again. Constant, unchanging, merely moving position. The oceans would always be here. The cliffs loomed behind her, craggy spurs of rocks, ready to tumble at any moment. They would always be here, falling back under the onslaught of the sea, revealing more and more history to whomever might be here to search for it.

That day Peer felt a part of life, and something much greater. The ammonite had made its mark in the world, however small. She knew, then, that she would do the same.

That seemed unlikely now. Yet Peer was still filled with a sense of change, a constant feeling that she was one step removed from the mechanics of what was occurring because she was here for something else. The disaster, the deaths, were purely coincidental. She had a further purpose, something painted in the clouds or scrawled in the rock, waiting to be uncovered.

And then another thought intruded, one that was far less comforting. Maybe they were all fossils already, just waiting to pass away and be absorbed back into the planet.

Maybe they were nothing more than rebellious ghosts, refusing to lay down anu die.

Chapter Eighteen

Room Full of Dead

Things are changing, Blane had said. Peer could hardly agree with him more. Indeed, few could disagree. Things are changing. It was the present tense that worried her.

She sat at a table with her chin resting in her cupped hands. Blane and Mary had gone in search of others, with the intention that they would try telephoning someone—anyone—from the offices. Mary had seemed desperate to accompany him, something that Peer could understand. Blane was small and tired and sad, but he radiated power in an almost visible wave. It was not charisma; Peer could see that he was not comfortable among people. It was strength of intellect.

And, perhaps, the underlying allusion that he seemed more aware of what was happening than anyone.

Holly and Paul sat at the table behind her, talking quietly, continuing the discussion they'd had as soon as they reached the services. Snippets of it came back to her now, words she could barely understand, ideas she did not want to hear.

"Something's put a slant on nature," Blane had said. "Bent it askew. Shifted it sideways. Do you feel it? When you look around you, can't you see that things are changing?"

Peer thought she could see more than was readily apparent, and that terrified her. It had taken this man to point out the subtleties of the changes, but now that it was spoken they were there for all to see. She stared out at the trees in the parking lot, wishing that they were normal. Not bent like they were, gnarled, wild.

"I never feel more at home than I do in nature," Blane had continued. "But today, I'm homeless. It's rejecting me. I'm no longer comfortable among the trees and the fields and the birds. There's an air of change there. And as well as that, an intimation of violence. We've seen what's happened already. Those people . . . they never stood a chance."

Never stood a chance, thought Peer. They were attacked from all sides, mutilated and eaten. By cows. And birds.

It might have been those same birds flurrying past the windows now, darting between the decorative landscaping and finding invisible crumbs of food along the curb edges. Peer was sure they threw more than an occasional glance at the service buildings.

As though they were waiting for the humans to exit.

"Sleep," Paul had said. "That seems to be the connecting factor. I had a dream, I was falling, I hit the ground. A snow bank. When I woke up, I was bruised and battered. Other people . . . I don't think they were so lucky with their dreams. Maybe not everyone had dreams of falling, but whatever's happening, it's killing lots of people. So, I think we have to try to avoid sleeping until we know more of what is happening. Or until we find help, and they can tell us."

"How long can we stay awake?" June said, panicked.

"I don't know."

"What? Days? A week? What happens then?"

"I don't know. Maybe we can sleep in shifts, watch over each other. Wake each other up when we show the first signs of dreaming. You know, twitching, REM."

"You haven't got a fucking clue."

"I'm trying. We've all got to try. Stick together."

"But how the hell . . ."

"You haven't got a fucking . . ."

"What about . . ."

It had gone on. For an hour, two, random discussions deciding nothing, conjecture, shouting, moments of hysteria. And all the while Mary sat watching Blane, staring, barely taking her eyes from him. Even on the few occasions she spoke, it was as though she was addressing only Blane himself, not the others. Holly sat next to Paul, backing him up most of the time but still objecting when he suggested staying put in the service station.

"That's crazy! If that was a good idea, we wouldn't be alone here now."

"Think about it, Holly. It's secure from . . . outside. No animals will get in. There are phones, toilets, fridges, cupboards full of food. Radios, TVs in the offices. Cars outside. Petrol station. It's a regular holiday home, if you think about it."

"This can't be everywhere." Her voice, desperate.

"It may be."

"Whatever's happened, however far it stretches, it's messed everything up for a while. All I'm saying is that we need to keep on the move. Travel. Explore, if you like. I take your point about being safe here, but we'd be living a lie. Waiting, on edge. We'd always be expecting that police car to come cruising into the car park, an army helicopter to land with some scientist who'd tell us, 'Okay, everything's sorted, you can all go home now.' At least if we're on the move, we're looking for help. We can see how bad things are. Christ, I just can't sit here. Well, if you all do, I'm going anyway—"

"Hold on, Holly. Calm down. Vote. We vote."

So they had voted, a show of hands, and in the end even Paul had relented. Holly had talked him around.

Peer glanced back to where they were sitting. Holly smiled over Paul's shoulder, and Peer returned the smile. She seemed nice. Head screwed on. Unlike Mary . . .

Mary. What was she all about? She'd acted as if she had recognized Blane, out there on the road, and ever since she had barely left his side. And that dog of hers, Spike, always trotting along behind her, sniffing at that damned chain she carried around like a set of murderous rosary beads.

Peer stared through the window, trying to tie

down exactly how things were different but finding it all but impossible. It was the sum of the parts, a thousand minute alterations that combined to form an oblique picture of reality. The old reality, at least. The trees grew slanted, as though the earth had moved suddenly, tensioning the trunks against their fixed points in the sky. The air above the river was hazy, bright, sunlight reflecting through thin layers of moisture to hide the wispy clouds higher up. The shrubs planted between parking bays had a threatening sharpness about them, promising gashed flesh and rashed skin if one approached too close.

Birds no longer flustered and fought over stale crusts. They gave the impression of rooting and eating merely to waste time, divert attention away from themselves. . . .

Peer snorted. Now she was being stupid.

"I've always loved nature," Blane had said. "Always felt I was an integral part of it. A puzzle piece that only truly fitted in when I was away from humanity and their fake constructs. That puzzle's changed, and I haven't. I don't fit any more. Tell the truth, I don't think any of us do."

None of us fit, Peer thought. *We're all rejects. Nature's refuse. Damaged goods.*

Jenny, with her broken neck. The burning town, blasting its human history at the sky in a thousand tons of ash. The skinhead, belying his image, dead in the road, eaten.

In a way, the thought seemed to fit everything together.

Peer smiled.

*   *   *

The little dead girl smiles. Her mother smiles back, distant and preoccupied. The little girl feels sad.

They are sitting on a cloud high above the patchwork countryside. Houses are tiny, cars almost invisible. A river snakes its way between hillocks and higher ground, its ten-million-year trail obvious and wondrous from this height, almost spelling secrets. The little girl thinks of times long ago, when all manner of creature must have wandered the land and drunk from the river as it wore its path through soil and rock.

Her mother stands and walks to the edge of the cloud. The little girl follows, not wanting to leave her mother's side in case she suddenly turns to find her gone.

They both look down, down, and see an airplane passing by far below. She thinks of waving to it, but suddenly wonders whether anyone would see her anyway. She is dead, after all.

She turns to her mother, but she has gone, vanishing straight through the cloud and drifting slowly Earthward. The little girl jumps up and down, but the cloud is impenetrable to her. She thinks she sees a rainbow, but then the clouds turn black, ready for rain. All color is washed away.

She wants to cry for her mother, but she cannot find her voice. It has hidden itself well.

As she stands, she feels something beneath her feet. There is an explosion in the cloud and something dark and gleaming bursts up through the insubstantial floor. A chain, dressed in hooks and blades, whispering death at the sky.

It whips around her neck. It does not hurt because she is dead, but when it starts to tug her to the edge she begins to panic. Her mother has gone, true, but she had floated. The little girl knows that she would not float. She would fall. She would plummet, reach terminal velocity and pass it in an impossible desire to bury her dead little body deep under the ground.

The chain rattles and jerks, the cruel barbs snagging on her windpipe and spine, hauling her closer and closer to the edge. She holds on, but her heels skim across the cloud as if it is ice cream.

She is plucked over the edge.

She tumbles as she falls, glancing back at the cloud. The underside is dark with whipping, writhing chains. Millions of them.

She finds her voice and screams.

Not real.

She is going to hit the ground, make her own grave.

Not real. Wake up now! Peer, wake! You're needed. More than anything . . .

Something tickles her ear, something other than the air storming by. Like a voice, a whisper in a hurricane.

Wake . . .

She jerked awake. Someone shouted. Then a scream.

She'd hit! Impact! She was dead!

"Peer, wake up!"

She sat upright, looked back at Paul and Holly where they were reaching over their seats.

"Christ, Peer!" Holly gasped. "Christ. One minute you were there, the next your head hit the table. Asleep. Christ."

"I was falling," Peer said. "You saved me, Paul. Thanks. You saved me." But she thought it was more than Paul's shaking and Holly's shouting that had woken her up.

There was a sudden row behind them, running feet and June's voice calling out in fear.

"We have to leave!" Blane shouted. He skidded to a stop. "What's wrong?"

"Peer was asleep," Paul said.

"Sleepyhead." Mary laughed.

"We have to leave," Blane repeated.

"Dead bodies," June panted. "Lots of them. Twenty, thirty. In the plant room."

Paul shrugged. Yesterday, this would have shocked him to the core. Now he needed more. They had all seen so many dead bodies already that he knew there must be more.

"Not the same," Blane continued. "They've been murdered. Some have their throats slit. Others . . . their heads are crushed."

"Oh, God!" Holly said. "What if the people who did it—"

"That's why we're leaving now!" Blane hissed. "Come on!"

The six of them moved through the restaurant, each with their own thoughts, each looking a different way. They reached the foyer without incident, Peer still stunned.

June reached the doors first. They slid open as she approached.

Outside, a bird sang.

The light vanished.

Chapter Nineteen

The Nature of Things

Fay had watched from afar when Mary and the bitch woman first met Blane's group. She had seen their stunned reaction to the animal attack, giggled at the woman's hesitancy when Mary called her back to the car. So you should be worried, bitch. Wait until Mary knows the time is right, when I tell her. Then you'll wish you'd gone with the others. Too late to worry then.

She had watched them leave and then skipped across the acres of mud to the river's edge. The water was rough today, as though reveling in a world no longer dominated by humankind, but she had run across the riverbed where the movement was less violent.

There had been a group of people in the services. They had stared at her in surprise at first, then shock. Then, when she moved at them, fear. But none of them had been fast enough, fattened as they were on the lethargy of modern life, and only one or two had put up token resistance. It was like stamping on ants, except less cruel.

She had to have a clean stage for her play. Nobody else could be allowed to intervene. And besides, their pathetic bodies would leave another signal and move things forward.

By the time the three cars reached the services Fay was sitting comfortably behind a screen of shrubs at the edge of the car park, chewing hungrily, and needlessly, on a still struggling pigeon.

Plants withered and shrunk around her, but only because she willed it so. If she wished, they would simply continue in their slow, inevitable transmutations, twisting into some bastardized idea of their former selves. She was merely a catalyst for the power of ruin and change previously unleashed; but even that was enough to enjoy.

She liked the smell of decay. She loved the tickle of dead leaves scratching her skin in the springtime. The taste of the pigeon, rancid and askew, was Heaven on her tongue. She shivered in ecstasy, just to see what it felt like.

The stench of death wafted from the building; fresh fear, newly opened bodies. She hoped the group would see it in all its terrible detail. Blane deserved it.

The cars drew up outside the building and they went inside. Blane led, with the tall black man and the bitch woman following. Another woman next, then Mary and that ridiculous dog she'd adopted. The final woman paused, looked around for a while, scanning the grounds for movement. Fay ached to be seen, to give a fleeting glimpse. But not here; now was not the time. Now it was time for something else, a little game, a play in the big match.

Time to throw another spanner in the works.

You, Fay thought, looking at the woman, grinning. *Standing there with your hands on your arrogant hips, tits thrust out. Bet you want some of his cock, don't you, shoved deep into you while he squeezes those tits, gnaws your neck. Don't you? Don't you?*

The woman turned to watch Paul enter the building. She ran her hand through her short hair and followed them in.

Yes, you do. But who's to say you'll get out alive?

Fay remained in position for two hours. She could see the group through the restaurant window, arguing, disputing, spending pointless time planning their route when it was she who would steer them until it was time for Blane and his bitch to learn the truth. Then, soon after they knew, it would matter no more. Mary would take the woman, and Blane . . . that was up to him. If he was as strong as he had been in the past, he would accept Fay and everything that was happening. There was really no denying or escaping it. But weak, as he now seemed to be . . . lessened, drained . . .

. . . maybe he would have to go too.

The birds had begun to gather. At first even Fay was surprised, because she was exerting no influence. But then she realized that things were progressing quickly, and the ruin had set in deeply in this area. The fact pleased her, but also frightened her a little. There was still some of her old self inside, despairing at what was happening, mourning the loss of so much. But her new self—the better, improved, evolved portion of her old soul—loved the idea she had become. She was a great idea. The thought pleased her, the analogy amused her. She would have to remember that for when she finally confronted Blane.

She grinned, enjoying the sight as thousands of birds of all shapes, sizes and varieties alighted silently on the roof of the service buildings. Canny they were, too, sending a handful of their number down to the ground to divert the attention of those inside with the usual, boring routine. The roof was soon covered with a living, fluttering carpet of life, vying for space, arguing and pecking at one another, waiting for the doors to open, looking for a signal from those down below. They could smell the people inside, perhaps the dead ones as well as the living.

So the birds gathered, and soon Fay began to wonder which one would be the first through the doors. She had no doubt that some of them would escape, because Blane was with them. No matter how much he had forgotten, or chose to forget, he still had power. Perhaps one or two of them would stay there, dead, torn up, but that was just the nature of things. The nature of the new nature.

Fay stroked the chains on her face, feeling the tiny tug at her insides as she did so. She relished the idea of revealing what they held. She loved the thought of Blane seeing the final, inextricable truth. His face. His eyes.

The foyer doors opened.

A woman stepped through. She paused for an instant, as if sensing what was to come. But fate gave her no more time to think. Like a huge black sheet waved from one end to the other, the birds lifted from the roof. If there had been a sort of order in their patient wait, it vanished now that the waiting was over. They plunged headlong at the door, twisting and spinning down around the roof overhang and smothering the woman, like dirty water spinning into a plughole. There were thousands of them, tens of thousands, forcing their way into the opening, with thousands more battering their brains out on the glass walls on either side, feathers flying, many of them peeling back and coming around for a second run when they realized that their way in was blocked.

Fay frowned.

From this distance the services resembled a giant bees' nest, with the workers humming around the opening. The foyer was literally full of birds, and now they were impacting with the inside of the windows as well as the outside, washing it red with blood and brains. A drift of dead birds soon built up around the opening, piled against the glass like stained snow.

Fay scratched at her chin, drawing blood. There were so many of them, more than she had expected. The ruin was advancing quickly.

Blane had to survive.

She left her hiding place, the time for concealment now passed. Several birds approached her, crying angrily into the hot sky. She hissed impatiently, and they fell with a patter to the tarmac, wings twitching in death. She walked, then ran toward the violence. The main entrance was a maelstrom of swirling, diving, crashing and dying birds, the windows now so obscured with their blood and feathers that she could no longer see inside.

Blane *must* survive. Surely he would not let something like this finish him? Not now, not while the great match was still being played. Surely nature would not be so unkind?

But then, Fay knew that it would. She knew how, and why, and when it would stop, and she became scared for the first time in a long, long while. She had never been alone. Blane had always been there, whether he knew it or not. She didn't know how she could face things, not without him, however remote they now were from each other.

She closed her eyes, concentrating. She felt sick. The chains pulled at her temples, stroked the inside of her stomach and moved the load they carried there. She squeezed her fists tight, feeling the ruin roiling haphazardly around her, trying to catch some of its manic energy and then letting it go again, boosted, amplified into a sudden wave instead of a steady background noise.

She hissed. Her front teeth broke and scattered on the pavement. Replacements began to grow instantly, but older, yellower, dulled by the ruin she too was experiencing.

The cacophony of the attack ceased. It was replaced with the sound of thousands of birds dying in one instant, dropping to the ground, twitching uselessly as their final breaths were suffocated by those above them.

Fay turned, sighed and ran. Within seconds she was away from the car park and running aimlessly out into the fields. The way she had used to run with Blane.

Once again, silence reigned.

Chapter Twenty

Toys

Peer heard the mechanical hiss of the outer doors open.

Above her head, outside, she sensed a weight. A living, breathing mass, pressing down, pushing back, compressing the air with its multitudinous life force. The confusion she felt over her strange dream vanished instantly, swept away by the intense dread that flooded her system like an injected drug. Knowledge was clear and true to her then, but a terrible knowledge, a certainty that death was mere seconds away. She did not want to become the little dead girl; she did not want to feel that lost.

June stepped through the doors. Peer saw the birds scattered across the parking lot look up as one; heard the loud call as they opened their beaks in unison.

Across the foyer there was a toilet door. Ten

227

steps. "Run!" she shouted. She did not have time for more.

As the deluge roared through the open doors, she turned and headed for the men's toilet, grabbing Holly's hand and hauling her along.

The wall of birds hit them, flowing warmly around them, beaks lancing at their skin like sharpened hail. Peer closed her eyes and tried to scream, but something entered her mouth and jabbed at her tongue. It tasted of stale bed linen. She gagged, unable to dislodge the creature, and she eventually bit down hard to clear her airway. She vomited as she ran, feeling warmth splash down her front. Claws scraped across her scalp like a hundred uncut nails, moving down onto her face and neck, searching for her eyes. She pressed one forearm across her face. Things caught on her ears and lips, ripping them and spitting blood into the air.

Blane saw the sky darkening and knew exactly what was happening. "Run," a voice called from behind him, but it was too late. He saw the first wave sweep into June, and the second it took them to pass her by gave him time to fall to his knees, arms crossed over his head in an attitude of pious prayer. He heard a scream from June; only brief, because it was quickly muffled. The wall of bodies hit him, forcing him over onto his back.

"No!" he screamed, teeth gritted. There must be something he could do. He felt there had to be something. But whatever it was, panic swallowed it. He kept shouting until he felt the first exploratory beaks jabbing at his chin and cheeks; then he pressed his lips tightly together. All over his body, hard beaks jabbed and tore. In places they felt like needles, puncturing his hide, then searching for virgin skin to do so again. Sometimes, when a larger bird like a crow or pigeon was the culprit, the pounding remained in the same place. Wounds were opened and widened, and Blane had the sickening vision of being eaten alive.

Run where? he thought. He used his feet to turn on the floor, then started forcing himself along the slippery surface—made more so by spilled blood and bird shit—toward where he remembered the toilets to be. *Should be doing something,* he kept thinking, but the thought itself was alien and strange.

The noise was tremendous. Blane was reminded of how the kids in the village had used to tape playing cards into the spokes of their bike wheels to produce a snapping, humming sound. This was like a thousand bikes, a cacophony of explosive wing beats and impact thuds as birds dashed themselves against walls or windows. Intermingled in this were other noises, even more ominous; the scraping of claws and beaks across hard surfaces; the insistent wet smacking of birds hitting bodies; moans and shouts, muffled by protective limbs or intrusive, pecking bodies.

He hit something. At first it did not move, and he wondered who else was dead. Then a voice came through the noise.

"Who?"

"Blane."

"Paul."

They were economic with their words; the birds were wild with their beaks, seeking any opening.

Blane nudged against Paul, pushing him toward the wall. "Move!" Something big scampered over him and he groaned in dismay. Badger? Fox? Heavy jaws snapped several times in the air around his face, and he wondered why he felt no pain. Then he risked a glimpse—just quickly—and saw Spike with matted feathers and blood on his mouth. The dog moved away snapping, growling, spinning, howling as beaks and claws found their mark. There was Spike, but where was Mary?

Mary, too, had sensed a change as soon as the doors slid open. Even as the bitch Peer shouted for them to run, Mary was turning and aiming for the kitchens behind the restaurant. They were a good thirty feet distant, she knew, but they were also away from the others. And while whatever came in the door was occupying itself with Blane and the rest, she could run and hide. She did not wonder what Fay would think of her actions; she did not consider whether or not this was the "right time" to get rid of Peer, or to attack Blane. Such thoughts, even powerful ones instilled by Fay, were driven out by terror, and a sense of self-preservation Mary had thought lost forever. With Roger and the gang it had been living because she was too afraid to die unwanted. Now she wanted to live because she saw a full, rich life ahead. One where she was needed, and respected.

So she ran.

And the first wave of birds caught her halfway across the restaurant.

She swung the chain around her head, feeling the soft thuds of multiple impacts and hearing the pained squeaks of damaged birds. Within seconds the chain had slipped from her hand, handle slick with blood.

She went down, shaking her head to dislodge the flapping creatures caught in her hair, crying out as cruel beaks and claws scraped at her eyes. A smell enveloped her, warm and musty, and rich-smelling shit pattering down around her. Something was hanging onto her eyebrow, a small bird, pecking at her eyes as though they were caged nuts. Dipping its beak, twisting, jerking its head down again, twisting . . .

Mary flung herself at the floor head-first. She felt the delicate crunch of bones as the offending bird was crushed. It remained attached to her forehead as she rolled across the floor, colliding with chairs and tables. Bodies crushed and popped beneath her, but there were always a hundred more to take their place as she came out of the roll. Soon she hit the food counter; there was nowhere left to go. She curled into a ball and protected her head. Beaks pressed into her back, her buttocks, between her legs. She thought of Fay.

Peer struck the toilet door and pushed her way in, dragging Holly through behind her. With their combined weight they managed to shut the door, but already hundreds of birds had gained entry. They began to dive-bomb the women, uttering no noise but loud nonetheless, their wings sounding like a huge sheet being flipped and waved.

Glass broke. A stream of birds gushed in, as if spat through the window from outside.

"Oh, no!" Peer screamed. The birds fanned out,

striking the line of urinals, hitting the wall and twisting, dazed, to the floor. They slowed their attack. "Stop it!" Peer shouted, and those assaulting Holly lessened their violence. Soon, they were simply hanging from Holly's ears, her torn clothing, heads jerking and beaks red and gleaming.

"Peer!" Holly whined.

"Stay still."

"What's happening?"

"I don't know." Peer put her ear to the door. Someone was screaming, Spike was barking and growling, the roar of the attacking birds outside continued like a violent waterfall. She readied herself to open the door. She felt she could do it. She did not know what "it" was, precisely, but it had worked in here.

She opened the door.

Holly screamed. "Peer, no!"

The birds poured through, a pent up flood, knocking Peer back. She felt like she was suffocating; every breath gave her a mouthful of feathers, each way she turned was darkened with birds.

And then the noise stopped.

The silence was shocking. The birds dropped out of the air. A few mild twitters or an occasional flapping wing were the only signs of fleeing life. Within seconds, Peer and Holly were surrounded by a thick carpet of dead birds, three deep. Feathers floated in the air, a gentle snow flurry compared to the blazing blizzard they had just experienced.

Blood dripped into Peer's eye. She wiped it hurriedly away and looked out into the foyer, terrified at what she would see. She remembered the dead people from the Cavalier and the Mercedes, the gleaming white of bones, the raw red of exposed flesh. A whine escaped her, an unconscious sound of desperation and despair.

The whole area she could see—foyer, shop, restaurant—was a vibrating sea of birds. Some still moved, on top and underneath, giving the appearance of waves and ripples. The walls and ceiling had been blooded and feathered. The glass on either side of the entrance doors was cracked and starred, and the doors themselves were wedged open, whining in frustration as they tried again and again to close.

There was movement in front of her. Peer stepped back as two bodies broke the surface, gasping and spluttering, spitting out feathers and blood.

Blane and Paul.

"What the hell?" Paul gasped rhetorically. He looked around, rubbing blood from his eyes and wincing as he scraped his hand across a dozen tiny cuts on his eyelids.

"They all died," Peer said. "Dropped like something stepped on them."

Blane shook his head. "We're being toyed with," he muttered. He did not elaborate, and nobody asked him what he meant. He realized that he was not entirely sure himself. What he did know was that this transgressed every law of normality. The birds were dead, not merely collapsed in a heap. The attack, though extraordinary, was at least believable. The synchronized death of thousands of birds was patently absurd. Yet here he was, kneeling among the pathetic bodies.

Yes, they were being toyed with. Like mice,

tossed around by a cat before the coup de grace was delivered.

"Where are June and Mary?" Paul asked.

"I saw Spike a few moments ago," Blane said. "June . . . she was at the door when the birds came in." They all turned to look, Holly stepping up behind Peer and holding the woman's arms as she looked over her shoulder. They were panting with terror and exertion; blood blew from their lips and misted the air.

The doors were moving slowly back and forth, motors humming as their attempts to shut were foiled by the dead things in the way. The piles of birds were deepest there, where they had still been struggling to get in from outside, and a diminishing heap fanned across the pavement and out toward the car park. Across the parking lots, individual bodies stippled the surface like boils on dark skin.

"I'll go," said Paul.

"Paul . . ." Blane began, but the big man ignored him and started for the door.

He took the longest steps possible. He could hear and feel the crunching bones and splitting bodies, feel fluid warmth soaking into his jeans and tipping over the rim of his low boots, but there was no other way to move. He stared resolutely ahead. The farther he went, the more it looked as though he had been blooded and feathered. A sick cartoon character, designed to disgust, not to amuse.

As he reached the door there was a loud noise behind him. He spun round and saw Spike bounding through the birds like a lamb in long grass, snapping here and there, his muzzle holding a hundred feathers on slick whiskers. The mutt kept biting, no matter how much Blane and the two women tried to calm him down, and Paul turned away from the sight.

So much blood, he thought. *Never knew there was so much blood in the world.*

The humming doors had frozen open now that he stood beneath the sensor.

"June?"

It was ridiculous. There was no sign of her. No hand above the pile, no streak of hair protruding like a safety line through an avalanche. Even if she was down there, she would be suffocated by now beneath the weight of dead birds. Calling her name was pointless.

"June?"

No answer. No alternative. He pointed his fingers and curled his thumbs into his palms, then forced his arms into the birds where they were piled the highest. Here, they were almost up to his thighs. He twisted his hands in a drilling motion, scratching them on beaks frozen open in death, sickened by the sensation of smooth feathers against his skin. He touched the floor, bent at the hip so that his face was only inches above the top layer of birds. He withdrew his arms, glanced around at the others. Their expressions did not change. He could see that they were suffering with him.

"Just like lucky dip," he said. He dived in again, farther to the left, and this time his hands found something more substantial. He grabbed hold, tugging, forcing himself upright. Straining, lifting, the shape he was holding finally broke surface.

He heard their mingled gasps. He was facing the

ceiling, eyes shut with the effort. "Oh, Jesus Christ," Holly said. Paul did not look down. He did not need to see.

"Is she dead?" he asked. Nobody answered for a moment. He opened his eyes and stared at the ceiling. The fiber tiles were pitted and split where the birds had struck them, splashes of blood marking a thousand points of impact. A sparrow and several tits were impaled there, their beaks stuck fast. A sprout of black and white feathers marked one large dent in a tile. Magpie, Paul thought. The scrounger of the bird kingdom. The thug. Vicious, beautiful, scavenging, one of his favorite birds. The magpie had character.

"I hope so," Peer said at last. "Let her go, Paul."

Paul let go and turned around. The others had already averted their gazes.

"We need medical supplies," Holly said, wiping blood from her eyes and wincing as her arm rubbed against her tattered ears.

"Lost your earrings," Paul said. "I'll buy you some new ones."

"New ears would suffice. I think I've grown out of jewelry."

"Spike!" Mary was standing at the entrance to the restaurant, bloody, hair plastered across her face. There was a dead bird pinned to her forehead somehow, leaking its own blood to mingle with hers.

"June's dead," Peer said.

Mary glanced across to where Paul stood over the tattered body, then smiled as the dog emerged from the shop, still snapping at birds. He sank up to his stomach whenever he stopped, so he continued bounding across the grotesque floor, bouncing around Mary and accepting her friendly pats.

At least she's lost that bloody chain, Peer thought. "You all right?" she asked. "You've got a dead bird on your face."

Mary looked over at her but did not answer. She grabbed the pulped thing hanging above her eye and pulled, grunting as a flap of skin came away with its clasped claws. She offered the bird to Spike, who snapped it from her hand, shook it and threw it down among its dead cousins.

"They must sell medical kits in the shop," Blane said. "Mary, you're nearest. See what you can find. Paul, you go out and bring the Mondeo up to the door. We'd better check the fuel. And fill the trunk with food."

"Blane, let's just get out of here before we start planning," Peer said, not unkindly. "Sort ourselves out. We're alive. We'll worry about everything else once we're out of this shithole."

Blane looked at her, nodded. He glanced across at Mary, nodded to her as well. She waded toward the shop, paying no particular attention to the dead creatures she was forcing her way through. Spike followed.

"We'll go to the petrol station," Blane said. "Clean up. Stock up. Then get the hell away."

"Where to?" Peer asked.

"I don't know," he said. "Just away."

He stared around as the others headed toward the doors. The noise of crashing shelves came from the shop as Mary searched for medical kits.

* * *

Someone's toying with us. In all the confusion and terror the others seemed to have forgotten the murdered people they'd found only minutes ago. Some horrors were greater. Blane just could not help connecting the two.

He remembered laughter, musical and sweet, accompanied by bird song. And as it replayed in his memory, it mutated into the chuckle he had heard in the woods. The sneering chortle that could so easily have come from the woman in the field.

However much he hid, however much he ran, he still felt spied upon.

Chapter Twenty-one

Into the Wilds

"Gas? Biological weapons? Germ warfare? I don't know." Holly paused. "Act of God?"

Paul shrugged. "I think the last is most likely. Hold still." They were in the disabled toilet of the petrol station. Blane had gone into the men's with a first-aid kit and locked the door behind him; Peer and Mary were cleaning each other up in the women's. Holly had insisted on coming in here with Paul, saying she had to talk to him. Mary had grinned past torn lips, but they had both chosen to ignore her.

"Mary frightens me," she said, changing the subject quickly. "She's weird. Shifty. And that dog of her's . . . Ow!"

"Sorry." Paul was dabbing the blood from her ears with damp toilet paper, wincing when he saw the torn skin. "You need stitches."

"You any good?"

He shook his head. "Oh, no, not me. Well, I've never actually done it. But if you want . . . ?"

"I've seen worse stuff today," she said absently. "Just put a bandage on, I'm not too worried about scarring. Just living."

They remained silent while Paul carefully applied antiseptic and sterilized bandages to her ears. "I'll have to stick it down to your neck," he said. "You'll look a bit weird for a while."

"No problem."

Another pause.

"Mary," Paul said. "Hmm."

"And what does that mean?"

He shrugged. "I'm not a good judge of character. Really. I'm not qualified to pass judgment on someone I met a couple of hours ago."

Holly stared at him until she caught his eye. His bloodied face made his eyes stand out, stark and wide and friendly. She had trouble stopping herself from smiling at him stupidly. "First impression, then. Now. Don't think about it, just say it."

"Spooky," he said. "Insecure. Demanding attention. That bloody chain thing is enough to tell you that. Strange how she hooked up with Peer."

"How do you mean?"

"Well, Peer seems . . . nice. A little lost, but aren't we all?"

Holly thought over what he had said. "So who's in charge out of those two?"

"If anyone, Mary. But only because she feels she needs to be. And only because Peer is too gentle to exert authority, even though she's the one who really has it."

"See?" Holly said. "Not such a bad judge of character. Potted psychoanalysis in five minutes."

"Come on now," Paul said, "only opinions. Not for human consumption, you know?"

"Don't worry," she said, "I won't tell a soul." She shifted away from him slightly, caught the hem of her sweater. "I hope you're not bashful. I feel like a fucking pepperpot, and blood is trickling everywhere." She lifted the sweater over her head. She was not wearing a bra.

"Oh . . . hey . . ." Paul muttered, turning away.

"Paul," Holly said, touched and angry at the same time. "I'm bleeding. I've seen more dead people today than I've ever had friends. The last thing I'm thinking about is . . . what you may think I'm thinking about. Are you thinking about it?"

He glanced at her face, could not help looking down at her small breasts. They were bleeding in several places; there were cuts on her stomach that in better times would demand stitching; around the base of her neck, it looked as though someone had tried to perforate a line to make her head detachable. Blood had dribbled down and soaked into the top of her leggings, which were similarly holed. "Oh, Holly," he said despairingly. He began to clean her wounds.

Later, when he had finished, she cleaned him. He stripped down to his briefs and turned slowly as she washed each small cut and put a plaster on the worst ones. As well as the assault by the birds, his body was bruised and sore from his dream impact. He looked like a plane crash victim.

They dressed together, smiling at one another, both enjoying the silent company. Suddenly, Holly did not want to leave. They could stay in here, venturing out to the petrol station shop now and then for chocolate and crackers and canned drinks, wait for help to arrive and rescue them. That ever-elusive help . . .

"Do you think this has happened everywhere?"

Paul paused in doing up his belt, looked at Holly for a moment, staring past her, seeing something far more distant than her lacerated face. "That's why we've got to keep moving, I suppose. To find out."

Holly nodded. "I suppose."

Outside, Blane was waiting for them. He was chewing slowly on a Mars bar, sipping from a bottle of water. He was still wearing his old clothes, though the cuts on his face and hands were now covered by small sticking plasters. "We've all got to learn to shave properly," he said.

"Blane," Paul said. "A million birds attacked us. What's going on?"

"I don't know," he said. "I know as much as you."

"So who's 'toying with us'?"

They were silent for a few seconds, three people thrown together by disaster, as different as random choice could have made them. Blane seemed to be struggling with some inner block, but soon he began to talk. He spoke quickly, throwing frequent glances at the women's bathroom door.

"I don't know much about anything," he said. "In fact, nothing. It's all a confusion. Ever since this morning, I've had the feeling that I'm being followed. No, not even that." He shook his head, sipped more water as he thought. "Orchestrated.

Controlled. In the woods this morning, a deer died before me. It's throat had been crushed. Then there were screams from the village, and I saw someone in the graveyard as I ran across the field.

"It was the same someone I saw just before we found the dead farmer."

"The boy? You saw the someone who arranged the boy in the graveyard?" Holly spoke quietly, her voice shaking. She remembered the grotesque display, the hints of witchcraft and sacrifice.

Blane nodded. "For me to find, I think." He shrugged. "I know. And when I saw the woman in the field, next to the lane, she seemed to know me. She did know me. And I knew her. But I couldn't place her." He shook his head, looking down at the water bottle in his hand. "There's so much about me you don't understand."

"Well, help us understand—" Paul began, but Blane cut him off.

"I can't, because I don't understand it myself. My memory stretches back only to encompass my time in nature. I can't remember childhood, or parents, or family. Nothing. Only sitting in woods, wandering around fields, loving nature and feeling a part of it. Until today. Now, everything's alien. Even you." He half smiled, taking away any offense implied in his last statement.

"Who is this woman? What the hell could she have to do with what's going on?"

"I don't know. She's strange, familiar, but not as she is now. It's as though I knew her in another life. . . . I have memories. . . . It's difficult."

"Try."

Blane took another swig of water, washed it

around his mouth as though tasting truths in its mountain-spring falseness. "She's hardly normal, barely human. Sounds foolish, I know, but it's how I perceive her. She had these chains, bolted into her temples. They go into her mouth. I'm sure they hold something."

"Oh, hey, this is getting weird," Holly said. "And besides anything, what the hell has she got to do with killing people in their sleep and hordes of animals suddenly eating us alive?"

Blane stared at her. He could not answer because he did not know the facts. But he knew the truth. "Something," he said.

The door to the ladies' opened, and Peer and Mary emerged. Spike trotted at their heels.

"I think maybe we should lose the dog," Paul said abruptly. "After what's happened in the last few hours, I don't want him suddenly turning on one of us."

"Spike goes, I go," Mary said.

Go then, thought Blane, but he said: "Keep him close to you, Mary. We'll keep an eye on him. Tell the truth, he helped me."

"Good dog," Mary said, patting his head. Something rumbled in his throat, a growl or a grumble of pleasure.

The five of them stood that way for a moment, and then Holly spoke up. "So, what do we do?"

"Keep moving," Paul said. "Arm ourselves, if we can. Look for help."

"Guns won't do much against the likes of that," Holly said, nodding through the large window at the service buildings.

"It's not only that," Blane said. "We found those bodies."

Silence. Even Mary looked worried. She stroked her dog like a comfort charm.

"Who do you think did it?" Paul asked. Blane could see the question in his eyes. *Her?*

"No idea. But I'd bet they're not the only murdered people lying around today." He shrugged at Paul.

"Why do you say that?" said Peer. "That's a horrible thought."

"It's the three-meal scenario," Paul cut in. He popped open a bottle of water and slaked his thirst before going on. "You heard it? Take away three straight meals from the population, and you've got anarchy. Basically, if normality slips sideways, for whatever reason, so does society. Falls from the knife edge; some of the people will impale themselves on the spikes beneath. Others will climb back up."

"I can't believe that," Holly said. "People are basically good."

"Sure they are," Peer said. "But in Newport this morning, a man fired a shotgun at me. He was wandering the streets naked. I saw him blow a dead driver's brains out. And there was the fire. Something that big must have been started on purpose. It can't have been just a coincidence."

"One man," Holly said. "Not everyone, surely. Us? We're all right. We're helping each other."

"And what happens if there's one car and two groups of people who need it?" Blane said. "Would you shoot someone for it?"

"Of course not!" Holly scoffed. Paul shook his

head. Peer averted her gaze from them all, and Mary simply stared.

"Then eventually—if this turns worse, and there's no outside help for a long time—you'd succumb. You'd die."

"Because I won't shoot someone for a car?"

"No. Because eventually, you'd be faced with that choice over food. Or clean water. Or medical supplies. Things run out. Things decay."

"Survival of the fittest," Mary said.

"Survival of the most vicious," Holly mumbled.

"Both." Blane began grabbing chocolate bars and crackers and canned drinks, dropping them into a carrier bag. "But let's hope it doesn't come to that. Help me grab some food, then we go."

"What about June?" Peer asked. "We can't just leave her there. We've got to . . . bury her. Or something."

There was silence. None of the group wanted to say no, though they were all thinking it. There were so many bodies, and the false promise they were all laboring under was that they would send back help.

"Okay," Peer said quietly. "Okay. So, where do we go now?" She bit her upper lip.

"Any objections to London?" Nobody answered. It was not because Blane's idea was good, it was just that there were none better.

Blane wondered whether the woman was already ahead of them, planning the next atrocity. And in an instant of clear thought, he decided to try to fool her if she was. They would turn southwest, away from London, down into the country. She would not be expecting that.

Take her by surprise, as she had done to them over the last twelve hours.

They took two cars. At first, Blane wanted them all in the Mondeo. It would be uncomfortable and cramped, he acknowledged, but he felt that they would be safer together. There was a large trunk for food and other supplies, and it was the newest car. But Holly had insisted that she take her Mini. What if the Mondeo broke down? she asked. And Paul had volunteered to travel with her, much to Mary's amusement. Blane had agreed, eventually, though he could barely see them all in the Mini if anything did happen to the big Ford.

They stocked up on food and drink from the garage in the services, not wanting to venture back into the main buildings. Other creatures had already started showing an interest in the car park: carrion birds pecking at their dead cousins; a family of foxes sniffing at the edges of the pile of dead birds. Even a pack of pet dogs gone feral, which Spike growled at but wisely did not approach.

They pulled back onto the motorway, Peer driving the Mondeo with Blane in the front, Mary and Spike in the back. Holly drove her Mini while Paul sat next to her, slowly stroking the many plasters on his face and neck. He was starting to feel as though he had a massive dose of chicken pox, and each slight cut was a spot aching to be picked. The pain was a heavy overall glow, always there, always ready to cut in with a sharp reminder if he shifted position the wrong way or rubbed the wrong plaster. In truth, he felt like a human punching bag. His back and limbs were heavy and aching from the impact in his dream; his left shoulder seemed almost to have seized up.

"Where the hell does he think we're going to find guns?" Holly asked.

Paul shrugged. "I think he was thinking farm buildings and the like. Shotguns. Though I don't much fancy venturing near any farms for a while."

"Why?"

"Large concentration of animals."

Holly was silent for a while. "Just what the fuck is going on?" It was rhetorical, and Paul did not grace it with another uninformed guess.

They drove in silence, Peer keeping them to below seventy, though the roads were almost completely empty. Once, a big BMW passed them, doing at least one hundred and twenty, youths waving bottles of spirits from the side windows, jeering, giving them the bird.

"Can you believe that?" Holly asked.

"The knife edge," Paul said. "People act differently. At least they weren't waving guns."

"But they'll kill themselves. Where are the police? Where do you think they are, Paul?"

He reached over and placed a big hand on her left knee. It was an unconscious gesture, born of a need for contact and comfort, and Holly did not visibly react. So he kept it there. "That's been worrying me a lot," he said. "A hell of a lot."

After a while: "So, are you going to share your worries with me, mister?" Holly took one hand from the wheel and squeezed Paul's, briefly. Then she lit a cigarette and waited for him to talk.

"Think about it. Something happens to people when they're asleep. Everyone has seen it, this morning. From the numbers of people around, it seems that it happened to everyone who was asleep."

"You survived."

He flexed his shoulders and winced. "I landed in a snow drift. Freak occurrence. It has happened, I'm sure, but how many people fall from great heights and survive?"

Holly did not answer.

"So, all those who were asleep last night are now dead."

"Oh, God." The full implications, the statistics involved, hit Holly. She swerved across the road until Paul's hand squeezed slightly and she brought the car back on course. They could see Peer staring at them in her rearview. Paul raised one hand, thumbs up.

"How many?" she asked.

"I just don't know. If there're sixty-odd million people in Britain, how many of them sleep through the night? Who can tell? There are lots of night jobs, people who wouldn't have been sleeping last night for various reasons. Insomniacs. Night people. But say half? Thirty million?"

Holly shook her head, her face pale, knuckles white where she grasped the wheel. "So where are the other half today? Why aren't the roads full? No, must be a lot more than that. Fifty, I reckon. Fifty million people. Fifty . . ."

"That's only if it's happened everywhere," Paul cut in. "It may be localized. It may just be here, South Wales and the South West."

"But the phone call to London."

"Yeah," he said, "yeah. There is that."

"The emergency services are always there at night. Where are they now?"

Paul shrugged. "I just don't know, Holly. No idea. Maybe they just quit?"

The thought was sobering, chilling. "Peer said she saw fire engines fighting the fire in Newport."

"Good. I hope they still are."

"But the roads are dead." Holly's turn of phrase was more than appropriate.

They drove in silence. Paul tried the radio several times and swept through all the medium wave and FM bands but found mostly static. One station seemed to be broadcasting "God Save the Queen" on a continuous loop, with no broadcaster intrusion. Another, for some strange reason, was playing and replaying "Good-bye T'Jane," by Slade.

"Think the queen's bought it?" he said. "Think Noddy Holder's still alive?" Holly did not reply.

It was almost five o'clock when they approached the junction with the M4 and M5. The Mondeo indicated left long before.

"I thought we were going to London?" Holly said.

Paul looked up. "They're heading left. Midlands or South West, do you think?"

"Let's flash them to stop. I want to know what's going on; it's not fair them making decisions without us." Paul nodded. Holly flashed the Mondeo and slowed down.

Peer seemed keen not to stop. Holly braked, and the Mondeo came to a halt farther ahead on the slip road. It reversed back to them and pulled up on their left. Peer's window was open, and Paul wound his down.

"I thought London?" Holly called across.

Blane stared at Paul intently. "I thought we should go southwest, Somerset and Devon. Maybe Cornwall."

"Why?" Paul was trying to read the signal he was sending.

"Just in case," Blane said. "Don't want any more surprises."

If he could not say what was on his mind, it was because of Peer or Mary. The latter sat in the back of the Mondeo, patting the dog, humming quietly to herself.

"Right," Paul said. "We'll follow you."

Blane nodded. Peer pulled off quickly.

"Hey!" Holly shouted. "What the fuck is this, misogynists incorporated?"

"Holly, he's got a reason," Paul said. "Calm down. It's the woman."

"What? How do you know?"

"He didn't want to say anything because of Mary. Maybe Peer, too. I think he wants to do the least obvious thing in case that weird woman of his has set up any nasty surprises on the way to London."

"She's following him," Holly said.

"Seems that way."

"So why are we as well?" Paul did not answer. Holly continued: "If there's some fucked-up weirdo following him and setting . . . traps . . . why the hell are we still tagging along with him? Wouldn't we stand a better chance on our own?"

Paul stared straight ahead at the receding rear of the Mondeo. It was on the slip road and starting to swing right, and in a few seconds it would be out of sight, crossing the M4 and heading south. He looked across at Holly. "Safety in numbers."

Holly slipped into gear and moved off, saying nothing. For the next thirty seconds, she could have gone either way. Paul sensed her inner struggle in the motion of the car, a stress in the steering that perhaps was a translation of her own doubts. They approached the final point at which she could go straight on—London—or mount the ramp taking them toward the South West.

They took the ramp.

Paul suddenly wondered whether she was right. Would they be safer on their own? Let Blane get on with his own strange stuff, when the world had gone bad enough already? He leaned across, gasping as pain flushed through his body, and kissed Holly on the cheek. She smiled shyly.

"My, on our first date, as well."

"You've already shown me your boobs."

They both laughed. It felt good.

The landscape changed. Not just geographically, as they passed through the huge conurbation of Bristol and its satellite towns, but physically. It felt all wrong.

On distant hillsides trees squatted like waiting armies, twisting without any apparent breeze, limbs scoring the sky. Hedgerows splashed out of line, spreading their wild contagion across newly planted crops and creeping along the plowed furrows of virgin fields. The growth was unnatural, extraordinary, and seemed to expand and eat up space even as the cars passed by.

The sense of things changed as well. The sunlight

began to fade, but faster than usual, swallowed by the land and denied the natural death it was used to. Darkness was smearing the horizon by seven o'clock, and stars spotted the sky even though a vague, resilient blueness still remained. The moon appeared, proud and arrogant in its fullness, already imparting its borrowed light and silvering the landscape. Yet light remained, slumped into valleys and hanging low over the ground like a morning mist. It gave the impression of a freeze-frame snapshot of the landscape, with the residue of a lightning flash just fading into darkness near the ground and nighttime already swallowing the upper atmosphere.

Peer indicated and left the motorway, followed by the Mini. The cars stopped on the hard shoulder just before the exit roundabout. Blane jumped from the Mondeo. His expression was stern, worried.

"I think we should find somewhere to spend the night," he said when he came to the Mini. "We'll eat, talk. Watch out for each other, make sure none of us sleeps."

"It's going to be a long night," Paul said, leaning across and resting his elbow on Holly's shoulder.

Blane nodded. "We'll have to find something to do. Something to keep us all occupied. I reckon we should look for a farmhouse; may find some guns there as well."

"What about the animals?"

Blane did not answer. He shrugged.

"Lead the way."

They drove into the country, took several smaller roads and passed through a seemingly deserted village. Cars remained parked in driveways. Lights still burned in some houses, but silence reigned everywhere. Peer stopped and tooted, Blane shouting that they were here to help, don't be afraid, come out. But no one showed their face, no curtains twitched. It must have been a peaceful village, once. No cause not to sleep at night. Moonlight reflected from cottage windows, giving them the impression of being lit from within by a ghostly radiance. One window hung open, its clasp being scraped back and forth across the sill by the slight breeze that had come with the night. It added to the haunted atmosphere of the village, a creaking door in a spooky mansion.

They moved on and soon left the village behind. They turned from the road onto a lane, which itself slowly grew plants and ruts and degenerated into a mud track. The Mondeo bounced and threw exploratory beams of light forward, but the Mini began scraping its belly along the ridged central part of the road. Holly guided the offside wheel into the center and drove with one side of the car constantly scraping along the rough stone wall abutting the track.

After a while the lane opened up suddenly and, silhouetted against the near-dark sky, a farmhouse marked its end. The cars stopped; they left the lights on, bathing the buildings with their brash luminescence.

Blane and Peer climbed wearily from the Mondeo.

There was a noise from one of the farmyard sheds and a huge shape, black against the darkness, rushed out toward them.

A gunshot barked out. A flash lit the scene.

Blane and Peer fell.

Chapter Twenty-two

Forgotten Ideas and Dead Roots

In the fading light she could see everything.

Fay passed across fields, leaving newly plowed furrows in her wake. She parted hedges, sending twigs and leaves and startled creatures pattering down in a living rain. Once she would have done this without interacting with the landscape, transferring herself from one place to the next with little more than a shrug and a smile. She was a breeze in the hair, the glint from a corner of the eye, a forgotten idea in the morning. She had moved but not flowed, remaining a constant wherever she went. Now, everything had changed. She flowed so quickly that nothing could keep up with her, making her mark and scarring nature as it had scarred her. She told herself she had a choice, to make an impression or not. But inside she knew the truth: that this was the only way for her to move, because she was failing. Slowly, like the world around her, she was changing. Shifting away from what she had been, passing the thing she had become and heading off toward some unknown, distant horizon.

She skirted hills instead of passing over them. A herd of baying cows appeared and she sheared through them, shaking off the mess of blood and viscera as she went. A road stood across her path, the tarmac bubbling and blistering into black pustules as her shadow flitted by.

She was finding it more difficult to remember how they had been, because the emotions necessary to do so were slipping through her grasp. She could recall locations, conversations, but not what they meant. She was at a disadvantage, because years ago she had chosen to eschew the feelings and ideas that had made her who she was. By shunning her former self, she had effectively denied herself full access to her past. She was feeling a little of what Blane was experiencing; but only a little.

She liked to think she did not care, but if that was the case, why had she transmuted into what she was? Why take on a form of vengeance if there was nothing to avenge?

She knew why. She would take him with her. It was not fair that he could forget it all.

She would take him with her.

"Bastards've been like it all day. They was all right this morning, y'know? Milked them, shoved them back into the field. They just stayed there, stood watching me. The dog, Boris, he wouldn't come out of the house. Then he did a runner. Bloody thing. Haven't seen him since.

"You get a feeling, y'know? Been with them all my life, and I know when there's something wrong. Rang the vet; there was no answer. Phoned Peter, who helps me most days, to see why he wasn't here. No answer. Rang the milk board, to see why they hadn't turned up for the morning's takings. No answer. All dead, you say?"

The old farmer sat furiously puffing his pipe, clouds of smoke billowing out and obscuring the already weak kitchen light. His lips worked on the stem like those of a goldfish.

"Lucky I shot that one. She had a calf last year; I sold it for six hundred. Lucky I shot her. Otherwise, you'd be dead as well." He roared laughter, but it was a hollow sound, with no emotion to back it up. "Crushed you senseless, that one would have. I expect she's licking her wounds somewhere, now."

"It's not only your animals, like I explained," Blane said. "We were attacked by birds."

"Birds?"

Blane nodded. "All sorts. They flocked and attacked. Then they just died."

The farmer nodded wisely. "I'll be out to shoot the chickens, then." He stood and picked up his shotgun, but Blane restrained him with a gentle hand on his arm. "Sit down, Gerald. Take it easy. There's no way in for them, and if there's anything to be done it's best to do it in the daylight."

The farmer shrugged and nodded. The others sat around the huge oak table picking at the bread, ham and cheese he had laid out for them. Paul and Mary swigged at the bottles of dubiously cloudy scrumpy he'd hauled from the cool pantry. "Right. I'll be settling down for the night, then. You all make yourselves at home. Nice to have visitors." He stood and walked wearily to the curved staircase in the corner of the room. At first Blane went to stop him, but then he followed him up the stairs, deciding it might be easier to talk to him on his own. Tell him why he couldn't sleep.

"Crazy as a fucking loon," Mary said, none too quietly.

"He saved our skin," Peer hissed.

"Don't you mean saved our bacon?" Mary, pleased with her burst of humor, rolled up a chunk of cheese in a slice of ham and stuffed it into her mouth. Spike sat below the table, snapping crumbs from the air as they fell.

They sat silently for a while, listening to the murmur of voices from upstairs as Blane spoke gently to Gerald. Mary's expression was unreadable. Paul took another swig of rough cider, gritting his teeth.

"Maybe you shouldn't drink much more of that," Holly said, nodding at the green-tinged liquid.

"Why?"

"It might make you fall asleep."

Paul's expression dropped.

Mary laughed out loud, shaking her head and leaning across the table to grab Paul's half-finished bottle.

"I suppose we're under siege," Peer said. She had been quiet up until now, sitting with her legs curled up on a chair by the fire. A plate balanced on her knees, still laden with food. She stared into the flames, trying to piece together all the impossibilities that had manifested themselves over the last eighteen hours.

"Come morning we'll be all right," Paul said.

"The old man's got two more shotguns, he says. If the worst comes to the worst—"

"Understatement," Holly cut in quietly.

Paul continued: "Well, we'll shoot our way out. Shoot the cattle from the upstairs windows, wait until they're all dead or gone. The chickens we'll just have to use knives on, if they trouble us getting to the cars."

"Ever fired a shotgun?" Holly asked. Paul shook his head. "Any idea how many shots it would take to kill an enraged cow?" she continued. Again, his head shook.

"I've killed a cow," Mary said. "Whipped it to death with a chain with spikes on it. At least, watched it done." She munched contentedly on another sandwich, dropping crusts and chunks of ham for Spike. The others glanced at her but ignored her statement.

"I didn't really mean that, anyway," Peer said from by the fire. "I mean everywhere, we're under siege wherever we go. Once we're in the cars, that's it. Everywhere else is out of bounds."

"I really did," Mary said.

"It just can't be all that bad," Paul cried, despairing. "The birds must have been a freak. Something from the river, maybe. Chemicals."

Peer gazed into the fire, silence her telling answer.

"I think we're all going to die," Mary said, staring at Peer's back as she spoke.

"Just shut up, will you?" Holly burst out. "You're too fucking spooky for your own good. What's happened to you today, huh? You don't seem so cut up about your dead folk now."

Mary merely shrugged, smiling slightly, chewing on a sandwich.

Paul squeezed Holly's leg under the table, told her by touch not to pursue it. Waste of time. Waste of effort.

"Everything's changed," Peer said, apparently ignoring the exchange from behind her. "Can't you feel it? Can't you sense the difference in the air? On the drive here today, from the services, the fields had altered. The trees looked menacing, instead of pretty. The hedges . . . it looked as though they'd spread, been out of control for a couple of years. Insects were bounding off our windshield like it was mid-summer, not spring. And most of them didn't splat. Didn't you see?" She unfurled her legs and reached forward, grabbing the poker. As she continued, she moved the end of the poker within the flames, shifting burning logs to see the glowing caves beneath, imagining being in there, melting. "Nature's taken another step," she said. "No particular direction. Just another step."

Mary had stopped smiling now and was paying attention. Spike nuzzled at her hand, but she slapped him on the snout. He wandered away to a cool corner of the room and curled into a ball.

Peer sat back abruptly as a shower of sparks spat from the fire. "Nature's changed, moved on or back, and humankind's too wrapped up in its own world to notice. So, we've just got left behind." She turned to look at the others and saw that she was the subject of their rapt attention. She grimaced, a little embarrassed. Paul and Holly sat close together, eyes wide, her fears mirrored in their eyes as they considered what she'd said. Mary stared at her as if she was looking at someone else, seeing a different face.

"I'm feeling more and more that we're invaders," Peer said. "Ever since I've come out of Newport, things have felt more and more askew. They've even looked different, I think, but it's hard to say how. It's like I'm seeing things for the first time in years; I've seen it all before, but now it's viewed from an aspect I can't explain. Or . . . if you've seen a place in magazines, photos, or on TV? Then you go there? It feels like that. I recognize everything, but everything is so changed. Some of it's obvious, like the birds and animals attacking. Horrible. But everything now seems so unwelcoming, like we're invaders seeing things we shouldn't see. I've felt strange for a while, now . . . like I'm one step removed. Maybe now I know why." Peer ran a hand through her hair, flinging it across her shoulder. She rubbed absently at the dozen scratches and cuts on her face from the bird attack. The fire crackled in agreement with everything she was saying. "Those birds today . . ." She did not finish, but it seemed a complete statement anyway, an expression of disbelief beyond words.

"She said you'd be like this," Mary said.

"Who said what?" Paul asked.

Mary shrugged. "Spike. Ham." The dog sauntered across, tail low, expecting another slap.

"Who said what?" Paul repeated.

"Leave it," Holly said. "She's just trying to cause trouble. As though we weren't in enough shit, we pick up someone out to cause more."

"I'm not causing shit," Mary said, but everyone ignored her. So she continued: "Yet."

Stairs creaked as Blane came down. "Gerald's upstairs. Sitting in a chair in the bedroom, looking out for anything approaching the house."

"Anything?" Holly asked.

"Animals. Cows. I told him what we saw today with those cars. There's always the chance they might try to break down the doors."

"So what do we do now?" Paul asked.

Blane shrugged. "Well, we need to eat, rest. But stay awake. We should be together, or in pairs. I've already told Gerald that I'll sit with him, though I've never fired a gun. We can chat; he obviously knows the district, so we can talk about where we go tomorrow, where we can pick up a few essentials."

"Like?" Paul.

"Guns. Ammunition. Camping stuff. Food. All the usuals." Blane tried to smile, but it did not work.

"Peer and me will stay down here," Mary said. "Won't we, Peer?" Peer glanced across from the fire and nodded, looking quickly back at the flames as if hypnotized.

Holly went to say something, but Paul nudged her again. He helped her up and they went upstairs without saying anything. There was an embarrassed silence in the kitchen until Mary giggled.

"Go fucky-fucky," she said quietly. Nobody answered her.

"Don't fall asleep, anyone," Blane said.

"Don't worry," Mary said, "we'll have a good old chat, won't we, Peer? I'm interested in what you said, about moving on and us being left behind. I've felt like that before. I don't feel like it now. Maybe you can tell me why."

Blane dumped some food on a plate and followed Holly and Paul upstairs. As he reached the landing a door down the corridor snicked gently shut. He handed the plate in to Gerald, then went back out and walked heavily along the corridor. No time for embarrassment, or coyness.

He tapped on the door. "No sleeping," he said.

"No. We'll stay awake," Paul's muffled voice said. There was no irony there.

"I'll give you a knock in a couple of hours, check up on things."

"Right."

Gerald was still smoking his pipe. He had turned the bedroom light off so he could see out into the yard, and the smoke gave the air a solid feel. Blane pulled up a chair and sat beside him, taking a lump of cheese from the plate.

"You live here alone?" Blane asked.

Gerald grunted and nodded.

Blane could just make him out in the moonlight. "You weren't asleep last night?"

The farmer shook his head.

"Me neither."

They sat silently, looking out into the yard at where shadows constantly seemed about to detach themselves from leaning walls and open doors.

Holly sat on the bed. It was an old four-poster; musty, damp and unused. The room had curtains, but they were tattered and torn by a decade of sun and moths. Framed photographs were molded to

the dressing table by dust, colors faded and edges
yellowed like vague memories. Prints hung from
the picture rail, bland colors blending in perfectly
with the dusty room. All in all it had the air of a
shrine, left as it was since the day someone had
died or vanished years before. Holly suddenly had
a partial understanding of what Peer meant about
feeling like an invader.

"What is it with Mary?" Holly asked, exasperated. "It's as though she's enjoying all this. And that
spooky fucking dog . . . what dog do you know that
doesn't plop down in front of a real fire whenever
it gets the chance?"

"I think it's a bit of an adventure for her," Paul
said. "Tell the truth, I think she's a bit lacking upstairs."

"She seems pretty sharp to me. That's what
makes it all the more upsetting."

Paul glanced around the room, recognizing the
opportunity to go and comfort Holly but letting the
moment pass. "I wouldn't worry. I'm pretty sure
she's harmless; just a little lost."

"Harmless?"

Paul sat next to Holly. "She's a kid. Insecure, misplaced. See how she's attached herself to Peer? In a
strange way, I grant you, but she recognizes the
strength Peer has and she's been attracted to it."

"And you're no judge of character?" Holly smiled
sadly, then sighed. "I can't believe what's happened. Do you think we'll find help tomorrow?"

No, thought Paul, but he nodded silently.

"I don't." Holly leaned against Paul, resting her
head on his shoulder.

He winced as pain flared from his bruises but

managed not to cry out. He liked what was happening; he did not want to discourage it. Although he preferred time alone with nature—following Jenna's death, close contact felt too much like betrayal—sitting like this comforted him more than he would have thought possible. The pain was still there, both physical and mental, biting in him every time he moved or breathed. But when Holly rested her head on his shoulder, a gesture of pure trust, the shaking ceased. It was as if they were fear sinks for each other. He knew that tomorrow would bring the terror back again, new and refreshed by the night. And if Peer was right, it would be richer and more varied than today. But for now they had to get through the next few hours without sleeping. They needed time to regroup their senses before the next onslaught. What better way to do it than with company?

He stared through the window at the moonlit landscape. Trees stood silhouetted like soldiers marching up the ridgeline of a distant mountain, angled branches as weapons. No sign of life marred the stillness of the view, other than the occasional mysterious flitting of a bat or a bird caught on the wing by the dark. He knew that the building they were in was subject to a constant bombardment from bats' sonar, too high-pitched to hear. The image, for once, was not a pleasing one. It was a secret of nature, an inaudible language that could be saying anything, plotting a move against the besieged humans.

Paul wondered how many other secrets remained undiscovered; codes beyond human sight or hearing or understanding, constantly passed through nature by those in the know. The thought made him feel very small and unprotected, however many shotguns the old farmer professed to having. There was a whole language out there, spoken by dogs with an extraordinary sense of smell, bats seeing by sound, birds communicating through whistles and chirrups. Whales too, singing through the sea to cousins a hundred or a thousand miles distant. How much secret plotting, stories, mocking of the weakness of mankind could go on without him knowing? Even now, a million creatures could be surrounding the house, preparing an attack by smell alone, plotting the downfall of the few measly humans inside with a glib sniff.

Paul had a healthy respect for the natural world. He thought he knew the reality of things, the fact that life and death were merely incidental events to the living planet, certainties requiring neither moral contemplation nor regret.

But until today, he had never feared nature.

"What are you thinking?" Holly asked, without moving her head from his shoulder.

"I'm wondering how we're going to stay awake all night," Paul lied, then realized he had a point.

Holly was silent for a long time. The only sound in the musty stillness of the room was their breathing. "Want to check my wounds?" she said at last, not looking up.

Paul smiled. He could feel the dampness of tears through his shirt. "I don't know if this old bed could take it." For a moment, he was terrified that he had misread everything, and he closed his eyes in readiness for the embarrassment.

Holly was silent for a moment. She curved her

arms around him and buried her face in his neck, breathing in his smell, breath shuddering past her tears. "There's always the floor," she said.

Gerald did not wish to talk, which suited Blane fine. Though he knew he should be planning for the next day, Blane wanted time on his own. To think. To try to discover where his fears were coming from, and whether there were any more hidden away preparing to spring out on him unexpectedly.

His memories consisted purely of his time with nature, though he had always been aware that there was something more, something forgotten. Since things had gone bad, a new suspicion had been worming its way into his thoughts: that these memories were not neglected, but hidden.

There was a Voice. It earned a capital in his mind because it was not his present voice, not really. It spoke in his tongue, it bore his intellect, but it communicated from outside his perceived history. It was like a recording he had made decades ago, reminding himself what it had been like. It was the Voice of someone else. The Voice of his forgotten self.

It was vague. It had manifested that morning, along with the memory of the musical laughter he could not place. She can't laugh like that any more, the Voice had said. No music left inside now. No sweet tunes, just slow death marches, where voice has no power and song has no strength.

She is not immutable, though she once was. She's a root gone bad. She's an idea that has changed itself, when in truth it should not, could not have done so.

Tim Lebbon

Blane gazed out into the moonlight. What dark secrets did it hold?

It's the ruin. The end of things. The woman had looked so familiar, but still a stranger. He had known her differently, of that he was sure. She had told him so little, but also so much, and it was obvious that she knew him. The chains from her temples down into her throat held a secret, she said, and Blane had known at once that it was something he could never bear to understand, not as he was now. This reaction in itself should be a clue as to who she was: Why dread knowledge if it comes from an unknown source? The only facts worth worrying about are those half-known truths that could lead to something more terrible.

Find her, the Voice said. Blane glanced around, so struck by the sound that he was certain there was someone in the room with him. He looked for shadows, for hints, even for her. But there was only Gerald, puffing on his pipe, staring through the window with moonlight swimming in his rheumy old eyes.

Find her, track her down. She's doing the same to you. Go on the offensive. The nearer you get, the more you'll remember. By the time you reach her, maybe you'll know. Forewarned is forearmed.

Know what? Armed against what? He needed to understand now. The Voice was his own, but if that was the case, then was he hiding the truth from himself?

Know the truth of things. Know the feel of sand between your toes as the sun glides down into a purple sea. Know the smell of a fresh autumn morning, while birds gather on high wires in readiness for migration. Know the satisfaction of seeing them arrive at their journey's end, flocking in from the sea or fluttering down to re-energize their depleted bodies. The sound of an elephant mourning the death of its mate; the taste of fear as a gazelle tries to outrun a trio of lionesses; the reptilian coolness of a crocodile's mind. You'll know all this, Blane. You've never really forgotten, but you'll know again. You have to. It's essential. You were a great idea, Blane. You can be again. You so nearly had it right; don't let your fall distort the truth of things. If it does . . .

I wish I had some great ideas now, Blane thought in his own, familiar voice.

Track her down, the Voice said. It won't be difficult. She's following anyway, so it's just a case of making contact. She's got a secret to show you, but by the time she does, you should have an inkling anyway. You'll have the upper hand. And you may need it.

Who is she?

You know that. I know that. But it's . . . buried. It's something that should become clear as you approach her. Try to remember. Try to recall. Remember her laugh, her face, her voice, her body. I can't tell you yet, but the memory is there, waiting to surface, waiting for you to grab it from the depths. Don't let her mock you with it. Find it out yourself. Then you'll have the upper hand.

"The upper hand," Blane murmured. Gerald did not react, obviously lost in his own thoughts.

Go soon. Go now. Preempt her. Find her and confront her. Don't let her torture you like this.

Is this all her doing? All this death, all this change?

But the Voice was silent. He could still sense it there, ready to throw more hidden memory back at him.

That terrified him more than anything else. What was so bad that he could not bear to tell himself?

"At least you're keeping me awake," Gerald said, shifting to find a comfortable spot again.

"What?"

"With your mumblings."

Blane apologized and closed his eyes. The woman had frightened him, but there had also been a sense of belonging, more than he felt with Paul and the others, almost as strong a feeling as when he was alone in the woods. The Voice—his memory, he was sure, returning to help him recall all those hidden truths he had been seeking over the years—had told him to go and find her. His instinct did likewise. Why lie to himself? Why deny himself? For although he believed that she had a part in what had happened to them today—Henry, dead in his trailer; the bird attack; the cars and passengers destroyed by wildlife—he was also certain that she would not harm him.

Or could not.

"Gerald, I have to go."

The farmer jerked a thumb over his shoulder. "Out the door, first on the left."

Blane shook his head. "No, leave. Go. There's someone I have to find."

"Oh! Wife, is it?"

"No. Not wife. Gerald, I feel involved in all this. Not responsible, but a bigger part of it than the rest of you. And because of that, I have to find out why. It's complicated. Believe me, you'll be safer with me gone. I seem to attract death."

Gerald looked at Blane and nodded slowly. "I'm not one to argue with another's wishes, never have been. And you seem set on this. Well, you'll be needing food, then. And a gun. And I've a Land Rover, if it takes your fancy?"

"I can't drive. But food, yes, and a gun . . . I suppose I should. I've never fired one, though."

"Point it," Gerald said, demonstrating with the shotgun in his hands. "Pull the trigger."

Blane stood, patted Gerald on the shoulder. "I have to tell the others. I'll leave in half an hour, but I have to talk to the others first. Tell them a few things. But only those upstairs. Get my drift?"

"Don't want the pretty girls downstairs to know, huh?"

"Pretty much."

Gerald nodded again, paused. "That one's strange, the one with the dog. Full of hidden stuff. Right, I'll go down and chat to the ladies. Come down when you're ready; I'll get some food packed for you."

Blane smiled his thanks and stepped out onto the dark landing. He stood silently for a few moments, listening carefully for any sounds from Paul and Holly's room. He did not want to barge in on anything embarrassing, but at the same time his need to leave was urging him onward. He felt the Voice holding its breath, ready to shout at him if he delayed any longer. And perhaps if he started out now, the Voice would start breathing the truth once more.

There was only silence behind the door. He knocked, waited for the reply and entered.

Mary had taken a seat opposite Peer at the fireplace. Spike lay by her side, slowly cooking himself in front of the voracious flames. They did not speak. Peer seemed fascinated by the fire; Mary was equally interested in Peer.

So this was the woman Fay was so afraid of? Why?

Peer was attractive, true, compared to Fay's more earthy look. But at the last, just before she had left Mary alone to her task, Fay had gloried in her own luminosity, glaring brightly in her voluptuousness. She had been beautiful, her radiance reflected in the pools of blood spreading out from Rupert's tattered throat.

Peer could not match that; not here, not now, surely not ever. Her face was rich in character but flawed as well, sporting a nose too long, a mouth too wide. And her eyes were empty vessels compared to Fay's blood-rich gaze, her frown a clown's concern against Fay's godlike countenance.

There was more than looks, Mary knew. Much more. There was spirit, humor, energy, ambition. All of which Fay had in abundance; none of which Peer possessed, this sad, depleted creature staring into the flames as if they would transport her back to a place and time before this nightmare began.

So this was the person Fay had asked her to kill? When the time was right, when the sign arrived? Mary smiled. It would be easy.

Watch her. Mark her. Wait for the right time.

Well, she was watching her now. She had marked

her, though there really was little to see. Peer claimed an attraction to nature, yet still she was covered with cuts and bruises just like the rest of them. No love lost there, surely, even if she was right. Now, all Mary waited for was the right time.

She had lost her chain in the bird attack, but she still had Spike, and she still had the fire. If the signal came now, she would have the bitch's head pressed into the flames and hot coals before anyone could pull her off. She would have the pleasure of seeing the bitch's hair burn and her eyes pop and melt before they could haul her away. By then it would be too late. She would have done Fay's bidding. For once in her life, she would be a success.

But there was no signal. Not yet.

Footsteps. The old farmer came downstairs, groaning as his knee joints grumbled at the descent. "Cup of tea?" he asked.

Mary nodded. Shrugged. "Make it coffee," she said. She was feeling tired.

They had tried. It was not the best of places for such an encounter, and surely not the best of times. Their failure, if anything, drew them closer together, made them realize what a change had been wrought over the world in a matter of hours. Fear and trepidation conspired to dry their lust. Though their hearts told them they wanted to make love, the reality of events soon persuaded them otherwise.

A passion had developed from the dark, surprising both with its intensity. Paul whispered that they might be the first to make love since the world had moved on, and Holly breathed heavily into his neck as she unzipped his trousers and held him tight. It felt right, it felt naïve and innocent, as though they were two teenagers experimenting instead of two adults. Paul thought of Jenna but experienced no guilt. Holly thought of her dead boyfriend Tommy, but he was from another time.

Paul pushed her down and undressed her, kissing her between the legs and biting her thighs, always gentle, both of them wincing as their new wounds were knocked or scraped. She pulled him up and held him, but he went soft in her hand.

She had tried for a while, with her hand and her mouth, but in the end they simply dressed and sat at the foot of the bed, arms around each other, enjoying the shared warmth. Neither of them mentioned the failure, and as the minutes rolled by time seemed to mark it more as a success. There had been no shyness, as is often present in a first sexual encounter. Their bodies had seemed familiar to one another, designed to fit, molded together from afar. Destined always to meet. The fact that they could not finish what they had begun seemed coincidental, as unimportant as the memory of a bad meal. Good meals would always follow.

And it was this mutual acceptance of failure, without embarrassment, without any of the usual intense angst involved in human couplings, successful or otherwise, that drew them together until they felt unable to ever part again. It was a comfortable feeling, one that should exist between two old lovers rather than people who had known each other for a day. They were both aware of why it was there—desperate times provoked extraordinary responses—but this was unimportant. For the first time that day, they both felt safe.

Paul spoke of Jenna, his dead wife, and how she had drowned back in the Dominican Republic. Car accident. Flipped onto its lid in a river. Stupid. Holly told him about Tommy, their young love, his anger and fury at the fact of her sterility, the crash that had killed him years ago. They swapped tales and their tears merged.

Then they fell silent, but they moved constantly. Fingers stroking, arms squeezing, knees nudging, in a constant concern that the other might have nodded off. Sleep loomed over them like a huge, blackened demon, once an angel but now scorched by the fire of death and the threat of unknown fates. Fear of what they would find, should they close their eyes and cross that ambiguous barrier between waking and sleeping, ensured that their eyes stayed wide open. Sitting next to each other, knowing for certain that any lapse in concentration or descent toward sleep would be instantly noticed, made it easier.

Paul had never been afraid of death. He supposed that he was like many people who claimed this, in that it was the manner of his death that terrified him, not the assurance of death itself. Now, sitting in a badly lit room next to a stranger who he had just failed in making love with, he was as scared as he had ever been. Not of death, as such. But of sleep.

He did not want to fall.

Fear seemed a theme for the day. Paul felt bereaved as much as anyone who had lost a relative, because the nature he so adored had vanished. In its place was a bastardization of what he had loved, a cruel sham, exposing only the grim side of the world, displaying nothing of the wonderful balance that nature used to support. Now there was only death and violence. It upset him more because he knew it would not last. Nothing could live like this. Whatever had gone wrong would be the end of things, unless circumstances changed very quickly. Nature had not only turned sour, it had also gone into decline. Humanity seemed to be the first victim of the catastrophe, perhaps because it was so removed from nature anyway and could not hope to cope with such an aggressive change. But Paul would not mind betting that soon, perhaps within days, they would begin to see the change exerting a detrimental influence on other species. Perhaps trees would start to wither and die, or birds . . .

Like today. The birds had fallen from the air on cue. Dying instantly without having to sleep and dream of a momentous impact to kill them.

Paul groaned.

"What?" Holly glanced at him.

"Nothing. There's nothing. No hope."

"Paul . . ."

Then there were footsteps, a knock on the door, and Blane entered.

"Glad I didn't disturb anything," he said. Holly smiled; Paul shrugged. Blane strode in and closed the door behind him, turning out the light and going straight to the window.

"I feel responsible," he began, staring outside. His breath misted the window and faded again instantly.

"We're here to help each other," Holly said. "Nobody said you have to make decisions if—"

"I didn't mean that. I meant this." Blane nodded at the window, at the landscape splayed in silvery light and impenetrable shadow. "I feel I had something to do with it. I feel that it's following me. Everywhere I go, people are dying. Things are dying."

Paul nodded.

Holly, exasperated: "But the animals. They're doing this anyway; it's nothing to do with you."

"The two carloads of people were massacred just before we got there," he said. "Message for me. The boy in the graveyard: message. And Henry the farmer had his throat ripped out. For me. By her."

"Who the hell is she, Blane!" Paul almost shouted, but it was fear- rather than anger-driven.

"I don't know," the sad man said, "but I feel I should. My memories are crying out for me to understand what's going on. I don't know what good it would do if I did, but that's no reason not to find out. Knowledge begets knowledge. I tell myself that I can find out, so I must try to do so."

"How?" Holly still held Paul's hand, clasping it harder now, as if she was watching someone walking to their death and felt powerless to prevent it.

"Well," Blane said, "that's why I'm here. I'm going to go out and find her. I think she's more aware of what's happening than I am. That she's even causing some of it."

"That's ridiculous," Paul said. "You're getting into the realms of fantasy stuff here, Blane. You need . . ." He smiled grimly.

"Sleep?"

"Blane, nobody on their own can cause what's

happening here. Not unless they're some mad professor with flyaway hair and a hunched associate who's created the ultimate death beam or doomsday bug. And I don't believe that for a second."

"Explain, then," Blane challenged. "Tell me what's wrong. Tell me why there are millions of dead people rotting around us, and the animals are eating the survivors."

"I don't know."

"There."

"All right, but listen. I can tell you a story that sounds far more plausible than some madwoman running around the country setting birds and sleep demons onto you for some vague reasons you don't even know. Try this, and this is off the top of my head! Right: sunspots, storms on the surface of the sun. Send out electromagnetic waves that mess around with the human mind. I don't know, cause mass embolisms that bleed into the dream center of the brain and trigger delusions. When those people sleep, they all have a similar dream, caused by disorientation, fucked-up balance glands, whatever. When they hit the ground, their brain is so certain its for real that it mimics the wounds the body should receive. In effect, the person's imagination kills them."

"Paul—"

"Holly, hang on. I'm on a roll. Let me finish, then we'll hear what Blane thinks is happening. So, okay, you've got fifty million dead people hanging around, and the survivors—the ones who weren't asleep and who therefore haven't yet used that damaged portion of their brain assigned to dreaming—they've still got these embolisms, waiting to kill them as soon as they nod off. Their own bodies are ready to kill them. Just shut eyes, sleep tight, kapow!" He slapped his hand on his thigh and winced in pain. "I'm a case in point," he said. "My own mind tried to kill me. Luckily, there was a snowdrift handy."

"The birds?" Blane said. "The animals?"

Paul shrugged. "Same cause. Different reaction. They wake up to a world with ninety percent fewer people, their brains fried by the sun explosion. Go on the rampage. Then drop dead."

"You're grasping," Blane said.

Paul held up his hands. "Hey, this is just a thought. But it works, don't you think? It could even explain the phone lines going down, and why the TVs don't seem to work anymore. Electromagnetic pulse. Wiped out all the circuit boards and electrical gizmos." He shook his head. "Bullshit, I know, but Blane, listen to yourself. You see some fucked-up woman in a field who hints that she knows you—"

"She knew my name—"

"Yeah, she probably heard me calling you from the car. You're getting paranoid. I can hardly blame you, but hell, it's just plain daft. And as for feeling responsible for any of this . . ." He waved his hand in the general direction of the window.

"I think," said Holly slowly, "that what Paul is trying to say, in roundabout terms, is that he doesn't want you to go."

Paul nodded. "Safety in numbers, Blane."

Blane sat on the windowsill, looked down at his scuffed shoes. "I want to believe you," he said.

"Good."

"But I don't. I know I'm right. I can feel it. I have to find this woman, Paul, and you're going to have to let me go."

Paul did not answer. He knew now that he could not talk Blane away from this course, and for a moment he had the idea that he should keep him here by force. But what good would that do? He recalled what Blane had said earlier, about slipping from the edge and having to be prepared to fight, to kill, for what was left. He would never go down that route.

Never.

"Humor me, then," Paul said. "Arrange to meet us somewhere in a day or two. It'll make me happier. And, if anything, it'll give us both a target. Something to aim for if . . . well, if it's all as bad as it seems."

Blane nodded. "I can't promise anything."

Paul shrugged. "Don't want a promise. Just a commitment. Let me know you're still with us, even if you are off on some fool errand."

"Where, then?"

"I don't know this part of the country? Holly?"

"Not me."

"Gerald does," Blane said. "We'll arrange it with him when I go."

"Which is when?"

"Now."

Chapter Twenty-three

The Ruin

Fay sat in a field a mile across the valley from the farm. It was still dark, but she could see clearly by moonlight.

Spread around her, like frozen ripples in a sickly pond, were concentric circles of dead and dying grass. At the edges of the field it clung on tenaciously to life, and the hedges were as lush and explosive as ever. But in the field, brown and diseased plants withered quickly into the soil. They spread their poison, giving the ground an acidity that shriveled worms and suffocated the most hardy of bugs. Scattered around the field lay several dead foxes, their auburn pelts stiff and dull in the silver light, legs pointing skyward in one final sprint. A badger snuffled among them. Fay glanced its way, saw that it had a horn growing from between its eyes, decided to let it be.

281

No need to destroy art.

She had been there for several hours. In that time she had not moved, since each action brought an opposite reaction of pain and discomfort. Her skin was sallow and rough and hung from her bones like a drying hide draped across a frame. Her body, hidden within loose clothing, sprouted growths and lesions that wept and stank. Her new teeth had begun to fall out, leaving nothing but hollows full of pain in their place. Pressure pulsed behind her eyeballs, like madness seeking escape.

She knew what was happening, had been expecting it ever since the ruin kick-started the day before. But not this quickly, surely? Not so fast that she would have no time to tell Blane what he really was, show him the proof and cut the bitch with him down to size? She was determined to progress, to transcend the physical disablements that threatened to ground her, and to attain her true aims. It was all she had left.

She cursed the land, as she had for a decade. But now her curse held power. She spat, and a slug caught in her spittle shriveled and turned black. When she exhaled, poison condensed in the air and drifted away to lay its fiery web across a tree, or a bird, or a nest of insects. She preferred it like this, when darkness hid much of the landscape from view. This way, there was only so much she had to see; like the badger, malformed and changing already.

It had not always been like this. Once, she had laughed with Blane and been accompanied in her song by the birds in the hedges and trees. Nature had caressed her with its gentle touch, in turn letting her provide a solid counterpoint for the flowing of life through the world. She had laid herself truly open to its influences, reveling in the trust that existed there and wallowing in the two-way relationship keeping her whole. Time had swept by them, touching them only lightly, turning them around and swirling about them in its everfluctuating journey. They had been together, then, inextricably bound by the love of what had made them, certain never to wane. . . .

Until the bad days when it had all ended, when nature was no longer fair but vindictive.

Fay had a cause for celebration. Revenge was not a word she was used to—she was not a sadist—but now it sounded good, tasted right. Things had to be righteous and reasonable, and certain shadows of chance just could not be allowed to become reality.

Moves were being taken, even now.

Fay's eyes, though hidden beneath eyelids drooping like melted wax, were bright and hungry. Full of a terrible intelligence, and a complete knowledge of what she wanted now that the ruin was in full swing.

She was patient. Time might not heal, but it would tell.

The farmhouse door opened. Two figures came out, guns pointing warily ahead of them. Blane followed, a shotgun resting across his arms, glancing around. Even from this distance, Fay could see that he was changed. His shoulders slumped, his head hung low. Perhaps he knew already, and he was leaving to do the decent thing?

If that was the case, he had to be stopped.

Fay stood and felt the thing in her stomach shift position, scraping away more of her stomach lining with cruel, sharp edges. She started across the field, passing through hedges and fences as if they barely existed. Within a few seconds she was hiding behind the hedge adjacent to the farm buildings, and she could see the three men at the door. The old farmer, the tall one and Blane himself. She could see now that his shoulders were only slumped because of the rucksack he carried, and if anything his eyes burned with a purpose they had been lacking for many, many years. He seemed uncomfortable carrying the shotgun, and Fay would be most interested to see him faced with shooting something of nature. Paradoxes had always fascinated her, even before the ruin began. This would be one of the greatest.

The three men remained on the doorstep, not talking, trying to pierce the dark with their weak eyes. Fay felt like rattling a bush or darting across the yard, too quickly for them to focus on but slow enough to trail a fleeting shadow behind her. But she was tired, her bones ached. And besides, she did not relish the possibility, however remote, of being peppered with buckshot. She was in enough discomfort.

She waited for Blane to leave. The two men walked across the yard with him to where the farm lane began, then exchanged a few hurried words and watched him move away. They went back to the farmhouse, dragging an air of dejection with them. Fay giggled—it came out as a hiss, involuntary and unrestrained—and both men looked across at where she hid. One of them, the farmer, raised his shotgun to hip height. The tall man touched him on the shoulder and indicated the house with a nod of his head, and they reached the front door without further incident.

As soon as the door closed behind them, Fay set off after Blane. She kept her distance at first, gliding back over the fields until she was watching him from the heights of the surrounding hillsides. Then curiosity and a warped sense of affection overcame her. She slipped down the slope as dawn splashed redly across the eastern sky. Clouds caught the sunlight and bent it, filtered it, refined it before it struck the changing earth. Birds flitted across the brightening sky, not as many as usual, some of them hissing or sweeping in unfamiliar flight patterns. Insects emerged from hedgerows and grasses and trees, buzzing the air, finding many more dead things than usual to show an interest in today.

Soon, Fay had fallen into step half a mile behind Blane. She could smell him; there was fear there, and also a sense of determination.

He was looking for her.

She laughed. High in the branches of an elm tree, a crow tumbled dead from its perch.

The little dead girl is running. Her feet pound clouds of dust from the dry earth, kicking up the remains of crops and the twisted, desiccated bodies of dead birds. Feathers flutter down behind her, marking her path across the landscape. Sometimes, things squeal beneath her feet. They are either not quite dead or impossibly alive, but she does not look down to see.

Her arms ache, her legs beg to crumple her to the

ground, but there is no breath. Try as she might, she cannot draw the stagnant air into her lonely lungs. She is dead, so it does not matter, but it still frustrates and terrifies her. Her hair is long and lustrous, and she flicks it back over her shoulder as she runs. Doesn't hair keep growing after death? How long had she been dead? How long had her hair been when she died?

Ahead, bright in the blazing sunlight, there is a door. It stands in the field, stripped of paint by exposure to the weather and surrounded by a frame looking set to rot. Its base is set in the surface of the soil. There is nothing around it, no wall, no surround other than the frame. She pauses before it, knowing it is pure temptation but unable to resist anyway. She glances around at the other side and sees the same thing: a door; rusty handle; timber raw and dried from ages in the sun.

She glances around, conscious of the silence and hating it. In the distance, set against the light brown of the dead hillside, a white farmhouse points wrecked walls at the sky. Its roof timbers stand out against the background like the ribs of a dead giant, the windows gaping wounds in its sides, giving a view into nothing. Scattered around the farm are vague humps in the landscape, the bodies of cattle disintegrating back into the earth and poisoning it forever.

The dead girl reaches out for the handle. It is stiff with rust and time. She strains, but it does not move. Perhaps, she thinks, it will not open for dead things. Why should it? Whatever is beyond is obviously worth protecting from the terrible blight that reigns here now, so why should it open for her, just another dead thing? Still she twists and works at the handle, scraping her hand against the rusted metal.

This side of the door the dead little girl must remain dead. On the other side, who knows what may happen? Could life return to static bones? Can flesh be reformed, flooded with fresh memory and made to breath and pulse and revel in life once more?

There is something behind her. It breaks the silence of the landscape, a noise approaching from miles away. A whisper at first, then a buzz, and then a roar of clanking metal like a continuously crashing train. A shadow disassociates itself from the darkness farther along the valley. It is huge, a rolling monolith of metal, a million chains intermingled and twisted together like a child's elastic band ball. Loose Medusa chains whip at the air as it rolls, snatching sunlight from the sky, swallowing it into darkness. They are sharp, filed to make a point, and rusty-red with the remains of victims.

She is dead already. But she knows that this monstrosity will kill her.

She heaves at the door, raising a foot and kicking at it, hauling at the handle in case she's wrong, in case it opens into this terrible land instead of out of it. The rumble of the approaching thing is increasing, the ground begins to shake and the dead girl realizes that it is far, far bigger than she had thought at first.

Then she has an idea. The door is locked, so it must have a keyhole. She bends down and looks. The hole is a bright light in the body of the door.

Sunlight bathes a burgeoning hillside, encouraging buds to sprout and baby birds to take flight. Rabbits explore the long grasses at the edge of the woodland, and a huge stag deer peers between the trees with wide, intelligent eyes. A stream tumbles out from under an ancient folly on the hilltop, watering a hundred species of plants and flowers along its banks. A woman stands on the hillside, hands on her hips in a casual show of nonchalance. She is tall, naked, attractive. Nature does not pass around her; it flows through her.

Something plucks the girl from where she squats in front of the door, and she realizes that the monster is upon her. A slinging chain has grabbed her, burying its claws into her dead flesh, and is sucking her back and up. As the huge ball rolls over the free-standing door, driving it into the ground and crushing it beyond salvation, the dead girl is flung high into the sky.

She spins upward, and there is a brief instant of weightlessness—and realization—as she reaches the zenith of her flight. Then she drops, plunging down toward the ground, which is no longer ground.

The ball has flattened and spread. A thousand tons of chains and hooks point skyward, ready to pierce and rip her. She cries out and the sound, a real sound, is so much louder than anything in this dead land.

Wake up, the voice says, but she is already waking. She stays for another second, watching. The chains are melting into the ground. Grass is growing through their links, choking them. In a way, she realizes, the door has already opened.

Peer opened her eyes. The room was still in semi-darkness, but the pinkish light of a cloudy dawn smeared the window. The fire had burned down to a faint glow.

Mary sat in the chair facing her, a faintly bemused expression on her face.

"You left me to sleep," Peer said.

Mary sat bolt upright. "Were you asleep? I didn't notice."

Peer shook her head. "I wasn't asleep. But I could have been. I thought we were supposed to be looking out for each other."

"So would you have seen me nod off with your eyes closed, huh?" Mary shouted.

"What's up?" Paul said. He and Holly were sitting at the big kitchen table, chatting quietly. Gerald glanced around from where he was preparing a fried breakfast for them all but looked back quickly to what he was doing.

"Nothing," Mary called in a singsong voice, smiling sweetly.

Peer shivered. It was not cold, but the memory of the dream drew a cool finger down her back. She'd been sleeping. After everything that had happened, she'd allowed herself to fall asleep.

Or perhaps not.

She remembered coming back to the fire after Blane had left, sitting down and gazing at the burning logs. She felt hollowed out by his leaving, as if life and hope had fled with him. Paul had smiled at her and tried to calm her, telling her that they'd be meeting up with Blane in thirty-six hours. But for Peer, he did not carry the same authority as Blane. He looked fitter, spoke as confidently, if not more so, but there was something about Blane that reached deep down inside Peer, and held her up.

She had never met anyone quite like him. So strange and distant, yet so familiar as well. She did not know him, yet there was a familiarity between them, not in the way they spoke or acted but somewhere deeper. It was as if he had the soul of the person she so wanted to be. That brave, intense, meaningful individual who had somehow eluded Peer all her adult life. She had tried, of course, but a succession of bland jobs and duller relationships had soured her to ever becoming the person she aspired to.

And she was sure Blane felt it as well.

Maybe that was why Mary seemed to dislike her; though, in truth, the dog was the only thing she *did* seem to hold in any regard. Mary spent minutes at a time staring at Blane, her expression unreadable, balanced somewhere between mockery and longing. Silently asking, perhaps, for the same invisible, indivisible link that existed between him and Peer to also spring magically into existence between the two of them. Peer was sure that this could never happen, as certain as she was of the existence of her own link with him. But this conviction scared her more than comforted her; it made Mary not only unpleasant and objectionable, but dangerous as well. What lengths would a person like this go to in normal times?

What lengths now?

"It's getting light," Paul said. "We'll be moving out soon, I reckon."

"Right, okay, fine, yep," said Mary condescendingly. "So who the fuck put you in charge?" She stood, and Spike stood with her, melded to her leg. The animal seemed to sense the tension and stayed close to his mistress's side.

Paul shook his head at her. "Nobody. I'm not in charge. No one is; it was just a suggestion. I thought we'd all agreed to let Blane go on his way, and meet up with him tomorrow night. If we're going to do that, we really should set out and see if we can find anyone else hanging around, waiting for help. Or maybe we can find some help ourselves."

Mary glared at him, and for a terrible moment it looked as if she was going to rush him. Her eyes blazed with inner turmoil, the muscles on her arms clenching, back twitching. The air was thick with anticipated conflict, still and silent and heavy. Peer gasped. Holly half stood behind Paul, but paused when the dog growled.

"Down, Spike," Mary said, waving her hand, breaking eye contact with Paul and severing the tension. "Down, I said."

The dog continued to growl. It was staring directly at Holly, and as she eased herself back into the kitchen chair, the creature's eyes followed. Its front lowered toward the floor, its haunches flexed.

"Spike!" Mary hissed. The hound did not break concentration.

"Paul?" Holly was half hidden behind Paul, her fear for him as well as herself. Paul shifted the shotgun in his arms, slid his hand back up to the trigger guard. The dog took no notice. It paid attention to no one other than Holly, now sitting slouched down in the chair.

Mary knelt next to the dog and slapped it around the muzzle. Paul winced, but the dog merely turned its head stupidly and stared up at Mary. "Stop it!" she said. "There's a good dog." She stood, glanced smugly at the others and led the hound back to her seat by the fire.

Peer stared at her. She did not return her gaze.

"Damn dog's dangerous," Gerald said.

"What do you know, old man?" Mary hissed. "You've been spending your day shooting cows."

"Yes, my bloody cows," Gerald shouted. His eyes watered, and he turned to the window facing out over the valley.

"Don't know why we have to follow the fool, anyway," Mary continued. "He wants to go get himself killed or eaten, fine. Don't know what the hell he's up to anyway, wandering off like that."

"He thinks he knows something about what's happening," Holly said. "He's going to try to find someone."

Mary froze visibly in her chair. Her expression became that of someone shocked beyond words, but striving desperately to contain that emotion within. It was a poker face that gave away her whole hand.

Peer, sitting opposite, saw. And noted. And wondered just who Blane had gone to find.

Chapter Twenty-four

Damaged Flesh

Blane felt reality distorting once more.

With the others, survival was the prime concern. Now, wandering along this farm lane with secret noises following his progress from behind hedges, more important matters besieged his confused mind. The emphasis had shifted. Countless millions might be dead, but he was on his way to meet someone more important than any of that.

The sun had just begun to bleed into the east. This had once been Blane's favorite part of the day: dawn, when there was a great changeover in nature as humankind woke to see what the dark had left in its wake. The night animals crept warily back into their holes or nests, cautious of the sun and distrustful of humans through experience or race memory. They left behind signs of their activities: blood-spattered plants where a kill had been made;

the tattered remains of dead prey; flattened grass or broken stems where rough mating had taken place. They left also the memory of their existence to those who had not seen them but heard them, or heard of them. As well as screams in the night, startling people awake from troubled dreams, there was the frequent image of a darting creature paralyzed between twin headlights. And occasionally, the grim memory of the sound of wheels passing over that creature.

Every morning, country roads shone pink with the smear of fresh roadkill, tire splashes receding beyond the mess in a barcode of death.

But not this morning.

This morning, the roads were clear. There were some squashed animals, but they were dried out, flattened, victims of days ago rather than mere hours. And the sun rose on a very different day.

Blane's distraction was allied to a growing sense of predestiny; the conviction that he had to be in a certain place at a particular time. As yet he did not know where that place was and, notwithstanding what he had arranged with Paul about where and when to meet, when that time was. But there was a sense of purpose about him now, smoothing out but not erasing the knots of confusion he had carried for years.

On leaving the farm, he had begun to realize how much more nature had been bent out of shape overnight. It terrified him.

The hedges bordering the road hid much of the landscape from view, but even they were twisted, distorted parodies of their former selves. Leaves, newly sprouted and shiny green two days ago, were now a thousand shades of autumn, cracked and split where their veins had dried, decorating the ground in an unseasonable display of passing on. Berries had grown and popped, hanging on their stems like tiny destroyed heads atop wounded necks. The bushes and shrubs making up the hedge had sprouted spiny tendrils that crept out across the lane, burrowing through compacted stone and sending up weird, pale-looking shoots. So as death struck the plants above, pulling them through half a cycle of seasons over the space of twenty-four hours, down below life clung tenaciously on. It was not the natural life of the plants, but bastardized, as though the DNA had been nudged into some parasitic, prehistoric sequence by the dark.

In wheel ruts, puddles glinted from a midnight shower. They were stirred up and muddy, as though a car had already passed this way today. Blane soon saw why. As he passed one puddle, something slithered from it. He stopped and watched the tentacle-thing twist its way onto the dry ground. It was bright red, the thickness of his little finger, small filaments growing from its head and blowing mucus bubbles as they breathed. Its body was ribbed, about six inches long, and on some of the segments suckers puckered and kissed. Blane grimaced, but in fear. This thing should not be. There was nothing like it. It was a travesty.

He thought it might be a huge, fat earthworm. Mutated, somehow. Changed. Ruined.

He raised his foot.

Then lowered it. He had not knowingly killed anything in his life. This thing, horrible though it was, *was*. It existed. Something had allowed it to become, no matter how altered that something was. He had no right to arbitrarily condemn it to death. If anything he should protect it, because if this type of extreme mutation was occurring everywhere, there was a good chance that this creature was one of a kind.

He turned and walked away.

He was shocked numb. If a mere worm could have changed that much, he thought, what else was there? What other bizarre freaks awaited him in this disturbed countryside? As the hedges opened up on both sides and Blane approached a junction with a B road, his fears were answered.

A badger, normally a creature of the night, appeared at the end of the lane. It was twenty paces from him, sniffing at the ground, its rough tongue licking at the pale pink splash of an old kill.

Blane halted. He raised the shotgun and clamped his hand around the stock, just behind the trigger. He had never used a gun—he found them repulsive—but his instincts cried out at him to shoot.

The creature was misshapen far worse than the worm. It had three black horns growing from its head, one from just below each ear and another from its forehead, curving inward so that they almost met before its nose. Where they sprouted from the skull the dirty white fur was raised and parted, revealing the raw pink of damaged flesh beneath. Further along its back, slicing through the black-and-white-speckled fur like a shark's fin in the sea, rose a sharp bony ridge. The badger's paws had changed into rough claws, cutting scrapes into the tarmac as it worried at the corpse. Its rump had shed most of its fur. In its place, skin was rupturing into hard, shiny scales.

As Blane stared, openmouthed, the animal looked up.

Then it ran at him.

Badgers were not as fierce as their reputation held them to be, he knew. Rather, they were shy creatures, always eager to avoid contact, undertaking most of their business at night. Their cousin, the weasel, was the fighter. Usually.

Blane raised the gun, aimed and pulled the trigger. He gasped with shock—both at what he was doing, and the anticipation of the explosion—but there was no recoil or explosion. Still the beast ran, its claws tapping a tattoo of promised pain on the ground. Blane realized that he had been carrying the gun unloaded, patted his pocket for the shells and knew he would not have time. He turned the gun and held the barrel in both hands, preparing to use the stock as a club.

The badger stopped. It was no more than four feet away, snarling at him past its wickedly pointed horns, scraping one claw on the ground like a bull aching to charge. Then it turned and trundled away, sniffing along the hedge until it found an opening to slip its malformed body through.

Blane did not pause to wonder at the sudden change in attitude. He ran past the gap in the hedge, watching warily in case the animal had gained slyness as well as a more ferocious body, and was planning an ambush. When he reached the road he broke the gun, loaded it and snapped it shut. He walked quickly, pleased for once to feel the smooth artificiality of a road beneath his feet.

Today, he thought, he did not much fancy walking in the fields.

The sun bit his neck as he walked. It was already unusually hot, and sheets of steam rose from the fields, hiding whatever mutations crawled or slithered therein. Blane despised the weight of the gun on his shoulder . . . and yet welcomed it. It was a device specifically built for killing things, taking away that one true miracle that science, theology and logic had always failed to find the real answer to, no matter how much they claimed to be the true voice. Its gruesome barrels were constructed to minuscule tolerances, designed to guide a hail of deadly lead to the target, to rip it to shreds, tear through flesh and seek internal organs vital for sustaining life. On silent nights in the woods, Blane had often mused upon the mystery of existence: what it was; where it was; why it was. For him it was something both incredibly strong and pathetically weak. Strong, because not only was it the driving force of the universe, but also the means by which progression would take place. Evolution rode on the back of life, and progression—toward whatever final aim nature deigned—tagged along behind. Weak, too, because the focus of life itself depended upon the pitiful constructs of biology to support it. There was, Blane believed, something total about existence, and after death the individual passed on to that totality. But for the years that individual existed, and took part in the great play of nature, there was merely flesh and blood keeping it alive. And as he had seen only too well over the last two days, the flesh was weak. Life could not be sustained in bad flesh.

The gun was hated, then. Reviled and despised. But today of all days, Blane felt a comfort in its weight. Minutes before he had actually attempted to kill with it, blast the badger into a messy shadow of its old self. Only the fact that he had failed to load the gun had saved the creature's life. The thought of killing made him shiver and feel sick, and he was glad he had failed to do so. But what if the badger had not stopped in its attack? He could have been injured, gashed, killed. And more than anything this morning, Blane felt that he had a purpose to fulfil. He was being drawn by some strange instinct, much like a swallow will follow lines of magnetic attraction in its long trips to the warmth each year. The import of this attraction felt massive, and that was why he had left the others. To find what was calling him.

To find the woman with the chains and the secret, and discover what that secret was.

As Blane approached a bend in the road he heard the sound of a car engine. He was instantly on edge, and it was much more than his usual uneasiness at meeting or being around other people. This was a fear of the unknown.

Take away three square meals and you have anarchy. Civilization treads a knife edge, and sometimes it slips. Order is just one particular form of chaos.

Sometimes disorder is much more likely.

The car came around the bend and dipped its nose as the driver stamped on the brakes. It was a powerful, souped-up Escort, engine growling and shaking to be released from its confinement. Blane stepped onto the verge, lowered the gun and smiled. He saw movement in the car, heads turning and shaking in animated discussion. He tried to stand as casually as possible, attempted to imagine that the gun was not with him, but he could not forget it. Perhaps he should not.

He would never shoot anyone. If the car pulled up and someone jumped out shouting and screaming and pointed a gun at him, he could not shoot them. It was not in his makeup. The instinct to survive was there, but the thought of murder was reprehensible. He was, he suddenly realized, at the mercy of people he did not know.

The car crept forward, a lion stalking its prey. Blane smiled, waved. With a roar, the engine powered the car along the road toward Blane . . . and past him. Frightened faces stared through grubby windows, two kids holding dolls and a woman with an arm around each child. The driver sat staring grimly ahead, face pinched in anticipation of the shotgun blast. He accelerated the car down the road, past the lane entrance and around another corner.

Blane listened to the sound of the receding engine, feeling helplessly ashamed. The looks on the kids' faces had tugged at his heart. The glance the woman had afforded him—the way she had looked down fearfully at the gun—made him see himself from their eyes: a man on his own in a world gone mad. A gun at his side. His strained face, his sad eyes, reflecting whatever terrible sins the casual observer would care to see in them.

He sat on the verge and dropped the gun, not caring about the damp grass. He could still hear the faint sound of the car in the distance, such was the silence pervading the landscape today. He wondered where that engine would stop for the last time, and how the occupants would move on from there. Today more than yesterday, Blane knew that an irrevocable change had been wrought across the land, affecting not only the wildlife and landscape but, more intensely, the people who lived there. He was walking through a country full of dead people, lying in state in their beds where they had died two nights ago. There were those who had survived, as he had seen, but the finality of everything, even the marked difference in the sunrise this morning, only helped confirm that normality had changed during the past thirty-six hours. Now, the old times were no longer the norm. Everything had changed.

As if to illustrate, the land around him burst into strange life. From the field opposite a flush of ducks rose noisily into the air. They swooped and dipped in flight like swallows, their calls sounding more like the screeching of crows. They changed their direction of flight suddenly and headed over the road, dipping down and passing only a few feet above Blane. One of them shit on him dismissively. He went to grab the gun, terrible images of yesterday sending his heart into overdrive, but the birds darted away across the fields.

As he stood, Blane glanced down at where he had been sitting. If he'd remained there for a few more seconds a line of yellow ants would have reached him. The leading insects were huge, at least the length of his little fingernail, and as he stood they paused, as if watching. Blane smiled ruefully and shook his head, but the idea of them observing him was sustained when they all turned, as one, and filed away.

Surely they had not been coming to attack him? Ants?

Surely not.

Blane moved on. The hedgerows to either side whispered with life, occasionally disgorging something for him to see: a rabbit with huge pustules in place of its ripped-out ears; a hedgehog with several fat beetles impaled on its thickened, lengthened spines; a murmuration of starlings, living up to their collective name as they chattered like old men, strutting along the grass verge, heads jerking their way forward. All following Blane, or leading him, or dancing around him.

In a field, two horses stood touching muzzles. They seemed not to notice him, involved as they were in each other. He smiled, imagining that they were kissing, enjoying the spectacle even though he felt something of an intruder. Then one of the horses reared up, emitting a terrible sound and striking at the other with its front legs. A hoof caught the second horse in the mouth and sent it cantering away in a wild panic. The aggressor stood still. Breath puffed from its nose. Around its mouth, foam bubbled and dripped.

Two sides to everything, Blane thought. Good and bad. Malignant and benevolent. Maybe, he realized, there were even two aspects to what had happened over the past couple of days. Maybe somewhere in this mess there was something to be grateful for. His job, he knew, was to find it.

He had no idea which direction to take, so he let fate decide. At the next road junction he walked on without thinking. Secret sounds continued around him but did not change tone, so he thought he might have gone the right way.

It was not until late morning that he had the sudden certainty he was being followed. The feeling might have been there forever, but once realized it stayed with him overtly, a million pinpricks on his back and scalp, impact points of a malevolent gaze. He did not try to spot the pursuer, but he guessed it to be the woman. He listened for the tinkle of fine chains, but nature conspired to hide the noise with bird calls and other, stranger sounds from hidden fields.

When he stopped for food at midday nature paused with him. He had the overwhelming sensation of being at the center of things, and that something was holding its breath while he sat on the verge and ate the sandwiches Gerald had made for him. In the distance birds dipped and dived in the soft breeze, but all tended toward him. Somewhere behind him, perhaps where he had been walking not ten minutes before, something else waited, like his disassociated shadow. A shadow with sharp teeth and a cruel, hated and hating laugh.

Lunch eaten, Blane headed off once more. Everything followed him.

Late in the afternoon he found the village. And he realized, at last, how quickly and irrevocably everything was falling apart.

Now that Blane was on his own Fay had an unbearable urge to confront him, finally and completely. Rip out the chains. Show him what was inside her. But her plan held sway and kept her on her secret trail behind him, constantly changing and refining itself even as she followed.

Fay was tired. Enlivened by the change around her, but tired to the pit of her stomach. The thing in there moved with every step, aching to be released, and if crying had been possible she would have wept at the pain. But she had lived ten years of agony, and a tad while more would make little difference. Except, perhaps, to give her some sort of respite in the pain of others.

Sometimes she would approach close enough to see him walking along the road, though she always kept herself well hidden. She knew that he knew, but it was all a part of the pretense. Part of the game.

Soon it would be time to show more of her hand.

She grinned. Her poker face began to bleed from the strain of the unfamiliar expression.

Chapter Twenty-five

The Heart of the Beast

On the farm all was quiet, but tensions were at the boiling point.

For a while after Blane left them, Mary was distant and melancholy. She had moped without moving, bemoaned her loss without talking. But it did not take very long for her mood to change

Now she was as intimidating as ever, frowning as she sat next to the waning fire with the ever-present Spike. She petted the dog, though Peer reckoned he was as far removed from a pet as any hound she'd ever laid eyes upon. He was about as tame as a wolf could be, or a tiger, or a Komodo dragon. He allowed himself to be touched and stroked because it suited his needs, and this made the intelligence in his obsidian eyes all the more disturbing.

"Any chance of helping us?" Peer asked once again.

Mary smiled sweetly up at her. "What would you like me to do?"

Paul took over, for which Peer was glad. "We need some eggs," he said, "and some milk."

"I thought Farmer Giles had shot all his cows." Gerald winced visibly, and Mary seemed to take pleasure from this. "Anyway, as I said before: Who put you in charge?" She was mocking, not asking.

"I'm not asking you to milk a cow. There may be some milk left in the tank from yesterday; it should be all right. If it isn't, we'll have to leave it. Gerald will go with you and show you how to work the valve."

"So why can't he do it?"

Paul glanced around the room. "Safety in numbers." The phrase hung heavy, but contained little comfort for any of them.

"Well," Mary said, "I think I'm just as happy staying here, in this cozy room. Here. I'll butter some bread." She stood and walked to the table, Spike tagging along at her heels, and sat down next to Holly. There was a fresh loaf and a sharp knife, and Mary set about slicing it with blatant relish. She grinned as it crumbled to pieces before her. Peer wondered whose neck she was superimposing over the loaf.

"Mary, we've got—"

"I'll go," Peer said. "I could do with some fresh air."

"Come on then, girl," Gerald said. "Milk, then eggs. Two sheds, next to one another. I'd have been out in the fields by now."

"On any normal day," Mary said.

He looked at the strange girl and nodded. "Yep. On any normal day."

They scanned the yard from the windows as best they could, then opened the door. Nothing rushed them, and the noises outside did not change. Strange noises, Gerald said. Weird. Peer could see the truth of the statement in his eyes.

Crows picked at the bodies of two dead cows in the yard. Their hides lay open, glistening pinkly in the fresh air. It reminded Peer of the artwork she had seen on the *War of the Worlds* album cover, but the analogy suddenly made her shiver. At least in that story, the enemy was visible. Here, whatever was arrayed against them had come from the dark and remained there still.

"Come on then, girl," Gerald said, and stepped out into the yard.

The smell hit Peer as soon as she passed through the door; shit and rot. Guts and blood. The dead cows displayed the pepper-shot scabs of Gerald's shotgun, but they were also holed in other places, their insides trying desperately to escape through the fresh, fly-covered wounds. "What did that?" she asked, but Gerald only shook his head. Peer was sure he was crying and he did not want her to see. She did not ask any more questions.

The doors to the milking shed hung half open. Inside there was silence; all the noise originated outside, seemingly beyond the boundaries of the farmyard. Coughs and snorts from the fields. Loud cries from miles away, human or otherwise they could not tell. Heavy breathing from the cesspit, which was probably the popping of gas bubbles. And laughter. Everywhere, the sound of nature laughing at them.

Peer wondered whether she was the only one to

hear this and identify it. Since nodding off in front of the fire and dreaming of the safe world behind the locked door, she had felt even more removed from what was happening. It was not just the unreal feeling of waking up after an afternoon nap, when the body seems to protest at an unusually short sleep, but more a sense of being singled out. She had seen past all the badness and into the good that, perhaps, resided beyond. The problem lay in where to find the key ... and then, more importantly, the door.

She felt chosen, true, but that terrified her. It made her wish that she could tell the others of the hope she had glimpsed. And it made her wonder what there was to do the choosing.

Perhaps the dream had been her own peculiar nightmare. Torturing her with impossibilities, while all around the world had died in its sleep.

They reached the milking shed and Gerald plunged into the dark. Peer halted in her tracks, suddenly terrified, feeling ashamed at her self-indulgent fear but still unable to go any farther. She heard the sound of the farmer scampering through shadows, felt the gaze of Paul, Holly and Mary urging her on. And she tasted the danger in the air.

Imminent danger.

"Gerald, let's get back," she said.

"Nearly there, girl. Just tasting." There was the sound of fluid splashing onto the ground, then a satisfied grunt from the farmer. "Hmm, milk's fine. Good herd I've got here. Always said that. Always said I'd spent my money well. Good machines, too. A clean tank is important. Keeps out all the bugs."

Laughter again from over the hedges, as if the

landscape was finding leading them astray amusing. "Gerald, let's get back. Something's coming." She turned and stared desperately at the farmhouse. Paul tensed at her expression, looked around with the shotgun pointing out from his waist, raised his eyebrows when he saw nothing. She did not know what to say. "Gerald!"

"Eggs," he said. "I'll leave the churn filling while I find us some eggs." He was back in his element, out of the house and into routine, his attention grabbed once more by his farm, rather than distracted by the strangers who had so rudely disturbed him last night. He leaned his shotgun against the shed wall and hauled open a squealing door.

The secret noises from around the farm continued but were interrupted by a rhythmic snapping sound. Gerald plunged into shadow once more, leaving Peer in the yard. She hated herself, but she just could not follow him in. In there, things could be hiding.

A bird called, mockingly.

Gerald burst back through the door, a dozen huge moth-shapes silently jumping at his head.

He did not make any noise. The chickens could not remain airborne for long enough to do much damage, so they were an annoyance rather than a threat. He waved at them, and Peer kicked out, covering her face to protect her eyes. It was almost comical, but Gerald's tears were not funny. Tears of anguish, not pain.

"What's wrong with the world?" he asked desperately, when the chickens had at last calmed down. "What's gone wrong?"

The snapping noise finally resolved itself. A bull

sauntered into the farmyard, glaring at them with rabid eyes, hide caked with mud and filth. Its breath was ragged and uneven, the clipping sound the steady impact of its hooves on the pitted concrete. A series of spines stood out along its backbone. Sparrows and blackbirds were impaled there, some of them still fluttering uselessly. Teeth curved from its mouth, pushing the lower lips down and out. Fresh blood dripped from their self-inflicted wounds.

Gerald's jaw dropped.

Peer felt much the same. She heard Paul whisper something from the farmhouse door, but he was too far away for her to make out, and Peer did not want to turn her attention away from the bull. It was huge, a mountain of meat, and it was about to move their way.

"Gerald," she whispered, but the farmer was already reaching for his shotgun. The bull followed his movements with terrible, intelligent eyes, seemingly gauging distances, weighing chances. Breath snorted from its muzzle, and it lowered and raised its head several times.

"He's coming," the farmer said. "In the shed when he does."

"Hey!" Paul had stepped into the yard and stood with the gun held above his head. Holly was aghast behind him. Mary's expression was an unreadable blank, her eyes centered on Peer, not the bull.

The animal charged. Paul shouldered the gun clumsily, paused with his eyes squinted, then looked in disbelief at the stock. The bull was nearly upon him when an explosion came from Gerald's gun and the creature's rump darkened with blood.

It spun around, amazingly agile for such a huge creature, and charged its new aggressor.

Gerald fired the second barrel and a hole appeared in the bull's shoulder, blood hazing the air. It seemed not to notice.

Peer screamed. She could almost smell the breath of the thing, and like a painting in a large room its eyes seemed constantly to bore into her. She wondered what it saw. She could not move. Her feet were twin flames of pain.

Gerald had broken his gun and now struggled to pluck out the spent shells. A strange keening was coming from his throat as he worked.

Paul fired twice in quick succession. The bull slipped and stumbled as one of its back legs snapped and spewed blood. Peer blinked in surprise as she felt stinging pain in her lower legs.

"Come on!" Holly was shouting.

"Run!" Mary screamed.

Peer looked up and saw Mary waving her toward the farm. Her. Not Gerald and not Paul. The bull was roaring in pain, and for a surreal moment she thought the sound was coming from Mary's wide-open mouth.

As the angered creature shivered and raged, Gerald managed to load his gun once more. "Run," he said. Peer shook off her paralysis and obeyed. Her legs burned as she hobbled in a wide arc around the edge of the yard, trying to keep close to the buildings in case the bull rushed her.

Paul raised his gun again, but once more blinked in surprise as nothing happened. Gerald's twin barrels coughed into the stricken animal. And it chose that moment, when both guns were empty or out of action, to come at Peer.

It seemed to have been feigning the amount of damage done it, because it was upon her in seconds. Shouts came from the farmhouse, the sound of running feet, metal scraping on stone. But Peer could see nothing, because her daylight was blocked out by the bleeding beast.

It slid to a halt before her, regarding her with rolling, mad, sad eyes. Its malformed teeth dripped pink saliva. A constant shiver rippled through its body, shaking its jowls and sending a fine patter of blood to the ground. Peer could not breathe; she could not move. Shouts came from a million miles away—or from behind a thick door—and the pounding of running footsteps could not outdo the thumping of her heart. The bull stared, blood now flecking the foam of every snorted exhalation.

For an instant there was just her and the bull. The sense of dislocation she had been feeling for weeks thrust her toward infinity, the bull following, everything else left behind. She held the bull's gaze; it held her. She was certain that to break contact would allow it to complete its stampede and crush her into the dirt. Its legs were covered with its own blood. She felt her own blood trickling down her shins.

The wounded animal turned away and charged Gerald once more. Explosions shook the yard as four barrels emptied themselves into its body, but still it raged and bellowed in anger.

Peer ran for the farmhouse, the spell broken. She felt nothing as Holly hauled her through the door, no emotion at all as Mary knelt by her side and looked carefully into her eyes, as if to make sure she was still alive inside. Spike scampered across her stomach and raced into the yard, joining in the fray by snapping at the bull's heels. The taste of blood seemed to excite him; he became as frenzied as the dying beast.

"Christ, Peer!" Holly gasped, tears running down onto her top lip. Paul shouted outside; a gun roared metallic death against the side of the farmhouse.

Mary ducked, a glint in her eye. "Almost had you then," she said. "Bastard almost had you." She reached out and laid a casual hand on Peer's shoulder, watching the slaughter in the yard.

More gunshots, more roars of pain, the slippery sound of something dragging itself wetly across the ground. Gerald said something with a hitch in his voice; then there was the sound of the guns being reloaded and another volley of shots. Then, after a dull thump, nothing more.

Peer lay back on the kitchen floor, staring up at the cracks in the ceiling and trying to make sense of things there. Spike trotted in and sat at Mary's feet, foam drooling onto the quarry tiles.

"You were so lucky," Holly gasped, kneeling at her side and putting her hand on Peer's forehead.

It didn't feel like luck, Peer thought. It didn't feel like luck at all.

When they cracked the eggs to scramble them for lunch, they were all bad. The yolks were a sickly pink, spotted with dark flecks, leaking through split membranes into the grayish white. It was as if they had been fertilized by the corruption in the air and then left to rot.

Chapter Twenty-six

· *Crying Blood*

Blane stopped outside the village. From a distance it could have been an optical illusion, but this close in he could see the truth of things. The place was abandoned and had the appearance of a lost Amazonian city.

Nature had smothered it.

Directly before him an ancient stone bridge spanned a chuckling stream, the tarmac road crossing it as incongruous as a striplight in a cathedral. The stream itself was a dirty brown color and as thick as oxtail soup, visibly heavy with the load of silt and mud it carried. Its banks were comprised of raw rock, soil and plants having been washed away in a surge. The bright scars of recent exposure to the elements were still evident on the stone. The gulley it had formed was deeper than it should have been, as if the waters had taken on some exaggerated abrasive quality. In the bank nearest the town an old stone structure had been uncovered; solid walls, a portion of a staircase, hints at foundations. An archaeological oddity that no one would ever have the chance to study. Detritus still tumbled into the stream from the unsteady, sheer walls of the gulley, causing lazy splashes in the thick water.

Blane leaned on the parapet and stared down. He felt as if he was seeing something never meant for human eyes. Something time had abandoned for a while to leave to its own devices. Turning, he walked into the village.

That same thought struck again and again, at every sight.

The road ended at the bridge. At first it was cracked into crazy patterns, but only slightly farther on it had been completely clothed in a carpet of grass, crawling weed and low, wide shrubs. In places the pitch was still visible, frozen into fluid snapshots as if trying to escape its own suffocation. The spread of vegetation did not stop at the road but hauled itself up garden and building walls, skirting them with bright green and occasional splashes of colored flowers that looked all wrong. The colors were there, as bright and attractive as usual, but the flowers themselves were deformed out of shape, pointing away from the sun, swollen as if full of pus. There were some colors that Blane had never seen.

The first few houses on the left had been demolished by trees. Moist, creamy trunks sprouted through walls and roofs, darkened areas of weathered bark yet to appear to protect the sudden growths from the elements. One tree was twice as tall as the house it impaled, holding twisted scraps of carpet and broken furniture high in its branches like trophies of some age-old conquest.

But this was not age-old; none of it. This was all recent. Trees growing in a day. Plants spreading and breaking the ground, the stream carving itself a deep niche in the sick land. All in one day. Blane was terrified; but he also felt something else, something that tugged at his melancholy heart.

Pride.

Fay was unafraid, yet she did not follow him in. This was all for him to see. It had only taken her a brief visit the night before to arrange the messages for him, and now it was down to him to wander through the village and find them.

Then he would find the messengers.

Fay watched him at the bridge and wished they could talk. But that time would come soon; for now she had to prepare for it.

There was a chance that she would not live for much longer. She could almost feel her flesh being consumed by her own body, in whatever frantic hunger it mistakenly felt. Her clothes hung on her like rags, defining narrow shoulders, sticklike arms, points of bone stretching the skin fit to burst. Blood leaked from every orifice, a bastard mockery of the rhythms she had once been the mother of. She let it congeal and harden into crisp brown scabs. Life was fleeing her, slowly but surely, but she did not care.

Inside, she felt wonderful. She would be with Blane again soon, if only for a short time. She would tell him her secrets. Then, let nature do as it would. Let it finish the job.

It was Blane's turn to go mad.

There was a body stuffed into a thatched roof next to the village pub, perhaps to keep cats at bay. A tree had pierced it with its rapid growth, lifted it from its resting place like some divine miracle worker, and hauled it Heavenward until the roof structure caught it. Blane could not make out whether it was a man or a woman, but he could see where the tree had grown straight through the still-cooling flesh and exited the body in a claw of ribs. He was tempted to go closer to inspect, but other sights called him. And something else was here, niggling at the back of his mind with insistent whispers. A laugh, half cackle and half song. Something from before his memory began, struggling to break through.

He had a sudden image of the woman, coughing up whatever secret lay in the pit of her stomach, hauling on the thin chains and gagging on blood as it revealed itself. Would she show him, when they met? Was he meant to see? He tried to picture the songlike laughter coming from her mouth, but the image would not gel.

There were three more bodies in the shattered windows of the pub, but these seemed to be arranged. Each stood naked, spread-eagled, pressed into the frames by whatever grew inside and pushing them outward. It was as if nature was trying to exclude them from the building, and only the remnants of the window frames kept them in place. Wood pressed into their flesh and puffed their skin into spacesuit bulges. Pale green weeds had wrapped around their legs from outside and now pulled in concert with the expanding foliage within. The pub had been called the Crown & Anchor; its sign was still visible atop a white pole in what used to be its garden. A magpie sat on the sign and set it swaying. The black-and-white bird had two sets of wings, one feathery and natural, the other a thin, brightly veined affair. It had something in its mouth, but it was wet, not shiny.

Grass grew in the gutters of buildings, thick and green, resembling prairie grass more than the shorter, brighter version found in Britain. Its edges looked sharp. It gave the dilapidated buildings a punkish fringe, shimmering in the breeze like lines of green fire. Cracks in walls had been found, aggravated and expanded, belching forth gouts of purple moss in malignant profusion.

Blane followed the road, although he could barely see it. He stepped carefully, always certain that in this bastardized version of the nature he so loved he would find, by accident, a mutated Venus's-flytrap or other vengeful plant. Each time his foot set down he waited for pain to intrude into his shock, acid to start eating at his old shoes. Most carnivorous plants killed by slow digestion, he knew. Once, he had thought that this was simply the most efficient way, that there was never any cruelty intended by nature. Now, doubt pressed in. What more terrible way to kill something? Humans often felt guilty about the remains of cute lambs or cuddly calves on their plates, but at least these animals were killed quickly. Nature was not nearly as efficient in killing its food, often stretching a death out for hours on end while the hunter ate into the living belly, gnawed through bones even as the victim writhed in agony.

He had never thought this way, and it was uncomfortable. But now it seemed right. In this place, nature had gone mad. Here, a hunter would toy with its prey instead of using it to fulfil a need. A fox may chase a human for hours until exhausted; a stag likewise. They had already seen what farm animals were capable of.

Blane hoped that Peer and the others were all right. Especially Peer. There was something about her that struck him as odd but also familiar. She did not seem to gel with the group like the others, always remaining on the periphery when it came to discussion. Mary was aggressive and antagonistic, but Peer was different in deeper ways. She seemed guided, not by decisions made within the group, but by something else. Her eyes held a constant state of subtle shock, a shock deeper set and more age-worn than mere terror at recent events.

The road curved sharply to the right, curling around the high stone wall surrounding a church and graveyard. Blane heard the occasional musical tink of something striking metal and saw dozens of black flapping shapes hovering around the belfry. Blackbirds, orange beaks mostly replaced by something gray that looked so much like metal, dive-bombed the bells in the church tower. The result was a part of the song of nature. Random, unseasoned and careless, but full of order. Until now. The sense of wrongness came, Blane realized, not from the idea that the creatures around him were alien, but that he was an alien visitor to their world. It felt like things had always been this way. They had simply waited this long to be noticed.

As the road rose and the wall dipped, his view opened up into the churchyard. He found his attention drawn there, even though he could still remember the last one he had been in.

There were a dozen bodies scattered among the graves, and for an instant Blane feared that he was seeing more of what had happened in Rayburn. But these bodies were old. It seemed the dead had sprouted; their remains had been forced through the compacted soil of decades or centuries and displayed to the sunlight. Their limbs projected in grotesque arrangements, sickly gray plants entwining them with thin stems, thicker roots disappearing down into disturbed graves and holding them aloft. Headstones had been pushed aside and tumbled, splintered wood showed wetly through the frozen eruption of soil, myriad small creatures crawled around in the damp mud, as yet undried by the sun. They were unwilling zombies in a film never to be made, slack-jawed skulls sad rather than threatening. Today, this was the acceptable face of death.

Blane walked on and found what must pass for the village square. A shop huddled in one corner, a garage in the other, benches in the center overturned by the agitated roots of the old oak that grew there. Its fresh bursts of growth, thrust out over the last couple of days, hung whitely on its ancient withered trunk. New leaves were green and vitally fresh, but they did not match their older cousins in the strength of their appearance, nor did the new branches harbor that mystic spread possessed by those there before. They did not reach for the sky, but twisted and pointed at all angles, directionless.

A stream trundled along at the edge of the square. Blane went to it, half hoping to see clear water that was fit for drinking. But the water was the color of sick urine, and stank as bad. He turned away and headed for the shop, wading through plants knee-high and armed with cruel, curved barbs. They nicked at his skin through his jeans, but he ignored them. He was afraid that to notice their presence would encourage them more in their attack.

Foolish thoughts. The thoughts of a madman. But what he could see around him were the visions of a madman, and he felt infected with the bizarreness of the scene. To change, he thought, is to understand—

An idea came, unbidden and shocking in its sudden intensity. A madman . . . or a madwoman.

The more Blane looked around, the more he saw order in chaos. A body had been lifted by the rapid growth of the barbed plants, the cruel shoots piercing the natural openings of the naked corpse and emerging from new, forced splits in the skin. But the way the mouth hung open, surprised in a scream, seemed false. Manufactured. Created. Other things, too, pointed at the artificiality of the scene. Not the disruption to living things, which was apparent everywhere, though more pronounced and advanced in this place. But the way the dead lay, in eternal mockery of the manner of their passing and the world they had been taken from so suddenly, shouted sham. Someone had been here before Blane. He thought he knew who.

A shape stepped from the shadows of a tumbled-down house. It was a woman, her mouth open in a sick grin, part pain, part hate. She was crying blood.

Blane turned to flee, but another shape joined the first; then they came from elsewhere. In a matter of seconds he was surrounded, and the people with blood for tears closed in on him.

Chapter Twenty-seven

Good Dog

Holly insisted on trying the telephone one more time. It was midday, the sky was clear and there were no vapor trails marring its perfection.

Gerald had an old rotary-dial phone, a genuine antique rather than an affectation. Holly dialed 999.

Paul stood behind her, hands resting gently on her shoulders. He could feel by the tension there that she had found nothing. He had not wanted her to try the phone again, because he was dreadfully certain of the results.

Paul partly hated himself for it, but he was more disturbed by the obvious changes in nature than the fate of untold millions of humans. Perhaps because people had removed themselves away from their environment by shunning it, burying themselves in redbrick prisons and soap operas, using it as a convenient picnic place rather than respecting it for what it was. Now it was all changing, and Paul felt life's purpose changing with it. His life was no longer clearly defined. All he could do was go with the flow.

"Maybe the lines are down," he said, knowing it was no comfort.

"Random number," Holly said, ringing in the area code for Cardiff, then a random six-figure number. "It's ringing."

Peer sat by the fire, staring into the renewed flames, legs bruised and swollen where stray pellets had struck her. Her jeans had prevented the penetration of all but a few, but dark blood bruises pebbled the skin of her shins. She had hardly spoken since tumbling back into the house. Mary sat opposite, staring at Peer, Spike at her feet. She was guarding Peer, Paul thought, though more as a captor than a bodyguard. Every now and then Mary would look up at the ceiling, frowning, as if reading shocking tales into the cracks and scratches thereon.

"Still ringing," Holly said needlessly.

"If they answer, tell them my cows need milking," Gerald said.

Holly went to say something but felt the squeeze of Paul's hands on her shoulders. "Don't worry, Gerald," he said, "they'll be here soon."

The ringing continued, hypnotic, hopeless. Holly counted them out loud, every one of them. At thirty rings she hung up and dialed again. A Manchester code this time, followed again by random numbers. Unavailable. She tried one more time with the same code and a different number. "Manchester. Ringing."

Paul stared out of the kitchen window. The dead

bull lay off to the left, dive-bombed occasionally by carrion birds he knew, and those he did not. He had never seen blue tits or robins rooting so relentlessly inside dead animals. He felt alone and betrayed, estranged from the nature he so loved and thrown in with a bunch of people he could barely relate to. Peer was distant and almost removed from their gang, worse now that Blane had gone. Mary was scary. Gerald seemed to have been losing it ever since coming back in from killing the bull. He talked of plowing the wild fields, milking the dead cows, eating eggs rotten with whatever had corrupted them. Paul had serious doubts whether Gerald would agree to leave with them, once the time came.

Holly . . . He felt an affection for Holly that he was not used to dishing out onto any casual passerby. She was brusque, much younger than he, but possessed of a tenacious strength that he respected. Like now. None of the others wanted to try the phone because they were so certain of what they would find. Holly had to try it for herself. She did not want to take anything sitting down.

"Still ringing," she said wanly.

Paul felt a chill pass through him as he contemplated trying to telephone home once more. He only spoke to his family once or twice each year, not because he did not still love them, and not even because the calls ostensibly cost too much to make. It was simply a habit he had fallen into. Now it was something he had been putting off. He had tried from Rayburn, but he put that down to a bad connection. He had to. He had to believe his family was still alive. It was his hope, and he did not want it dashed. The Dominican Republic was such a beautiful island. So much wildlife . . .

"Try home," he said. He could remember the number like guilt.

Holly dialed the number as Paul recited it. She heard the creak of interest as Mary and Peer moved forward in their chairs to listen. Gerald was peeling potatoes. After she had finished the dialing there was a series of clicks, mysterious sighs, pauses interrupted by more static.

"Well?" Paul asked.

"Hang on." Everyone held their breath. The scraping of Gerald's knife was the only sound in the room. "One long tone," Holly said quietly. "Unobtainable."

Paul gently took the receiver from her, suspecting she had dialed wrong. He rang the number in himself and waited, and the same tone spat into his ear. He tried one more time. Then he looked up another foreign dialing code and tried a random number in France. There was ringing, but it went unanswered. He tried Australia, but that too was unobtainable. America did not answer.

He tried about twenty numbers, moving into Holly's chair when she vacated it for him, feeling her hands on his shoulders now, roles reversed. She squeezed, and pain bit through his muscles, but he welcomed it because it proved that he was still alive.

"Everywhere is dead," he said. He turned around and said it again. Even Mary seemed shocked.

"Can't be everywhere," she said. "It must be the phone. The phone's broken."

"It's possible," Holly said.

Paul turned back and rang the talking clock. The voice was calm, assured, soothing. He wondered what state the woman who had spoken these words was in now. Now that everyone else was dead. He put the phone down gently. Through the window he could see the midday landscape, hazed with a threat of violence. He wondered whether it would ever feel like home again.

"So?" Mary asked. Spike grumbled as she spoke, as if echoing what she said.

"So," Paul said, "we do as I suggested. Head off toward where we're meeting Blane tomorrow. See if there's anyone else around." His words sounded empty, even to himself.

"What's the good in that?" Holly said. There was an edge of panic to her voice now, slipping in like a sharp knife through skin. "Why not just stay here? There's food, a big house, a stream to drink from. Why not stay for a while?"

"Then what?" Paul said, but wished he hadn't. It had too much of an air of finality about it. "Look, we said we'd meet Blane and it would be unfair if we didn't. He'd be on his own, Holly."

"He left us on our own," Mary said.

Peer looked up from the fire, her face still red from its glow. "He's gone for a very good reason. He thinks he knows what caused this. Do you think he'd just sit back and let it continue?"

That seemed to settle the argument. They would wash, gather as much useful equipment as they could into the two cars and head off toward their meeting place. Gerald seemed to agree, but Paul thought that they would have trouble with him when the time came to leave. This was his farm, his

327

history. Paul decided there and then that he could not force Gerald to go with them. It was not fair.

Nothing was fair.

Paul and Holly had the same room as before. It had a small washbasin in one corner, and Holly stripped off shamelessly to wash. Paul stared out of the window, but the splashes and the sound of a towel rubbing skin drew his eyes back.

He went to Holly and hugged her from behind. She went limp in his arms, started to cry, shaking uncontrollably for a couple of minutes.

"Is it really everywhere, Paul?" she asked. "Can it be like this? All in one day? Can everything change so much in one day?"

"I think so," Paul whispered into her neck. His own tears dropped onto her shoulder. She turned around and kissed him.

This time, they had no problem.

Peer and Mary remained downstairs while the others went up to wash and freshen up. Peer started to gather together provisions, leaving them on the kitchen table for now until they could be bagged up and put in the cars. In the pantry there were several lumps of cheese on a cold slab. As she picked one up a dark shape scurried from behind it and found shadow behind another. A spider. But it had far too many legs.

"The spiders have changed," she said casually.

"Why should they be different?" Mary was at the window, looking out into the yard, not just staring. Spike, as ever, was at her heels.

"I wonder whether we'll ever see a do-do."

"Hmm."

"Or a unicorn."

Peer opened the fridge and paused, bathed in white light and cool air. For an instant she was opening another door and the light flooding around her was fresh sunlight, the air tinted with the smells of spring. She stood that way for a while, as hypnotized by the fluffy frost on the shelves as she had been by the caves of fire in the grate. The world moved around and then away from her, distancing itself even more as her thoughts drew inside.

Her mother had always told her that she had an overactive imagination, but then her father said imagination was a good thing. She had been left feeling guilty and invigorated whenever she had a flight of fancy, as though dreaming was masturbating. She knew that her father was right, and she could never dream of a situation where her mind would not benefit her. Slowly, over the years, imagination was replaced by adulthood, the curse on the innocence of wonder and awe. Peer had thought that remarkable vein of ideality purged from her mind for good, or at least driven deeper than mere memory could redeem. She had mourned it, but not too much—the loss was gradual, and other changes in her body and environment were enough to keep her mind diverted for a time.

Now she had found it once again. Her mind was wide open. Every sensation had many meanings. Nothing seemed literal any more, and the strange distance she had been experiencing simply allowed room for her to see, taste, feel so much more than she ever had before. She wondered what her mother would say.

Tim Lebbon

* * *

Mary was staring at Peer. Peer was staring into the fridge. Once more, Mary found it difficult to come to terms with the fact that this weak, dreamy woman was, or could ever be a threat to beautiful Fay. But from bitter experience Mary knew that it was always the weakest, slightest-looking ones who were the worst. In a supposedly civilized world, size was complemented by temperament. Now, with civilization foundering on an unknown beach, nothing was quite as it seemed.

She tapped her leg and Spike stood to attention, stumpy tail erect. Time suddenly bore down on her, now that she had decided what to do. The others were upstairs, but they would not stay there for long. Decisions had to be made, threats issued, and once they were on their way they must never stop or permit the chance of being caught. Mary had to fulfil her promise when the time was right; it would be easier to do so if she and Peer were alone.

As for Blane . . . Fay must surely have her own plans for him.

"Peer," Mary said quietly, using the hated woman's name for the first time, "I think we should go."

"Go where?" Peer said.

Mary had begun to shake. She tried to keep her voice low, frightened that she would alert those upstairs, but she had little control. She felt guided by Peer, not in control of her. "Away from here," she said. "Away from these. They're fools, and they're hanging on to the past. And Blane is the worst of them all. They're better off without him, and we're better off without them. Will you come with me?"

She tried to sound forceful but felt more like a puppy begging for favors.

Peer looked at Mary with her thin arms, scrawny neck, wide blank eyes surrounded by stress lines where laughter lines should be. A stern face, acting the hard thing when really she was the most vulnerable of them all. "Of course I won't go with you, Mary," she said. "You hate me. I feel safe with Paul and Holly. And Blane has something about him that makes me feel important. Like I've something to do, but just haven't been told yet."

"You're a fucking whore," Mary spat, shoulders twitching and tendons standing out on her neck. "Spike!"

The dog trotted over to Peer and, before she had a chance to move, stood and placed his front paws on her stomach. She held her breath, looking down into the dog's obsidian eyes. Spike growled, a low, continuous noise that sent subtle vibrations through his legs and into Peer's body.

"He'll rip you open in a second," Mary said. "He's a good dog. Good dog, Spike. If you make a noise or a movement, I'll tell him to attack you. By the time those idiots upstairs get down here, you'll be damaged beyond help, trying to stuff your guts back inside. Is it worth it? Do you value your freedom that much?" Mary had a sudden memory of a deer they had caught once, how Jams had bashed its head in with a sledgehammer while the others prodded at it with sharpened sticks.

How she so wanted to do that to this bitch.

She shook, clenching and unclenching her hands, wishing she still had the chain. She came close, so close to telling Spike to savage the bitch, and realized how much she would love to sit back and watch. She was aware of a dark presence in her mind and she opened it up and spread it out. She thought she would find Fay there, an influence burned in forever from their brief meeting, a duty waiting to be performed. But when she realized what was inside her, she was shocked. Shocked, and amused, and greatly excited.

The blackness was her. She wanted to kill the bitch and rip her up, and not because it was the duty bestowed upon her by Fay, but because she wanted to do it for herself.

"I'm so close to killing you," Mary whispered, and she saw outright fear in Peer's stare. She was glad. "Come on."

Mary grabbed Peer's arm and squeezed, enjoying the sharp intake of breath by the other woman. As she led her to the door Spike followed on behind. "Sexist bastards keep the guns for themselves," she muttered, but she opened the door anyway. She snatched a set of keys from a hook next to the jamb and pressed them into Peer's hand. "Take these. You're driving."

"I can't drive."

"Don't fuck with me."

Mary led Peer across the yard, Spike's nose tapping against her leg as he followed close behind. She had not picked up food, drink, maps or any other supplies. She had walked them both into the yard without checking for any danger. She was not even trying to be quiet about it.

"You're mad," Peer said.

Mary giggled. "What's mad? Falling asleep and breaking your neck?"

They reached Holly's Mini. Mary waited until Peer had strapped herself into the driver's seat before motioning Spike onto her lap. He sat very still; so did Peer.

"Rip your face off," Mary said gleefully, knowing that soon it would be true. When the time was right.

Then Fay would welcome her with open arms.

"Let's go, James," Mary said, jumping into the passenger seat, "and don't spare the horses." She laughed, realizing the irony of her words and relishing it.

"I can hardly steer with this dog on my lap," Peer said.

"Try." Mary giggled again.

Peer started the engine and eased the car around in a tight circle. She was aware of movement in an upstairs window of the farmhouse, and she saw Mary glancing up as well.

"Oh, the lovers have noticed us," Mary said. "How nice." She gave them a little wave, smiling sweetly. "Put your foot down."

There was no longer movement in the window. They must be coming down the stairs. Peer stalled the car.

Mary grabbed her throat. "Start it again and drive us away. One more trick and Spike will have you. Then I will." She kept her hand around Peer's throat, allowing her fingers to sink into the skin with a little more pressure than was really needed. Peer grimaced and started the car again.

The farmhouse door opened and Paul stood there in jeans and an unbuttoned shirt. He had a shotgun cradled in one arm, still broken. Holly appeared behind him, and Gerald's pale face materialized at another upstairs window. Paul shouted something, but his words were lost in the screech of the laboring starter motor.

Peer drove slowly toward the lane, steering around the tattered body of the bull, trying not to look at the birds feasting on purple meat and staring dismissively at the car. She thought about stopping; about how long it would take Paul to reach the car if she did so; how much damage Spike would do to her face in the few seconds it took him to cross the yard, raise his gun and blow the hound away. The chances did not balance in her favor, she knew that. But she also knew that she was in the car with a madwoman. The chances that way were worse.

A flock of birds parted from a tree next to the barn like leaves coming to life. They streamed through the air, passing close over the roof of the Mini and causing Mary to duck involuntarily. Peer sat still. They would not harm her, just as the bull had not. She was not really here for them, just as sometimes she did not even feel here herself. All this was happening to someone else, someone she no longer knew that well. She had changed.

In the rearview mirror she saw the birds collide with Paul and Holly in the doorway. Almost as if they had been sent here, for this purpose, at this time.

"Now drive!" Mary shouted.

Spike growled. His breath stank.

Peer drove into the lane, glancing in the mirror, seeing the farmhouse door slam shut on light feathered bodies. She hoped that they were all right in there.

"Where to?" she asked.

Mary looked at her blankly. Then she glanced through the windshield at the lane curving its way to the main road ahead. She had no idea where they were going. "Turn left at the end," she said. "Then I'll tell you when to turn again. You just drive. And don't mind Spike." She scratched the dog behind his ear and he groaned in appreciation. "He's a good dog really."

Peer glanced down at the hound. Then she stared at him. For the first time, he averted his eyes, and she realized there and then that, like the bull in the farmyard, he would never attack her. But she kept the advantage to herself.

Chapter Twenty-eight

The Lidless

The woman stopped several feet away, ignorant of the thorns stabbing bloody pearls into her bare legs. She wore a short summer dress, had long auburn hair and graceful limbs, and she was quite mad. Her eyelids had been sliced off and she glared at Blane with boiled-egg eyeballs, her pupils ridiculously small in the expanse of glittery white. Tears of blood ran across the surface of her eyes from the unhealed wounds. Her grin was a grimace. She must have been in immense pain.

"Don't your eyes hurt?" Blane asked.

"Pain is better than sleep," the woman said. She had a deep voice, which some men would call husky, and she must have once been beautiful. The others stood behind the woman, perhaps deferring to her because of this erstwhile beauty. They all fixed Blane with obligatory stares, regarding him maniacally through masks of dried and drying blood.

"You're Blane," the woman said neutrally. "I'm Gabrielle. We're the lidless."

"Where is she?" Blane asked, horrified but equally excited at the idea that the woman was nearby. All that he could see suddenly seemed relevant, but he did not know why. There were huge secrets straining at the stitches of reality, blatantly laid out for his perusal in the lay of the land and the twisted thing that nature had become, but he could translate it into nothing except death and corruption. He needed someone else to help him see what was staring him in the face, and perhaps had been for many years. His memories awaited their final revival.

Gabrielle was still. Blane could not hold eye contact for more than a few seconds. He glanced around at the others, all of them young, all possessed of a handsomeness now despoiled by the brutal wounding they had suffered. The women wore dresses, the men wore jeans and shirts, as if dressed for a visit to an informal restaurant. Looking closer, he could see their cheeks twitching as muscles ached to cleanse their eyes. He could barely imagine the pain they must be in.

"Can you still see?" he asked.

"Who said that?" one of the men said, laughing harshly. A couple of the others smiled pained smiles, but Gabrielle's expression did not change.

"Gabrielle," Blane said, "I'm looking for someone. You know my name, and so does the person I'm looking for, so I know you know where she is. She knows what's happening—"

"Of course she does," Gabrielle said enthusiastically. "She is the queen of it all. She caused it. She's the artist. Somewhat abstract, I'll grant you, but genius nonetheless. Come with me."

Blane followed Gabrielle, while the others followed him. He looked down at the ground, trying to step between plants rather than through them, desperate to not see the occasional gray things slithering beneath the shrubs. What Gabrielle had said should have shocked him, he thought, or at least comforted him and confirmed his suspicions. But given voice, it no longer rang true. There was so much more to what was going on than simply the woman. So much more. If only he could see it.

"Why did you do this to yourselves?" he said, but the answer was obvious. Gabrielle seemed to know that; she did not respond.

They headed toward the garage in the corner of the square and took a path next to it. It led in between the buildings, curving around odd-shaped gardens and ducking under old trees. "How many of you are there?" Blane asked.

"Fifty. We few are the only ones who haven't gone mad."

Blane looked at Gabrielle's back. From behind, with her mutilated face out of sight, she was indeed beautiful. He tried to liken her to the strange woman he had seen in the field outside Rayburn, but he could draw no real parallel. "Why are you helping her? You said she caused this. All the terrible things that have happened. So why help her?"

Gabrielle answered without turning. "You should see what she can do! She's in control, and she's the only one now. We need someone in control, for when the real changes come. That's why she welcomed us when she found us."

"You did this thing to yourselves?" Blane asked, aghast. He had been imagining that the woman had forced these people to slice their eyelids away.

"Of course. Survival of the fittest now, Blane. Those who do not sleep are the fittest, by default. Because they live. Everyone else dies, they all die, and in the end there will be only a few left. We . . . I, intend to be one of those few. At her side. Working with Fay."

"Fay." He whispered the name and it was like acid on his tongue, sweet yet deadly. It hit him like a punch to the heart. Fay. The fairy. He tried to ally the name with the woman he had seen in the field, and it fit in some peculiar, depraved way. She was as far from the fairy of myth as anyone could be, and yet the description seemed to echo what she had done and was still doing. A fairy gone bad. Rebelling against the land having shed her wings, or had them shorn.

"You were beautiful once," Blane said, not knowing why he said it. To appeal to her vanity? Ask her, subtly, to shift to his side, for when he really needed her?

Gabrielle stopped and turned around. They were under a tree, and the sun came through and speckled her skin like pustules waiting to burst. "What's beauty?" she said bitterly. "Was I beautiful because men wanted to fuck me? Or is she beautiful because she has survived, and is turning things to her own way? It's in the eye of the beholder."

"And you behold everything," Blane said, half question, half bitter statement.

Gabrielle smiled. Her wounds were bleeding again. "I see everything through blood. Quite apt for these times, don't you think?" She turned and continued along the winding, overgrown path.

Things skittered out of their way; small gray shapes like frogs with six legs and fur. Plants squirmed at their presence, withdrawing back through the hedge like the tentacles of some great beast. Gabrielle seemed not to notice.

"Did you lose someone?" Blane asked. "Fay caused all this, you say. Oh, how clever of her. Did you lose someone? Did someone spill their blood across you as you lay awake?"

Gabrielle paused but did not turn around. She kicked idly at a shape on the ground, a dead magpie with a watch in its mouth, the watch still on a severed wrist. Maggots the size of peanuts were glutted on its flesh. "That was in the past," she said, and walked on.

They proceeded in silence. *Fay*, Blane thought. The name was so misleading, yet so suited to the woman he had seen. The light laughter that had been haunting him since seeing the deer die in the woods could have come from a Fay, yet he could barely associate it with the Fay he was going to meet now. Perhaps, somewhere in his past, there was a different version of the same woman. Someone who could laugh sweetly, and mean it. Someone who did not love and court death the way this woman seemed to.

Now that he knew her name, perhaps he would recognize her when they met.

* * *

After watching Blane cross the stone bridge and enter the village, Fay moved through the fields and placed herself just where she wanted to meet him. Here she would reveal all. Here she would cough up the secrets she had been harboring for so long, and watch his face drop, and see the impact of cruel realization tear him to pieces.

She did not want to hurt him. Really, she did not. But why the fuck should she suffer all alone?

The building was old and had been abandoned for years, but it still stank of death. Its purpose was slaughter, and that had seemed to imbue it with a killing air, a haze of murder coating all its surfaces with memories of violent, incessant death. Fay imagined the stains on the concrete floor to be spilled blood because that pleased her.

She had seen plenty of blood in the last couple of days, like the gorging at the end of a long, slow feast. Her feast had lasted for ten years, and the nibbles she had taken during that time still lay in shallow graves or under indifferent gravestones around the world. There were plenty of bodies to bury now, but few left to bury them. Sometimes Fay craved the hot tang of blood at her lips, but now she was sure that it would no longer serve any purpose. In the past it had simply been an affectation, not a necessity. The panicked trickle of it down her throat pleased her, because of where it came from. How often she had dreamed of allowing Blane's own into her system.

But what purpose was there in replacing same with same?

She was tired from her rush around the village. She was not as strong as she had once been. Blane

341

must be halfway through by now, approaching the square and that fool Gabrielle who called herself lidless. Brainless, more like, but she served a purpose. Just like Mary.

There were still some chains bolted to the wall, several hanging from the ceiling. The hooks had long since gone or been stolen, but Fay grabbed a fat metal link in each hand and took some of the weight off her legs: slumped like an offering of meat. She let go of the chains and leaned against the wall: casual and in control. She sank to the floor and sat on one of the worst-stained areas, running her hands across the gritty old concrete. She waited there, one hand on each bony knee: contemplative and concerned.

Like a schoolgirl about to meet her first date, Fay tried to decide how to greet Blane into the slaughterhouse. The thing in her stomach shifted in anticipation of its imminent revelation. She coughed, and felt the tint of rank blood on her tongue.

Minutes later, she heard footsteps.

Then she felt Blane thinking of her, and she cringed in terror at the unconscious authority of his thoughts.

The door slid open on rusty runners.

"Brother," she said.

Chapter Twenty-nine

Mother's Intuition

Soon after the Mini left the farmyard, the birds that had made it through the door settled down. Some perched on high plate shelves and the picture rail; others sat on the stone floor, puffing ruffled feathers as if having just finished a long migration. Paul and Holly stared at each other wide-eyed, memories of the attack in the service station all too fresh. Their wounds ached with the recollection of probing beaks and angry claws.

Gerald blundered downstairs, bare feet slapping on threadbare carpet. "What the bloody hell?" he asked.

"Mary's taken Peer," Holly said tonelessly, as if to convince herself.

"Who?" Gerald stared at the birds lining his picture rail and shelves like animated Toby jugs: sparrows, tits, siskins, finches of all sorts and several tail-wagging wrens. His shirt was buttoned unevenly. He looked older than he had earlier, his hair grayer, his eyes more pale.

"What do we do?" Holly asked. She looked at Paul. Her look was different from before they had made love. Her cheeks were still flushed with the effort of not making a noise.

"I don't like these birds in here," Paul said. "Let's try to shoo them out." They sat staring at him. Their heads moved with rapid jerks, like a bad stop-motion animation.

"Don't open the door again," Holly said. "Please. We don't know what will come in next. Let's just wait here until it's all over. Just wait . . ."

Paul went to speak but held back. He knew that she knew it was never going to be all over. There must be survivors everywhere, begging phone lines for rescue, huddled in small groups trying to decide what to do, arguing about who was in charge, making friends, losing lovers. All waiting for a rescue that would never come.

He cradled the shotgun in the crook of his elbow so that the barrel pointed at the floor. He thought briefly about firing at the birds, but how many could he kill with two shots? Five? Leaving dozens more agitated and angered, beaks sharp and quick. Some of them had changed, too. A blue tit had turned green. A woodpecker had three beaks. A sparrow had bulging pustules on either side of its beak. They reminded Paul of poison sacs on a snake.

"Gerald," he said, "can we go into the other room? I think we need to shut the door to this one and stay out. I don't know how long—"

"Not the other room," Gerald said. "Nope, I can't have strangers in there. Patty wouldn't like it. Haven't dusted in there for months; she'd never be having with that."

"Who's Patty, Gerald?" Holly asked.

"Patty. My wife. Patty."

Holly glanced at Paul, but he shook his head slightly.

"Upstairs, then," Paul said. "Is there any way out of the house from upstairs?"

"No doors upstairs," Gerald said, as if explaining to a small child.

"A window onto a roof," Paul said. "Anything. Gerald, we have to get away from this room and leave ourselves a way out of the house. Holly, bag up a bit of food from the table. I'll get some stuff from the fridge. Say if you see our feathered friends doing something different."

"That's all I have seen lately," she said. There was a carrier bag already half full on the table, and she only had to throw in a loaf of bread to fill it. She tied the handles together and started filling another. She tried to turn her attention away from the birds, but they were always at the periphery, watching her from the shadowed ceiling, emotionless and full of menace. They were silent, too. Somehow that was worse.

Paul went to the fridge and took out milk, cheese and a chunk of ham. He was shaking and confused, and he wanted more than anything to curl up and go to sleep. Tiredness was held at bay for now by the adrenaline flooding his system, but soon he would come down with a crash. How long did they have left? he kept thinking. How long before they all had to sleep? He'd survived his dreams once; he was certain he would not be so lucky a second time. The terrible idea came that they were all living on borrowed time anyway, and escaping, evading and running from death were only delaying the inevitable outcome of these dreadful couple of days. Wherever Blane had gone he was obviously losing it, involved in some strange personal fantasy that bled to those around him via his beliefs and his peculiar, indefinable charisma. He would not help them. Paul had already begun to doubt that they would ever see him again. Still, he had made a promise. They would go to meet Blane, however inconceivable it was that he would make it.

And if Blane did meet this mystery woman whom he thought had some hand in what was happening to them all, what then?

He leaned his forehead against the fridge door, breathing in the chilled air to calm his feverish thoughts. Over the last hour he had made love, faced death and seen a madwoman kidnapping someone he felt partly responsible for. At least if he did only have hours to live, he was making the most of them.

He giggled, surprised and perturbed at the same time.

"What?" Holly said.

Paul shook his head. "This is all mad," he said, summing everything up in one word and seeing Holly's understanding. She shrugged, nodded and continued to pack food.

"What are we doing?" Gerald asked.

"Following them."

"But the cows need milking. They're late already,

poor beggars must be hurting. And the fence in the
east field has been broken, been telling Patty I'll fix
it for ages. Years."

Paul went to Gerald and put his hand on the
man's shoulder. "We've got to leave the farm. To
help Peer, if we can, and to meet Blane. Every second that passes, Mary's taken her farther away."

"But the cows," Gerald said. "I didn't shoot them
all, you know."

"I'm sure they wouldn't let you milk them if you
wanted to," Paul said. Gerald glared at him, looking ready to launch a fist, but he started to cry instead. The tears looked out of place on his old face.
He turned and stalked back upstairs.

"You don't really think we can catch them, do
you?" Holly asked.

"We owe it to Peer to try."

"She's weird, anyway. She was with Mary when
we met her; why not let them go off together?"

"I don't think Peer had really decided to go off
with her, do you?"

Holly did not answer.

Soon they had three bags filled with food. Still
keeping one eye on the birds, they backed out of
the kitchen and shut the door. They were in the
hallway, the stairs behind them and a closed door
on their left. To their right, another door leading
outside. They would have to walk around the side
of the house and across the yard to get to the car,
a trip neither of them was relishing. As Gerald said,
he had not shot all of the cows. Sometimes, they
could still hear furtive movements from the milking
shed.

"I'll get Gerald," Paul said.

"No. I'll go. I think you just offended him."

Paul smiled at Holly and pecked her on the cheek. They hugged in the hallway for a while, both taking immense comfort from the contact and the knowledge that they were helping each other.

"Why couldn't I have found you years ago?" Holly said. She expected no answer, and received none.

She hurried upstairs, softly calling to Gerald until she heard him moving around in his room. She tapped on the door and waited until she heard his grumbled reply before going in.

He was sitting on his bed, his head in his hands. On the table next to the bed stood a photo of a gray-haired, smiling woman. Patty.

"Are you coming with us, Gerald?" Holly said. "We want you to. We can all help each other."

"You expect me to, don't you?" he said. He looked up at Holly, determined but not unkind. "Why would I ever want to leave this place? Patty and I ran this farm for over forty years, you know. Never made much of a profit, but we made a living, a life for ourselves. We were more than happy with that. Today, I killed my animals. I destroyed my life. To help you. No, I don't think I'm going with you."

"You know you can't sleep—"

"I can do what I damned well want in my own house," he said. He rubbed callused hands across his face, and Holly heard the rasping of dry skin.

"Are you sure, Gerald?" Holly asked, but she already knew that they had lost him.

He looked up at her again, his expression softer

now. "Just go," he said. "Please. I'm an old man."
As if that explained everything.

"Thank you, Gerald. Take care."

Downstairs, Holly shook her head at Paul. He
went to go up himself, but she held his arm. "We've
got to go if you want to catch up with them," she
said. "They've been gone five minutes already.
We've probably lost them as it is."

Outside the air was warm and dry as the sun
began its long journey earthward. The farmyard
was silent. It only took them a minute to reach the
car, but it seemed longer. Breath held, eyes wide,
they expected an attack at any second. Fear
stretches time.

As the Mondeo engine came to life a flock of
birds appeared from behind the barn and swooped
low across the sky, alighting on the farmhouse roof.
They could see Gerald's face in the upstairs window, and he raised a hand as they pulled away.
Holly was crying. Paul was silent. The land
watched them leave.

Paul motored along the farm lane, confident that
they would not meet any traffic coming from the
opposite direction, taking blind corners at a suicidal
speed. The puddles were still cloudy from the disturbance of the Mini's wheels. Holly held on to the
hand grip above the door and pressed herself back
into the seat, gritting her teeth as the car hopped
and jumped from one pothole to the next. The car's
suspension rattled and screamed. The exhaust
screeched painfully as it struck the ground.

Around the final corner before the main road
there were several rabbits standing in the lane.

Their ears drooped arrogantly. Their eyelids were half shut, as if regarding the world for the first time with an uncanny, unnatural intelligence. One of them was gnawing at a mess in the mud, something still oozing blood. They stared at the car but did not move, obviously expecting it to stop for them.

"Paul," Holly said, but she knew he was not stopping. She did not look in the mirror once they had passed.

At the junction Paul instinctively braked with the car pointing left. He looked at Holly and shrugged. She opened the door and jumped from the car.

"Holly!"

"Hang on." She ran along the verge for a few feet, bent at the waist, examining the tarmac. Then she turned and ran back, leaped into the car and pointed left.

Paul gunned the engine and winced as the tires howled before gripping the road and launching them forward. "What was on the road? Blood?"

Holly nodded. "Rabbit stew."

They were traveling through a foreign country. They had been in the farmhouse for less than a day, but in that time things had been changing. Not only did the landscape itself feel loaded with antagonism, but it was promoting change in the creatures living upon it. Hillsides seemed rougher, ridges sharper, hedgerows and clumps of trees larger and able to hide more. But nothing was hidden because now, with humankind undergoing its own struggle, there was no longer anything to hide from.

A heron flew majestically across the road ahead of them, carrying a small black lamb in massive, incongruous claws. The lamb struggled, but to no avail. The heron seemed unperturbed by the extra weight. Paul wondered whether it even recognized the change it had gone through.

"We're being watched," Holly said, summing up the feeling perfectly. Paul knew that even if the heron was not overtly aware of its change, its behavior had altered in accordance with the atmosphere of everything around it. Humankind had been excluded. For Paul, the countryside no longer felt like home. He was an invader, an alien in a foreign land where he did not know the customs, the laws and, least of all, the dialect.

Over the years he had discerned a language of the land. Simple things like whether cows faced in the same direction, the patterns a flock of sheep would make in a field—spread out or clustered together—were often omens for other things, like weather or behavior. People would have mocked him, he knew, but he was certain that he had begun to perceive a pattern in things. He was still an amateur, and he knew that it would take a dozen lifetimes to become fluent.

Now, he was strictly *no comprende* once more. And he had the horrible feeling that he was being talked about in ways he could never understand.

"Paul, you're doing ninety," Holly said.

Paul glanced at the speedometer and eased his foot back slightly. It was a snaking road, and while he hardly expected to meet anything coming from the opposite direction, there were still unknown bends and trees that could be their undoing.

"What do we do when we catch up with them?" Holly asked, verbalizing something that had been at the back of Paul's mind ever since they left the farmyard.

"Decide when we do?" he said lamely.

They passed a small turning and Paul braked, slewing the car across the road. "Have a quick look," he said.

Holly ran back to the junction, bent low and looked at a puddle at the head of the narrow road. Then she jumped back in surprise, ran to the car and slammed the door, breathing heavily.

"What?"

"They didn't go that way."

Paul drove onward. "What was in the puddle?"

"Water."

He glanced at Holly with a smile ready, but she was staring straight ahead, ashen-faced and moist-eyed. "Holly?"

She shook her head.

They drove that way for twenty minutes, stopping occasionally at side roads to see whether there were any clues as to which direction Mary and Peer had taken. It was mostly Paul who checked. Holly was quiet and contemplative but kept telling Paul there was nothing wrong.

At a junction with a dual carriageway, Paul turned left. Holly did not argue, though she had a feeling he was right. A feeling she did not like, because it was verging on a certainty, and there was no way she could know. Was there?

She had seen her reflection in the puddle. It was her, but it was someone else as well. Like a face from the history books, she recognized her own features as those of someone important. It was not ego, not personal. She had stared into the eyes of someone destined for greatness. In a way, she felt she had glimpsed herself weeks or months in the future. And it terrified her.

In truth, she felt different anyway. Altered, added to. She sensed a responsibility dawning that she could not put a name to, but that felt spectacularly important to her and those around her. It was a niggle in her chest, but she was not sure whether it was physical. A screen in her mind, drawn back to reveal something she still could not properly discern, but she was unsure as to its reality. Perhaps she really did not want to believe.

For want of a better name, she called it mother's intuition.

Chapter Thirty

The Next Catastrophe

"Remember when we used to run through the woods?" Fay said. "Swim in the oceans? Sprint across the savannah?" She sighed. "They were good times. Then you left me."

"No," Blane said, "I don't." But he did. Not whole memories, but fragments: the feel of rough grass underfoot, but no sight or smells associated with it; the tang of saltwater on his tongue, but no recollection of movement or pressure. Her laughter, too, bright and carefree; but he could not correlate it with this thing before him. This thing with leathery skin, protruding bones, razor teeth and slashed lips.

"I planned so much for today," Fay said. "I was going to tell you everything, in such a wonderful way. Call it revenge, or spite. Or unrequited love. You were going to suffer. You still will, maybe, but it will be your own suffering. Not that visited upon you by me. I think, maybe, I'm too far gone for that."

"You're dying."

Fay laughed, an echo of the noise he had heard while holding the dead deer in his arms. "I've been dying for decades," she said. "Don't you remember? Don't you remember telling me, all those times, that I had to do something about it?"

"No," Blane said, "I don't." But again there was something there, a third-hand memory of what she was alluding to, like vague impressions of pages read years ago and long since forgotten; a feeling, rather than a memory. And perhaps it was best left that way. If remembering would make him like Fay . . .

Fay let go of the chains and slid slowly down the wall. Now that he was here before her, confused but slowly recalling his past, she had become so tired. Not only tired but useless, shallow. Ashamed. A century ago she could have pitied herself for what she was doing. Now there was no pity left, only hate. But she had suffered. All these years, shunned by nature, welcomed only by the mistakes inherent therein . . . she was a mistake. A blot on the landscape. The runt of the litter. Destined, she knew, to survive no longer. Her resilience had been through anger, not strength, and that anger was fast waning.

Now, with Blane here, she was his little sister once more.

"Why did you do this?" he asked. "How did you do this? How many people are dead?"

"You're blaming me? You haven't remembered as much as I thought." She rested her hands on her knees and her head against the wall, closed her eyes. How easy to slip away now, to let the world finally have its way. But then she would be wronged, and the last ten years had been about righting that wrong. It would take minutes to finish it, and she would only be cheating herself by ghosting away now.

"Leave," she said to Gabrielle. The mutilated woman turned and slid the door shut behind her. They were alone in the slaughterhouse, Fay and Blane.

Blane was confused. Not only by what was happening now, but by what had happened in the past. Memories swirled in his head like jigsaw pieces in a hurricane, and he strove to grasp them, piece by piece. But at the moment the winds were too strong, the forces set against him too powerful. Fay, it seemed, still held his history in her grasp.

"Fay," he said, "tell me."

She opened her eyes. "Oh, Blane," she said, "you really don't want to know."

He sat opposite her, crossing his legs, keeping eye contact. Everything felt replayed, life on a continuous loop.

"How often have we sat like this?" she said.

"Often?" Blane said, a question and a statement.

"There was one time," Fay mused, casting her gaze at the corrugated ceiling, "in Austria, in the mountains. Before the tourists had found the place—before people set their scars on the land—when we ran for days. The snows melted in our wake, because we willed it so. The lakes filled and splashed with the jumping of mating fish. Hillsides were awash with flowers, like colors splashed from an artist's brush. Do you remember, brother?"

Blane shook his head but felt the cool kiss of snow on his heels, saw the staggered teeth of mountains bringing the horizon in close.

"There were goats and birds, and nature ran wild. *We* ran wild." She closed her eyes and sighed, and for the first time in years she thought of those times without bitterness. She was excluded, but she had lived them, she had been there. They were her memories as much as his, however much she had changed. "We followed a stream down into a valley, came across a herd of deer and let them run with us. They left us soon after, because they could smell what we could smell. Sulfur in the air. Blood. Violence, not overt, but inherent in the senses of nature."

With each description, Blane felt some of what Fay was saying. He wondered whether she was mesmerizing him, but the memories must have been his; they were so personal, so pure.

"They were mining," she said. "We sat and watched them for days, tunneling into the ground, ripping out the Earth's innards, dumping them on the surface like useless organs. We both knew what it meant, because we had been seeing it for ages. It was a foretaste of what was to come, the raping of the world. You shrugged and said it was progress, humankind were destined to do so, nature would make allowances. I hated it, even then. Hate tears you apart, brother.

"We watched for a while, then left. But it stayed

with me for years, that image. It was only on a small scale, but to nature scale is nothing. Intent and progress are more important, not incidental moments in history. From that moment on, I think I was doomed to this. And so were you, because you're my brother."

"I don't remember parents," Blane said. "I don't remember childhood. I don't remember . . . learning."

Fay smiled. "We're always learning."

"When I saw you days ago, you'd killed. As a message to me, you'd killed people. Why? Why do all this?"

Fay glanced away, her gaze alighting on dangling chains, once used to hold cattle while their brains were pulped or their throats slit, their meat ground down and fed to the masses while their hides were cured and worn as status symbols and fashion. "Everyone is dying anyway," she said, "and I'm jealous. I'm a cruel and jealous god."

"You're no god," Blane said.

Fay shrugged her bony shoulders. "No, of course not. If I were, I would have done all this ages ago. And I would have left no chance."

"I still don't understand," Blane said. "These things you're talking about . . . some of them I think I have memories of. But I don't trust them, because I don't trust myself. I have no memory, as far as I can make out. No past. I just sit in a wood, watching things. I don't know why you're doing this. I don't know what's going on."

"But you think maybe you should, don't you?"

Blane nodded. "I came to find you because I felt

I had to. I thought you'd know what was happening."

The evil glint returned to Fay's sad eyes. "Irony fucks us in the arse once again," she said. "I know everything that's going on, because I'm no longer part of it. You . . . you're stuck in the middle, and you know nothing. Sweet irony. Who said God hasn't got a sense of humor?"

"I don't believe in God," Blane said.

Fay laughed. A giggle at first, then racking coughs that seemed to cause her pain. "Blane," she said, "brother, how I love you and hate you so. You have to believe in God. You're part of It."

She continued laughing, and Blane leaned back on his arms and stared at the ceiling. He closed his eyes. He wanted to sleep.

"What's your secret?" he said, nodding at the chains disappearing into her mouth.

Fay's expression turned sour. "Proof," she said. "Something to make you believe. But not yet. I promised myself I'd take great pleasure in telling you all this, seeing your reaction. Your horror. Now, I'm not so sure."

"What? You're not going to tell me, or you won't take pleasure?"

"I'll tell you. I have to. To not tell you would be the worst torture, and . . . well, you're my brother. I hate you, Blane, but we were made to love each other. However much I try to convince myself that I've moved on from that, I'm still basically how nature made me."

"So tell me."

"I'll tell you," she said. "I'll tell you now. But you're not going to like it."

*   *   *

Outside, for a time, things paused. Gabrielle and the rest of the lidless hid away in their adopted homes, glaring at the walls, yearning sleep. The air turned heavy, like the atmosphere before a storm.

Birds roosted at an unnatural time. Insects crawled beneath rocks. The fish in the stream aimed their noses at the current and floated, still.

It was a held breath, a paused step, a space between heartbeats. The world balanced on the blade of a knife, teetering on the edge with mysteries awaiting on both sides. The blade was keen and already slicing into things. More pain was promised soon.

"We're so very old, Blane. We have control, you and I. We're the ideas of nature, the basic forms of male and female. The controlling influences. Only . . . I went mad. I saw what humans were doing to the world, and I couldn't stand it, and I went mad. I have been for a long time. I went mad, and you couldn't stand it, and you went mad too, in your own way.

"But while I was mad and bad, you were just ruined. So nature tucked you away in a wood somewhere, where you could still be what you are, and me . . . it disowned. I'm homeless, Blane. I've been kicked out of our family home, and you're running it all by yourself.

"You've forgotten so much. But over time, you'll remember it."

"Is that why all this is happening?" Blane said, aghast. "You're destroying everything because of what humankind has done? Surely that cannot be."

"No," Fay said, shaking her head and rattling her chains. "No, not at all. For a start, things are changing, not being destroyed. Nature would never commit suicide, just alter itself to suit. Secondly, I'm not doing anything. It's all down to you, Blane. You're the powerful one. You're the cause of everything. It's all coming from you. Ironic, really. All this death, and you don't even know what you're doing."

This was the moment she had been waiting for, the time when she revealed to him what he had done. She wanted to see him rave and cry. She wanted to revel in his sudden, terrible knowledge. But in the end telling him was as painful as the last ten years had been for her. It was an anticlimax, in a way.

"No," he said, "I don't believe you. You're planting this in my mind. I didn't cause all this. I can't have. I wouldn't."

"Nature discarded me," Fay said, "and it was on the point of losing you. Without you, it would be chaos. It needs a balance, and you and I were it. Losing me disturbed it, and losing you as well would have killed it. It had to even the field, and you had to come back. Now you're back. And the field is evening up nicely."

"Even the field? What, by killing everyone?"

"Why not? Everyone is the cause of what's happened, in a way. Humankind is the next catastrophe. I couldn't help hating it, but I was pushed to one side. Every breath you take, Blane, kills another million people. Humanity has had its day." Fay's smile went from vicious to sad, stretching her face into patterns of compassion it was no longer used to. She suddenly felt so ill now that her defenses were down. She realized that she had been dying for a decade; she just hadn't known it.

Blane stood and paced the room, feeling a weakness of the spirit but a surprising strength of the body, channeling in through his feet, enlivening tired muscles and aching bones. He was suddenly plugged in. "I don't believe you," he said, but memories were crowding to be noticed. He tried to turn away from them, but whichever direction he looked in they were there, struggling to be let loose, aching to reveal the awful truth of what Fay was saying. The truth that, Blane knew, he would have to come to terms with soon.

"I'll prove it to you," Fay said weakly. She stood up slowly, her movements pained. As she bent down and placed her hands on her knees, she stared to cough. She clenched and unclenched her stomach muscles, feeling movement in her guts, a keen squirming as something began its journey back into the open for the second and last time.

Fay knew what she was doing. She knew that once revealed, her secret would destroy her and also destroy Peer. Its revelation would send a message to Mary, and she would do away with the bitch. The poor bitch. But if Fay couldn't have Blane back, no one could. She did not regret it, she told herself. It was what she wanted. To die now would be to finish what had begun ten years ago, an inevitable turn of events that Fay was fully at peace with. Suffering would end. The torture of her knowledge would end. Peer would die.

Everything was turning out just as she had planned.

Now there was one more pain to go through. A twisted birth from a body that should never have given birth. A turning inside out of history, a revelation of something hidden for eons.

One more pain.

Blood began to dribble from her mouth; Fay kept coughing. She had known worse. Mental anguish was far more dreadful than physical discomfort. Besides, she was perfect. Nature had made her that way. She grabbed the chains and pulled, hauling the lump up into her throat, letting it drop to the floor in a splash of blood and mucus and vomit.

The thing looked alive, but was quite plainly dead. Fay ripped the chains from the bolts in her skull, stumbled back and leaned against the wall. Blood ran from her wounds, much faster than it should have. Fleeing someone already resigned to death.

"Blane," she croaked, "nature hates a vacuum. What have I done!" She looked truly wretched, blood doing little to hide her expression. "What have I done!"

"What have you done?" Blane asked, staring at the thing on the floor.

"Put her life at risk," Fay said sadly. "Oh, I've ruined everything."

The thing was shriveled and ancient, a mummified lump of flesh. "What's that?" Blane asked.

"Our final arrogance . . . our child. Our belief that we could put things right. Oh my brother, my twin, my lover, what have I done?"

"We're twins . . ."

"Of course." Fay sighed. Everything was receding. "Connected so closely. Bound together in nature's womb. Great ideas." Her senses began to fade, and she took one final look at their mummified child before she closed her eyes. "How could we have believed that such a thing would ever be allowed . . ."

And then she fell to the floor and died.

Chapter Thirty-one

The Marked Time

Mary's heart stammered. She felt queasy and weak. She saw Fay's face for an instant; androgynous and worn by life; then beautiful, shining with an inner power few could doubt and none could match.

Something obscured the image, something fleshy and fluid, warm and dead at the same time.

Then nothing.

"Fay!" Mary shouted, but now she could not recall the face of her mistress. It was hidden from her just as true happiness was hidden, always had been hidden, always would be. "No, Fay, no!" she cried, willing her memories back, shaking her head and punching the dashboard in frustration. Dark things were within her, screaming at her, scenes of unbelievable torment splaying themselves across the landscape of her imagination as she tried to find Fay's face once again: pains Fay had endured; terrors she had faced and mastered; dreadful deeds she had done.

Mary screamed again, but this time it was for herself. These images were beyond her comprehension, and all the more horrifying because of that.

Peer let the car coast. Mindful of the raving woman next to her, even more aware of the stocky dog on her lap, she applied gentle pressure to the brake. Mary's sudden screaming made Peer want to scream, too, the shock sending her stomach into gymnastic spasms. Spike turned his head and casually watched his mistress.

Peer tried to observe Mary without turning her head and attracting attention. She moved her right hand and began to gently stroke Spike's left flank, scratching under his ribs until he growled in gentle contentment.

Mary screamed, kicked, elbowed the door window again and again until it ghosted obscure under the impact. Fay had gone, either left her or taken from her, and if ever the time was right, it was now. There would be no signal, there would be no message to spur her on. It was now. She stopped thrashing and spun on Peer.

"Kill the bitch, Spike!" she said, voice dripping venom. "Kill! Rip out her fucking throat and . . ." But the bitch was stroking the dog, petting him, and the stupid mutt was acting like a teddy bear. After all she'd done for him. After letting him feed on the remains of the bastards who'd beaten her and ignored her and hated her. "Spike," she said, trying to inject a note of command into her voice, "kill her! Bite!"

"The dog won't do me any harm," Peer said. She scratched at the tattered ear, and Spike drooled happily.

Mary tried to talk, but she was speechless. Now was the time! She knew it, she felt it, she saw it in the dreadful visions that had appeared unbidden in her mind's eye. Her commitment to Fay, her promise, must not be broken, because it was her meaning and her mission. To deny that would make her survival pointless; it was the thing she had been saved to do. Fay had made that quite clear.

To find Fay again—to regain Fay's image into her heart—she must do her bidding.

"Well," Mary said, smiling, trying to sound calm, hoping her manner would disarm Peer, "I wouldn't really want him to." She reached out and patted Spike's head. The dog began to pant. She punched Peer in the face, using all her wiry strength to smash the back of her fist into the bitch's nose.

Spike growled. Peer felt for the door handle, unable to see anything through the pink haze of pain that had exploded behind her eyes. She felt winded even though she had been hit in the face. Her head was one big agony. Salty fluid dribbled down across her lips, blood diluted by tears.

She felt another blow to her head, this time followed by white-hot lines of pain as nails raked ragged paths in her skin. She had the overwhelming sensation that her heart had adjourned to her head, because there was a pumping, pulping throb coming from within and around her skull and blood seemed to be filling her eyes. More blows, more scratches, fingers probing at her throat, then the dog's weight left her lap and she heard a shout.

In the blindness of pain, when sensations were ambiguous mimics of the truth, Peer thought she heard the car doors opening. Warm blood cooled. Fresh air made her retch.

There was a growl, then another; one canine, one human.

Shouts. Screams.

The thump of bodies against metal.

The explosion of a gun.

A gurgling exclamation of pain, a scream dying in rent flesh.

Pounding footsteps.

Confused and terrified—not knowing if she would ever wake up again, or if a dreamed fall would crush her to pieces—Peer could not prevent her slide into unconsciousness.

Chapter Thirty-two

Lost Treasures

With Fay's death came knowledge. Acceptance of her words, and their expansion into others. A million ideas flooded Blane's mind, and at first he was terrified that they would drive him mad. But he knew he had been built this way, to think these things, to see these images; if ever madness had threatened it must have been during the last ten years. Ten years spent in a vacuum. Nature abhors a vacuum.

Put her life at risk.

Blane knew who she had meant. Peer was in danger because she was different. Now Blane could recognize that she was as he had been before today, a confused harborer of nature and secret things. But whereas he had always been that way, Peer was new. She would be scared. She would be confused. And somehow, Fay had put her at risk.

Blane began to cry. He had found and lost a sister in one day; an astounding revelation and then a terrible bereavement. He knelt next to Fay's corpse and gently ran his fingertips across the leathery skin of her forehead. He had been with her forever and now she was gone. However accursed she had become, he forgave her, because even nature was not perfect. He damned it for allowing her to evolve into this bitter creature, for creating something with such an in-built flaw.

But he did not know whether he could forgive himself. He looked at the fetus but could not touch it. *My child,* he thought, but it was obvious it had always been destined for this. *Our final arrogance . . .*

He, too, had been at fault. Now, knowing the truth, he felt whole again. He felt reborn.

Fay's blood had already dried to a crisp. Her long hair had started to drift from her scalp, like leaves in autumn. Blane backed away to the door, fearful that the thing she had brought out of her would begin to squirm and live. But it was as dead as she. The chains hooked into it had already begun to rust.

He bumped into the door, feeling strong for the first time in years but unable to use that strength to haul it open. To leave this place would be to move on, and for a moment he did not want that. For a brief instant he wished he could die, too, to find his sister wherever she had gone. He felt nature rebelling at this thought, but he let it. It had kept him locked away in the prison of his own mind for so long, it could wait another minute while he harbored impossible fantasies. He put his hands to his temples, feeling ghost pains there in sympathy with his twin, a phantom madness threatening to spill from her into him. And what then? If he, too, went insane, what then for the world? For those who had survived the cataclysm?

The cataclysm he had caused.

Her revelation to him that he was the focus of this change was a heavy truth, barely digestible, hardly perceived. It was too awful to contemplate, but its reality was leaking slowly into his awareness, the drips of an intravenous nightmare. It was another cruel irony forced upon him. But irony was a human conceit. If he was the male idea of nature, then he was far more than human. He was far more than anything.

As Fay had said, he was a part of God. Though today, he felt more akin to the devil.

The sun was stagnant. The air was heavy and thick, the village quiet. There were no signs of the lidless.

Blane looked out upon a brand new world. Truth cast conjecture aside and painted facts in a new, starker color. The pavement here was cracked and crazed by years of neglect, hardy weeds poking their heads through from where birds had dropped them or shat them: Blane felt responsible. Opposite where he stood there was an old timber archway into a back garden. Spiderwebs hung heavy and lumped with prey, the spider a fat presence in the corner: it was Blane's spider.

Cirrus clouds strung out high in the atmosphere, parodying the aircraft trails that would not taint the sky again: Blane's clouds, Blane's sky. Hours earlier he had hardly felt a part of the world. He had been excluded, remote. Now, the world was a part of him.

He sighed.

A sigh of relief.

Nature let go its held breath.

The old slaughterhouse disintegrated. Masonry burst up and out, raining down around Blane and forcing him to the ground. Sheets of corrugated metal leaped skyward, then spun slowly down. Rust had made their edges ragged and sharp. The ground below him leaped and punched him in the chest and stomach, throwing him into the air to land awkwardly on his left side. He gasped, felt dreadful pain, and wondered if he must now suffer the torment he and Fay had brought onto the world through their waywardness. Worse still, would he now be victim of the ruin that had overcome Fay?

A ripple of destruction spread out from the site of Fay's death. It passed through the village, a wave of sound, power, anger. Buildings collapsed, trees split down the middle, streambeds cracked and drained their contents into hidden depths. Roads waved and split, the church tower tumbled, its bell ringing for the final, unheeded call to worship. The air was suddenly filled with birds escaping the tumult, but the ripple passed through the air as well. Fluttering shapes tumbled after the shockwave, others spinning through the disturbed air, disorientated and forever changed.

Blane felt and heard the destruction spreading out. Perhaps it was nature's grief at the death of its rebellious child. Maybe it was his own.

Or maybe it was Fay's soul fleeing her weak body, casting one last angry look across an altered world that she had come to resent so much.

The sounds of chaos receded into the distance. Bricks still tumbled, tiles slid off roofs, those buildings that had been completely demolished settled into their final resting pyres with creaks and groans. Blane stood unsteadily, hoping that Fay had not left any more surprises.

"Where is she? What have you done to her?" Gabrielle emerged unsteadily from behind the wooden arch, several more of the lidless following close behind. Blane did not feel scared; he felt tired.

"Fay died," he said.

"You killed her!" If Gabrielle could have blinked away her tears, she would have.

"She died," Blane said again, unwilling to explain the intricacies of his sister's life and death to this wasted person. "Now you can go."

Gabrielle was shaking, eyes crying blood once more. She had chewed her lips raw with the pain. Her short dress was an incongruous statement of the past, a wedding dress on a zombie. "She was our only hope," she hissed.

"She never had any hope," Blane replied, "she can never have been one." He felt tears welling in his eyes but knew that they would do no good. His sadness was nature's sadness.

"I should make you join her." The lidless behind Gabrielle pushed forward and stood beside her, faces wracked with agony.

"Fay wanted to die," Blane said. "She was ready to die. She's been dying for a long time. She only wanted to see me before, then . . ."

Gabrielle glanced over Blane's shoulder at the ruin of the slaughterhouse.

"Listen," he said, "there's another like Fay, as special as her. But she's in danger, too, now, and I have to reach her before something dreadful happens."

"But who have we got to follow now?"

Blane sighed. They were doomed, and they knew it. They were unfit, and in this new world only the very fittest would survive. Already they were consigned to the past. Their wounds were constantly open, untreated, exposed to the elements, inviting infection. Fay had used them. They still loved her for it, and he could see no way to disabuse them of the fact that she had been their leader. Their messiah.

"You decide," he said, "I'm leaving."

He started back along the path, treading on loose ground disturbed by Fay's death. His feet crunched on gravel and sucked at freshly turned mud. He could almost hear the indecision in those behind him, but he did not turn. In a way he had created these people, but he felt more sorry for the dead magpie at his feet than the tortured souls who had damaged themselves so. He saw a cat with two heads urging its body in opposite directions at the same time and felt a lump in his throat. But when Gabrielle called after him, her voice now devoid of anger, full of wretchedness, asking him what were they to do now? ... who do they worship now? ... he felt nothing.

Soon he was back in the square. It was a far different place to that he had left hours before. The stream's course had been diverted by a change in the topography, and now it was in the process of flooding the square and surrounding streets. Tiny black fish flapped their last amid low shrubs, trustingly following the course of the waters.

Blane was responsible.

The question, *Why now?* never entered his mind. Why anytime?

He knew what he had in his mind, his vastly expanded mind, but he was terrified to view it. The memories and knowledge had always been there, of course, but hidden away like him. Shoved into a dark corner where they could do no harm, traces of them haunting his darkest hours over the last ten years and driving him to distraction and disaffection. It was as if they had been piled behind a weak door and the keyhole left open, allowing a dribble of their vastness out at a time. Now that door was smashed from its hinges, and like a man among lost treasures, Blane was wading into the new, dark room. But along with the treasure were skeletons, and next to the skeletons were the swords by which they had died. Pride; anger; hate.

He would have to be careful.

As Blane walked back through the village, a memory began to form. A South American settlement centuries ago, buildings burned or smashed, bodies already merging into the hard ground, crops looted and pulled and left out to die in the sun. Needless murder in a slaughter where children were considered acceptable targets. Babies, swung against trees. Left in a pile.

He recalled the disgust he had felt, but also the sense that he could do nothing about it. He was unable to act in any matter, existing as he did as a model more than an overseer, a cast for the imperfect creations he saw killing each other and slowly raping the world.

Fay's reaction, too. Even then she had been changing, Blane realized. Preparing herself, either consciously or subconsciously, for the shift that would eventually possess her.

Another memory . . . Fay screaming at the world as she gave birth to a dead thing . . . his own madness driving him away, abandoning her to the fate that had overcome her . . . But he closed his eyes and shoved the memory inside. That was for later.

The stone bridge had fallen into the stream, its back broken. Blane did not hesitate to wade through the waters. As he emerged onto the other bank something dived at him from above, flapping and screeching murderous threats. He flinched, but at the last minute the bird veered away and snatched a small fish from the upset waters. He watched it move away across the ruined village. For a moment he wished it had attacked him. At least then he would have felt real.

Chapter Thirty-three

Taking Account

The sunlight felt fresh on Holly's skin. It fingered through her eyelids, urging her to open them and accept its touch, but they were all that shielded her from the sight of reality. She was unsure whether or not she really wanted to see it.

Every part of her body tingled, from the underside of her toes to her hairline. Her senses seemed sharper; either that or the smells, sounds and tastes of nature had intensified directly after the earthquake. She opened her eyes and sat up. The tremor had flipped the Mini over onto its side, exposing its rusting underside. Oil dripped like thick black blood. Somehow she had been thrown clear. "Paul," she called, but she knew he could not answer. Gingerly, she touched the side of her head. Her hand came away sticky with blood, speckled with grains of tarmac like black fleas. She felt dizzy, hardly able to sit up let alone stand. So she crawled to where Paul lay slumped on the grass verge—hand holding his throat as if strangling himself—and saw that he was dead. Blood stuck his hand to his skin. The worst of the bite marks were hidden.

Spike lay farther along the road. Paul had shot the dog as it hung from his throat, blowing its body away with a mouthful of his neck in its spasming jaws. The dog had crawled while it was dying, leaving a smear of itself across the road like an exclamation mark. It had crawled the same way its mistress had fled.

Peer sat farther along the verge, rocking slowly back and forth, hands clasped in front of her. She did not appear to notice the blood caking her lower face. She did not seem aware of anything.

"Paul," Holly whispered. "Paul. Paul."

There was a sudden flurry of activity from above. A flock of birds appeared, flying low across a field and lifting over the hedges and the road. Their wings flapped in complete unison, changes of direction instantaneous, as if they were separate facets of the same consciousness.

Holly's wounds from the service station were still sore and itching. She went to cry out, but then the birds disappeared into the distance, mumbling to themselves about how much things had changed.

She lay down next to Paul. The stimulation of her senses continued. She could smell heather, though she did not know how near they were to the moors. She could hear a heartbeat; she placed her head against Paul's chest in excitement, but all was still. She tried to discern whether it was her own heart beating, or another, or some other pulsing noise, like the life sign of the land. She rolled onto her back and still heard it. It was a comforting sound, almost soporific, an invisible metronome driving strange ideas into her head and encouraging her to accept them.

She felt a sudden affection for Peer, poor battered Peer, but it was a motherly love. Peer remained sitting on the verge, rocking to an unseen rhythm. "Peer," Holly said when she reached her. "It's all right, love. Mary's gone away. Things are different now."

She finally stood up and looked around, and saw just how right she was. A clump of trees in a nearby field sprouted huge flowers, waving fronds whipping at the air and snatching insects from flight. Birds larked in a fresh new sky. A gang of blue tits, twice their normal size, swooped down and pecked a frantic jay to death before eating it. Rough, but nature. Even the sky seemed different; a clearer blue, with higher clouds diffused gold by the sun.

Holly sat next to Peer and put a comforting arm around her shoulders. The shocked woman stopped rocking at once and leaned against her. They sat there for a long time, exhausted, Holly vaguely aware that they should be moving in case Mary came back. She stared at Paul's corpse, a heavy sadness weighing on her heart like iced rain.

The day carried on around them, ignoring them at last.

By the time Holly realized that Peer was asleep, she, too, was on the verge. A warning rang urgently in her mind, but it was muffled by tiredness and shock, and another feeling altogether: a sense of belonging.

Leaning together, Holly and Peer sat with their eyes closed, their breath slow and deep.

A fox trotted along the road in front of them. It sniffed at Paul's corpse and passed it by. Its auburn pelt was speckled with spots of gold.

The sky is a deep blue, a color richer than she has ever seen. It looks so solid that, for a moment, she is afraid that it may fall in upon her and crush her. Fat clouds bobble its pureness. The sun is a bright button high overhead.

The field around her is sad, in pain. Its crop droops, trying to bury itself in the sick earth from whence it came. The seed is rotten. Hedgerows divide the fields like the spines of dead behemoths, trees slump in secretive clumps, farm machinery rusts itself back into the ground.

When she was here before, this place was in upheaval. Now the ruin has been and gone, leaving behind this changed, dead land. But ahead of her there is a door, and she realizes that this is a possibility, not a reality. Change need not mean end. Mutation is the prime driving force of nature, not something to fear and abhor.

She approaches the door, glancing over her shoulder as she does so. No clinking shadow bears down upon her. The door is old, inlaid with iron bracings and smooth from the touch of a million hopeful hands. It whispers open almost before she pushes, inviting her in, hauling her from the dead world she no longer wishes to inhabit.

She steps across the threshold. Realization strikes. She sees the vibrant, alien landscape spread out like the map of a surreal dream, and she opens her eyes.

* * *

Blane was standing before her. Peer smiled up at him, and even though he looked smaller and older than when he had left them, she could see nothing but good.

"Hey," she said.

"Peer," he said. "You're bleeding."

She raised her hand to the dried blood covering her lower face. "I was. I'm not anymore."

"You were sleeping."

She nodded. "I was. But I think it's all right now. I think it's passed." She turned her head carefully and kissed Holly on the top of her head, trying not to wake her. "See? Sweet as a baby."

Blane sat next to Peer, groaning as strange aches made their presence known. His joints thrummed, feet throbbed. He had seen Paul as he approached the two women, and for a terrible moment he was sure that they were all dead. Paul was cold, but the women were still warm. The mere thought of Peer's death had sent sparks of terror into him, creating a rich, plump fear more awful than that connected with anything that had happened over the last few days. Sometimes the future can be lost in the present. Even now the momentary fright was still a stale taste in Blane's mouth.

"Mary?" he said.

Peer nodded at Paul, waking Holly in the process. She stirred and stared at Blane through dazed eyes.

"What?" Holly said. "Where are we? Oh, shit!" As events caught up with her, she turned pale, recalling the sight of crushed, impacted bodies in Rayburn's village square. "You let me sleep!" she said to Peer, but remembered at the same time that the truth was actually the reverse.

"You can sleep," Peer said. "It's better. Blane has made it better."

"I've made it all bad," he said, but he found it impossible to continue even when prompted by Holly's raised eyebrows. "I found her," he said instead. "She showed me some things, made me keen to come back here. Then she died."

"Was she close to you?" Holly said.

"She was my twin sister." *And my lover.* But some things could never be said.

They sat chatting quietly for a while, the women telling Blane what had happened with Mary and Paul. Holly fetched a blanket from the Mini's trunk and covered Paul with it, kneeling at his side for a long time and resting her hand on his shoulder.

"It all happened at once," Peer said. "Paul and Holly. The dog. Mary. Then the earthquake . . . or whatever it was."

"A shockwave," Blane said. "Nature shuddering." He looked at Peer and Holly and wondered whether they knew the full import of what they were. It was not his place to tell them, he thought. He had been the focus of so much heartache and destruction. How could someone so corrupted talk to those so newly pure?

They lay Paul in the backseat of the Mondeo and headed back toward the farm. There was a calmness about things now, a serenity in the air where before there had been nothing but threat. The world was a stranger place than before, but it was a place at peace with those in it, including these tired travelers. Holly sat behind the driver's seat, Paul's head resting on her lap. She fell asleep with him like that, an arrangement that hours ago would have been impossible. Now, it seemed like the right thing to do.

Blane sat back and closed his eyes, letting the memories continue to flood back in; strange, wonderful, bizarre memories of his time with Fay, from long before the ruin began. It was as if the reminiscences were inherent in the landscape, forming the backbone of nature. Only now were they released to him, whereas before, when nature and all in it suffered, they had merely been able to offer clues and vague outlines.

But with knowledge came a terrible tiredness. Fay was dead, and the echo of her death had settled itself into his bones. Blane began to feel himself slip away from his surroundings, blending more into the background. While his mind was active, challenged, enraptured with the miraculous revelations being laid out before it, his body was failing. An endless darkness loomed; Blane almost welcomed it.

The car wound its way through the lanes to the farmhouse. It was deserted. There was no sign of Gerald, no indication that he had ever been there. It was as if he had vanished into thin air. The inside of the house was sterile and clean, all personal effects gone, the smell of bleach rising from every surface. Holly, Peer and Blane sat at the kitchen table, sighing dejectedly, staring around as if expecting Gerald to appear with a sumptuous feast at any second.

Outside, the Mondeo rocked slightly on its suspension. The armrest flopped down in the backseat, resting at an angle against Paul's body. Two hands squirmed through the opening, then a head. Then a shout, as a madwoman was born from the dark womb of the car's trunk.

Chapter Thirty-four

To Sire the Future

"Did you hear something?" Blane whispered.

"What?"

"Car door."

"Gerald?" Holly half-stood, hands splayed on the table like a piano player. "Paul?" she whispered impossibly.

Blane glanced at a shadow against the window. "Oh, no."

The glass erupted inward, merging with splintered timber and lead shot to make a lethal concoction. Blane fell back like a bird in a storm of stinging things, choking a scream through a ripped throat. His hands went back to lessen his fall, but his wrists folded under his weight. Shards tinkled to the flagstone floor like frozen rain.

Holly screamed and stepped back from the table, coming to a halt against the wall adjacent to the cold fireplace. Peer remained seated, watching the shattered window, waiting for whatever was to come.

Mary came. She leaped into the room with the unconscious grace of a ballet dancer, rolling across the glass-strewn floor and standing in one sweet movement. Blossoms of blood opened on the back of her shirt, flowers feeding on chaos. She held the shotgun straight out in front of her, eyes wincing against the imminent recoil and explosion. It was aimed directly at Peer.

"Bitch!" Mary hissed through bitter tears. "Fucking bitch! What makes you think you're so special?"

"Nothing," Peer offered.

"Shut up! Shut up, shut up, shut up!" Mary was manic, but the gun did not waver an inch. Her eyes burned behind the tears. She was useless once more, and it was a feeling she hated. It was a feeling she was unbearably used to. "Where is she?" she shouted.

"You've just shot the person who can tell you that," Peer said calmly.

Holly's hands were pressed to the cold stone. She wondered how long it would take her to reach the madwoman. Push herself away from the wall, not worry about falling, use the forward momentum to stumble across to Mary. What then? Stand in front of the gun? Her muscles twitched as the seed of the idea struggled to germinate.

Mary glanced down at Blane. He was squirming, like a landed fish barely alive in its own leaking juices. "Where is she!" she demanded, but Blane either did not hear or could not answer.

"She's dead," Peer said then. "Whoever she was,

she's dead. I don't know what control she had over you. I've got an inkling of why, but just sit down and we—"

"I don't want to sit down! I want Fay!" Mary's eyes squeezed shut. Her knuckles had turned white around the shotgun stock and barrel. Her biceps quivered with the weight; her forefinger felt like a brand of hot iron, waiting to cool and contract around the trigger. Peer sat tall and still in front of the gun.

"You bitch!" Mary said quietly.

"I did nothing," Peer said.

"Mary!" Holly shouted, not knowing what she was doing, what use it would be to attract the woman's attention.

Mary did not answer.

"Mary, it's all pointless!" Holly cried, angry at how it could all come to this.

"I don't care," Mary said. "It makes me feel better." The comment had an air of finality to it.

There was a sound from the broken window. A growl. Mary turned with a smile on her face. "Spike!"

It was a fox. Bigger than normal, more heavily muscled, its tawny coat interrupted by tigerlike stripes of yellow fur fleeing down across its ribs. Its teeth were bared.

Peer watched, motionless and expressionless. She felt other arrivals, though she could not yet see them.

The fox leaped. Mary screamed and tried to bring the gun to bear upon it, but it fired and chewed a lump from the table, spraying splinters. The recoil pulled her arms over her head. The fox hit her in the midriff and clawed its way up her body to bite into her throat. She gurgled and screamed.

More shapes rushed in. Mad spring hares kicked at Mary's legs. A buzzard, shrinking the room with its size, pecked at her eyes. Smaller birds joined the fray.

Peer sat still, a step away from the carnage. Unafraid. Holly watched, stunned. Blane was unmoving among blood-splattered glass.

Mary screamed, but it merely allowed access to her mouth. A bee went in and did not come out again. Insects swarmed across her skin and brought her features to life. A muffled shout could have been Fay's name, but it was difficult to tell above the noise. The farm kitchen was transformed into another domain of nature, absorbing its smells and sounds, bearing witness to the hunt. Mary stumbled toward the door, the fox still clawing at her front to maintain its grip on her throat. Blood merged redly with its coat.

Mary became a sculpture of living things, a work of terrible art. Her sounds of distress combined with the noises from the animals to form a symphony of death—gurgles, grunts, howls, the snapping of teeth, the subtle ripping of flesh and, eventually, the crackling of bones. She reached the door and moved outside, allowing larger animals to join in the fray. A cow sauntered over, its udder hideously swollen and split, knocking Mary to the ground with one nod of its head. It walked across her, crushing whatever lay beneath its hooves. Birds swooped down from out of nowhere. Rabbits and hedgehogs zeroed in on the struggling mass.

Some mink waved across the yard and became blurs of teeth.

Peer watched from the doorway, unafraid. Holly stared through an unbroken window. Blane stirred on the floor and managed to sit up, though he could surely see nothing through so much blood.

The chaos in the yard eventually died down. Animals left to be replaced by others, darting in to snap up any of the spoils. Birds took off with scraps in their beaks, to feed whatever strange brood they had. The fox sat by the cow shed, panting, muzzle black with blood. It stared disinterestedly at the observers in the farm.

"Poor Mary," Peer said.

Holly went to Blane and helped him into a chair. Her mouth hung open. His weight was unreal in her arms. She did not say anything, because she felt no pity for Mary. If Peer wished to mourn her loss, she could do so on her own. There were too many dead people, and someone who wished only to add to the list deserved whatever came for them.

And what, Holly thought, had come for Mary? What precisely had happened these last couple of minutes? She felt a sting in her stomach like an answer, but that was no reply. Not yet, not here. Surely that was no solution. A new life for old, she thought, but felt uncomfortable swapping Mary for whatever might lay within her. Paul's final gift to a lover he had barely known. A miracle gift to a barren womb.

Blane was not badly injured. He bled a lot, but most of the cuts were superficial. Bruises measled his face and neck where the spent pellets had struck. His wounds were already drying when

Holly helped him up, and by the time Peer turned away from the yard Blane seemed himself again.

Another strangeness for Holly to ponder.

"I'm special," Blane said to her unstated query, with no arrogance at all. "So are you. And Peer. We're all special now."

They buried Paul behind the farmhouse. Gerald must have tried doing the decent thing for his livestock, but most of them lay half burned in a shallow ditch. Slowly rotting away.

"Should we say a prayer?" Holly asked.

Blane said nothing. Peer shrugged. Holly stepped uncomfortably from foot to foot, conscious that she was more than just one person now. Now she had someone else to think about.

"In the short time I knew Paul . . ." she began, but she did not finish the sentence. After a long silence: "Look after him, wherever he is. He's the father of the future."

Blane smiled at this, put his arm around Holly's shoulders and hugged her. His bruises had vanished like dark snow. He looked a hundred years old, but the cuts on his face were now little more than pink smears. Special, he had called himself. All of them.

Holly felt more than special. She felt important. They were two different things.

"You already know who you are, Peer," Blane said, a statement rather than a question. He thought she had probably known since the shockwave of Fay's death.

He could see the settled, comfortable look in Peer's eyes, which he recognized from his newfound memories of Fay, countless years before. Indeed, there was much about Peer that was now familiar: her calmness at things; a vibrancy, shaking the air around her with almost physical waves; the impression that she was aglow. The sheer absurdity of the idea that she could ever, ever die. He had thought that about Fay once, when everything was good and the rot was not even a cloud of smog on the horizon.

Blane realized now how utterly relieved he was that Peer was still with them, because without her, he had no idea what would happen.

As for him . . . he was failing. He would not be around for much longer.

"And you, Holly. Your baby is going to be someone very special."

Not around much longer; but perhaps long enough to bring up someone to replace him at Peer's side.

"He already is," Holly said, hand flat on her flat stomach. "He's Paul's."

Chapter Thirty-five

The Open Door

Blane and Holly left the farm in the Mondeo. Peer remained in the farmhouse, because she could not be with them. She had much to do, she said. A whole world to discover. And today it was a new world, moved on by a giant kick rather than the smooth glide of evolution, forced into mutation and change by the trauma that had changed it forever.

Peer was a changed woman, too. Now she was a part of everything: the land; the sea; the animals. She was the earth, the wind, the fire, the water. She was special.

Holly drove quietly, with Blane slumped in the seat beside her. They did not talk much on the journey; Blane had told her there would be plenty of time for that later. They would see Peer again, she knew. When her son was old enough to join her, Peer would come to them. There was a satisfying balance in the outcome of things. A rightness.

They passed several cars going in the opposite direction. Two of them flashed for them to stop, but Holly kept going. They were too special to risk confrontation; she would not endanger her unborn child.

They reached Rayburn in the early evening. It was much as they had left it. They passed the tractor and trailer containing Henry's body, used now by the animals. Blane glanced from the window as he remembered meeting Fay here; only days ago, but it felt like decades. The first time he had ever seen her, he had thought then. If only he had recalled the truth instantly, instead of letting her play awful games with his mind. How much of this could have been stopped? But, by then, most of the damage had already been done.

Holly parked in the village square next to the burned-out car. There were no bodies, and no one came out to greet them. Rayburn was a ghost town, haunted by the memories of better times. Or perhaps just different times. Definitions had changed radically, and who was to say what was for better or worse? A breeze blew gently across the village, sweeping up the ghosts and depositing them in memory and legend.

"Let's go to the forest," Blane said. "I want to show you something."

Together they walked through the churchyard. Holly glanced at the gravestones and saw them as remnants of another era. When they had buried Paul, he'd gone into a new earth, governed by new rules. These old graves were already monuments to lost times. They had left Paul's grave unmarked.

The sun sank ahead of them, and they strolled across the field as if trying to catch it. Peace surrounded them in the smells of the plants, and the sounds of animals in the nearby woods perhaps watching their approach. Holly looked down expecting to see a well-worn path, but the field was virgin. She glanced at her stomach and wondered what he was thinking, how different he would be. But Blane was as human as anyone—more human than everyone—and she harbored no fears for her child. He would be good. He would be strong. He would be a fitting student for Blane.

"Here," Blane said. He did not pause at the forest's edge, but plunged straight in. There was no halt to the birdsong, though much of it was strange. The rustlings in the bushes continued, evidence of new things finding their feet. He and Holly were a part of nature now, not excluded from it; here to be welcomed, not feared. "Let me show you."

The old oak stood wide and gnarled and diffident. It was home to a multitude, a small ecosystem in its own right, from the smallest insect to a family of albino rooks nested in its highest branches.

"I used to sit here for hours on end," Blane said, "before I knew who I was. Even then I knew I was a part of nature, much nearer to it than most. I reveled in it. I tasted it, listened, felt it wash over me." He closed his eyes and stuck out his tongue, the tastes both familiar and strange. "Lots has changed," he said. "That's good. That's how we advance."

Holly sat on an old fallen tree, leaned back and looked up into the branches above her. They spread out to fill her entire field of vision, and for a moment the tree was the whole world. "It's lovely," she said.

"Four hundred years old," Blane mused. "At least. And this year, the most important ring ever will be added to its trunk. I'm so damn old, Holly. I know a lot more than this tree." He sounded exhausted.

They sat silently for a while, letting the darkness creep out from permanent shadows deeper in the woods. Holly moved next to Blane, sidled up against him, sharing warmth. She went to ask when they were going home. But then she realized with a pleasing jolt that they were already there.

There was no door in the field, but still she recognized the scene.

She stood naked on the slope and stared across the strange, wonderful countryside. Already the roads were becoming clogged and overgrown by plants excluded from them for so long, and the houses spotting the landscape would soon be subsumed beneath the rapid sprouting of this new spring. A spring of rebirth and regrowth, more so than any other.

The sinking sun bathed the hillside in golden light. The hedgerows were spilling across the fields, exploding into flower and bloom. A family of rabbits scampered at the bottom edge of the field, their fur spotted with splashes of yellow, some of them with four ears. Peer turned slowly, tracking the stream tumbling from beneath a folly higher up, and then she saw the stag.

It stared at her through doleful eyes. It was larger than any she had ever seen, but it was in place; it was right. Peer put her hands on her hips and smiled. The deer turned and wandered away.

Nature did not skirt around Peer; it flowed through her. She had much to do, a whole world to learn about and introduce herself to, and for the first ten years she would be without help. But then she would visit Holly, and meet her and Paul's son, and she would have company forever.

Two halves of the same whole. Twins in nature, if not in the flesh. Where she was now, ten years was barely the blink of an eye.

IN THE DARK

RICHARD LAYMON

Nothing much happens to Jane Kerry, a young librarian. Then one day Jane finds an envelope containing a fifty-dollar bill and a note instructing her to "Look homeward, angel." Jane pulls a copy of the Thomas Wolfe novel of that title off the shelf and finds a second envelope. This one contains a hundred-dollar bill and another clue. Both are signed, "MOG (Master of Games)." But this is no ordinary game. As it goes on, it requires more and more of Jane's ingenuity, and pushes her into actions that she knows are crazy, immoral or criminal—and it becomes continually more dangerous. More than once, Jane must fight for her life, and she soon learns that MOG won't let her quit this game. She'll have to play to the bitter end.

___4916-3 $5.99 US/$6.99 CAN